EAT

THE

RICH

for my father

EAT THE RICH

Brian Dillon

Intangible Books

©2012

www.intangiblecollective.com

t.m.m.r.o.j.m.i

<u>1</u>

If there is a wrong way to start the day it's got to be watching an eighty-seven year old woman blow her brains out on her front stoop.

A full minute had yet to pass since Bobby Collins, chief managing partner of First Freedom Mortgage Company, had watched as the owner of the home he was at that very moment just beginning to auction away made her appearance from behind her front door. Nigella Smithson wore white shoes and stockings. A skirt's hem met them between her knee and ankle. It was also white, with tiny embroidered flowers: red, yellow, and blue. She wore a great hat with a sunflower in its paisley brim. Her white gloved hands clutched a small red purse, sequined with a purple dragonfly. She clearly had somewhere to be.

After a minute or so Nigella gingerly opened her purse's clasp, pulled an ornate, polished revolver from its mouth and pushed it under the veil. In one thunderous bang, the back of her skull blew away, great hat and all, and the rest of her slumped to the porch, dumping buckets of blood on the pale blue word through the hole at the top of her neck.

Collins was dressed in flesh. There were pieces of her in

his teeth. A hat full of white hair spun in his shoes...then stopped. The bidding parties, speckled with gore, fled for their lives.

Needless to say, Bobby was now panicking like a kitten in a rickety canoe. He finger-painted bloody thumbprints onto his blackberry, dialing his boss all the while whimpering and blowing beads of sweat off the tip of his long, bulging nose.

No answer.

He tried again. He even went so far as to scream at his employer's voicemail recording. Like he was practicing for a conversation he'd never muster the stones to have.

He was only doing his job. The old bat had stopped answers phone calls and letters months ago. The mortgage hadn't been paid in a year. What was he supposed to do?

Bobby ran a clammy mitt through his thinning blonde mane. He swore. Bobby swore often. He treated the word "motherfucker" with the enthusiasm of a ten year old boy. The current application of that phrase certainly wasn't out of joy. He chose the term simply because he didn't know how else to express the fact that thanks to his aggressive collection policies a senior citizen had just offed herself on the very porch he was trying to sell to the highest bidder.

His colleague, a freshly graduated young man named Adam Brewer was sitting Indian-style on the lawn of the property, shoes off, sobbing like a schoolgirl who just saw a pony thrown off a cliff. It was his third day on the job. Bobby swore again. He walked over and patted the kid absentmindedly on the shoulder, leaning over the rocking, weeping Wharton grad. A big pearl of sweat rolled off the tip of Bobby's nose and plunked Adam in the knuckles.

"It's alright kid. We were doing our job. She couldn't pay the fucking bills. What are we supposed to do? It ain't our fuckin' fault the bitch killed herself. Right?" Bobby ended the sentence with a cheerful inflection. Like he had just solved the problem by blaming a woman whose face was spread over the lawn like she was a gerbil who had made the mistake of hiding in the microwave.

And it wasn't like he just rolled up in her driveway and started raffling her home off. They had tried desperately to get her to understand that the home had gone to judicial foreclosure and that there was to be no more discussion. He offered assistance in finding alternative housing – but was stiff in his promise that the home was indeed going to be auctioned to satisfy the terms of her mortgage. That despite the fact that she still stored her family's history in its closets and windowpanes; she no longer possessed the deed to the property. When Bobby, accompanied by officials from the bank associated in the foreclosure and the local Sherriff's department arrived at the Smithson home on the morning of the auction, just past sunrise, they attempted reason.

They knocked. They knocked and knocked on every door and window. They spent an hour peering through the thin glimpses her shuttered blinds gave them on every rotation of an oscillating ceiling fan's cageless blades. A cyclone of knives. She was watching Family Feud and drinking pink lemonade.

Bobby yelled into the slicks of glass. By the time interested buyers were coalescing on the scrubby fringes of a dead lawn, he had resorted to swearing and banging on things. She gave him nothing.

Soon the business day had opened its ceaseless maw. Murmur and chatter filled the avenue. The sheriff now got involved. He made much of the same remarks with the sole exception being he threatened to break down the door and carry her out in foot irons. Bobby intervened and thought it wiser to simply start the auction. She'd have to leave eventually and there was no sense in further disturbing his curious group of potential buyers.

In his sweeping need to impress, coupled with a fear of confrontation, Bobby Collins seemed to miss that the worst possible thing he could have done at that moment was sell Nigella Smithson's home from under her feet while she sipped lemonade in the living room.

The Sherriff Whittaker, Bobby and his colleague Adam stood on the porch. As the wide-bellied Whittaker spoke, he gestured with his hands and explained the process to the willing bidders sprouting across the Smithson lawn like dandelions in neckties who had each lost a fistfight with outlawed pesticides. After some time, the sheriff asked if there were any questions before turning to hand over the affair. As he turned behind him, those closest to the home's front heard the click of a very old doorknob's lock.

What happened next, of course, was loud and messy.

By the time the police arrived, Bobby was sitting next to Adam in the grass. While his younger colleague stared, puffy-eyed off into the distance, Bobby continued trying to contact his boss, David Drahtman. The VP of Acquisitions at Ohmco, a vast multi-national holding company which owned many mortgage companies, Drahtman was a special man. And boy was this going to be a special day.

2

David's face was so deep in his pillow that the great cotton poofs swaddling each side of his head made it look like he was performing oral sex on an angel. David had terrible sleep apnea. But unlike most sufferer's David didn't just stop breathing in his sleep. He appeared to be attempting to outright suffocate himself by force.

It was nearly noon when he leaned up in his sprawling bed, yawned like a hyena and scanned his room. The first thing David did was look for his phone. Ignoring the fact that his wife was missing, David tottered around the bedroom naked until he spotted the red blinking eye of his handheld in the bathroom. He yawned a second time and looked into the mirror.

David Drahtman ran two hands through his thick black hair, mashed his knuckles into heavy lids and yawned for the third time. David's thick and glossy hair sparkled. Like a pair of ducks who choked to death on crude oil had been stapled to the top of his skull. It was something that gave him peace of mind. At 39 years old, David had successfully navigated the black waters of human aging with grace. And it didn't hurt that he could finance the journey's more fiscally troubling whirlpools. Not unlike his wife, David was becoming less human by percentage points every year. Chemically scraping off layers of unsatisfactory skin, boiling off unsightly bumps and ripples with requisite gusto. Of all the improvements, the only one with which he attributed any modicum of regret would be the first he had performed.

At 25 years of age, David Drahtman was an up and coming junior vice president at a monolithic multinational corporation called Ohmcom. He was the pride of his generation and his family. A strong-willed, pretty-on-the-eyes, cock of the walk. His father Victor had helped him snag the job out of college so that his son would fit snugly into each of his footsteps. He was a broad-chested man with thick black eyebrows and a prominent chin. He could have kept his wallet in its cleft if he was so inclined. Victor was a first generation American, born in the densely Bavarian enclaves of Northern Queens County to a domineering set of parents. He was taught to fight and claw his way to a point of power, and did so obediently.

Victor Drahtman had worked at various corporate institutions on his own path to success, stomping and spitting on the heads of those around him all the way. He was a callous, baseless man who raised his son in a similar mold. The elder Drahtman womanized and abused his wife, and encouraged his son to join him. One Thanksgiving they took an overcooked turkey into the yard and urinated on it in tandem. Victor laughed and patted his son on the back until he did the same. It was a veritable super-villain origin story.

By the time he was twenty-seven David had more money that he could swing his dick at it. Unfortunately for David Drahtman, he could not under any circumstances swing his dick at anything. This was of course due to the fact that when flaccid David's penis resembled a button mushroom, or an oversized clitoris. He had, since the age of seventeen had needed to shave his pubic hair. Even the scrawniest bush would make him look like he had a vagina. He and his father had many things in common. Having mini-muffins for genitals not the least among them.

To alleviate half of these issues, David had a phalloplasty performed. A phalloplasty is most often performed on biological females who wish to be men. These women, born with the mental outlook of a lumberjack and the bodies of ballerinas, hire surgeons to build them a penis out of other parts of the body. David, being born without a vagina but certainly without enough penis to qualify him as an actual man had skin and flesh taken from his buttocks which was used to form a shaft to insert between his mushroom cap and the base of his pelvis. This surgery now left him with a longer but equally useless noodle. To transform his floppy little man into a big, strong soldier worthy of combat, a second procedure was performed. This operation placed an inflatable bladder into his scrotum which was attached via tubing to air sacs running the length of his member. When David Drahtman wished to perform sexually, he squeezed his testicles thrice and suddenly, like a balloon-animal, his pseudopenis would inflate to full rigidity. It was certainly a sight to behold.

And so he beheld it. Staring in his reflection David squeezed his balls. He stared at his penis for a minute, chuckled smugly and then deflated himself.

Then the phone he had forgotten was in his hand shook. It was Collins. David loathed the man and pressed "ignore". He threw a robe around himself and walked up to his office on the third floor of the palatial Long Island home. He stopped to make coffee on the way, having to ignore Collins three more times before he made it up the stairs. Little did he know then that in southern NJ there was a man he had never met waking up as well. And in one week's time that simple-seeming man would change David's life forever.

3

Thomas Jones was an absolutely unremarkable human being. His life had been a series of failures wrapped like bad beans and limp wet lettuce in the soft corn tortilla of occasional middle-management responsibilities. He ran fast-food restaurants with casual aplomb and got fat on cheeseburgers. He masterfully assisted in the management of convenience stores slash pharmacies and got high on bootleg Vicodin... He even supervised the work of gas station attendants until he stopped arriving to work under the suspicion that one of his employees would hijack a customer's Buick and drive it into the Pentagon.

Thomas Jones was raised in a small house in the southern New Jersey resort town of Wildwood. Built like so many sandcastles on the Atlantic, Wildwood was a place in constant flux. Between September and April, she was a ghost town populated only by locals who had existed here before the boardwalk and the chintzy art-deco hotels. When the sun began to quickly cook this small enclave in June and a new year's worth of high school seniors were released from the clinching grasp of Social Studies and Arithmetic, they would arrive on the boardwalk in troops prepared to baste her beaches in flavored rum and teenaged semen. Thomas Jones, like many others his age, was mortally frightened by this annual migration of coke-snorting, hot-tub sexing Long Islanders, and did his best in the summer to get to bed early so as to avoid the inevitable 3AM retreat of hooting , half-dressed, bottle-smashing adolescent armies from the boardwalk.

Thomas Jones scratched crumbles of sleep the size of bran muffins from his eyes and clapped twice. The lights in his bedroom sprang to life at this command, as did almost everything in his house. Thomas is a member of that rare breed, the Clapper owner. Whereas most of us became bored with the novelty and soon resorted back to the all-too-tiring task of flipping switches, Thomas Jones saw this technology as the obvious future of mankind and bought twelve of them. This decision did not work out well, as the machines simply get confused and turn one another on, or worse, turn on when a sound even remotely reminiscent of a clap is heard anywhere near one of them. For example, the curiously similar sound of a man's lap smacking repeatedly into the inner thighs of a woman. Needless to say, that particular woman was less than impressed by Thomas's improvised strobe-light (strobe TV, strobe Stereo, strobe garage door opener) and had her jeans back on before he could clap them back off.

Thomas sat up on the side of his bed and took off the socks which he wore to bed in the broiling clasp of deep summer on the Jersey Shore, where even the dogs walked around naked. This was all on account of a touch of foot phobia so flagrant that he found it quite nauseating for his own feet to touch one another unsheathed. In middle school Thomas contracted a particularly severe case of athlete's foot after trying out for the swimming team. At the behest of his mother, poor Thomas was forced to wear swimmies to the try out. Even with the aid of inflatable orange tubes around his coffee-stirrer arms, young Thomas still nearly drowned to death. After being laughed out of the pool, he must have plodded across some feisty microbes which infected his tootsies. Thomas was reminded of the disaster by cracking, itchy toes for the next week and a half. Subconsciously, this might be why Thomas so avoided feet, but it made it no more rational to wear sweat-socks to bed in the smothering heat of mid-summer. It wasn't as if there were a gang of mean-spirited twelve year old boys waiting at his bedside every night to ridicule him into a pair of galoshes.

Nevertheless, Thomas Jones was not a bad-looking man. If anything he was quite good looking when he was shaven, showered and wasn't talking. That last bit was much of his trouble with women, since only the most brilliant of Casanovas can slide themselves between the legs of a lady without saying a word. When Thomas did manage to copulate it was less sliding, and more tripping and falling dick-first into a vagina. He was, as you might imagine, average as one could be: 5'9, 180 pounds, brown hair, brown eyes, and a penis that when flaccid was three and a half inches long. For those not working in the adult film industry, this number is sound and appropriate. Anyone in possession of something in excess of that is fortunate to the extent that they should consider more than regular trips to Wildwood's glitzy sister, Atlantic City.

As this was a Monday, Thomas Jones, currently unemployed following an incident with a roller-skating dinosaur the week before, went to fetch the morning paper off the lawn in front of the house he had been raised in. There he found a teenage boy and girl spooning on his front lawn like an old married couple who had lived there all their lives. The major difference being that these two had empty bottles of rum in each hand. Both wore bathing suits and were smattered with wet sand, thanks to Thomas's automatic sprinkler turning on earlier that morning. They seemed completely unfazed, but were breathing, so he left them there.

As he walked back into his childhood home Thomas thought of all the times his mother had beaten boozy teenagers off her lawn with a broom. He was certainly not the sort of person to employ a broom as a weapon, and certainly not against two individuals who were clearly brandishing empty bottles of Bacardi.

Nowadays his mother was an aging, spare-haired, Alzheimered old dear named Abigail Jones who had some five years earlier required help beyond his ability to proffer and had reluctantly departed for the greener pastures of Shady Days Nursing Home. In her last year at the home on Sandy Circle, she had taken to calling him by his deceased father's name. Soon enough, this had logically evolved into her believing that her son *was* her late husband and regularly attempting to sexually assault him. Desperate for intimacy and amoral as our Thomas was, he was certainly not so far gone to consider tongue-kissing his seventy-year old mother to achieve erotic fulfillment. Alzheimer's is one of the gods' queerest innovations. His mother, who was beyond the ability to comprehend that at her age strutting around the house she shared with her middle-aged son wearing nothing but pearls was not in good taste, but could without hesitation name all the state capitals in alphabetical order (and occasionally to a tune) was certainly testament to the disease's persnickety nature.

Her final morning in the home they shared began like many others. Thomas, dressing for work at the pharmacy at which he developed an, albeit temporary, taste for prescription pills, heard the familiar mating-call of his mother. Abigail, as Thomas had been made to learn, preferred her coitus by the light of morning.

"Ohhhhhh Jaaaaaames", his mother squealed Thomas's father's name. Knowing that this meant his mother was about to attempt mounting him, he instinctively grabbed a down comforter with which he would try to collect his confoundedly amorous mother. The plan was to wrap her up quickly and then use the comforter like a shopping bag with which he could deposit her back in her bedroom. Lastly he would wedge a kitchen chair under the knob and run from the house.

Thomas, being all too familiar with the sight of his mother's droopy, deflated body turned the corner and made to head her off before she could get a hold of him. In an especially playful mood on this particular spring morning, Abigail giggled into her bowed and crumpled fingertips and turned her back to him. Like the post-war vixen she might have once been Abigail threw him a furtively come-hither glance over her shoulder and bounced off down the hallway. She snickered playfully, trundled up the passage to the kitchen, where Thomas noticed her step was more crooked and hackneyed than normal. Looking down, his squinting eyes caught sight of his mother's feet and noticed that she had added to her normal ensemble by donning the most ridiculous red heels he had ever seen. For a second, Thomas thanked the lord on high as he had had quite enough of her knotted tree root toes sliding up his pant-leg at the breakfast table. Distracted, he failed to reach her in time as she toppled to her right, crashed loudly into a mirror and then the floor with a decisive CRACK.

Her hip shattered like a hip shatters when you're seventy some-odd years old, wearing three inch heels, and attempting to copulate with your thirty-something year old son. While he was appropriately aggrieved for his mother's suffering, Thomas could not help but feel somewhat relieved as he called an ambulance to their home that morning. This hip injury would allow him to feel less guilty for placing her in a nursing home, whereas previously he would have needed to explain to a nurse that he had to lock his mother out of his room at night so she wouldn't board him like DC-9. After her hip was replaced with a Tupperware drawer full of plastic and she was able to be pushed about comfortably in a wheelchair, she was rolled three miles from the hospital and into the room in which she now resides, sloppily kissing a framed picture of her only son like a silly little school-girl. A school-girl in a diaper, that is.

As Thomas pondered these and other pleasant memories,

he flipped absently to the want ads in his paper, hoping for a position not unlike most others he had ever had in his life. A position that would utilize his major skill set: his age and how that age engendered fleeting respect in a job most likely populated by young teens still in the grips of their squeaking, pimply, erection-maddened days. As Thomas's community college degree was unlikely to boost his chances of finding work outside of the terminable, soupy, middle-management purgatory that he so willingly bobbed about in each day, his job search was normally quite brief. Typically, he would be name-tagged and having arguments in what he believed was serviceable and functional Spanish with a dishwasher/housekeeper/grill cook by noon on Wednesday. This morning's search, however, would be perhaps the fastest yet. On the second page of the classified section was this ad:

WANTED:

Keepwater Holdings Group is looking for a full-time operations manager to work in the New York and New Jersey area managing various operations and projects. Ideal candidate will be generally unremarkable.

Qualifications include:

* Amorality

* Willingness to act against one's better judgment

* Lack of taste, character and conscience on the job

*Fondness for swear words, alcohol, and tobacco off the job

Responsibilities will include managing personnel in the act of a myriad of projects, all of which are in some way remarkably classless, money-motivated, and morally reprehensible. Qualified candidates should call our offices during normal business hours (12am – 12pm) and ask for Jameson (212) 539-5667 ext. 2569
Pay will be commensurate with experience in the business of being a salty bastard.

For an individual who spent as many days out of the year perusing classified ads as did Thomas Jones, this was most unusual. Apart from the employer's affinity for boozy, black-lunged, sailor types, Thomas had never in his life seen the term "salty bastard" used in a newspaper, much less by a businessman looking to hire. And while Thomas could hardly call himself salty, to his knowledge he was no bastard, and truth be told he had not once in his life used the word 'fuck' in public (Thomas was an avowed user of the more diluted 'frig' variations: "Mom get your tongue out of my friggin' ear!"), he was enchanted by this ad, and spent the rest of the day re-reading it and working up the courage to swear openly in front of his mirror. Thomas had not been this excited about something in his entire life. And while he was picking up his phone, David Drahtman was throwing his out of a window.

<u>4</u>

Actually it wasn't technically a phone. It was the Bluetooth wireless earpiece David wore everywhere he went and sometimes while showering. After hearing Bobby tell him the story of the Smithson house whilst simultaneously explaining the situation to local policemen, David scrunched up his eyes like frustrated little assholes and scratched the blue-tooth wireless ear piece from the side of his head – nearly tearing the ear off from his face like loose-leaf - and threw it clean out the window of his home's third floor office.

Before he could even sit back in his chair and stem the mounting rage which was syruping up his throat, David heard a distinctive plink and then the all too familiar beep beep beep – woop woop woop – honk honk honk of a car alarm cutting through the silence of mid-morning in East Hampton Long Island. Drahtman strode to the massive bay windows on the wings of a veritable sermon of cuss-words so masterfully strung together they would make the most ardent of Tourette's sufferers bow to his swear-word supremacy. Not to be outdone, David leaned this litany, and torso, out of the window and bellowed to whom-ever would listen.

"TURN THAT FUCKING SHIT OFF

GODDAMNIT!! STACI, I SWEAR TO GOD, TURN THE
FUCKING THING OFF! OFF!!" David continued, "STACI!
WHERE IN THE NAME OF GOD ALLMIGHTY ARE
YOU!! ARE YOU DEAF?! ARE YOU FUCKING DEAF?!!"

At that very moment a beautiful, lithe little woman
galloped around a white marble corner. Her long, sun-streaked
blonde hair trailed behind her as if Rumplestiltskin himself were
holed up in there somewhere, churning out an ever-increasing
wash of gold. She was wearing a white bikini and god-awful
strappy white heels which gave her a sort of awkward canter as
she ran at top speed around the house, hands swinging on their
hinges in front of her like she was waving excitedly to invisible
friends all around her. The only things not jostling about as she
ran towards her husband's voice were her breasts, which stood
like bags of wet cement wrapped in bar napkins despite all the
trembling and wobbling the rest of her body was enduring.
Following her around the corner were four equally beautiful
human beings, though some a bit older than she, and most of
them wearing more than tea-cozies and coasters.

Staci Drahtman stopped within earshot of her husband,
whipped off monstrous black glasses and screeched up at David,
"WHA? WHASSA MATTA BABY?!" David drew his head back
within the window's frame and mashed his fingers into his face
again, squishing his beady black eyes together while trying to
decide which sound was having a more calamitous effect on his
brain: the BEEP WOOP HONK or the shrill, 'lawn guyland'
accent pouring out of his wife. The latter was combined with a

baffling lack of awareness as to the possible reason why he might be calling her name in the first place.

BEEP BEEP BEEP!!

"BABY!! WHATCHA SAY BABY?!"

HONK HONK HONK!!

"BABY!!", turning to her friends, each smiling widely like a dentist's mannequin and holding drinks of various shades of pastel pinks and green, "Gawd, thas' loud, no?"

WOOP WOOP WOOP!!

"BABY!! WHASSA MATTA BABY?!! YOU CAWL ME?!"

BEEP BEEP BEEP!!

David Drahtman's black-brown eyes opened, they were now tinged with thin angel-hair lines of blood from the strain of squeezing the bridge of his nose to death while listening to his wife's hollering senselessness. David closed his eyes again and blew hard air through pursed lips. Opening them, he calmly wrapped two hands around the large flat-screen computer monitor off his desk and whipped it, ultimate-Frisbee style, out of the window.

Below Staci and her friends, who were now sipping their icy pink drinks again and laughing as if there wasn't a remarkably loud, howling car alarm bellowing a warning of theft next to them, jumped slightly at the sound of the flat-screen hitting the marble steps leading up to the glacier-sized home. As Staci, who spelled her name with an I at the end, "because it's cuter" (despite the insistence of her family and husband that her name was indeed Stacey, as her birth-certificate certainly could testify), held up a long, French-manicured finger to her friends and smiled, as if to insinuate she was going somewhere. Turning back toward the house in her tottering trot, she stopped again suddenly when her husband's twisted, red-eyed face appeared again in the window. In his mind David momentarily considered leaping down at her in an effort to murder her, or at the very least himself.

"STACI!"

"YEA MUFFIN?" she inquired, completely oblivious.

David took another breath this time, and then in a single, scratchy, high pitched burst - head shaking up and down and back and forth,

"TURNOFFTHEGODDAMNEDALARM!"

"OFCAWS BABY!!" Staci proceeded, smiling, to bob and weave through six or seven cars which were parked out front. All but two were unregistered, uninsured playthings; monuments to excess. Staci leaned her tousled golden head nearer to each to discern which car was the offender.

It was another two or three minutes before the sounds of his exceedingly high-performing alarm system were put to rest. David blew air through his lips while squeezing the bridge of his nose. He began to evaluate the situation at hand, trying to find the best way to smother a no doubt boisterous response from his superiors and surely the media. Not a minute of storming in his brain later, what sounded like a six fisted centaur rapped furiously on the double doors of his office. David ignored the three-headed dog of war momentarily, considering the plausibility of scaling three floors to the ground and speeding off in one of his vehicles. This, he knew, was most impossible. After the incensed hammering on his door by the poly-limbed arthropodic fire-monster whom David was sure awaited him had eased, he knew what was to follow.

"DAAAAAAAAD", cried three voices at once, at different pitches and tones. They truly did sound like the collected voice of the Leviathan, male and female, high and low, all at once in a horrifying, searing, wail. Once again, David ignored them, until they each in turn began to scream individual demands at him while thrashing what sounded like their entire bodies against his door.

David, calm as a man of his character can be when charged with the task of parenting, strode to his doors and swung them open with two hands. They were immediately silenced.

Before him stood his three children. In the forefront were his twin boys, Theo and Leo. The eight year olds were both gangly little monsters with black mops of unyielding hair and they both had inherited their father's empty, toilet eyes. They were missing several teeth which each brought them a hundred dollars apiece. David had become convinced that after being rewarded for the first time by the Warren Buffet of tooth-fairies, the two had begun punching one another in the mouth regularly to thicken their bankrolls. They were also both presently covered, head to toe, in white paint. Behind the twins stood David's daughter. Sophia was an utter clone of her mother. Long blonde hair and a thin face and body were offset by breasts which were clearly outside the normal range which a 16 year old girl could possibly hope to squeeze into her baby-t. Her left hand pressed a tiny, pink, rhinestone-dotted cell phone to her face, which brought to mind the question of how she could possibly carry on a conversation while simultaneously evoking the wrath of Odin at her father at the tippy top of her lungs from behind his office door. For three children who were only moments before launching a campaign of open warfare against two sheets of reinforced plywood, they were remarkably calm. His daughter spoke first.

"I need the car", she demanded, still yet to say a word into her cell phone since he had opened the door.

"Sophie, you don't have a driver's license."

"IM SIXTEEN!" she leaned over her brothers and roared at her father. David, ever the patient father, screamed back at her leaning close enough to smell the smoke on her breath.

"YOU FAILED THE FUCKING TEST THREE TIMES SOPHIA", he bellowed, ignoring the mentholated tobacco stench on her tongue. David could care less if his daughter smoked. David Drahtman could honestly care less if he walked in on his twin eight-year olds smoking a hookah. Sophie Drahtman, while far more sulky and miserable than her mother, was equally incapable of functioning mentally, and unfortunately for her, this translated to her inability to operate a motor vehicle. Her three tests had ended with a mangled stop sign, a missing side-view mirror, and a dead cat, respectively. Still she seemed to believe that because her father had bought her a Bentley on her sixteenth birthday nearly a year ago, that she was in any condition to operate said vehicle. Finally, she spoke into her cell phone.

"I told you he's an asshole." David Drahtman, who had been called only two days earlier by this same teenager both a "cock-sucker" and a "fucking pussy" was not fazed by this comment and simply ignored her as he turned his attention to his two be-spackled sons.

"What?" he spat at them, ignoring the fact that they looked like they had been molested by a manic Jackson Pollack, as his daughter screamed and swirled back down the hallway, phone still stitched to her temple. Theo spoke first.

"The TV is broke." David chuckled at this.

"No, no Theo. That's not a TV. That's a flat-screen plasma computer MON-I-TUR. Can you say mon-i-tur?"

"No, no, MY TEE-VEE" He leaned down to their level with his hands on his knees and replied as calmly as possible.

"Which TV?"

"MY TV!!" Theo roared back at him.

"And why would that $1,800 television be broken Theo?"

"We painted it and now it doesn't work" Not for a moment doubting the ability of his children to paint a television, he strode off between them toward Theo's room. Leo's room was on the floor below. As he approached the double doors which opened into his son's room, he distinctly heard the blaring sounds of car crashes and gunshots emanating from a plainly operable television. David turned into the room and saw that the

24

twins had emptied several cans of white paint (which were being used on renovations to the upper levels) onto the floor, couches, bed, and television. The television of course still worked fine, it had simply been bukkaked into uselessness. There were white foot and hand prints on everything as they had evidently completed the Sistine Chapel of finger-painting. David, in the grips of an entirely awful morning, leaned down to his sons and in a manner not unlike his final exchange with his wife earlier, burst into a head-banging, epileptic fit from the neck up.

"WHYTHEFUCKDIDYOUDOTHIS?!"

The two boys looked back at him, appalled, mouths agape. Then, Leo swung back and punched his father in the crotch. The boys ran up the adjoining steps and disappeared.

Lying on the painted floor of his son's room, David Drahtman was, despite the agony of being jabbed in the scrotum, now one-third of the way to a full erection.

<u>5</u>

Thomas began dialing the number in the paper and stopped. He was nervous. Thomas tried to convince himself that there was no need to be scared, it was just a matter of asking for an interview. Lord knows he had enough practice at that given his whirling-turnstile approach to employment. Still he was stalling.

The sound of an air-conditioner his mother had bought in the days he was wooing a stuffed unicorn whooshed and dripped overhead, sputtering short bursts of tepid, bleachy air into the room. Now, sweating as if every pore in his body had been spun open like ten thousand faucets, Thomas got out of bed and paced his bedroom in his sock-feet. Turning on his heels Thomas saw on his windowsill the newspaper and turned to the ad which he had already been over what felt like several hundred times that day. It felt heavier, like the newspaper itself was sweating. Thomas slid the paper under his arm and clapped twice. Like the Judeo-Christian deity with which he had an awkward, unfamiliar relationship his entire life, Thomas Jones let light into his world. As his pupils jumped noisily in his eyes, adjusting to the majesty that is fluorescent lighting, Thomas Jones noticed something on this advertisement which he had not previously seen.

Squinting nervously and practically punching himself in the face in an effort to see more clearly, Thomas reread the hours between which one could call the offices of Keepwater Holding Group. "Qualified candidates should call between the hours of 12AM and 12PM". It had to be typo. The only businesses whose normal hours of operation would fall into this territory generally employed individuals whose uniforms customarily included nipple tassels. And if there was one thing Thomas Jones would never do in this lifetime, it was glue glittery plastic baubles to his nipples.

Considering these new developments Thomas read the article for the seven hundredth time. "There's no way I can manage operations in a variety of facilities in nipple tassels. No, certainly not." Thomas Jones thought to himself. Clearly it was an error, and he would need to just suck it up, get some sleep and call in the morning. But what if he was wrong? What if this was a clever rouse by the management of Keepwater to see if a candidate was capable of paying attention to detail? What if many others had already called to speak to Jameson tonight and he was to be stuck having to wait a whole day more to express his interest in the position? It was, after all, five minutes to noon.

It rang once. Twice. Thrice. Fourth ring now and Thomas Jones was considering hanging up again. Clearly, no one was going to answer the phone, and to let it ring off the hook like this was not only rude, but seriously –

"Yello." A hard, smoky voice croaked from the other side of the line. There were other voices in the background, both male and female.

"Er…Hello?" Thomas had swiftly lost any remnant of

saltiness in mere moments. Whoever this was had dissolved Thomas Jones's testicles by the sound of his voice.

"Yeah? Hello?" said the gruff voice on the other end, "Hello?! Anybody there?"

"Um, yes sir, I am looking for Jameson. I mean, I'm sorry but" he was interrupted by the man on the other end.

"This is Jameson, who is this?"

"My name is Thomas Jones."

"Tom Jones! I'll be damned", the voice become muffled as if Jameson was covering the receiver and speaking to the others in the room, "Tom FUCKIN' Jones on the phone guys!"

"Well actually, my –", he was interrupted by the sound of four or five men and women singing sloppily like they had all just had Jagermeister omelets for breakfast.

"IT'S NOT UNUSUAL TO BE LOVED BY ANYOOOOONE", they held onto this last note particularly long. Another voice was humming the trumpet parts, "Da dad a dad um dum" Thomas waited for the hooting, thigh-slapping laughter to soften before speaking.

"I'm sorry, but maybe I have the wrong number?"

"How many Jamesons do you know?"

"None", Thomas answered honestly.

"Well then I assume you're interested – hang on", he muffled the receiver and spoke to his friends. "Hey, HEY! You can all go home, nice work," the voice returned in full scruffy volume, "So Tommy, where were we, I assume you're looking to become involved here at Keepwater?"

"Actually, my - I - prefer Thomas," he attempted this in hope of coming across as deliberate and tongue-puckeringly salty as possible, however, did not.

"I would too if I were you Tommy-boy". Thomas paused briefly and gave up on this defense. He needed work and wanted this job worse than any he had ever had in his life. Although, in all honesty, he hadn't the slightest concept what the job would entail outside of drunken lounge singing.

"Um, ok then, Mr. Jameson, I was just calling to inquire..." he began before being interrupted again.

"No 'mister' necessary Tommy, call me Jameson. Full name Jameson Moxy." Thomas Jones seriously doubted this, and considered giving himself a sturdier middle name. Thomas Agamemnon Jones crossed his mind.

"Ok, Jameson, I was inquiring as to whether or not you – we, I mean – could set up an interview, perhaps today."

"Well Tommy, as I am sure you are aware, given the times specified in my ad we are currently closed for business today, and believe you me, it's been a doozy of a day," Thomas thought he heard the sound of a single man laughing, but played it off as a television. Thomas noticed that Jameson's voice was beginning to open up a little, into a smooth flow of words that carried a assured, effusive poise. This made Thomas's penis shrivel and retract like a farting balloon, "Sooo, if you'd like you can come in at the start of my next business day, which will commence at 12PM this evening. Let's say 11pm so we can get this interview in before the rush. That's not past your bedtime, is it Tommy-boy?"

"It's, um, Thomas, sir." He couldn't believe he had said it again.

"Sure it is Tommy, well see you around 11ish -."

"But sir…" Thomas now cut off Jameson and was absolutely disappointed in himself for the outburst. Hearing the silence between them he continued, "Where am I supposed to meet you?"

Jameson let the question float unanswered in the electric current they shared before answering in a voice that sounded distinctly like it was pushed from behind a smile.

"When all else fails, Google it." There was a loud smack of phone on receiver then silence. Despite being flatly out salted by the mysterious Jameson, Thomas felt proud of his performance under such duress. It was now well after noon and Thomas was hungry. He had a big night ahead of him.

Seeing as how this was the latest Thomas Jones had woken since his lap-vomiting days at Wildwood Community College, he was quite unsettled in his daily schedule. Gone were the soothing tones of early morning TV news and the audible thwap of newspaper on wet grass. Gone were the sticky, forlorn purple prophylactics melted to the sidewalk. To counter this Thomas Jones made breakfast. A pancake of defiance to gods of afternoon responsibilities! Fie on the noon-time!

Somewhere between bacon and a blueberry muffin, Thomas Jones' phone rang. Messily slopping brown splotches of grease on his bathrobe, Thomas rolled his chin and lips down on their terry-cloth shoulders and scampered to the phone. He had seven messages (eclipsing the previous all-time record by six) and was in danger of an eighth were he to continue admiring the fireworks display that was the blinking red, digital '7' on the answering machine.

Snapping out of a fantasy in which each of those messages were from a different person, Thomas swiped the cordless from its base and answered, tongue still smacking pork fat from his lips and gums. "Hello?"

<u>6</u>

By the time David has recovered from being kicked in the soccer balls by his eight year old son, he could hear the office phone ringing again. Waddling like a bald monkey with a load in his diapers, he made his way to the stairs and the office. It was his superior, Ohmco CEO Alexander Prewitt. This wasn't going to be a friendly call. Clearly news of what happens when the Golden Girls meet Ichabod Crane had reached his employer's pruned visage. He walked past the phone and to the windows.

Staci was hurling their children into a large black SUV in their driveway. The boys looked thrilled. Sophia, not so much. He had no idea where they were going and he could not have cared less.

Beside the black SUV was his wife's car. A vehicle so clearly intended for a woman that it even smelled like a vagina. The car was the color of a newborn baby girl in a diaper made of double bubble. The pinkest of pinks. The pink of a princess's pussy. The car was also a Hummer. A pink Hummer with spinning white rims that had a large red heart in the middle of each tire. The color of that monstrosity reminded David that there were to be workers in the house today to paint murals in the newly renovated first floor. He made a mental note to remind her as he began getting dressed for no particular reason. Perhaps in an attempt to ignore the constant ringing of his desk phone he

32

tied his tie three times. Behind him he heard the shuffling heels of his wife become louder until stopping.

"Baby."

"Yes?"

"Where are my baby's?" David considered strangling her with her own hair in the spirit of Porphyria if she said the word 'baby' again.

"Staci for Christ's sake you just put them in a car and it drove away right in front of you."

"No no, no, no, my BAYYYBEEES!" she sputtered, wiping her golden hair out of her eyes, "The doggies! They have school today!"

His wife's two snaggle-toothed, rat-sized Chihuahuas, Dolce and Gabbana, were to be picked up that morning for "doggy day care", a family institution his wife unremittingly referred to as 'school'. Before they could be picked up Staci would first need to find the microscopic, barking loofahs. This 'doggy day care' cost one thousand dollars a day. Not that the money mattered, but he questioned why on earth dog-sitting cost so much. At this thought, his wife seemingly ripping the thoughts from his head - spoke excitedly, hopping up and down.

"It's the finest doggy school in the world bayyybee!! You saw the brochure: they get one-on-one contact with a professional doggy person who plays with them alllllll day! They get fed the finest food. Filet Mig-nown!"

"The 'G' is silent Staci. It's French", his wife stood, hands-to-hips and huffed with a mingled drink of feigned offense and genuine deflation.

"Well… you just shush, who cares?" she paused, staring at the floor for a moment before looking back up, "Now," returning her attention to the echolocation of twin Chihuahuas, "Where are my little bayybeeeeees", this last word squealed like the voice of a staked witch from between her milk-toast teeth as she scuttled from the room, still in swimwear, on the hunt.

Sliding his well-pressed body into the leather bucket driver seat of a two-year old baby blue Lamborghini Murcielago, David grabbed the scissor door's overhead handle and pulled it down. The engine turned over with a swampy, throaty snarl. Spitting pebbles behind her, the powder blue dragon slid off the driveway and into the street, heading west. Though he owned two dozen motor vehicles, some doubtlessly priceless, he drove and in fact insured only two: his wife's monstrous pink SUV and his own.

As the Long Island Expressway wove and wound round his growling beast. David Drahtman, sitting like dragon's brains at the wheel, began to consider how to approach his meeting with Mr. Prewitt. Drahtman's primary responsibility was to manage the handling of what can most appropriately be considered 'monopoly money'. David played each day with funds invested primarily in the business of buying other businesses. He bought out the competitors of the companies owned by Ohmco and then either destroyed the business outright or turned the property into some other brand of money-making machine related to one of Ohmco's many sub-corporations. This rampant, Viking-style fiscal pillaging was of course quite commonplace in the American market. This is why industries as specific and singular as coffee can have a villainous, nocturnal, troll-like figurehead. Starbucks, despite what David's wife would tell you, does not, in fact, make the best coffee in the world. Stylized advertising and slick-smooth property and logo design aside, what makes business thrive is a lack of competition. And rather than out-pace and out-perform the other coffee makers of the world, Starbucks' board of directors simply put money into the business, advertised itself as the trendy choice among rich, white Americans, and summarily entrenched itself in every corner in the United States. Carving bent creeks of cappuccino into neighborhoods large and small, the drink with the sea-queen cup teaches us that nothing begets money like money.

The issue, today, however – had to do with an entirely different problem. One of David's underlings had inadvertently brought about the very public suicide of a little old lady, and this was by no means an occurrence Ohmco was in need of.

Ohmco, while being one of the most valued institutions of business and finance in the world, was not the greatest in terms of size and assets. Massively powerful holding groups like Wetra International and The Fletcher Group were infinitely wealthy and kept thousands of businesses in their quilted pockets like so many gum wrappers. It was the great mission of Ohmco, as bushels of memorandum would tell you, to be better, get stronger, and improve their image. Being responsible for what happened at the Smithson house was not going achieve this end.

Before David knew it, he was pulling into the garage below Ohmco's world headquarters in Manhattan's financial district.

The elevator eased to a stop at the eighty eighth floor of his building and let David off. This floor was devoted to the cavernous, labyrinthine offices of Ohmco's upper management. The only thing above this floor was the office of the company's chairman of the board, Alastor Shank.

Mr. Prewitt was a stuffy, puckered sort of man. His lips, not unlike David's eyes, pursed back and forth when he wasn't talking like he was gumming a lump of taffy, or kissing prudently at some corporate guardian angel.

"Come in Mr. Drahtman", said Mr. Prewitt as if David was some level of janitor, rather than a major executive who would likely take his job in the years to come.

"Hello sir, how are you?" David said with a not insubstantial dose of submission.   If he had a tail, David would be wiping his ass with it.

Prewitt moved imaginary candy around his mouth and paused before speaking, unhinging his jaws widely so that thick ropes of spit thinned and lengthened betwixt his teeth. Congealed yellow meatballs pulsed in the corners of his crackling gray mouth.

"Not well, Mr. Drahtman. Not well at all." Prewitt drew long on the words, staring dead into David's eyes.

"Yes, well – clearly what happened wasn't expec-"

"Clearly unexpected! However, Mr. Drahtman.

Regardless of what was or was not expected, we now have quite the situation. Don't we?" David might have suspected that his superior expected no answer to this question. His lips parted but before the words could tap and the back of his teeth, Prewitt raised his voice again. "The press is swarming, Mr. Drahtman. Ravenous little beasts on the phone," he swatted a crooked, leathered hand to his desk phone, "at the door" waving the hand to the door, "and on the blasted inter-web!" he thwacked the monitor with all the strength he could muster.

"I'm sorry Mr. Prewitt, but I really had nothing to do with it. Bobby Collins manages that company on his own, maybe we should be speaking to him."

"You are his superior, and under your watch a senior citizen blew her skull off.", Prewitt's face was beginning to flush when his phone rang. He ignored it as long as he could.

"Oh DAMN IT ALL!!" with a great backswing Prewitt swept his arm across the desk and struck the phone. It skidded about a foot but stayed on the desk. Prewitt steamed.

"Mr. Prewitt, what is the difference whether the old bag offed herself or not? It's not like Bobby pulled the trigger himself, he was doing his job. And if I'm not mistaken, now that she's dead with no heirs, the home goes to the bank regardless. Mission accomplished, no?"

"While I appreciate your brilliant assessment of our circumstances, the situation is not so simple. Companies such as ours cannot afford to have such public relations disasters. We are now going to be seen as some sort of corporate monster, a heartless pack of villains!"

"So blame it on Collins and can him!"

"DO NOT RAISE YOUR VOICE TO ME!" Prewitt pointed a rickety, knobbed finger at Drahtman that shook violently before composing himself and pulling his lips back over his gray teeth, "You do understand that we cannot afford to be seen in such a negative light. The Chairman is very disconcerted by all of this. While Ohmco increases our profits every year, we are in constant combat with the giants of the corporate world. Wetra International, for instance, is not only privately owned, but maintains assets that some industry insiders claim may nearly double ours. That being said, an old woman's head being blown to pieces on company business is NOT GOING TO HELP US."

"Okay. So like I said: drop Collins and the press and our partners will blame him."

"Mr. Collins has been removed from his position at Freedom Financial. At the direction of Chairman Shank, he has been moved to a new position within the company. You however may not be so lucky. Your lack of oversight is deeply troubling."

"Fine, fine. You're right. I'm sorry – I should be keeping tabs on Bobby." David winced. The phone rang again. Before Prewitt could wind up again to attempt another feeble swat, David reached over, lifted the receiver and then hung it back up.

"Mr. Prewitt." David paused to give his superior the opportunity to exert his authority again, and not seeing cords of spittle snake in his maw, continued, "I apologize for what happened and promise to work harder." He stopped short of cleaning Prewitt's shoe-tips with his mouth.

"You're quite right you will Mr. Drahtman, Go." David Drahtman rose from his chair and walked back to the elevator, nodding happily at the floor's receptionist/secretary. The girl, a tiny, black haired 22 year old, turned to watch him walk past her with an eyebrow up and mouth open. She was obviously insulted.

"Where the hell do you think you're going" she whispered angrily back at him. David turned, sighed heavily and walked slowly to her desk. Leaning down and placing his mouth close to her ear, he whispered over stuttering anger.

"Shut - the fuck – up Dana" he turned, clenching his fists and forcing himself not to stomp at the carpet and steam from his ears, he made his way to the elevator.

David Drahtman drove home slowly, enjoying the time away from his children and sound-track-of-the-apocalypse that was his wife. He resolved to better himself in the cause of business, and be more like the big-boys, more like Wetra International, more cunning and crafty in the business…of doing business. The image of him sitting in Prewitt's desk was interrupted by the sound of his cell phone ringing. Ever the playful child with his many technological appendages, each person in David's phonebook had an assigned ringtone. His wife calls alerted him by a running chainsaw; his children's' the Imperial March of Darth Vader, depending on the person. This person however, was Dana Jenkins, with whom he shared oft-frequent and illegitimate coitus with not only in that office, but that elevator and that car. She therefore had no ringtone, so as to not alert his children with the tune of Motley Crue's "Girls, Girls, Girls" every time one of their daddy's baby-sitter aged girlfriends started calling. Preparing to curse her into a coma and remove any sense of self-worth the young lady had (the term "cum dumpster" sprung bouncily to mind) he realized he wasn't wearing his earpiece, which went beep-woop-honk only the day before.

Driving in a Lamborghini with the top down on the Long Island Expressway (where cell phone use is illegal on the road) at 85 mph (also less than legal) and insulting an employee who quite regularly has her mouth on your genitals is no simple chore. It requires deft handling and the ability to shout clearly. Pinning his cell phone on the steering wheel and prying it open, he one-handed the phone to his shoulder and pressed his head and cheek down on it while in between shifting gears. Now two-fisting the very concept of lawlessness, David licked his wind whipped lips to sufficiently lubricate himself for the task at hand. He took a deep breath in like he was about to commence playing the tuba before beginning to scream from the dimly lit basement of his lungs. If not only to be heard over the blustering insides of an open backed dragon on the highway, David also wanted to be sure that he made a point.

"DON'T YOU FUCKING CALL ME YOU LITTLE SLUT!" he began and then stopped momentarily as he changed lanes without checking the blind spot (which is pretty much everywhere when you're using your face as a phone-hand). David corrected with a short jerk of the steering wheel and clipped the

back of a long, dusty eighteen-wheeler with Yosemite Sam mud
flaps. The semi hardly felt the toy car flick its steely rear. The
dragon spun out violently; twisting and sputtering off into the
reeds, gouging sandy circles along the shoulder. As the centrifugal
force abated David lost his grip on the phone and allowed kinetic
energy to blast it into flight. It tore off in a line drive, whipping
off into the distance like a ninja star, sending little tornadoes of
digitally rendered swear-words pirouetting out over the shoreline.

When the car stopped, David vomited all over the
steering wheel and much of his lap. Ignoring this momentarily, he
tried to turn the engine over, but it wouldn't, since it was full of
beach vegetation and a healthy portion of crumbly, white sand.
David Drahtman wailed a scratchy cry and punched his pukey
wheel, cutting through the silence of the Long Island morning
with short, angry bursts of honk and muffled cursing.

After a few minutes of this epileptic car-fighting, David
Drahtman ran out of steam. Wiping his palms on the front of his
slacks, David slid open the driver-side scissor door. It was a most
peculiar vision from the road. The long, whippy reeds of the
Long Island Expressways eastern ends occluded the entire
vehicle. After four minutes of honking and cursing and vomiting,
the top of the vegetation had sprouted what looked like a
levitating, blue shield, springing vertically into the sky like a great
sapphire middle-finger. From beneath this, the head of David
Drahtman appeared. Puke in the corners of his mouth, gutters
cut into his brow and assholes for eyes, David was the picture of
curmudgeonly self-loathing. In a moment of impossibly perfect

timing, a fat gull from the sound effortlessly sloped down in a valley over the car and released its sphincter's load of chalky bird-shit squarely in the center of David's sandy dome.

Moments like this, nay, a temper like this was responsible for much of David's premature aging. Why, right this instant, David was forming deep, heavy fork-like folds of crinkled skin on the sides of his eyes. These were more eagle talons than crow's feet. As if rather than an accident and some bird shit, David was standing atop the north tower on a beautiful Tuesday morning. David was nothing if not self-pitying.

After all, none of this would happen if David Drahtman were an honest, faithful person who did not regularly force a balloon animal inside the tight confines of his secretary's sluices. David makes a messy bed. And avoided lying in it like it was his chosen profession.

<u>7</u>

"Hello Thomas, it's Jane." said Thomas's younger sister flatly into the phone.

"How are you Jane?" said Thomas with as much warmth and familiarity as possible. For two people who came, genetically, from the very same pair of testicles as did these two humans, they spoke as if they had met only weeks before. . While Thomas and Jane Jones shared one another's plain, aloof outward persona and not dissimilarly mousy, tow-eyed bodies, they could not possibly be more uncomfortable around one another.

"Fine Thomas, why didn't you pick up the phone this morning?"

"Sleeping in, I had a late night", Thomas imagined her laughing under her breath at the notion that he had been doing anything other than sleeping and masturbating past 9pm (which was partly true). He silently cursed her like he was 14 again, calling her flat-chested and 'fugly' in his head.

Thomas certainly held very little logical animosity towards his sister. Their relationship appeared to be a not uncommon result of sibling rivalries since time immemorial only that this particular rivalry had stretched into the sibling's mid to late thirties.

If anyone had been responsible for the discord between them it was Jane. The elder sister had always been a brutal influence on the more soft-hearted Thomas. She had made it her life's work to convince Thomas he was not only adopted, but not even human. His real father was a rabid wolf and his mother a smelly, homeless dog. This ceased temporarily when she left for college.

"I'm sure it was quite the wild evening, Thomas. Now come open the door"

"Huh? What door?"

"Oh I don't know. The front door? We need to talk and you haven't answered all morning."

It took Thomas longer than it should have to understand what she was saying. Eventually he waddled over to the door and opened it on to the sight of his sister.

Jane Jones, four years older than her brother, had a body not unlike Thomas. Her breasts were indeed a pair of ravioli, small domes which could just have easily been the result of fifty push-ups. The rest of Jane Jones was as straight and narrow as a drinking straw. She was as sexy as a broomstick that wouldn't fly.

This was most unfortunate for Jane Jones, as her mind was quite the contrary to her body. Jane Jones, as plain as a Jane could be, was not what she appeared to be. In high-school, unable to seduce the popular boys with her closet-rail body; she used a far more powerful aphrodisiac: a glee-full willingness to handle with happiness any penis within reach. She, despite the ignorance of family and the few friends she had, was the obligatory under-the-bleachers fire-crotch of Wildwood High School. Her enthusiasm for activities of an ejaculatory nature was the doorway to the secret world she would call her own. Like an XXX-rated Narnia.

Unwilling to bite the bullet and just take a job in the adult film industry servicing English Bulldogs, Jane Jones had committed herself to a life of excellence in clerical workmanship. As she soon became aware, her inability to conduct herself on a phone for eight hours a day without fantasizing about places in which that phone could, properly lubricated, have erstwhile probed would prohibit her accomplishment of that noble end. She began, like her brother, to shift swiftly between opportunities on the open market, eventually landing herself in the sufficiently non-customer service related domain of housekeepery. Jane Jones preferred, and thrived, in the business of cleaning rented rooms. And unlike her brother, once she found her calling, she never betrayed her first opportunity. Nowadays, she managed the work of several illegally employed housekeepers in the business of scrubbing down rooms which are purchased by the hour for purposes which clearly did not include bible study and quilt-making. Jane Jones could spot spots of vomit and see semen from miles away. She could smell the subtle distinctions between vodka and gin in a comforter. Jane Jones, in all her mastery, was privy to tales untold, the bearer of a mythology known only behind doors that would whisper the way out of town in case of a fire. She was most often the first of her cadre of cleaning ladies on the scene of a freshly departed room. Where most human beings would be stricken with fear at the sight of pantyhose on lampshades, splintered hypodermic needles in ashtrays, and night-tables sprinkled with glassy, white dust, Jane Jones was delighted. In her mind, she would carefully reconstruct the night's events. Cinching imaginary belts around her wrists and ankles to the bedposts, Jane would occasionally make more stains than she could clean. In her wildest dreams, Jane Jones was smelly, bloody-nosed prostitute.

It was this fondness for depravity that made Jane believe herself to be to polar-bear to penguin opposite of her brother. In her mind he was stiff and stale where she was moist and pliant. He was day-old bagels, to her warm, soupy bread bowl.

Nevertheless, when it came to the business of the family Jane was the one charged with the task of arranging the scattered Jones clan. Presenting herself, as she did so expertly, as the quiet and conservative Jane Jones of Christmas's past, she was often looked to in times of need as a leader. She had a steady job, unlike her perpetually unemployed brother. On the morning in question, she had called her brother seven times to relate to him the news that their grandfather, at the age of 100 had died the night before.

"Grandpa Jim is dead", she said still in the doorway in a voice that was as emotionally sensitive as she could manage. This was, after-all, a man who had been burped into the world when Teddy Roosevelt was still swinging his big stick. Ignoring the surging saltiness he had developed the night before, Thomas considered momentarily the response, "It's about time", but recanted for the more appropriate:

"Oh no, that's terrible. How?"

"He's a hundred years old Thomas" she said bluntly as she strolled to the kitchen table and pulled up a chair.

"Oh, well, old age then?" replied Thomas wondering exactly how a person died of 'old age' and what that felt like. Did you just hear an oven-timer go off and then POOF, gone?

"No. He stole a car and drove it off a bridge."

"WHAT? Well then why did you remind me he's 100 when I asked how it happened?"

"I reminded you he was a hundred because you said, 'Oh no that's terrible" she said pinching her nose.

"Well how the hell did he get his hands on a car? And what bridge? He's 300 miles inland and there's not a drop of water for miles"

While not the bananas-for-brains infirm that his daughter-in-law was, Jim Jones Jr. (but another unfortunate name in the Jones' family history) was certainly not playing poker with 52 cards, if you catch my meaning. As a young man, Jim went into the produce business. His own father, and his father before him had been in the fruit orchard industry, and Jim would be no different. When Jim's great-grandfather came over from England in the mid-19th century, they landed in South Carolina. This lasted only two years, as Frederick Jones was appalled by his fellow farmers' insistence on decidedly un-paid help. "If a man can't pick his own apples, then what in blazes is he good for?"

The former British Naval officer was so offended by the sight of his neighbor physically bullying the young African slaves that after roundly punishing the man with his fists ("Blast you Yankee scurf! A tough-tongued nickey with a whip you are! Blows on an unarmed young woman! In all my days!"), he made plans to correct the situation once and for all. Jones purchased a large horse-drawn wagon for four dollars and planned to depart for colder pastures. The night before the Jones family would embark; Frederick got out of bed before dawn, scaled his neighbor's fence and herded a family of nine African slaves into his wagon.

"You'll be expected to work, mind you, but you'll be paid like proper gentlemen and ladies." said Frederick, flicking a mosquito off the ratty collar of one of his new employees. "Course you could certainly do with some suits and skirts, if I do say so. Never you mind, all that will be straightened out properly once we reach our destination" Frederick Jones fed this family, gave them his own name and loaded them into his wagon with sights pointed for the promise land, New Jersey.

That family would work for Frederick Jones until they had saved enough to purchase their own land in the free north. They would be dear friends of the paler-skinned Jones clan for many years to come and even after the ones who made that journey on the wagon had passed, each year on his birthday; flowers dress the grave of Frederick Jones.

His family proudly retained an affinity for the fruit tree, and throughout that century and into the next each Jones man was to take over the business. Frederick's youngest son Charles managed the fields until his death on New Year's Eve in a Chinese firework accident. He was succeeded by his son, James. In 1925, Charles' only son died when he fell from a ladder in his orchard. His fall knocked loose a large crate of Macintosh apples from the back of a wagon and he was consequently buried in fruit. They found him several weeks later and laid him to rest beside his father, smelling like fresh apple pie.

It was at this time, that our century-old, demolition derby driver took over the family business. Jim Jr. was as proud as his grandfather and would gladly throw fists at those of his peers who looked down on him for this vocation. While many of his friends were doing the Charleston, smoking unfiltered Camels and drinking their evenings away, Jim Jr. manned the post at their main grocery, in New York City. This would prove fortuitous.

Then, oddly enough, on October 24th, 1929, many of his old friends ceased doing the Charleston and instead began doing Superman impersonations by hurling themselves of rooftops. The Stock Market Crash affected the great majority of Americans, but not the Jones's. Suddenly, nickel apples were all the rage and Jim Jones Jr. was rich on fruit-money.

Jim Junior's only son, James III, was unfortunately, not at all interested in the apple trade and refused to take over the family business when his father offered it to him in the late 1960's. Feeling insulted, Jim Jr. spent the next two decades of his life doing what he always did, growing and selling fruit. In the 80's, now into his seventies, Jim Junior took the same trip his father did. Head deep in the branches of his beloved trees, he took one wrong step, fell to the earth and crushed his hip and left leg. While his family thought it lucky that he survived, Jim Jr. was not at all pleased. After all, if a man can't pick his own apples, then what's he good for.

His son, not so enamored of the apple, convinced the lawyers that his father, now with one usable leg and a questionably useful brain, was out of his mind and was hence able to secure the sale of the family business. Jim Junior promptly disowned his son at this news and vowed to reclaim his apple farm. After years of careful planning, it was this end that drove him to wheel himself out of his nursing home at 3AM that morning. Having stolen car-keys the night before from one of the night-nurses pockets during a particularly invigorating sponge bath, Jim Jr. pressed her car alarm button until he found the right vehicle. Hurdling himself into the driver seat, Jim Jr. squashed the gas pedal with his good right leg and squealed out of the parking lot, bound for his beloved orchard. Crossing the Delaware River that morning, Jim Jr., as is customary for men of his age, nodded off while driving, jumped a curb, and plunged headlong into the whirling, foamy depths below. There was a note on his bed, penned in the scratchy hand of a man who had lived before the advent of the ballpoint pen.

Dear Sons (and Daughters) Of Bitches,

I've gone to reclaim what's mine, my bastard son be damned. Tell that harpy Jessica that rubbing an old man so vigorously is not good for his heart, and I apologize for taking the car, she can pick it up whenever she can find time to traipse her suggestive behind to New Jersey. It's been awful, really, and I hope that you all burn in hell.

Good Riddance,

James Archibald Jones Junior

"Whoa.", said Thomas Jones, after being related to the story of his grandfather's demise.

"Yes - so, seeing how he was already starting to decompose five years ago, we're going to do the funeral tomorrow morning and have him in the ground by dinner", said his sister as if she were relating a schedule of activities to kids away at camp.

"Um..OK… is mom coming?" Thomas crossed all ten fingers and ten toes in prayer that she wasn't.

"No, I don't think that's a great idea. I saw her last week and she spent the day talking about where she and daddy were going for dinner the next day. I think she's under the impression that he's still alive and they're both 20 years old."

"That so?" calmly, not wanting his sister to divine any hint of her and his mother's last few years together.

"And I also think she believes that you're her husband." Thomas forced a laugh and snorted.

"Ha! What makes you think that?"

"She kept flashing a picture of you"

"Flashing?!"

"Flashing, as in, pulling up her nightgown and shaking

her breasts at your picture" she said while pointing with two fingers to each of her breasts.

"Well, that's just crazy", said Thomas, knowing full well that if his mother had only flashed her socks-with-quarters-in-them breasts at him in the morning, it would've been a quiet day on the farm.

"I'm not saying it isn't crazy, she has severe Alzheimer's Thomas, and that sort of stuff happens."

"Yeah well, whatever, where's the funeral?"

"Maria Regina"

"Oh OK, sure." There was a moment of silence as they stared awkwardly at different parts of the kitchen. Thomas popped a cooling piece of sausage into his mouth and nodded, smiling at his sister. He chewed slowly to avoid the responsibility of actually having to converse with her.

"So are you working? Or still sore from what the rollersaurus did to you?" she said with a smirk.

Thomas swallowed hastily and sprayed his sister with salty-smelling orange juice just as he blurted out a response. "Actually, Jane, I have a very important interview tomorrow." There were few things he enjoyed more than sticking it to his sister. Jane, however, seemed unimpressed.

"Very important? Oh my! And where is this event of global consequence taking place Thomas?!" she leaned over the table as she said this, feigning a gripping interest in the topic. Thomas caught the sarcasm in the air and made a face at her.

"In New York actually. Saw it in the paper just yesterday

and they invited me straight in for an interview."

"Why would a very important company from the city be advertising in The Atlantic City Press? That doesn't make sense."

"How should I know? They did. The paper's in my room." Said Thomas defiantly, pushing a piece of toast into his mouth with a fork"

"Yesterday you said? Who eats toast with a fork? Jesus Christ. Yesterday yes?"
Thomas grunted over the softening bread. He nodded over his shoulder down the hallway.

"No need, I've got it here." Jane said as she pulled the paper from her purse. It was opened to a half-finished crossword puzzle.

She licked her thumb and leafed to the small classified section of the paper. She turned back and forth to a few pages.

"There's nothing in here Thomas. Something for the CVS across town. You certainly blew that job. Then there's a counter boy for Luigi's...You might get your ass kicked by a cheese-steak – that's no good..."

Thomas swallowed and snatched the paper away, greasy spots sopping in its corners. "Shut up will you! It's right here dangit. He flipped and flapped. Turned and twisted. But he couldn't find the ad. By the time he checked the date and realized it was definitely the same paper, his sister was getting up and making her way towards the door.

"Enough Thomas, keep it – there's a job for a janitor at the middle school. If you could do that without becoming addicted to Windex you might have something."

"But no, Jane-" before he could finish the door was slammed shut. He heard her yell back towards the door.

"AND DON'T BE LATE TO CHURCH!"

Thomas spent the remainder of the afternoon staring at both papers. Quite obviously they were the same edition of the paper. The cover both said the same thing. They both had the same articles. The only difference was that Thomas's paper had an ad searching for a "salty bastard", and his sister's did not. It made absolutely no sense at all. But it didn't matter; Thomas Jones had things to do. Despite incongruent periodicals, despite a family of incestual matriarchs and fruit mogul car thieves, our hero had an interview this evening.

Thomas was not worried about that elder statesman of sedans as far as the trip went, for he never drove the thing anywhere in the first place. In a decade of service, Thomas had put thirty thousand miles on the car, and more than half of that was from trips within the larger Wildwood community for groceries and gas. After plotting his course online via the ubiquitous Google, Thomas left his apartment at 6pm, hoping to ensure he would be there on time. He stopped for gas, driving five miles out of his way to avoid the one he had worked at in the months after September 11th. Thomas Jones was awkward like that.

<u>8</u>

Sitting on the hood of his powder-blue dragon, David Drahtman had poop on his head and puke in his lap. The early August sun baking every fizzling bead of life from the air around him, David considered suicide by cooking himself alive on his car. Too proud to ask for help on the roadside, and too lazy to look for the cell phone which was no doubt within a few paces of reed and beach glass, David stewed and steamed. Considering various applications of violence which he might employ to the body of Dana Jenkins, David thought – for a moment – that he heard a familiar sound.

Yes, he had. The brassy crash of horn and cymbal, the Wagnerian stomping and bass drum bashing, and of course, the mental image of a tall black helmeted man with dark cape billowing behind him, sweeping up the concourse of some brilliant cosmonautical vehicle, consorting with holograms and generally plotting the demise of his children, the theme of Darth Vader, "The Imperial March" was playing somewhere out in the dunes.

Making the connection between his idol Anakin Skywalker, and the person to whom he ascribed this tone in his cell phone, David scrambled off the broiling hood and tried to locate the source of the sound. Taking careful steps in different directions to be sure which way would take him to his Sith Lord wife, David found that the sound seemed to come from the direction nearest the water. Spattering the reeds with all manner of bodily fluid, David high-stepped his way through the reeds like he was in Vietnam (which he never was; not on account of moral objection and civil disobedience, but rather, because he was two years old and toddlers do not do well in jungle combat situations), or Desert Storm (where he also never was; on account of twelve different implants in his calves, chest, cheeks, lips, testicles etcetera. Notwithstanding these potentially flammable and combustible battlefield no-no's, David would never have went to Iraq in the first place. He was scared of being shot at.).

Quickly, the nearness of the cell phone became apparent, as David could almost taste the musky trumpet of James Earl Jones in the air. Finally, after scraping through sand and beach-garbage, David located his phone, snapped it open and pressed it to his head with two hands.

"Baby – you HAVE to see the mural! It's wonderful - blue and pink and"

"STACI! SHUT UP…"

"You don't like pink? I thought the blue would make you happy I mean -"

"No – no! SHUT UP AND LISTEN TO ME!"

"Ok.", his wife said as if her husband had asked her to change the station on the TV, rather than slap her squarely in the face with a forked-tongue.

"Staci. I was in an accident. I need you to come pick me up. I am at exit –"

"OH MY GAWD!! BABY ARE YOU OKAY!!" she was convulsing, screeching and hyperventilating. Feeling unusually humorous, David responded

"No Staci, I've lost both my arms." His wife let loose a wailing bawl at such a heavenly pitch that one might assume only a border terrier would be capable of hearing it. Baffled and astounded by the brain-blending stupidity that would be required to believe that a man with no arms was able to converse with his wife on a cell phone, David exhaled slowly. This only incensed his wife's horror.

"OHHH DAAAAYYYVID!! ILL FEED YOU AND WASH YOU AND – "

"STACI!! I DIDN'T LOSE MY ARMS GODDAMNIT! HOW COULD I CALL YOU! DO YOU THINK I DIALED WITH MY FEET?"

His wife went silent, breathed heavily – clearly stifling the urge to sob – and said, "Oh."

"The car is dead. You need to pick me up. I'm about a mile past exit 70, eastbound on the expressway."

"Do you want me to call a tow truck?" she was clearly insulted by his joke.

"No. Leave the fucking thing. Just come get me". His wife hung up.

Sitting in the reeds, smelling like an outhouse in high summer, David Drahtman mused on his life. Unlike most human beings, those who are possessed with feelings of concern and compassion for their fellow man, David did not consider either his wife or mistress's feelings. The true loss would be the dragon. Even this, for David, was easily corrected. Whenever David felt dejected or despondent in life, he remedied this by buying things that pleased him. Some of these things he put his body in, and other things were put in his body. David would go car-shopping tomorrow and would feel wonderful by noon.

Overhead the mid-day sun combusted and sputtered white hydrogen into the atmosphere. She blazed and cursed and screamed in all her glory – frying the earth in butter and leeching every drop of moisture from the air. David Drahtman leaned back in the weeds and white sand and lay on his back. Fingers laced behind his surgically reconstructed hair-do, David chewed his tongue and waited for his wife to come fetch her husband from the roadside. In the haze and blurry steam that surrounded him, David's mind wandered before drifting noisily to sleep.

David Drahtman dreamed of dead dogs, melting coins, and prostitutes. He imagined punching small Asian girls in the face and spitting in their hair. If he were awake and able to squeeze his balls, he would've had an erection. His dreams shifted and changed into nightmares that featured malt liquor and cardboard boxes. He was homeless, helpless, and alone. Then, a gun shot. In this landscape, David dreamt he had been shot square between the eyes, and had died on a filthy couch in a faraway land. A black cloak, a window, and a breeze.

David woke up. The moon, like the pearl in the universe's fishy oyster-box hung low overhead. He was still in the sand, alone. Checking his watch, it was after midnight and his cell phone's voice-mail alert (a quacking duck) was feverishly squawking like an early eighties Nintendo game. Digital, frantic, and confused.

David slapped his hand forcefully against his face and screamed. He had been lying in the sun for hours and his face was blistered and fatty like Jane Jones' greatest sexual triumph. Little did David know at this moment, thanks to the fact that he had been partially shaded by the whipping beach grass, his face and arms resembled that of a strawberry zebra. Lines of erupted sun sores were parted by slices of smooth skin. He was part lobster-tail, part corporate wunderkind.

David laid his phone against his head and squeaked. That ear was no longer capable of phone use, as it had been stewed and broiled by the August sun to the point of a jumbo sun-dried tomato. Shifting to the right David called his wife, knowing each and every message was from her. He assumed correctly, that she had simply confused east and west and driven up and down the expressway the wrong way for the last twelve hours. She answered, screaming like she had just had her eyeballs removed with soup spoons. However much low-mindedness and superficiality we can ascribe to Staci Jones, we cannot say she did not love her husband. For she was still, at this moment, driving up and down the expressway looking for her lost, armless husband. After a confused conversation, David walked gingerly to the edge of the highway and waved, painfully, his left arm. Soon enough a honking, swerving Hummer the color of lip gloss on a girl-scout screeched through the pebbly loam lain up against her husband's castrated dragon.

Staci was crying and sobbing wildly, mascara drawn down her face to the point that she resembled some late-nineties Marilyn Manson fan. She bobbed and weaved uncontrollably through the sand and threw herself on him.

"OHHHH BAYBEE!!!!"

"Staci," she refused to be consoled, "STACI!"

"OH! OH! Baby I yam soooo sorry!! I love you I love you I love you." she sputtered while kissing and rubbing his mashed pomegranate-potato face. He screamed and pushed her off. Snapping open her cell phone for light in the darkened shoulder she saw her husband's strawberry short-cake head. Her mouth fell nearly to her knees and she fell weeping uncontrollably.

When they finally arrived home, David, who was beyond reproach, anger, or concern for the fact that his face looked like a man-sized candy cane in a ten thousand dollar suit, was led in by his still grief-stricken wife.

"Do you wanna see the murals baby? Or do you just want to go to bed? I understand if you want to sleep baby I –"

"Sure", said David, who, thanks to natural pain killers, no longer felt the frenzied anguish that would be waiting for him by morning. Seeing the mosaic of senselessness that he was sure his wife had commissioned in their home would, perhaps, offer him a chuckle.

She led him ever-so-gingerly to the 'party room'. It was called so because they were uncomfortable calling a room in their house "The Sixth Living Room", which is exactly what this room was. The room opened into a large walkway so, technically, had only three walls, each of which looked like eight hundred Care-Bears has been nailed to them and subsequently disemboweled. Cotton-candy pink, baby-boy baby book blue and as pale-green as a leprechaun's scrotum, David Drahtman's sixth living room looked like a rainbow had been sodomized in it. About to unclench his peaceful, endorphin induced calm and resort to violence – David was interrupted by the front doors smashing open. It was now two in the morning, and his daughter was just coming home.

Sophia Drahtman burst through the house screaming for her parents.

"MOM! DAD! MOM! DAD! LOOK! LOOK!" she hollered, searching through the palatial home for her parents. David could hear heels clopping and clacking in all different directions as she sought her mother and father. Neither of them made any effort to alert her to their location. Whereas most parents would search for their daughter in order to lace their palms to the girl's cheekbones for coming home at such an hour, David simmered and stroked his crackling face. His wife giggled, clearly in the grips of a good game of hide and seek.

Finally, Sophie turned the corner. For starters, she was nearer to naked as one might imagine possible. A glittery piece of silver fabric, no wider than a necktie was draped diagonally over her hips. Apparently this was a skirt. Her top was comprised of what was clearly a close cousin of the brassiere. The pair of black cups hardly covered two massive scoops of caramel ice cream which were smeared with glitter. She was sweating, just slightly, and her blonde hair was falling in her face – painted like she had an invitation to Jezebel's Halloween party. In her hands was a wad of seven or eight one hundred dollar bills. Her mother spoke first.

"You look hot!"

Both of David's eyebrows jumped so high on his forehead that he looked like a cartoon character who had just had a cannon shot into his ass as he turned his head slowly, appalled, at the girl's mother. Ignoring the fact that her father looked like the hooves of Satan had been dragged across his nose, she spoke quickly, and quite plainly, drunk.

"MOM! You don't even know! I'm in the bar, you know, cosmos and small talk, and then this guy comes up to me. He's dressed in all black, SOOO FUCKING HOT (her mother clapped at this announcement), tall, dark hair, smokin' this big cigar – God! SO HOT! And he's like," at this point, Sophie imitated the voice of a man, "HI THERE LITTLE LADY. YOU WANNA DO ME A FAVOR? And I'm like: SHIT yeah I wanna do YOU a favor! So he's hands me THIS," shaking the bushel of decapitated president heads, "And he's like, go over to that guy over there and flirt with him for a few minutes. Mom this guy was like ancient. Gray, wrinkly, like AT LEAST thirty. And he's like, just go over and see if you can't get him to flirt back. If you do, you can keep this cash. So I'm like, SHIT YEAH!"

At this point, David sat down on the ground and rubbed his temples. Staci was listening with rapt attention to this story and laughing at every word that came out of her daughter's drunken mouth.

"So I push up the twins, you know," she winked at her mother at this comment while grabbing her breasts, her mother swiftly returned the gesture like some strange indigenous ritual, "So I go over to this guy and he just GOES for it, YOU KNOW? He's like touching my waiiist and brushing the hair out of my faaaaace.", David wondered if this gentleman had brought a forklift with him to the bar this evening in order to properly remove the full weight of his daughters blonde locks - which at this moment fully occluded her face to the point where he hoped this prostitute was in fact, not his daughter - from her face.

"So then outta nowheres the guy in the black suit comes back to me and interrupts my conversation with the old guy and pulls me over to his table. WHICH, is surrounded by like five more of these hot young guys in black suits. He hand me more of THIS," holding up the cash again, "and says thank you and goodnight. MOM I ALMOST PULLED OFF MY SKIRT AND JUMPED ON ALL OF THEM!!!"

David Drahtman is, and always has been, an evil little man. However, at this moment, we cannot help but pity his position. His sixteen year old daughter has just come home dressed like a stripper in a hurricane, reeking of vodka and brandishing nearly a thousand dollars she earned using her surgically-enhanced body. Unfortunately for David our pity cannot endure. He paid for that body, after all, and taught it's owner little in the ways of the human. Sophia Drahtman is a product like all things in David's life. A result of unfortunate circumstances set in motion by higher authorities who paid no mind to the consequences of raising children in a ball-pit brimming with diamonds and dirt.

David lay back on the marble, listening to the conversation curl and loop around him. Footsteps above his head sounded the sudden appearance of his sons, who were no doubt awoken by the brainstorming-in-the-brothel-bathroom session that was unfolding in the 'party' room.

Theo and Leo, wearing nothing but underwear, cowboy hats, and a sock each slid into the room, eyes crusted with dreamy tumbleweeds. Upon seeing the cash their sister was shaking about in the air, they both leapt in the air like Billy The Kid and Annie Oakley's illegitimate spawn. Having snatched a few spare bills from their sister's manicured paws they scurried into the hallway with haste. Mother and daughter clicked and clacked after them screeching and swearing around the corner.

<u>9</u>

As Thomas Jones traversed the jumbled loops, passages and tunnels which joined the states of New Jersey and New York like some clanking, iron, circulatory system, he became nervous. Thomas had never liked driving in New York City. The street lanes were almost entirely ignored by the locals, who treated the city streets more like bustling waterways. Cab drivers swerved in and out of lanes at will, cursing one another in more than a handful of distinct languages, pedestrians strolled through traffic like there weren't a quarter million cars crumpled and stacked into piles at every corner. Worst of all, to Thomas, was the sustained conch-of-war like sound that was twenty thousand horns firing at once.

All this commotion distracted Thomas enough that once crossing the outer boroughs of New York City and into Manhattan Island, he would typically park his car at the nearest unspoken for corner and then walk the rest of the way to wherever he was going. Cabs were of course, out of the question. The bus system mystified him, and Thomas would rather have his mother's ankles around his back than be caught dead on a subway. At the heart of this peculiarity was a deep, arresting fear of pan-handlers. He feared them like they slept under his bed.

The jangling, coffee cup maracas in the muddy mitts, the lingering odor of foot and pit, the lazy moan about having contracted cancer of the aids in Vietnam nearly gave Thomas an aneurysm. The first time this happened, he tried to change subway cars but when he opened the door between cars and heard the banging industrial horror-show that is what subway trains sound like while not actually inside one, he thought better of that decision. When that particular homeless man sauntered up to him, smelling like the inside of a dead cat's asshole, Thomas pressed his back against the wall, closed his eyes and pretended he wasn't there. Like the boogey-man had been laid off and needed a dime. Just as this individual had begun hollering at Thomas Jones for ignoring him, he was saved as the car came to a stop at Time Square, offering our hero the opportunity to escape. Thomas Jones never ran so fast in his life.

That day, Thomas spent the remainder of his afternoon lost, being chased by a naked cowboy with a guitar, and accosted by ethnically ambiguous salesmen promoting $5 copies of movies that hadn't come out yet. He wandered aimlessly, wearing two fraudulent Rolex's he bought for forty dollars until he found his car well past midnight.

Today, however, Thomas had a plan. He chose the bridge closest to his final location, parked immediately after crossing that bridge and got out his map. Thomas had been taught all his life that two things one did not want to walk around with in Manhattan were a map and a camera. New Yorkers, as his peers would tell him in early life, would stab him in the heart for being a tourist. He walked, his eyes like tacks on which the map was hung.

Turning the last corner, Thomas began counting off address numbers. The block on which he now stepped (which the author is in no condition to reveal) did not at first glance appear to be the location of a large, multi-national holding group. The road was narrow and dirty and seemed more residential than anything else. On his left Thomas saw several young Hispanic men sitting on their building's front steps, taking long pulls from brown-bagged bottles and eyeing him suspiciously. Thomas Jones, in black slacks, a pale green collared shirt and blue and gray striped tie, did not, in any way imaginable, fit into the scene normally set on lower Manhattan streets at 9pm.

Pulling the map out of his face, Thomas turned to his right and saw the numbers "731-80" in cheap, foil stickers above a black door at the top of several oily black steps. According to the address he had copied from the paper, this should be the place. Thomas looked both ways down an empty street and crossed swiftly, map waving in the air. Closer now, he saw tacked to the door a piece of white printer paper that read "Keepwater Holding Group, NY, NY" in small font. Now sure he was in the right place Thomas checked his watch. Nine-fifteen. He was indeed quite early for his interview. Not wanting to seem too eager, he folded his map many times and stuffed it in his back pocket and began to walk casually up and down the block, map scrunching in his pocket like a diaper. He even went so far as to whistle while he did this.

Not five minutes later, Thomas Jones was mugged. Whistling "Yankee Doodle" with his hands behind his back and doing one of the most extended jobs of pacing this world has ever known, Thomas did not see it coming when a young man with a wool hat over his face grabbed him from behind by his neck and stuck what felt oddly like a finger in his back. He could have been brandishing a hot dog and Thomas still would have wet his slacks

"Gimme your money bitch!" said the assailant quickly. Thomas emptied his map, wallet, cell phone and car keys onto the street, whimpering indistinctly as he did this. The mugger shoved Thomas face first into a light-pole, threw him to the ground, kicked him in the ribs, pulled off Thomas's shoes and stole off into the night with his wallet, phone, and loafers. Thomas Jones scampered on all fours and collected the keys and map while fighting off the urge to sob uncontrollably. Many people in this situation would ask for their mommy. Thomas Jones, however, did not.

Standing and wiping off his trousers, Thomas noticed that he had indeed urinated on himself. He considered briefly the excuse that he had spilled coffee on his lap. Looking at his reflection in a glass door on that street, he soon realized that unless that cup of coffee had punched him in the face, threw him onto a dirty street, and pissed on him, this excuse would likely prove inefficient. Thomas resolved to use the tie as a napkin and dab at his pissed-on Dockers. He convinced himself that a tie only subtracted from his salty-bastardness, and felt slightly better about this. As minutes ticked by, Thomas became convinced that he had broken at least one of his ribs as walking (and breathing) were becoming more and more difficult by the moment. He moved like a busted accordion.

Thomas looked down to his left wrist and found that he no longer had a watch. The thief had somehow relieved him of his timepiece while simultaneously pumping feet and fist into his body. Thomas Jones, battered and barefoot, black-eyed and pissed on, decided in that moment (for the first time in his life), to say in response to the situation he found himself in: "Fuck it". Completely unaware of the time, Thomas decided to cross the street in all his glory and knock on the door of Keepwater Holding Group. After all, he had an interview with a man named Jameson.

Gingerly lifting his body up the five steps that separated Thomas Jones from the door to Keepwater Holdings Group, he was taken aback when the door abruptly swung open and two gorgeous twenty-something young ladies stumbled out of the door laughing madly. Instinctively, Thomas sucked in his belly, puffed out his chest (which caused a sharp tearing sensation in his side) and smiled at them. They paused, holding one another up, and cackled madly at him. Staggering down the steps, they made their way down the block and around the corner before Thomas released his mating posture. Wincing and biting his lip, he used the door handle to pull himself up the last step and over the threshold.

In his present condition, Thomas Jones did all he could to reduce, at the very least, his limp and proceeded into a tiny waiting room grimacing, waddling, and chewing his tongue. He looked very much like he desperately had to empty his bowels. Seeing two chairs Thomas sat down, which brought his urine-soaked pants closer to his face. He smelled, on the whole, like he lived comfortably in an out-house. He thought he heard a window shut somewhere.

There was nothing in this room outside of the two threadbare chairs and another door. He fought the urge to cry for a little more than five minutes, debating whether or not to knock on the next door until it opened.

Out of the doorway walked a tall, ginger-haired man in a black suit with a bright orange tie. He was the type of person whom Thomas Jones would have attributed work of a Navy Seal or Top Secret Agent of some nefarious government shadow operation. Well-built and imposing, the fair-haired super spy from the year 2400 stared at him for a moment. Suddenly and smoothly he then broke into a smile and a wink like he was Johnny Carson, and walked towards Thomas confidently with his hand out to shake. Terrified (and covered in blood and piss),

Thomas stood swiftly in one jerking pop in his ribs and spine, and received the massive, bear-like paw.

"Tom, correct?" and not waiting for an answer he continued, "Name's Jonathan", said the man called Jonathan.

"It's Thomas, actually, -", he was interrupted again –

"Smell like piss and look like shit Thomas." said Jonathan matter of factly, as he pumped Thomas's right hand vigorously. "Well, Jameson is waiting for you inside, I gotta be hitting the streets, time for work you know buddy?" Jonathan smiled warmly and patted Thomas on the shoulder with a heavy, gladiator-like grip before donning a black fedora, tipping it back and striding out the door, whipping it shut smartly behind him.

If the man named Jameson was looking for a man like Jonathan, then the man named Thomas was not even going to cross into Jameson's room after being beaten severely and roundly by what Thomas was yet to know were a 15 year old boy and his little sister (the watch). Suddenly, Thomas, still standing where Jonathan left him heard another voice, which he immediately knew belonged to the man named Jameson, hailing him from behind the open door.

"Tom Jones! Get in here man! We're going dancing", Thomas heard a click, and then the song that was the music of a million miseries in his childhood filled his bleeding ears. *It's not unusual to be loved by anyone. It's not unusual to have fun with anyone.*

Waddling flat-footed around the door like a drunken penguin in man-clothes, Thomas followed the song into the office.

It was small, with a window at the back looking into an alley. Two chairs identical to the ones inside the 'waiting room' were set at the wall before an aluminum desk that could have held an algebra teacher. Behind that desk was the man named Jameson. He was about Thomas's height with sloppy, longish brown hair and thick eyebrows which sat above well defined, entirely unshaven face which was contorting in the effort of singing Thomas's least favorite song. He was wearing black pants, an un-tucked black shirt, and a loose red tie. He was dancing dramatically, slashing his hips through the air and waving the one arm he wasn't using to hold an imaginary microphone. He looked like he was in his early thirties and late for the Black Mass. He probably could have lost some weight and couldn't sing if he ate whole canaries and trumpets for breakfast. He was very likely high. At the least, he looked interesting, and happy. Ceasing quickly and abruptly, Jameson pecked a finger at an I-pod on the desk and shook his head, longish locks banging around in front of his young, crazy brown eyes.

"Jameson. How are you Thomas?" he said seriously, and then grinned again, "Hope you don't mind a little screwing around on our part."

"It's OK", he lied before adding truthfully, "I've gotten it all my life."

"Oh, the music, no I mean the wallet", he pulled from his pockets Thomas's wallet and tossed it at him, "cell phone…aaand the watch", he tossed the watch at a flummoxed Thomas, "oh, and the shoes…I am sorry about the shoes, sometimes they get carried away", he placed Thomas's shoes gingerly on the desk, straightening them so the toes pointed to Thomas. Jameson stopped momentarily and sniffed at the air before saying "And I must say, I don't ever remember Felix taking a piss on anyone, but, you know they're young and stupid…" he trailed off as Thomas wrapped his bruised head around the idea of Jameson sic'ing Latin-American children after him.

"Why, did you –", Jameson cut him off with a gentle hand in the air and spoke softly.

"I know, it seems brutal, but it's the best way of seeing what sort of job you're capable of. You met Jonathan on the way out, no?" he asked.

"Yes"

"Well do you want to do the same job he does?"

"No." said Thomas so quickly the answer nearly humped Jameson's question.

"Exactly", Jameson sighed with palms extended. Thomas gently interjected.

"Excuse me, but I was under the impression that I was here to interview for a job managing the operations of some sort of business or factory or store or something. I didn't know a black belt was required." Thomas thought this last part was funny. Jameson, for almost the first time since they met, stopped smiling.

"Well, regardless, we are looking to hire for all sorts of positions, some of which are beyond a description which we would be able to adequately outline in a newspaper without losing the full nature and character of the opportunity."

"What does Jonathan do?" Jameson seemed to think about this for a moment and responded as clearly and slowly as anyone could.

"Jonathan, besides having a very relevant capacity as a provider of security for various interests, is a member of the upper management of our enterprise. He deals with the 'big ideas', you see?" finished Jameson, lowering air-quotes into his lap.

"So, John works –"

"Don't call him John, he prefers Jonathan, and I think you can relate to the wish, no Thomas?"

"Sorry. Sorry…so Jonathan then - he would be my boss?"

"Oh Lord no!" Jameson exploded. He offered no further explanation of this outburst and spoke again, "anyway, sit down", he extended his left hand to one of the chairs in front of Thomas. He gingerly side-stepped in front of the small metal chair and leaned himself back on to the seat like he was pregnant. With twins

Jameson looked into Thomas's eyes for a moment, smiled widely and spoke.

"So, Thomas Jones, tell me a little bit about you, outside of an aversion for physical combat."

"Well, I have held many different positions in many different industries as a manager of –"he was cut off with a karate-chop-like hand gesture and Jameson's warm voice.

"No, no, no Thomas. What I mean is, tell me a little about *you*. What do *you* like? What do *you* do? What makes Tom, sorry, Thomas Jones, tick." Thomas looked down at his watch at the word 'tick'. Shaking his bruisy head quickly he responded.

"Um, I like to manage people. I enjoy being responsible for things" he had no idea what he was saying, "I like to be looked to in times of need, I like to be the one people trust with –", interrupted again.

"Ok, Thomas, you're a fucking middle-management wonder-boy", Jameson smiled away any offense Thomas could've taken from this sentence, "You, are a man without bias or complication, and you do what is asked of you, is that correct?" Thinking that an answer in the negative would be counter-productive, Thomas Jones nodded.

"Thomas, what I need to know is if you are someone who will, in the time of need, be loyal to me."

"Well, I, er, consider myself a very loyal person who will – "

"Thomas, I need you to stop talking like a resume, ok?" he was, for the second time, sounding very severe.

"Yes, sir"

"Wonderful!" returning to his wide, room-warming smile, "Thomas, my friend, let me tell you a little bit about what we do here at Keepwater." Thomas nodded again and swallowed some blood.

"Great. What we do at Keepwater Holding Group…" he paused thoughtfully and then changed direction, "Are you familiar with what a holding group does?"

"No", Thomas answered honestly.

"Ok. Well, a holding company is an institution that maintains a variety of assets in the form of other businesses. We own hundreds of different companies which do a variety of things. And while there are thousands of institutions like ours that fall under the umbrella of 'holding groups', we here at Keepwater believe that we are quite different than our corporate cousins. Do you follow me Thomas?

Completely and profoundly without the ability to honestly answer that he knew what Jameson was talking about, Thomas Jones said, "Yes."

"Good. What I mean is that some of the enterprises which comprise this noble and august organization might be in some circles considered quite abnormal. In even more disconcerting of moments, ours is a body to which some would even ascribe a certain degree of ethical ambiguity. Plainly, some of things we do might seem to the casual observer, of being, in some way, unfaithful to our clientele." Without Thomas noticing, Jameson had magicked a cigarette into his mouth. He smiled and rolled the thin white cylinder between pearly blocks; the center of which was framed by two front fangs which angled out slightly to form a slim teepee of black space behind an otherwise brilliant smile. The gap in his teeth pissed blue smoke into the air as he exhaled, waiting for a response from the applicant.

Baffled and astounded to every sparking, sputtering neuron in his body, Thomas Jones saw before him a man so salty he could dry the Atlantic with a single belly-flop. His brain smoking, Thomas said, as if this was a thing to say to a person, "Are you a mobster?"

Mouth huge and flapping, Jameson laughed hard and sharply. "Holy shit! No I am not a mobster? A mobster? Brother, I am barely a businessman, much less an organized criminal. Occasionally, we, in a blatantly unorganized manner may, possibly engage in an activity that might – no, not even. Truthfully, Thomas, our intentions are to the benefit of the species and planet. Most importantly you will never have to deal with such things. Any risk that we, of upper management may take is our own. You will deal with far less severe endeavors. Do you follow?"

"Well, what are we talking about? What do you do that is so risky for a company to do", Thomas blurted quickly. He was happy with himself for the question. Continuing seamlessly, Jameson answered.

"We murder people for personal gain."

"WHAT?!" Thomas squealed. Jameson laughed deeply, holding his paunchy stomach.

"STOP! Come on Thomas. I'm fucking around. Merely trying to be upfront with you, in the event that anything would occur in the future involving myself or anyone else who works for Keepwater. I want to make it clear that you are being told now, that this holding group, regardless of our present appearance of massive wealth," Jameson waved his arms widely at the bare, crumbly office, "may, at any moment, reserve the right to disappear. We offer no pension, 401k, or other such sundries, although, in the event that this group manages to succeed in the work of achieving its ends, you will be rewarded beyond the scope of your narrow, small-worlded imagination. We make new colors here, and we invite you to use them in the painting of your life on this planet", slipping a snake's tongue of white smoke through his lips, he continued, "Your impact on this group's future, is yours to decide. For now, however, all I am concerned with is whether or not you can be collected and calm in the face of circumstances which you might find unsettling or confusing. You will not be asked again to defend yourself against the applied violence of street gangs. Does this all seem fair to you Thomas Jones?"

"I suppose. What did you think I would be best suited for doing for Keepwater?"

"Well, what I think, thanks to your interview outside, and our brief one here, may be something you're interested in is the operations of a small business just outside the city, in north Jersey.", he handed Thomas a business card with the name Melvin and an address. "Ask for Melvin, he'll explain everything." Now thoroughly confused, Thomas couldn't control the stew of confusion and curiosity that washed his gums.

"I'm sorry – but what interview? We hardly talked? Who is Melvin?" Jameson smiled warmly again and spoke evenly.

"Melvin is the project manager for a small factory at the address below that produces items for auction or sale, online and off. This company is owned by Keepwater (he pointed to himself) and operated by Keepwater (pointing to Melvin's card). You are going to work for Melvin"

"How much does working for Melvin pay?" Jameson looked impressed and talking with his hands, answered.

"How's 50k sound?"

"Great!" he said trying not to sound too excited but nevertheless doing so.

"Done then, let's get you to a hospital," he leaned forward and yelled over Thomas's head, "CRANK!" A man dressed identically to Jonathan, but shorter and with spiky blonde hair entered. One of his eyebrows seemed to be permanently stapled in an upright position. Equally as imposing as Jonathan, Crank too looked like he could digest Thomas with his mind if he was so inclined. "Take Thomas to the hospital, and give him some cash to get where he needs to go. You start the day after next at 9am. Good luck Tom Jones", he laughed loudly as Thomas heard the door close behind him and the man named Crank lead him gently out the door.

10

As Thomas Jones left the offices of Keepwater Incorporated accompanied by a spiky-haired, black-leathered, sunglasses at midnight salt-lick, he couldn't help but think that the man, whom he was told to call "Crank", had to be an actual vampire. He even had the teeth for it: pearly, inverted mountaintops, nestled in valleys of gum, rolling pink hills that were always exposed due to the fact that Crank never seemed to stop talking. Or laughing. Crank thought Crank was hilarious. Where Jonathan looked tough as a nail gun and spoke like it also, Crank looked like a power tool, but spoke like a drug-addled macaque.

"Yeah man, you look like a bag of shit!" pointed out Crank before following the remark with a loud, abrupt cackle – a machinegun of *HAHAHA* which ended as briskly as it began. Now with a serious look on his face he pointed to a black sports-car on the corner of the block. They passed a scum-covered blue hatchback with a paunchy mustachioed man sleeping in the driver's seat. As he opened the door for Thomas to get in, the new employee responded to the gesture, "Why thank you kind sir", thinking he was teetering on the brink of smooth.

Crank stared at him blankly for a moment, still holding the door, smiled wildly and said, "HA… You're a *faggot*!", and slammed the door in Thomas's swollen face.

Thomas watched Crank laughing fiercely in the moonlight as he walked around to the driver side and opened the door.

"I mean, seriously bro, I totally support your rights and all, I do, I really do man," At this point, Thomas was confident that Crank was under the influence of cocaine, and judging by a nose which looked like a powdered donut hole under the interior lights, this was an accurate assumption. Continuing, Cokey The Wonder Dog went on, "All I am saying, dude - is that - is that – bro -" he paused to laugh, snort loudly and bark out another laugh, "Bro -All I am saying my man – is - doesn't having a dick in your ass, suck?!" Crank thought this was wildly humorous.

The drive to the hospital was a blur for Thomas Jones. The vampire named Crank went through a blow-inspired litany of topics ranging from hot dog machines and card tricks to windmills and Venetian blinds. At one point Crank told Thomas he loved him thirteen times in a row and at another broke down in tears over the death of his childhood pet, a male hamster named Amanda. He also spent a full three minutes singing the song "My Sharona", only he inserted the word "bro" for every single syllable in the lyrics. "Broooo Brobrona!"

It was clear that Crank was taking Thomas to a hospital closer to his home, in Wildwood. Besides the fact that he hadn't given Crank directions, Thomas connected the dots which separated his own car in New York City and how on earth he was ever going to get back to it, he asked.

"Um. Crank, sir. How exactly did you – I mean, my car is still in the city and I don't see how I'm going to get back to it."

"Dude – bro – dude. Don't worry about it. We'll figure it out. Well – I won't" quick laugh, "I mean – you know – bro – Jameson will take care of it bro"

Thomas was in too much pain to argue.

By the time they had reached the emergency room entrance, Crank was regaling Thomas the tale of how he grew psychedelic mushrooms in his bedroom when he was a teenager. When his mother asked him what the shoebox full of cow-shit and fungus in the corner of his room was, he told her he was growing potatoes. Thomas wanted to tell Crank that potatoes grew underground, but he didn't. Instead, he got out and told the lunatic to wait in the car.

"Oh sure man, sure, but hold on a sec", Crank reached into his leather coat and pulled out an envelope and handed it through the window to Thomas who grabbed it quickly. Inside was a credit card with the name Jameson Moxy on it. He assumed this was to pay for whatever repairs would be needed to his face, torso, arms and legs

The last time Thomas was in a hospital, he had just come to the realization that blue pajamas and red tablecloth tied around your neck do not a flying superhero make. As twenty neighborhood kids looked on, Thomas leapt from his roof; hands outstretched in the air, big drooly smile on his big doofy face, and fell quickly and awkwardly on his lawn. Little Thomas Jones had broken his legs.

That hospital trip was not unlike this one. The waiting room stunk like a funeral and was packed to the bricks with moaning, sweaty, half-dressed invalids – each one either bleeding or wheezing or heaving or crying. Worse than all this was the fact that unlike his last visit, the time was on this occasion by now nearly two in the morning. Much like a White Caste, a hospital's clientele is entirely dependent on the time of day. In the early afternoon, a hospital is populated by bee stings, snakebites, and sprained ankles, not unlike the way a White Castle is rife with little league teams, construction workers, and overweight video game champions. At two AM, however, a White Castle is stuffed with the stoned, the homeless, and those whose vulva are on sale for not much more than the cheeseburgers. Similarly, a hospital in earliest morning smells like a neglected litter box and is home to the diseased, the drugged, and the dying. Its sound, a rush of sobbing, wailing, squelching madness is full and horrible. By day, girl-scouts get stitches. At night, old ladies are munched up by cancer like a crinkly sleeve of thin mints.

Fortunately for anyone not standing on this reaper's porch, the hospital was also located in Wildwood. This alone would bring in a different sort of midnight injuries. However, the fact that they were not only in Wildwood, but in Wildwood during early August – the summer's smoldering centerpiece - was most important. The year's litter of pissy teenagers from Long Island were always up to the task of providing much-needed comic relief. Like a Falstaffian Messiah, nothing would break up the mouth-filling misery of a hospital waiting room like a 19 year old boy having his stomach pumped because he drank four gallons of milk in fifteen minutes on a dare. Or the girl who waddles into the room at four A.M like she had shit her pants, when she really had a bottle of Zima stuck in her honey-pot. Better still, the brilliant young genius who pierced his own nipple with a staple gun. That last one was especially amusing because he ran through the sliding glass doors in nothing but flip flops and khaki shorts, screaming at the very top of his lungs with an expression of utter horror – absolutely covered in blood. For about one second you might've thought he had been shot. But then you'd realize: Nope. He's just a fucking moron.

Thomas spent the next forty-five minutes reading a pamphlet about Prostate Cancer back to front at least thirty times. By the look of the hospital bulletin board, *Prostate Cancer Awareness Month* was upon them. There were pamphlets and posters of smiling, middle-aged men flashing thumbs-up signs. He couldn't help but wonder what precisely those men intended to do with those big, floppy, upturned digits. This was the last thing a man who used to give himself breast exams three times a year in complete terror at the prospect of being diagnosed with cancer of the boobs wanted to see.

He was horrified by what he read through his one functioning eye. Apparently, men his age should already be having annual examinations for this most deadly form of cancer. Early detection is key, said the pamphlet. Torn between living and having his rectal cavity probed by a hairy-knuckled proctologist, Thomas considered his options. Should he mention his concern to the doctor? He had certainly had plenty homophobia for one day and was not wont to stink up the thumb of a quarterback. Half-asleep and imagining a conversation in which he would ask another adult to put their hand in his asshole, Thomas was shook awoke by a hammy pink hand on his shoulder. The nurse, a portly little Irish sausage of a woman with big sloppy curls no doubt loosened by the stress of playing catch with the projectile vomit of a heroin addict someone found on the boardwalk, nodded motherly up to a waiting physician who was still calling his name.

"Thomas Jones."

"Yes", spluttered Thomas, trying to rub his eyes and finding that the left one was the size of peach meatballs. He picked himself up slowly and looked at the doctor. To his surprise, the emergency room doctor was in fact, flat-out gorgeous. She was tall, thin, and built like a Barbie. He hair was dark and pulled back like she had just awoken and her lips looked like two pieces of skirt steak had been sewn together. And despite the awful stink of all things around her, she smelled like cinnamon.

"Thomas, my name is Doctor Beckett and I will be helping you this morning."

"Excellent", said Thomas in a surprisingly calm and collected voice. Never having been so inadvertently sexy in his life, he was impressed with himself, although if he had remembered what he looked like at that moment (bleeding, blue, hair in all directions, smelling like urine, and with only one open eye) he might have thought better of it.

"Well, Mr. Jones, you look like you've been attacked by some pretty tough cookies?"

"Teenagers, actually" said Thomas in the same pseudo-sexy voice he had just employed on accident. Unfortunately, this time, the words did not match the voice and he sounded like an idiot. Worse yet, it was one teenager. And his little sister.

His confidence smashed to specks and sediment the patient continued more carefully, "Just kidding! Um - Anyway, - I have been beat up a bit tonight - mugged – really. I'm pretty sure

I've broken a rib and my face feels pretty sore," he paused before ending masterfully, "Ow."

The doctor sniggered on a smile.

"Well then Mr. Jones; let's get a look at you. You can get undressed in Room 23, right down the hall."

Thomas closed the door to Room 23 behind him and clapped twice. Unfortunately, this hospital employed light switches. Flipping it, Thomas began to undress. Owing to the dexterity required of disrobing, he was coming to realize the full depth of his injuries. He felt like he had fallen off a roof again, except it was a much higher roof, and he had been thrown of it by a 10 year old girl. Every bone in his body ached and he looked like he had swollen three inches in every direction. He could've gained 20 pounds on swelling alone. Once he was down to his stained briefs, Thomas gave up. It wasn't like he had any chance of seducing a beautiful, well-educated doctor looking like he had just wrestled a restroom and lost. The sight and smell of piss wasn't going to make much of a difference. Now near naked, shivering, bleeding and stinking of toilet, Thomas waited for the door to open. A day ago this situation may have given him cause for a nervous breakdown. But tonight, he was considering the best way to ask this woman to put her finger in butt.

She entered half-way through a sentence, "Smells like a urinal in here for god's sake –" she paused, flashed a look at Thomas's stained Hanes and said simply, "Oh.". Dr. Beckett placed a clipboard on the counter beside the table on which Thomas was sitting and continued, "Happens all the time Mr. Jones, don't even worry about it." She smiled wide and let her brownie-brown eyes lay cakey and frosted on his. Thomas thought for a moment she might be undressing him with her eyes. But then he remembered that he already was as undressed as he was going to get.

Dr. Beckett reached into her white overcoat pockets and handed him a blue ice-pack. He caught it and she pointed absently to his right eye which resembled, ever so slightly, a taco salad. Gingerly, he pressed the cool blue jelly bag to his face and sighed. Suddenly he felt the hot hands of the doctor running in tandem down his right side. His skin puckered at her touch and he immediately felt better, like hands of aspirin and aloe were melting into his side. Then, quicker than a computer counts to three, sudden stabbing pain shot through his side.

"Oh yes, yes. We've broken a rib indeed. Unfortunately there isn't all that much we can do for you besides prescribe you some medication for the pain and suggest a good deal of rest." She went on running her hot butter hands over his body, seeking like caramel ninjas dressed in gold rings and diamonds for bodily trauma. Bruised and sore as he was, Thomas Jones was clearly more ugly than injured. His rib was indeed broken, but beyond that, he had simply gotten his ass kicked. And no doctor known to man can cure that awful calamity.

As he considered these things, condensed water from his ice pack was running over his face an onto the beef balloon that was his lower lip. This cooling, refreshing rainfall was brought to a halt when Dr. Beckett reared in front of him. Momentarily realizing how absurd he must have looked in his pissed-on underwear, mouth agape in satisfaction by the blue Jell-O-filled condom he held smashed into his brow-line, Thomas straightened up, winced, and hunched again.

"Vicodin. 750mg. This will help with the pain. Do you mind me asking what sort of work you do?"

Two problems were apparent: The last time Thomas Jones used Vicodin on a regular basis, that period of his life ended with him showing up at one of his employee's Sweet Sixteen, uninvited and loopy to the belt on pills. When he woke up he was in the catering hall's janitor closet, handcuffed to an ice sculpture of the Eiffel Tower. Secondly, he had no clue what sort of work he did. Again, hardly aware of what he was saying, Thomas replied.

"Sorry, can't say. Top secret" If he wasn't already winking, he might've considered it as an appropriate ending to such a statement. It wouldn't have been appropriate. No more so than the ridiculous sentence that preceded it.

"Well, that's wonderful Mr. Jones, but I would suggest that whatever secret spy work you are up to, make sure you don't do any heavy lifting."

"Sure thing", he smiled, and it hurt like brushing your teeth with a pineapple. Despite his agony, Thomas thought he was really hitting this one out of the park.

"Lastly, Mr. Jones, I want to suggest that you consider seeing your own personal physician in the near future. At your age there are a lot of precautionary measures that men should be taking. According to the records I have here you are well behind on some procedures". Struck by the brilliance of his plan, Thomas pointed a crooked finger in front of his face and said abruptly.

"Yes! I was reading about prostate cancer, why don't we take care of that right now". Channeling the spirit of his employer, Thomas stood, smiling painfully, and bent over the examination table.

The old Thomas Jones would have been happy that he was taking a sensible health concern seriously. The Thomas Jones that had been vomited from the stomach of this evening was happy for another reason. He thought he was quite impressive with all his prostate cancer awareness. As these two figures wrestled to the death in the head of Thomas Jones, he heard the snap of rubber glove band on wrist and the squelchy splat of lubricating jelly being smeared on latex. Forcing himself to consider the benefits of the exam, Thomas began to imagine a prostate the color of sunset on Valentine's Day. Pink, shiny, and smiling – and then the bony index finger of Dr. Marlena Beckett squiggled its way into his asshole.

Almost immediately – as swiftly as dreams of ballroom dancing prostates left his mind, Thomas Jones sprung a rigid, thunderous erection than *plung* bouncily off of the underside of the steel table.

"Happens all the time Mr. Jones." He thought he heard her laugh. And he was right. Soon, she withdrew her finger and Thomas had the strange sensation he had pooped out an Eskimo. It was cool and living as it left him.

"Everything seems to be, in place", with the slightest hint of a grin, holding out the prescription.

Standing, stiff as a soldier and stinking of a gas-station bathroom, Thomas took his prescription from the doctor, slung his clothes over his shoulder and walked out of Room 23, half-naked and ready for love.

As he neared the front doors of the hospital, Thomas noticed that something strange was going on outside. Either the parking lot of the facility had been transfigured into a nightclub in the previous hour or there was a better explanation for the swirling blue and red lights that whipped through the glass doors and into the lobby.

The first thing he heard was a combination of laughter, swearing, and thumping. When his eyes were able to eat up the scene, Thomas found Crank being wrestled on the hood of his car by three policemen. On the trunk of the car was a plastic Ziploc bag filled with white rocks so large you could've used it to anesthetize a brontosaurus. If you closed your eyes you would've thought Crank was being tickled from the sheer hilarity he seemed to find in the whole affair.

Rather than walk, half-naked, up to the police and ask them politely what the problem was, when the problem couldn't be plainer, Thomas calmly kept walking in the opposite direction. He knew how to get home from here. It'd be a decent hike, but it was better than felony drug trafficking charges. Thomas slid his shirt back over his head as he walked, checking over his shoulder to make sure the cops weren't on to him.

Just as he had gotten out of range of the hospital grounds and to an intersection near a gas station, a car pulled up to the light and stopped in front of him. It was a crummy looking blue hatchback. It looked familiar.

<u>11</u>

David woke early that morning and dressed quickly, for two very different reasons. Firstly, he absolutely refused to arrive after his secretary Dana, whom he was sure was going to be hostile owing to the mathematics apparent in an equation in which one subtracts common decency from the sum of his and his employee's twenty-one-year-old genitals. If he could come before she came (pun well-intended), near seven in the morning, he might be able to cordon himself off in his office and conduct business via speakerphones and email. That, coupled with a locked door should do the trick. Surely, this was futile. Eventually he would have had to deal with how calloused and wriggling his heart had been. But not today was what he thought. Not today, and probably not tomorrow.

Secondly, David had made his mind as he lay in bed the night before, face slathered in creams, that he was going to appeal to his corporation's Chairman and Founder, Alastor Shank. The crusty veteran of global finance had always seemed to like David, although they rarely spoken in person. And after the Smithson debacle, David was mortally committed to ensuring that he was still in the good graces of the powers that be. The news the night before was ablaze with stories of the suicide. It appeared they had chosen to blame a new employee, one David had never met, named Adam Brewer for the disaster. He was fired, and forced to issue an apology to major media outlet. While a relief on one hand, David did not reach the stinky peak of the asshole mountain by being passive. He needed to keep his chairman happy. He'd ask for new work. He'd wink and smile. He'd suck a dick if he had to. He'd suck the skin right off it.

It was well known within the company that Shank himself never arrived in his office later than four in the morning and David saw it as an attempt to wedge his face into Shank's livered and dimpled backside with nary an interruption.

There would be problems, of course, and David hoped to carefully dip and slip around the obstacles before him. Avoiding his mistress and not bleeding from facial sores, while not the least of his problems, were certainly not the worst. His wife had a massage appointment at 5 a.m. and David would have to get Staci's heinous little beasts into a limo at 5:30 before he could leave. That odious pair of yapping, slipper-humping little monsters would be difficult enough to find, let alone capture and deliver to the day care service's driver. Furthermore, David was going to have to take a different car to work. Not that he didn't have a fleet of Italian sports cars at his disposal. He just didn't have insurance, registrations, or license plates for any of them. David loved his powder-blue Murcielago, and all his other vehicles were primarily collector's items. He only drove them on his property when he had them in front of the house on display for company. Since the car he loved more than any person he knew was still sitting on the side of the road, awaiting rescue, the only car he was going to be able to drive all the way to Manhattan would be his wife's. A vehicle so clearly intended for a woman that it even smelled like a vagina.

The car was the color of a newborn baby girl in a diaper made of double bubble. The pinkest of pinks. The pink of a princess's pussy. The car was also a Hummer. A pink Hummer with spinning white rims that had a large red heart in the middle of each tire.

David got in the shower, half awake and turned on the water. And then he screamed at the top of his lungs and fell into the tub, *clonking* his head on a rack suspended from the shower wall. Needless to say, his sun-banded face did not respond well to pulsing hot water.

David skidded from the shower at 5:00 a.m., still damp and dressing as he hopped out of his bedroom, with one more lump on his head then when he entered it. By the time he was downstairs his wife was already outside by the pool, stomach-down on a massage table. As he briskly streaked out to inquire when the last time was that she had seen her wooly, impish charges he noticed how early it was.

Staci Drahtman was clearly very relaxed as her hands lolled limply over the sides of the black leather massage table. Her head hung loose and jiggly over the front end of it and her long golden locks wobbled with the motion of the massage. If she wasn't moaning longingly he might have believed her dead.

The man who was going over David's towel-naked wife was quite short and had black hair. The masseuse had a bronzed, oily complexion and a moustache he curtained over a wide smile. He was not appearing to have a reaction to the fact that David's face looked like a referee at a football game between flowers and hand-fruit. And he wasn't massaging Staci at all. He looked like he was scratching her back.

"Staci. Why are you getting your back scratched at sunrise by a janitor?"

"David shut up!"

"Staci, you couldn't do this later in the day and find the dogs on your own?"

"It's a *very, very, very, very* exclusive massage style that was created millions of years ago"

"Oh for the love of—"

"And they were booked through October unless I took something this early. And he's no janitor; he's a practitioner of ancient Mongolian Exfoliation Therapy. It's *wooonderful.*"

"Staci, I swear to God—"

"And by the way, his name is Pepe."

"Pepe?"

Pepe smiled at the sound of his name and waved at David before returning to his work with vigor. He looked very serious and almost like he was playing Staci like a piano.

"A *Mongolian* masseuse named *PEPE?*"

Pepe smiled and waved again.

"Yes dear." Staci paused as if in thought, staring blankly

through a wall of blonde hair and finished, "It's by China!" David paused for a full minute with his thumbs in his eyeballs.

"Staci. Where are the dogs?"

"Well, Gabbana was with me in bed until I got up and I haven't seen Dolce just yet. Try the boy's room, he's always in there poking around for treats those naughty boys have left behind." she giggled through her nose at this thought.

David turned silently and headed back toward the house, leaving his wife with Pepe, the Mongolian back-scratcher. First he made his way back to his bedroom to see if Gabbana was still in bed where his brainless bride had left it. Sure enough, the dog was still sleeping on its little back with its little red turtle-head hanging out of his belly. He was panting, tongue flapping madly, eyes closed. Gabbana was having a wet dream. Imagine momentarily what sort of canine carnality was on display in the pooch's personal peep show, he recalled that he was actually being given a wonderful opportunity to quickly nip half of his dog-hunting problem in the butt. As he mused on a plot to snag the snarling little horn-dog, Gabbana's black, diamond-studded collar bumped and rattled in stride with the animal. At its front, a large diamond "G" bobbed in rhythm off the buckle.

David quickly formed a plan. Snatching a small dog kennel and a pillow case from their places in his wife's walk-in closet, David crept back upon the aroused Chihuahua who was by now humping rhythmically at the air, no doubt porking a Pekinese in his dirty dog dreams. David intended to wrap the beast in the pillowcase and stuff the tiny package into the kennel, pillowcase and all. Raising the silk fabric over the visage of his wife's spasming pooch, David took a deep breath. Just before he could lower the boom (and close his mouth), Gabbana gave a sudden *ARF!* and ejaculated on David's face. The thick, yellowy spackle thinned in strings between his teeth. It tasted like a dirty fish-tank and felt like snotty, salt-water putty had been blasted on the roof of mouth. Spitting and wiping the dog scum off his tongue with the pillowcase David woke the dog accidentally who sat upright with a start, *arfed* once again, darted off the bed and into the bathroom.

Cursing and convulsing, David ran after the now quite satisfied animal in the bathroom and began a frantic serious of swings and grabs. The dog bounced around the counter and shelves of the bathroom, finally landing in the toilet. David shut the lid and cursed the dog from above. It took all his strength to resist the desire to take a dump on the dog's head.

It took David another fifteen minutes to get a good enough hold on the wet beast with the pillowcase to yank him from the toilet and into the dog carrier. Swearing and muttering words of triumph to the animal, David stalked off with one kennel full of a wet Chihuahua that, given opposable thumbs, may have been lying on his back in the kennel smoking a cigarette.

True to her word, Staci's second puppy, Dolce, was indeed in the twins' playroom. Unlike his more sexually inclined brother, Dolce was a glutton. At this moment the dog was rolling back and forth on the parquet floor of the room, completely enclosed in a small garbage wire-mesh can. Either the garbage can had learned how to bark, or David had found what he was looking for.

Once again feeling fortunate to have caught this twin unawares, David set down Gabbana's carrier and stalked quietly up to the barrel, whose closed bottom was facing him. Hoping that the imprisoned animal would be satisfied by the earlier cum-shot facial he had provided David that he would not make too much noise, he moved closer still, intending to simply turn the can over and trap the dog between the floor and the receptacle.

Gabbana, however, had other ideas. He waited until David was as near the can as possible to begin a series of alarming *arf*s. Unfortunately, Dolce was not the brain-child that his brother was, and instead of exiting the garbage can he simply ran face forward into the back of it, speeding away from David like a wire-mesh homing missile.

With sharpness that belied his personality, David dove to his left and grabbed the black plastic garbage bag as it streamed behind the projectile puppy. Pulling hard, David had Dolce trapped. Now holding a garbage bag that was full of refuse, a ten-thousand-dollar diamond collar and a living Chihuahua, David tied a knot in it, poked two holes in it with a pen so the infernal rodent wouldn't drop dead and sat down, breathing heavily.

Not more than five minutes later a horn sounded outside the home of the Drahtman's. David sighed and carried the kennel and the garbage bag downstairs and out the door. Not stopping to explain, he quickly handed off both to the driver of a long black limousine and turned back to the house. The driver, an older, lanky man with wiggly jowls simply cocked a bushy peppered brow and put both the carrier and the *arfing*, thrashing garbage bag in the rear of the limousine without further protest. David could hear all sorts of assorted barking from within the vehicle and couldn't care less if the animals were torn asunder by wolves in the back of the stretch.

Climbing inside a vehicle so large and so pink that it looked like a tank that had been remodeled by Hannah Montana, David felt like he should have been wearing pumps. He turned the key and felt the engine turn and growl. There were three seconds in which the car didn't feel like the inside of a uterus on Mother's Day, and then the stereo came on. At a volume beyond the hearing of highly intelligent life from outer space, a song being sung by a woman who was happier than anyone David had ever met began scorching into his eardrums over a poppy, sloppy, frozen daiquiri sort of music than smelled of artificial flavors and blue food coloring. Screaming and punching the stereo in its stereo face, David Drahtman pulled out of his home in a pink hummer with red hearts spinning on white rims. He was furious about it.

By the time David had reached his building he had been honked at repeatedly for an hour, whistled at by at least five different cars at lights, and strangely enough, flashed twice by breasts unknown. Hers was a car that would not go quietly into the office. Billy the parking attendant even laughed so hard at the sight of Drahtman in the thing that he had an asthma attack and needed to scramble for his inhaler. David would take the mockery and insolence of his co-workers and colleagues for driving around the deepest, darkest desire of every nine-year-old girl on the face of this good earth; he would not, however, allow himself to be spotted by the leopard he had been of late pawing. At least not today, and probably not tomorrow. Dana normally arrived in the office right around seven. It was five of.

David ran flat out to the door of the garage elevator and smacked the 87th floor button with both hands like he was hammering nails. When he reached his floor David turned the corner like a ninja who had never heard of Coppertone and caught a glimpse of Dana's desk. Empty.

Sidling along an artificial cubicle wall like some special-ops desert storm trooper, David shamelessly shoved aside one of the newer interns in the office. This one in particular, whose name David couldn't be less interested in knowing, was his least favorite. He had more tattoos than David had money. Ignoring the bespectacled intern's queer stares at his fat, red face, David clambered to the door of his office, swiped a key card to open it, hurtled through and shut it behind him before sitting down on the thick black shag.

David spent the next hour peering intermittently through the thin black plastic blinds which shuttered oversized panes of glass. When Dana arrived she seemed unaware that he had even arrived, despite the closed office entrance. Knowing well that he needed to move his secretary in order to be able to reach the elevator again to see if he couldn't persuade Alastor Shank to a chat, David formed what might have been his fourth brilliant plan of the day.

Disguising his voice and covering the receiver of the phone with his $300 tie, David dialed Dana's extension on the inter-office phone and followed it with another two digit combination which would make the called appear as "Unknown" on her phone. He used it constantly.

"Ohmco, Dana speaking, how may I help you?" she sounded aggravated at the fact that only three minutes had elapsed in her shift.

"Yes, Mr. David Ratman please." he was sure to sound foreign in a way that smelled like curry and coconut milk and to mispronounce his own name. Hoping momentarily his secret admirer would defend him from such careless indifference, he was swiftly disappointed.

"Mr. Ratman is not in yet today." David thought he could hear the bile in her voice when she tasted the sound of his name on her lips. She sounded like she had just eaten maggoty cheese. Trying his best to ignore such an oversight on her part, David responded in what he hoped sounded as unlike David as is possible.

"OK. Well, yes I have a special delivery for Mr. David Ratman."

"I'll be right there for Mr. Ratman's package." Dana was nothing if not nasty.

As she slowly strolled off out of view, peering around her for a sight of the man with the makeshift gearshift, David waited.

When she had fully turned the corner he bolted, baffled he had been so slick and greasy and snapped back into the elevator. He nearly put his middle finger straight through the button with the number "88."

Alastor Shank's office comprised the entire top floor of the Ohmco building. It was cavernous. Mountainous. He could have installed an in-ground pool. Being modest, he had instead put a three-hole mini golf course in one of the yawning triangles he called "corners." Wall-less, it was without column or partition, division or divider. An open room with a fireplace large enough to cook Kong, a rug skinned and peeled from the cadaver of the Yeti, and of course, three holes of mini-golf complete with windmill and clown head. David could swear there was a hot dog cart, manned by an Arab salesman and an umbrella. Though, clearly, it would never rain. Not that it didn't look plausible through the twenty-thousand square foot gilded gold and glass ceiling. Outside, the morning's choking, smoky moisture had turned vicious, pissy, and black.

At the rear of the great room was Shank, behind a black marble slab that David knew to be a desk only by the fact that it had a phone on it. The chairman was behind the mountain of black stone and seemed to be having the time of his life talking to somebody on said telephone.

Before he could join in the festivities, David had to clear the desk of the only genuine barrier in the room. Behind a cylinder of green glass sat Mr. Shank's personal secretary, Marigold Humphries.

Marigold looked like a thoroughbred porn star. Like she had been bred for it from the loin and limb of Jenna Jameson and Ron Jeremy, Pamela Anderson and John Von Dong. Were she not staring at him and smiling, he would have thought her another pricey bauble. Some sort of twenty-third century sex doll. But Ms. Humphries was indeed real. And she could talk.

"Mr. Drahtman!" she was *very, very* excited to see him. "How *are* you?" Before he could answer she continued, "I haven't seen hide or hair of you since the Christmas party!" she winked, smiled and twinkled suggestively. It was on that night that David had discovered in a hotel bathroom that Marigold Humphries had seemed to inherit the equipment of a weathered, veteran porn-star as well. There was more traction on a slip and slide. It is not to be dismissed that the remainder of her looked as if the Almighty had borrowed his son's prodigious hand at carpentry and whittled this woman from wood. Cedar. She was solid and sweet-smelling, but below the equator she was a wallet of ham, a bouquet of bologna spilling in all directions. It looked like a bearded ax wound. And even David Drahtman, a man with, if possible, even more unsightly under-parts was not wont to swim in those waters any longer.

"Ms. Humphries. I'm so sorry, it's really been a very busy start to the year...you know how it is."

"It's August, David. And cut it with the Ms. Humphries. Call me Mary."

"Yes, of course. Er, could I possibly bother you for a few minutes of Mr. Shank's time."

"I suppose I could help you there. But first you need to tell me whatever happened to that pretty face of yours. David you really should be careful in the tanning booths. Set the alarm honey, you've got to—"

"Yes, you're right—got to be careful—so can you help me with Shank?"

she looked affronted by his interruption. "I guess. At the moment he's on the phone with a very important character."

"Any idea who?" David asked, interested.

"No but he seems to like me. He keeps calling me to ask for him, and they've been chatting every morning for weeks. I'm sure he could just call Mr. Shank directly."

"Hm. Probably family or friend then eh? I mean, he doesn't look like he's talking shop." David pointed to Shank who was slamming his fist into the desk in gasping, breathless laughter.

"Doubt that its family. He's only got his wife and the nephew." at this she swung a blue- tipped thumb towards a diminutive figure sitting behind the chairman in a small chair, "*And*, today he didn't even show up until after 5 a.m. He's never here—"

"Later than four, I know, I know. Well, thanks Mary, I'll just see how it goes."

"Enjoy Davey." she sighed, stretching the last wispy syllable until David was halfway to the desk where the Chairman and Founder of Ohmco was to be found.

Alastor Shank was in excess of seventy years old. He was squat, fleshy and pickled with freckles and livery splotches of brown and black. His round face was crossed with lines and dusted with black and white hair. His own head was a frightful comb-over, an east-to-west tsunami of long graying twine. Despite his snarky and dwarfish appearance he always seemed to be quite contented and calm. The man was persistently grinning and enjoying himself tirelessly in whatever task he might be set at, but today he was a great deal more pleased than David had ever seen him. He was still smiling and laughing broadly, the sounds whapping off the black marble sub-continent he used as a workstation. Behind him, Shank's nephew noticed David and looked up from a folder he was scribbling on.

Somersworth Omicron Battlefax was without a doubt one of the strangest and most unnerving men David had ever met. He was rail-thin and below average in terms of height. His hair was white-blonde and was combed back slickly on a diagonal against his skull. His eyes, sunken and set deep in hollow sockets, were a reddish brown that gave them the look of rust. His skin was as pale as his hair and sucked in around his cheeks. For a man of less than thirty, he looked like he had just been exhumed.

Somers was *never* seen outside Shank's office unless accompanied by Shank himself. His behavior was comparable to a talking lap-dog. He sat behind Shank and to the right on a rigid metal chair that looked suited for a dining room. Somers had only started at Ohmco within the last two years or so. To the employees of Ohmco who came into contact with him, Battlefax was little more than a sniveling, red-eyed ferret of a man. At the sight of David he hurriedly stuffed the papers he had been working on back in a folder, capped his pen, replaced it in his pocket and stood with his ghoulish nose pointing directly to the glass ceiling.

"Can I help you?" he said as if David were a Jehovah's Witness, knocking during the dinner hour.

"Yes, Somers, I need to speak to Mr. Shank." Somers waited, simpering over the request and none too pleased about being referred to by an abridged version of his first name.

"Well as you can see. Mr. Shank is rather busy at the moment." Shank laughed broadly, still not acknowledging David's presence or the conversation going on around him.

"Yes, yes! I've told you—when I get more information you'll be the first to know," Shank hollered into the receiver.

"Yes I realize that."

As the two men stood staring at one another in silence, Shank caught David in the corner of a pink, watery eye. His smile dropped away momentarily at the sight of him, then he nodded and spoke into the receiver, "I promise, my boy! All you want. The wife will be pleased…yes I suppose mine could as well."

"Well, I'll just wait then," said David defiantly.

"Oh stop! Like you're one to talk! Yes yes." Shank was still going on.

"I think not Mr. Drahtman; the Chairman's schedule is quite full today." Battlefax sneered while looking into a black leather planner, clucking his tongue.

"You've got my word sir. All you need…Thank you, thank you. I will speak to you at lunch." it appeared that the conversation was winding down in spite of David's arrival, and not because of it. "I will, I will. Thank you again, my friend." he laughed again and then finished, "Good day, you dog! Good day!" Shank replaced the receiver in its cradle on a black, ceramic-looking phone, folded his hands on the desk, smiled, exhaled and raised his face and eyebrows towards David. Sensing he was being given an opportunity to speak, David did so.

"Mr. Shank, sir. I was wondering if you had a few moments to speak with me about some things." not feeling like he was going to be interrupted, David went on, "I know that lately we've had some issues, and I feel as if my choice to do a certain amount of work at home has affected me. I—I really do want to encourage Mr. Prewitt, and yourself, to trust me. I have decided to make an effort here from my office to really have an impact. You can expect me to be here earlier and later than anyone—well, of course, not earlier than yourself. Not that I wouldn't be willing to come in that early! I'd be honored if you thought—"

"Who are you?" asked Alastor Shank plainly. Battlefax let a sneering chortle slip from his tight, white lips.

Thing clearly were not going according to the proverbial plan, but the idea that the man didn't recognize him at all seemed implausible. He was a senior vice president for God's sake!

"David Drahtman, sir. Senior Vice President of Acquisitions. I've been here ten years, Mr. Shank."

"Oh yes! Yes! David yes, you were the one—I'm sorry, old boy but you look like a circus performer with that face—you

110

were the one who had that very creative solution for the problem with the bee farmer. What in the name of all hell did you do?"

Immensely satisfied that Shank had recalled this memory of all those he may have been able to choose from, David began to reminisce.

Ohmco had been attempting to purchase the town of Patience, Mississippi. It was a small, dusty little crater that didn't even register a blip on any map you could buy in a gas station. Population four hundred and thirty one, Patience was an old, dying place. And Ohmco had been contracted by a casino business to lay a freeway over it to connect two of their outfits. To be accurate, Ohmco would not be laying the freeway. But rather, finding a creative solution to removing anything in the way of the proposed freeway.

The town's home-owners had happily agreed to sell their small place in the world for the substantial figure David was offering. Only an ancient, wizened old man, known to locals as Blackshoes, who had farmed honeybees all his life, refused to sell. And when he was informed that he had no choice in the matter, that David had already helped pass county and village legislation (via bribes) which meant the house no longer belonged to him. That that he could have the money or not but the land would be theirs regardless, the man holed up in his house and waited. When David ordered the demolition crews to his home, the old bastard sicced thousands of bees on them. This halted the process significantly. David, being the ever-resourceful young businessman, flew to Okinawa and purchased twenty thousand Japanese hornets. These bird-sized, armor-plated bee-eaters were then released on the house.

In the ten minutes before the house was finally demolished and swept away, the structure was draped in dead bees. The house's paint, a fading, sickly green, was now entirely shrouded in a furry blanket of black and yellow hair. The million or so honeybees were like a quilt that hung around the home's neck. The hornets, not likely to be flying home to Japan, settled in the area, erasing the county's agricultural systems and exterminating much of its insect wildlife. It was unclear what became of the bee farmer. He may have been swept away with the debris of his family's home.

As David was paraphrasing the noble tale of his victory over Patience, Shank cut in. "No David, I know about the hornets. When I said, 'What the hell did you do,' I was referring to your face."

"Oh!" sputtered David, smiling uncomfortably. If he hadn't been scored with magenta eruptions he might have been blushing, "Sunburn sir, the pattern I know is odd but—you see I was in an accident and fell asleep—"

"Yes, yes. All good and wonderful. Better question: *Why* are you here?" Feeling very unimportant, David answered meekly.

"Well. Well, I had been hoping to clear up any lingering concern over the Smithson matter. And perhaps ask if there is anything I can do for you? Any project I might be able to help you with or perhaps take off your hands?"

"For one, the Smithson situation is now a closed matter as far as I am concerned. Young Mr. Brewer has appropriately taken the blame, and absolved Ohmco of any legal liability. So do not fret yourself over our dearly departed friend Nigella. We've paid for the funeral"

"That's very generous of you"

"That being said. Be careful Mr. Drahtman. I don't want to pay for your funeral also. I encourage you to keep better care over your charges.

"Yes. Er. Sir I –"

"Enough," he cut through David's sentence with the fatty back-hand of his cleaver paws, "I cannot have you harping on this issue. Know that you shoulder some blame, but move forward. I do have something quite important for you, and I don't want you to fail out of some lingering concern for a septuagenarian housewife"

Shank ran his left hand over the knotty salt and pepper brambles that meandered around his skull and then out in to space. The result was to make him look even more peculiar than he was. "We have a problem not unlike the one you remedied in Mississippi." Alastor Shank began to rummage through some form of drawer that was chiseled into the space rock David stood before. Catching David's side to side glance, attempting to take in the full breadth of the thing, Shank offered.

"Igneous," said Shank, knocking with one hand on its top. Finally, he pulled a blue manila folder from its place and slid it face up in front of David. Drahtman, excited, leaned back to sit but missed, since there wasn't a chair on this side of the desk.

"Ho ho!" laughed his employer, slapping his palms loudly on the desktop. "Every time. I'll never understand how you people sit before being offered a seat. My word." still laughing, "funny, *funny* stuff," Somers was laughing so hard, mouth shut, he was crying. Shank told him to quiet down.

David got up, and forced a humble chuckle. Picking up the folder he opened it and as Mr. Shank began to explain.

"I am currently helping the City of New York in brokering deals for the acquisition of assets and real estate which will help facilitate the construction of a long-rumored subway line"

"The Second Avenue line"

"You are familiar with it then?"

"Yeah they've been trying to build it for a century haven't they?"

"About eighty years in fact"

"So this Melendez guy," he said pointing to a document in the folder, "what does he have to do with the subway system?" At this point Ms. Humphries appeared beside David and dropped a folder on the desk for Mr. Shank. Shank nodded to her and answered while Battlefax scrabbled around the corner to fetch it. He began to open the file but was rebuffed when Shank snatched the fat folder and stuffed it in a drawer.

"Mr. Reynaldo Melendez and his family have maintained the property in question since the turn of the century, and have used it as a restaurant, *Cocina Criolla*. This simple purveyor of fine Hispanic delicacies has been at the crux of the reason why the Second Avenue subway has failed to be constructed all this time. Each time a Melendez family member dies, city authorities and organizations that have an interest in the project's completion have seized repeatedly on those properties that are most crucial to the construction. Typically, we have very little trouble convincing owners to sell due to the significant figures we can provide as a purchase price. The Melendez family, however, staunchly refuses. Quoting heritage, tradition, and the like, they have refused astronomical figures for the space and continue to this day." Ms. Humphries, who had lingered at the desk ran a finger down David's back and promenaded back to her post. Flustered momentarily, David went on.

"So why can't we force him to turn over the property, like we did in Patience. The local authorities supported us one hundred percent—they welcomed the move."

"Surely you can see how the bureaucratic and civil structures are a bit better defined in New York City over Patience, Mississippi."

"Sure, but—"

"There is no way possible to force the issue. It would be unwise of us to act in an openly forceful manner in this regard as not only are their more civil liberties lawyers in this city than are desirable, but give the result of the acquisition: a major change in city transit structure rumored for generations, we cannot have anything to hide once the deal is announced."

"So is this man, Reynaldo, dying? Am I to convince his son or something?"

"No, his son is the problem. We have reason to believe his youngest is taken ill with a very rare kidney condition. Sources say the Melendez family is in a state of financial downfall due to hospital bills and are awaiting an organ for transplant, a significant fiscal investment in itself. Furthermore, I can find no record of them even having health insurance. Apparently they have a doctor in the family."

"Ah."

"I believe you will find him in a state more suitable for negotiation"

"And if he still doesn't budge?"

"Be creative. Delivering that property to the city is of the highest priority. It spells windfall for all concerned. Which now includes you."

David Drahtman was pumped, and we do not speak of his penis.

12

Thomas Jones pulled his Ford Tempo into the parking lot
of Maria Regina Catholic Church at nine in the morning.
Somehow the car had appeared in his driveway in the intervening
night. After what he had been through the evening prior, Thomas
wouldn't have been surprised if Jameson had left a flying saucer
on his lawn. He was dressed in a gray suit, black shirt, and white
tie. It was as hilarious to behold as you might be imagining. He
looked like he was wearing a mobster-costume on Halloween.

Thomas had been baptized in this very church many,
many years ago. He had been within its walls twice since: once for
his first communion, and again for his first confession.

For those untutored in the customs of the Roman
Catholic tradition, the concept of the Holy Communion is easy
enough to explain in one sentence. The central, most important
rite of the Catholic faith is that one in which the followers of
Jesus Christ ritually cannibalize his two-thousand year old corpse
by magically transfiguring a cracker and a mug of boxed wine into
the flesh and blood of the son of God. Simple enough, no?

As it is with any cannibalistic tribe, the age of seven is
seen as the optimal age in which to consume the body and blood
of God. For those lucky Catholic children who manage to avoid
parochial school, religious education is conducted within the

walls of the ever-feared Sunday school.

It was here that Thomas Jones first learned of the mystery of The Last Supper, and how that dubious event translated into the sacrament which he was soon to receive. Thomas's Sunday School teacher's name was Miss Wendy. Miss Wendy was a pale-skinned, house-dress-wearing Catholic who a decade earlier wanted to be a model. When she discovered in her late teens (like so many girls) that many of her more prominent features: a beakish, shark-fin-like nose, a single, Himalayan eyebrow, and a peculiar body odor which reminded one of garlic candy—would preclude her from being considered beautiful—she chose God. Not unlike many of his less attractive beasts, Wendy Fernowsky was drawn to God for solace, but perhaps more importantly, for a boyfriend.

At the time in which young Thomas Jones was a student of hers, Miss Wendy was charged with the task of preparing her gaggle of spitball-wielding, worm-slurping second graders for the acceptance of the flesh of the creator into their being. This transition was akin to changing menstrual blood into fruit punch. It was no tranquil venture.

Among the gossip of a second grade classroom, the eating of crackers and juice was not headline news. Heated discussions on whether or not open-mouth kissing could get your mommy pregnant, as to which superhero would prevail in a battle between Batman and Superman, about the myriad reasons why girls were not be touched or conversed with abounded. Thus, when the concept of eating God was presented to them, there was little reaction. Only after some time of preparation, as the rumors spread that they were in fact about to eat the toenails of the Almighty, did this pressing event become hot-topic in Sunday School.

It was Eddy Drummond, a boy the same age as Thomas, who scampered into and across the classroom one day still wrapped in coat, mittens, and rainbow colored beanie hat directly toward young Thomas. He grabbed him by his cheeks and screamed in one prolonged flutter of polysyllabic elementary school epiphany, "THEY'RE GONNA MAKE US DRINK BLOOD!"

Several of their classmates recoiled in horror at this revelation. Eddy went on to tell his classmates how his fourth-grade brother, a seer of unquestionable authority on such topics, had warned him that they would be expected to eat bones and drink blood. By the time Miss Wendy entered the room, she was stared at by her students like a vampire with the entrails of the Christ child dangling from her fangs. This is of course, not to say that these twenty-odd seven-year-olds were so possessed by the spirit of their faith that such an act would be offensive to them. It was more a case of mythological horror. She could have stabbed Santa and roasted the Easter Bunny over vegetables and gotten a similar response. God was no more real than the Tooth Fairy to them, and was accorded similar respect. Ignoring their horrified expressions, Miss Wendy sat and asked what the trouble was. Eddy, mustering all the courage he could, spoke first.

"Why do we have to drink blood?"

Calmly, Wendy Fernowsky responded,

"Because, Edward, that is what the apostles did the night before Jesus died"

Instantaneously, visions of Jesus being eaten by his best friends filled Thomas's head. If he was eaten the night before he died then how did they hang him on the cross? This was all quite baffling. As the internal dialogue swirled within young Thomas, he missed what was an illuminating discourse on the mystery of the Christian faith. Left with these strange images of half eaten men being nailed to a lower case "t" Thomas would face the sacrifice as confused as he had been the morning he caught his parents wrestling. That time, Thomas had been so excited his parents were interested in his favorite pastime that he ran to the bed with a big goofy grin and dropped a flying elbow on his father's back and attempted to put his mother in a sleeper hold. That, however, is an entirely other story.

On the morning of his first communion, pristine in a white suite and white tie, little Thomas Jones filed into Maria Regina followed by his mother, father, and as yet undefiled sister. As the ceremony proceeded, Thomas was soon asked to get in line to receive the host. When he reached the front of the line, camera bulbs were popping and rosary beads were clicking through his mother's thumbs. Thomas stood before the pastor. The old man of the cloth held a circular cracker before him and said, "The body of Christ."

Suddenly struck with the reality of the situation and unwilling to eat a person, regardless of how much that person looked like bread, Thomas screamed and ran to his left. The church fell silent at this response and our young hero noticed it. Mid-stride, he was faced by an older woman who held the chalice in which some truly offensive wine resided. Torn between his fear of eating the creator of the universe and impressing his family, Thomas resolved that blood had to be easier to consume than chewing on the tibia of the creator. He snatched the goblet from the lady, shuttered his eyes, and downed the equivalent of three glasses of red wine in a single gulp.

Absolutely and entirely drunk out of his little boy brain, Thomas had to skip his own communion dinner and was put to bed before the sun set. He vomited wine up for hours and took this as a sign that god was not at all pleased with his actions and would punish him by emptying him of all the blood in his veins.

It would be unnecessary to say that Thomas Jones did not for many, many years receive communion. On any occasion in the future in which he had to be in a church, he abstained from communion like an atheist. A seven-year old atheist.

It was not a year after the wine-quaffing incident that Thomas was faced with a second sacrament (his third, counting baptism). This time, it was the sacrament of Reconciliation, commonly known as Confession. It is odd that the Catholic patronage would insist on this event occurring so early in a child's life, as if these third-graders had cheated on their wives, developed a gambling problem, and smoked too much. While the logistics of Confession were easier to convey to children for Miss Wendy, it was no less difficult to provide subjects suitable for confessing. After all, what exactly, can an eight-year-old cop to? What sins could such a small person commit that would require the experience to which they were now headed. Unfair baseball card trading practices? Cheating in the role of banker at Monopoly? Genocide by means of magnifying glass?

For those members of this audience not so privileged to have previously experienced the rite of Reconciliation, allow this humble author to illuminate. The sinner (i.e., every single catholic ever) sits in a large, windowless phone booth which is kept conveniently void of all natural light by the creative choice to forgo windows. In this upright casket, the sinner (you, me, and everyone) will confess his sins through a small black pane of mesh wire. On the other side of this partition sits a priest who will listen to your ill deeds. Through this revelation, the Catholic believes he or she is forgiven for all their sins. The priest, in the role of some form of holy prison warden, will prescribe a sentence. This punishment is always a collection of prayers. For children as young as Thomas, one can be forgiven for punching their sister in the liver by, say, five "Hail Mary" and an "Our Father." For adults, whose sins may include burglary, assault, and adultery, the punishment might be as severe as an entire rosary (one hundred "Hail Mary" and ten "Our Fathers"). This tradition of retribution is perhaps most ironic for the fact that the confessional booth is historically notable for its value as an excellent location for activities ranging from altar boy-on-priest fellatio to priest-on-altar boy anal sodomy. We might, if we were so bold, assume that a priest engaging in such pursuits might be able to, after dismissing his ward, punish himself with two rosaries and be on his merry way.

This morning in particular, however, was not destined for forgiveness or cannibalism. Today was the funeral of Jim Jones, patriarch of the Jones family. As Thomas sat in his driver's seat, preparing himself for unavoidable conversations with relatives he had been free of for years and the accompanying stares fixed unwaveringly his swollen head, he considered his appearance in the rearview mirror. Thomas's color had lightened from the plum-like purple he wore the evening prior into a rose petal red which made him look more sunburned than anything else. His limp and beleaguered breathing was more of an issue at this juncture than anything else.

Nervously juggling an orange pill bottle in his clammy palms, Thomas elected to take two of the small white ovals with the remainder of a warm bottle of water from his cup-holder. He resolved to keep the habit in check this time and then took two more pills. He had, after all, built up quite a tolerance to the stuff and needed to keep himself from whimpering with every step on the way to his seat in the church.

When he had lumbered his way through the church's double doors David took in the space which he had not seen since leaving here so soused he was shocked he remembered a lick of it.

Indeed the church itself looked just as he remembered it. It was a wide, growling building which quickly closed upon the sun in dark wood beams; fettered and muzzled up the sky into tight knots of pine and iron trim. It peaked like the pope's hat and fell fat and wide-hipped to the grass. At its waist the belt of the building wore buckles of stained glass that told ancient tales and hummed hymns immemorial. She was a dome, a womb, a belly of belief in the great beyond.

At the back of the structure, before an altar, sat the shut brown-black wooden coffin of Jim Jones Junior. Lilies bedecked the breast of the catafalque, and to his left on the altar steps were four massive portraits. Each of the Jones men had had portraits painted of them. Grand, expansive things in oil depicting each man reclining on chaise lounges, smoking pipes and cocking brows. Each had a fat red apple in his left hand. Thomas recognized the first portrait as his Reconstruction-Era great, great, great-grandfather, Frederick Jones, as this was a portrait which hung over the fire of many a Jones family home. Frederick had made copies. Quite a few of them actually. And you might have made copies of your own portrait too, if you looked so majestic. The original American Jones was splendid in tightly tailored slacks and vest. His round glasses framed perfectly blazing blue eyes. His moustache, which would put Merlin's beard to shame, brushed bushy around his whole face- a wide swathe of bristling, golden shag that finished in curly points on blooming, smiling cheeks. He looked like the Emperor of Apple, and for some time it could be argued he was.

Noticeably absent was the third James Jones to live in the States, Thomas's father, now passed. Jim Jones III was no fan of his family and so his family was no fan of him. Besides, Jones III has no desire to have portraits made of him. That would be superfluous. Thomas thought that was madness.

The very first person whom he encountered after musing on these images of antiquity was his sister. Jane Jones was dressed all in black, a skirt halfway between knee and ankle, and a black blouse piped at the collar with white flowers, which was cinched strong round her throat.

"Oh Jesus Christ, what have you done?" she somehow managed to scream in a whisper. Taken aback, Thomas responded,

"I got into a fight." pausing as he wondered whether his next statement was going to be seen as hilarious or not he finished,

"You should've seen the other guy." She did not laugh.

"Oh I sincerely doubt that. It's more likely that you fell in a Slurpee machine somewhere because your employees pulled the foot-stool out from under you. You *are* working?"

"Sure am."

"Doing what?" And before he could make up an answer to the question, his Aunt Margaret grabbed him by a swollen, grapefruit ear and squealed at him.

"Tommy! Tommy! Tommy! Oh how good it is to seeeeeee you!" She flung her immense, beefy frame around him, engulfing Thomas in vanilla musk, polyester, and clip-on earrings. She kissed him hard and forcefully on the lips. "Little Tommy Jones, Oh how your Auntie has missed you!"

"Yes Aunt Margaret, it's great to see you too." He was

quite pleased, what with his sister already having forgotten her question and now chasing an un-known Jones child through pews, still screaming under her breath. Thomas was beginning to mull over excuses to his aunt as to why he looked like he had been bullfighting over the weekend, when he remembered that his Aunt was blinder than shit. Literally.

"You know Tommy, I saw your Mother yesterday. She misses you dearly; she never lets that picture of you out of her arms."

"Really? Strange!"

"You must go visit her Tommy. You simply must. I am going next Sunday, why don't we go together!"

"Oh, I'm sorry Aunt Margaret, but I have work that day, and I see Mother plenty often as it is"

"You're working again, are you? I always knew you'd shape up one day Tommy! So what exactly are you doing then?" Thomas Jones was about a third of a second from saying he was selling drugs to put an end to the conversation when he was rescued by another relative whom he hadn't seen in nearly a decade. This was his cousin Marty.

Marty Gorman was around Thomas's age and looked rather similar apart from Marty's more swiftly retreating hairline and dull, blue eyes. Marty wrapped an arm around Thomas's neck and led him away from Margaret in one motion.

"Oh, you two boys! Don't let me keep you!" their aunt bellowed behind them.

"We'll do our best Aunt Marge," said Marty casually,

without looking back at her. Turning into Thomas's ear, he said softly, "You're welcome." Marty was a rather unspectacular local cop, and often acted as though he thought he was in fact a member of the Secret Service. He often gave snapping glances over each of his shoulders as if he was being watched. He was not being watched.

"Yeah, thanks, Marty." His cousin took his arm off Thomas's shoulder and led him into a pew, as the service seemed imminent. They sat, Thomas rather slow and painfully.

"So tell me cuz, what have you been up to? It looks like you got your clock cleaned, buddy." This was Marty's word, *buddy*, he used it when speaking to men and women, young and old, human and non-human (a golden lab he owned was named Buddy).

"It's a long story. Maybe later."

"If someone's giving you trouble you let me know Tom, I'll take care of it." he then winked drastically, "if you know what I mean." He winked again, dramatically.

"Oh, it's not that big of a deal, I'll be fine"

"Yeah, yeah, you can tell me later over drinks. You are coming to the dinner over at Marge's, right, buddy?" As Thomas's brain began to swell with fradulent commitments which would allow him to avoid the disaster that would certainly be dinner at Aunt Margaret's he was saved, for the third time, by Father Joseph Nunzio.

"Welcome friends and family to the house of God."

As the service trundled and meandered through its many

stops and starts, stands and sits, kneels and prays, Thomas's head began to spin slowly. The room itself, staunch and stiff with old oak and stained glass, began to lose shape, its colors blended and the voice of the pastor muffled into an gurgling froth, a hum of hosannas, and whirring blur of blessed be's.

Within him, several thousand milligrams of Vicodin were dissolving into the membranes of his stomach and small intestine. This heady dose of pain killers certainly did its job in spades. After it had rendered the pain in his ribcage like pork-fat and annulled the union between the nerve endings in his body and those in his brain, the drug went to work on the rest of him. Vision increasingly crepuscular, hearing muted and indistinct, Thomas was flat-out, no-question, high off his rocker on Vicodin.

A more sober Thomas might have taken issue with the fact that he missed several responsorials, in which the rest of the mourners were saying in unison, "And also with you," which was in stark contrast to the "Where are my shoes?" that came out of Thomas's addled, kite-high brain. He napped through the Eucharist and when time came to exchange handshakes and "Peace be with you's," Thomas kissed his Uncle Ralph square on the mouth.

It was a blessing that his own father was already dead, his mother fantasizing about him in a hospital bed, and his sister sitting in the first row. Uncle Ralph was crazy enough to confuse Thomas for Elizabeth Taylor, and Marty thought the entire display hilarious. After all, Marty was the family member most noted for chemically induced displays of stupidity and was enjoying this matinee with gusto. This was but another reason to avoid his aunt's party. Marty would likely be more sauced than spaghetti by sundown.

When his cousin shook him awake at the conclusion of the service, snickering into his tie, Thomas thought first how embarrassed he felt. That feeling was rather easily dispatched but again, Thomas Jones could really do nothing with the situation at hand, and was losing patience with a sense of guilt.

As he and Marty shuffled down the aisle he saw at the rear of the church his sister, arms folded, plainly waiting for him. He was not in the mood for a scolding, though she clearly seemed prepared to deliver one. This from a woman who had spent the evening prior suspended by her ankles from a basement ceiling.

Fortune once again entered on behalf of Thomas as a short, pretty looking girl with a blonde ponytail burst through a side entrance. She was wearing purple hospital scrubs. This nurse, whose name was Jessica, grabbed Janet by her arm and began to point her finger and squawk. Neither Marty nor Thomas could hear the conversation over the din of bagpipes which had begun to bleat into the mid-morning as his grandfather's casket was exiting the church doors. As they got nearer, Thomas caught the words "car," "old cocksucker," and "off a goddamned bridge".

Passing through the doors, grateful to have avoided his second interaction with his only sister in as many days, Thomas stopped as he heard a familiar voice behind him.

"You look a whole lot better there, Tommy-boy." Thomas turned jerkily, which overextended even his noble supply of Vicodin, induced wincing, and found behind him the last person he ever expected to see at his grandfather's funeral. Jameson shot him a big pearly smile, then closed it severely, walked three paces to Thomas and extended his hand. "I am very sorry for your loss Thomas, I really am." They shook hands and Thomas believed every word of what Jameson had just said.

"My goodness, sir, thank you so much for coming. How did you—" Jameson silenced Thomas with a sharp slice of his open palm on the air.

"It's no matter Thomas. I happened to be in the area with my friend Cleo," he gestured behind him to a woman so staggeringly beautiful that Thomas had thought she was painted into the glass behind her, "and both of us had work to attend to in the area this evening." Cleo, taller than Thomas and dressed in a long black dress with brownish red hair pulled up smiled and nodded at him.

"Well, I do appreciate it—hi Cleo nice to meet you—I do appreciate it sir," Jameson raised his eyebrows, "Jameson, I am sorry, I am just not used to referring to superiors—"

"Superior! Ha! Superior indeed, Tommy-boy." He put a cigarette in his mouth and lit it. Thomas thought to consider the indoor smoking policy of the house of God and then realized he hadn't introduced Marty. Turning to bring his cousin into the conversation he realized that Marty was gone. Much of the family had exited to the cars, and besides the screeching of his sister and

130

the nurse, the church was quite empty.

"Anyway Thomas, if you're not doing anything crazy tonight, I would like you to join my associate for dinner. We had a reservation at a spectacular little place not far from here and I have to attend to some rather sudden business."

"With—you?" he said, pointing gingerly to the supermodel standing behind Jameson. It was his employer that answered.

"With Cleo, yes. You don't mind do you? It's on us."

'Well, of course I don't mind. I would love to. What time?"

"Figure about eight, Cleo will pick you up then."

"Great. I guess I will see you then." he smiled nervously at Cleo.

"I guess we will," she said in a voice that had the faint whiff of some faraway place Thomas would never visit, let alone spell the name of. She smelled like beach-grass and coconut-guts.

Jameson rolled the cigarette between his teeth, smiled and offered his arm to Cleo, who took it.

"I will be by tomorrow morning to check on your first day. You've still got the address, Thomas?"

"Yes sir."

Jameson raised his bushy brows again.

"Jameson...Sorry"

"Don't be, Tommy-boy," he said as he walked out into the mid-morning Jersey sun, "Don't be."

13

Clutching a thick blue folder to his breast David Drahtman barreled into the elevator on the eighty-eighth floor and depressed a white button. Alone, and unwilling to wait a full twenty seconds to investigate further the task that had been given him, David buried his nose in the various documents attesting to the difficulties between the family Melendez and the city of New York. His greedy little eyes swept back and forth across faxes and photocopies, swallowing memoranda beneath coal-black brows that turned in sinister curves round the bones of his eye sockets. If he had a moustache, David might have curled it mischievously between two fingers.

He did not even realize when the doors snapped open on his floor that he had arrived and was awakened from creepy daydreams by the voice of a co-worker whom he knew by the name Collins. Bobby Collins.

"Shit Dave. What the hell did you do to yourself?"

"What?" muttered David, still not acknowledging his colleague's presence. Bobby was a junior vice president at the company, although he was probably a bit old for the position, being only a few years younger than David. He wasn't an unattractive person, a bit long in the face and nose, though he seemed to be unaware of this. His dirt blonde hair was certainly beginning to dissipate and he had a mild sweating problem which often seemed to be focused, unfortunately for a man of business, in his palms. He was also a bit intense, always more excited about something than everyone else.

"David?"

"Collins," he said as if Bobby was asking his own name.

"For god's sake Davey-boy, get out of the fucking elevator!" He also had a cursing problem. Not like Tourette's, but as if he just said curse words almost constantly and always seemed to make them the loudest word in every sentence. Bob Collins treated the word "fuck" with the enthusiasm of a ten year boy.

"Oh, ha" said Drahtman, covering, "Sorry, heard about the issue with the old lady. Sorry bout that."

"No fucking sweat. Things are still looking up!"

They shook hands and David cringed at the sensation of Collins's swampy mitts souping around his like tentacles of old cold-cuts and hot dog water.

"What—did you go fucking tanning?" Collins thought he was being funny, but rather than acknowledge the humor or even reprimand him, David just ignored him.

"Something like that," said David distractedly, "listen, I need a minute to go over a few things, check back with me later, will you?" David smiled absently, still barely looking Collins in the eyes and pointed him away and down a hallway. But Collins did not depart—he turned back like a proud eight year old after a touchdown and waved at David in poorly-disguised glee.

"Wait – Davey – did you hear? Huh?" he asked as if David had missed out on an alien landing in the executive toilet.

"What?" he asked honestly.

"That whole business with the bottled water upstate—you remember? You know they gave me that file after the old bitch offed herself, and you heard what happened?"

"Oh, the—um—Creek Spring, or something—right?"

"Spring Brook, actually—but no matter. Fucking bitch actually reported us for health violations. We have the cleanest plant on earth."

"Wow. So she reported you just to fuck with us?" asked David incredulously. He seemed terribly offended.

"I offered her twice the value of the space, and we weren't even gonna use the buildings as is—it was for residentials." David nodded vigorously as Collins continued, "So I said fuck it, we've got the pharmaceutical plant in Brewster, not, what—fifty miles away?" He seemed to really expect an answer, as if David Drahtman dealt regularly with water-bottling old ladies from the Adirondacks.

"Yeah?"

"So now she's got a spring full of enough dead trout to make a bouillabaisse." They shared a laugh. David loved deeply these tales of conquest.

"Excellent, so they shut her down then."

"Oh we reported it ourselves!" they slapped one another on the back, "Nearly lost it at the last minute too. That fucking prick intern with the staples in his face fucking lost a fax from her and I didn't respond for a week.

"That shmuck with the green hair?"

"I think it's orange now. What the fuck is with that kid"

"I dunno, I can't imagine there weren't better candidates than these dirtbags they've got running around—"

"Whatever. Fuck em'. Anyway so last night she calls and sells for 400K, a tenth of the value from Monday. Four hundred g's for fucking Brook Creek!"

"Creek Spring?"

"Oh who gives a *fuck?* We're gonna pave the place on Friday!" A few people were turning and looking with horror at the two of them. David, being the first to ever notice the glare of his peers steered the conversation away from any situation which might necessitate the employment of the phrase "fuck," "shit," or "cunt."

"Going out with the wife tonight to celebrate." He paused and glanced over his shoulder towards Dana's still empty desk. "so long as I can keep that slut off my back." Collins finished with a big gummy smile and nudged David with his elbow, "If you know what I mean! Huh? Huh?"

David forced the laughter this time, and made it clear he was ending the conversation by swiping his keycard and opening the door to his office.

"Keep that chair warm for me, huh Davey?" said Collins, waving the pointer finger of each hand at David like he was brandishing revolvers and bearing a big sloppy grin.

"Sure thing, Collins," David forced this last line through clenched teeth. Collins blew imaginary smoke off of his imaginary finger-guns and walked away like John Wayne with sweat-stains and a sailor's tongue.

Strange as it may sound, David felt honestly jealous of a woman whom he was trying, and succeeding, to avoid at all costs. He couldn't imagine how he had made it to 10 a.m. without her knocking on his door like she was doing impersonations of his family.

Finally leaning back in his leather recliner, David exhaled slowly through pursed lips and closed his eyes. Reaching into his jacket pocket, David pulled out a thin tube of aloe vera gel his wife had left out for him. David extruded a glossy ice cream cone's worth of the bright smelling gel and ran it between his hands as if warming them. Wiping a few stray black chunks of hair back off his forehead, David gingerly applied the jelly and massaged it into the craters carved into his face. Sighing again heavily, he reclined back in his seat and hummed contentedly while he formed a plan.

The first move was pretty straightforward: he would simply apply his gifts as a speaker and communicator. He would begin easily and softly by giving the appearance of a friend who was only calling to offer help. Most Hispanics didn't understand him well enough to make out every word, but by using calm, gentle, even tones he would be able to engender some trust. It would be crucial to not mention the son; he needed to appeal to the man's fears without spelling them out. It had to appear as if his call was just a happy coincidence. A solution to Mr. Melendez's problem rather than a solution to Mr. Drahtman's. He had done it all his life and was confident this operation would run as smooth as any of the countless others like it which he had handled in the business of doing business.

If, by some infinitesimal possibility—some nightmare of epic proportions—David's application of this prodigious skill-set did not serve to extricate the desired result, then he would need a "Plan B." He would need to be strong. And creative. David's mind began to fire with images of solutions of all designs: fire, water, earth and air. Just before he had fully satisfied his dream to cast lightning bolts upon the evil-doers and smite them in their sleep, David was interrupted by his speakerphone. It was not, as his sinking heart-valves had supposed, Dana Jenkins—but instead it was David's immediate supervisor, Alexander Prewitt.

"Mr. Drahtman. Where is your secretary?" An excellent question, thought David to himself. She had left her desk hours ago as David had so artfully planned. If she had returned during his meeting with Shank he did not know, but by the sound of Mr. Prewitt, this was not the case.

"I'm not sure, sir. I was out for a few minutes earlier."

"I have been waiting for near an hour for some documents, Mr. Drahtman, and I am not pleased by the delay."

"Well, sir, I saw her head out earlier this morning to collect a package downstairs. I doubt she's been down there this whole time."

"I will call the front desk. There is no reason why she

should be away this long"

"Great, uh, let me know when she gets back."

"Good day."

David saw the light on the speakerphone go out and relaxed. Still gooey and viscous with aloe and ointment, he raised himself from his seat and made his way to his private bathroom to wash up.

When David was cleaned and settled back in his chair, he prepared for the task ahead. Being no stranger to the restaurant business (or, at the least, the business of buying restaurant businesses), David knew that the very perfect time to contact an individual in the trade was before noon. Calling a restaurateur during the lunch rush was not only frowned upon, but considered ignorant. Unlike the corporate structure of holding companies, restaurant owners regularly employ the pot and the pan, the mop and the bucket. David hadn't so much as boiled water in twenty years.

At a quarter to noon David dialed Cocina Criolla, preparing himself—steeling himself, in fact—to become the beast he had to be. As the phone rang, David prepared himself to break out his best Spanglish, if only to better open the paths of communication to a man who would no doubt not understand a third of what he was trying to get across. This was an art form, he thought. It's far more difficult to ply information and funds from people who actually comprehend what you're saying. Finally, a hurried and tired voice answered the phone after a prolonged series of rings.

"Cocina Criolla," said a young female on the other end of the line. Behind her David could hear the sloshing, clinking, sizzling music of the kitchen. A deep fat fryer was gorging itself on tortillas and belching in a sustained gurgle of pop and fizz.

"Hello. My name is David. Is Reynaldo Melendez there?" No need to fiddle with the language here, even a Mexican with one leg on the border fence could understand this most basic of sentences. The young voice on the other end did not respond but rather slammed the phone down on a steel table with a resounding *dong*. The sounds of the kitchen amplified off the countertop as David waited. He could hear the quick knocking of knives and the soft scratch of steel wool on cast iron.

"Hello," said a clear and much calmer voice on the other end.

"Hello. My—name—is—David. Is—this—Rey—naldo—Melendez?"

"Yes?"

Now David turned on the juice, nonplussed by the slightest whiff of suspicion he heard in Melendez's voice.

"Hello—Mr—Melendez. How—are—you—today?" David enunciated each word clearly and slowly, speaking a touch louder than he might have if speaking to an equal.

"I'm—fine. Who is this?" He was starting to sound more like a Raymond than a Reynaldo. Ever the one to press on, David did.

"My—name—is—David. I—*trabajo*—for—a—*senor*—who—would—like—to—buy—you

—beesness."

"Mr. Drahtman, I do not know who you are or where you're from but I am very busy and you seemed to be confused. Are you feeling all right?" This had to be their lawyer, or their Irish Catholic dishwasher. Did they put a customer on the phone? David was baffled.

"Um. Can I speak to Mr. Melendez, please?"

"You *are* speaking to him, Mr. Drahtman! What is your problem?"

"Reynaldo Melendez? The owner of Cocina Criolla?" David pronounced these Spanish words with a flourish. Like a freshman Spanish student first wrapping their teeth around the word *senorita*. Endlessly trilling the "r's" until the word lost meaning and became vibration.

"Ah. I see what's happening here. You expect me to *no speaka ingles*. Is that correct, Mr. Drahtman?" Busted, David considered his options, forced a chuckle and tried to cover.

"Oh Lord no, Mr. Melendez. The connection on my end is terrible! You wouldn't believe how bad it is, gotta talk like—a—moron—to be sure I'm heard." David faked a staggered laugh that fooled no one.

"I can hear you just fine. And unless your phone also translates crappy Spanish, then I am still confused."

"Oh you must have misunderstood me! I can't speak a lick of Spanish; I took French in high school."

"That may be, Mr. Drahtman, but I am very busy, as you can hear behind me, and I have no time—"

"It won't take a second. I'm not selling anything, I promise you that. Just give me until noon and I won't bother you."

"You have three minutes."

"I won't need that many! Mr. Melendez. My name is David Drahtman and I work for a small company here in the city. You seem pretty busy for this time of day, eh?"

"Well, we're a bit understaffed at the moment. Now, why exactly are you calling Mr. Drahtman?" Sensing chum on the waterline, David nosed around hungrily.

"Understaffed huh? I am sure you could get some help from the family, no? I'm sure with an establishment as old and renowned as yours you've passed on your delicious recipes—and if I do say so, they *are* delicious—to some of the younger generation?"

"To be honest Mr. Drahtman, we have some family issues which are taking precedence at the moment. Once again, I am very busy—why are you—"

"Oh, I certainly hope it's nothing serious?" It was a testament to his gift as a speaker and businessman that he could turn the conversation on its head from its rather auspicious beginning. "Maybe I can help?"

"I doubt it. What you could do is tell me why you are calling my place of business." He still gave off an air of stiffness, but was beginning to soften marginally.

"Of course. Let me get to the point. My employers are interested in possibly entering into a relationship with you. I think

141

that we can be of assistance to you—especially if you are having some family or financial difficulties. We would be willing to make you a *very* substantial offer for your restaurant." David heard the music of the kitchen drop away suddenly as if a thin door was snapped shut. Mr. Melendez had gone into his office to have this conversation.

"Mr. Drahtman, let me be frank. This restaurant has stood for four generations. We are a landmark and a pillar of our community. I have every intention of protecting this business as my fathers have done before me." David thought to interject, but heard an inhalation and allowed Melendez to continue, "However, my highest priority is my family and we are in great need of financial stability of the order which is unfortunately not possible to sustain from our customers. I will say to you, sir, that I am of a right mind to consider an offer, but allow me to clarify: this business will not come cheap to you. I intend to make enough off of its sale to not only take care of substantial bills with have accrued as a result of unavoidable circumstances, but to also purchase a new restaurant, perhaps more uptown." His shark nose now full of blood, David kept his calm coolly, took a moment to prevent the slightest hint of eagerness from creeping into his tone and responded.

"Mr. Melendez. As you can probably tell, I am not calling on behalf of the city, and I am not, as I suspect you may have supposed, interested in building over your restaurant. I may even be able to keep you on as a manager of it as it continues on into eternity, as I am sure your grandfathers would have wished.

Further, the funds which I am authorized to tender to you would be sufficient to fulfill any and all dreams you may wish. And lastly, if we were in a position to keep you on in the company—which I would surely fight in support of—we would be able to cover you and your entire family under a pretty spectacular health plan we have here. Of course, I am sure your family wouldn't need that, but I thought I should mention it."

Silence filled David's ears like sweet music. As deft and careful as ever, he ventured another word.

"Say, Mr. Melendez, there's no need to rush into these sorts of decisions. Why don't we meet for dinner tonight, on me, and we can get to know one another a little better. Maybe we talk a little business too."

"Fine."

"Traîtrise, say, six o'clock?"

"Traîtrise?"

"Oh, of course, why would anyone so lucky to work in a restaurant such as yours spend much time at other establishments? Central Park West—the corner of—"

"I am aware of the address."

"Oh—yes—of course a chef of your pedigree is familiar with—"

"Please. Mr. Drahtman" Melendez couldn't handle any more from this most prolific of sycophants. "Six o'clock?"

When he hung up David sighed through a grin. God, he was *good*. Granted, it wasn't perfect, but he had gotten Melendez to agree to a meeting and if nothing else this was an opening.

Feeling more invincible than he had all week, David decided to do the most arrogant thing he could think of: make his secretary bring him coffee.

David pressed the button beside Dana's name and in the most snide, authoritative voice he could muster, said "Dana. Coffee. Now"

But unfortunately for him, Dana Jenkins did not answer. Striding to his blinds he looked again towards her desk, expecting to see her laughing at how smart she was for ignoring him. Dana, however, was still nowhere to be found.

<u>14</u>

"So, Mr. Jones, tell me about yourself," said Cleo, leaning in over the table, eyes lit by a candle whose flame danced with its feet on the floor. Thomas, busy investigating the current state of affairs in the cavernous recesses of Cleo's dress-front, answered a bit late.

"Um—well. I am from Wildwood, New Jersey," he spat out, flustered. David had never smelled a woman as near perfect as Cleo, whose last name he still did not know. She was lithe, thin and long in the legs. Her long auburn hair fell around her shoulders in cascading sheets of black and dark red.

"Yes, I know Mr. Jones, I picked you up there". She did indeed. Cleo had pulled up to the house in a white BMW at around seven and they had not spoken the entire drive to the restaurant, which was over an hour. Cleo bobbed her head to increasingly voluminous music until they were parked.

"Oh—yes—you did, didn't you? Ha. Well, I don't know what else to say. I've had all sorts of strange jobs in my life, can't really say I liked any of them to be honest"

"Well if strange jobs are your game then you certainly came to the right place." She gave an I-know-something-you-don't-know sort of laugh and leaned back in her chair, and her nipples, fat and round, pushed their way through fabric. Thomas considered for a moment that Jameson was running a brothel, but then realized that he wouldn't make a very gifted prostitute. He supposed he could probably give a mean hand-job, having given so many to himself. Again, responding a bit late and blustery, Thomas jerked away from her dueling nipples and looked back into eyes formed from chewy caramel.

"Yes, I have to admit, I'm not sure what I've gotten myself into. Maybe you can fill me in." She gave another knowing chuckle.

"Well, firstly, I don't know what Jameson has planned for you. And as you are very new to the company it wouldn't be prudent of me to be divulging company secrets, now would it?" she said in a way that would have made you think she was winking, though she wasn't.

"Oh of course not," he said briskly, over-estimating any insult he may have caused her.

"Please, Mr. Jones, relax. You are perfectly entitled to some information. If I were to guess, I would say Jameson has something very simple for you, to ease you into the swing of things."

"He said I was going to work for a man named Melvin." Cleo laughed loudly and put a hand to her lips, stifling the bubbling giggle.

"Oh yes, that sounds about right. Melvin manages a very important part of the business. It is a division that deals with some of the core values we hold dear at Keepwater."

"Ok. And what, err—division, is that?"

"Luxury would be the proper word for it. Items for those with a discriminating taste." As he began to form his next question, a waiter arrived with the bottle of wine Cleo had ordered when they first sat. The server showed the bottle to Cleo, opened it and poured her a taste of the dark red wine. Wrapping a thick bottom lip around the glass's rim she emptied it, keeping one eye on Thomas. She smiled, nodded to the waiter who then poured a glass for each of them.

Thomas Jones knew nothing whatsoever about wine. He knew more about quantum physics and Chinese literature than he did that most ancient libation. It would be safe to assume he had not drunk a drop since his rendezvous with the blood of Christ so long ago. Figuring it couldn't hurt, Thomas took a big swig from the glass, keeping one eye on Cleo. He swallowed with difficulty and seemed, outwardly at least, unimpressed.

"It's warm." Before Cleo's eyebrows could return back to earth, Thomas was scooping ice out of his water and moving them sloppily over to the stemmed wine glass. Cleo did not bother to inform Thomas Jones that red wine was intended to be served at room temperature.

"Much better," said Thomas after a second, cooler sip. "So, luxury, you said. Like what, jewelry? Cars? What?"

"Oh, it will be more exciting for you to see for yourself, I'm sure."

After they had ordered their meals, Thomas decided he should be asking about Cleo, rather than going on and on about himself.

"So, what do you do for Keepwater?"

"An excellent question, Mr. Jones. I work in a very different capacity from yours. It's actually quite complicated, but I work in the, um, *Legal* department, I guess you could call it."

"Are you a lawyer?"

"No, but my job often involves dealing with them in an indirect manner." Confused by this, but undeterred, David finished the first bottle of wine with some help from Cleo, who was beginning to flush a bit in her cheeks as well. The waiter returned as they finished their glasses with the entrees.

"Could we have another?"

"Absolutely sir," said the waiter. Thomas then leaned over to the waiter's side and half-whispered, as if her were saving the man from some embarrassment.

"And a cold one too, if you don't mind"

"Um, as you wish," the waiter stuttered after a prolonged pause.

"Great! Thanks a million."

When the server returned, with a bottle of pinot noir in an ice bucket, Cleo chuckled again.

"So where exactly are we? That was quite a drive for dinner, no?"

"Well, I had business here this evening, so we figured you and I could eat here as well"

"Oh yeah, you mentioned at the funeral about having work in the area. How did it go?" She smiled at him while slippering a noodle betwixt her rose-petal mouth.

"I haven't done it yet." He shook his head, still confused, but was encouraged by the grape juice.

As Thomas continued to suck down the wine, he noticed that Cleo hadn't touched her full glass from the second bottle.

"Not thirsty?"

Not wanting to insult Thomas, or to drink cold Pinot Noir, she found a simple excuse.

"I've got to drive you home, Mr. Jones, don't I? And besides, you certainly seem to be enjoying it." And he certainly was enjoying himself. The bottle and a half of red that was slowly but surely replacing the blood in his vessels was working all manner of magic. If he had only drunk red wine when he managed the pharmacy, he might've avoided a lot of embarrassment. He also might've ended up an alcoholic but that is often the way the cookie crumbles.

As they finished up, both Thomas and Cleo leaned back in their chairs and sighed.

"So when will I see you again? I mean, will I ever work with you?" she let out a noise somewhere between a sigh and a giggle. A siggle?

"I think you're a way off from working in my department. But you never know. Jameson likes to move people around pretty quickly. If you make it through the first week, that is."

"I don't get why people keep warning me. It's not like I'm going to be asked to kill anyone." He laughed. Cleo didn't.

"Well, not yet at least," and then her face broke again into a big smile. Thomas didn't know if she was being serious or not, but at the moment, couldn't care less. He drained the last of his glass.

"So, shall we go?" Not answering, Cleo smiled again and stood. She lifted her glass and took his arm.

"You know you can't bring that in the car. It's illegal in New Jersey."

"It's not going in the car"

As they walked, Thomas felt better and saltier than he had in his entire life. Him, Thomas Jones, walking out of a ritzy little restaurant with the most beautiful woman in the world on his arm. For the first time, Thomas felt like *the man*. As he walked, he imagined what kind of silly life all these other shmucks lived. That guy with the stupid moustache and his fat wife. That other guy with the meat sauce stains on his shirt. And this guy right here, with the big nose and the bald patch with his pissed-off-looking wife. What was his problem? And why are we walking right towards him?

Cleo dropped Thomas's arm and walked up to the man with the big nose, who was at the moment pouring a glass of champagne and threw her full goblet of chilled pinot noir in his face. She looked him right in his eyes and said, "Nice, Robert. Nice." And then walked away, dragging Thomas behind her.

As they left, Thomas could hear glasses breaking and a woman screaming. As the doors closed behind them, Thomas, baffled, heard the man scream back at her, "I swear I don't know who the *fuck* that is!"

15

David Drahtman had not felt so good in days. While his favorite thing on earth (his car) was destroyed and still sleeping soundly on the side of a freeway, his wife and children were still living in his house, and his face was still the color and shape of a scoop of strawberry ice cream, David would not be deterred from a sense of overwhelming superiority. In all of his life, there was nothing that got David high like conquest. The internal visions of himself getting the better of another man, through deception, seduction, and a patent disregard for law and livelihood was to David what a jug of paint thinner is to a twelve-year-old in a tree-house outside of Birmingham.

As he strutted like a cock primed for fighting from the elevator and into the wide, open lobby, David was reminded by the sight of the building's two receptionists of the fact that he had not seen his own receptionist all day. Or at least not since he had sent her down here that morning to pick up a package that did not exist. In an effort David thought was most humanitarian of him, he turned as he passed the main desk and traipsed back to inquire as to whether or not the two women has seen Dana that morning.

Ohmco's main desk had been manned since long before David had been there by the same two women. They were sisters, known to everyone in the building, and one another it seemed, as Miss Marie and Miss Susan.

Both women were short, wide-bodied black ladies with great dark curls and big, happy smiles. Both women had a warm and gentle nature to them and seemed very much inseparable. If anything, Miss Susan had a bit more cheek to her and always seemed to have the louder response to any situation. Marie was more calm and motherly, whereas Susan was like the drunken aunt. Regardless of this difference they were both sweet and kind to anyone who required their services. As the two longest-tenured employees in the building, they had and almost preternatural knowledge of the building and its systems. Miss Susan had once saved an elevator full of colleagues by squeezing her thick frame in an unused ventilation duct she knew of and working her way to the elevator like the love child of Jack Bauer and Biggie Smalls. They did, though, look very similar and the difference between which allowed the many people who worked in the building to tell between them was that Miss Marie had an affinity for dogs and Miss Susan one for cats. The desk itself was cordoned and partitioned off into a battleground for stuffed puppies and kittens, puppy-dog picture frames, and kitty-kat keyboard decals. Coffee-mugs with chocolate Labs on them and mouse pads with tabby cats. Miss Marie, Dalmatian bow in her curls, was nearest David when he pulled up in front of her.

"Why, if it isn't Mr. Drahtman! And how are *we* on this

beautiful afternoon?" They both had vaguely southern accents, seemingly peppered with an inner-city slant that made them appear stuck between New York and Atlanta. Although geographically that would mean Pittsburgh, and there was no doubt in David's mind that neither woman had ever so much as set foot in the Steel City.

"I am just fine Miss Marie. And yourself?"

"Never better, dearie. What can I do you for?" Even David couldn't help but feel warmed within by being called "dearie" by such a woman. Her voice was hot chocolate in his cold, sticky mug.

"I was wondering, Miss Marie, if you happened to see my secretary at all today? Dana?"

"Dana? Hmm—that the French-fry lookin' one, yeah? Little whisper of a thing, dark hair?"

"That's the one," David replied, smiling back into Miss Marie's open, happy face.

"I thought I saw her out front with Mr. Jay this morning but I was tied up, got the grandson in with us today." She pointed behind her, smiling even wider, to a young black boy spinning furiously in his grandmother's desk chair, "Anyway, Miss Susan has been up front most of the day, let me see what she could tell you," She turned her head over the padded shoulder of a purple lady's jacket and bellowed, "Miss Susan!"

From around the bend tottered Miss Susan, who was wearing a similar-looking woman's business dress suit, only in red, with a huge, faux-jewel lapel pin of a large orange cat. In one hand she had a sandwich, wrapped in deli paper. She chewed, swallowed, and yelled back.

"What? What do you want Miss Marie, I told you I was going to eat." She swatted the boy in the chair behind his ear. "Scoot Freddy. Oh, hello Mr. Drahtman, and how are we on this beautiful—"

"Oh hush up Miss Susan, help the kind sir out. He's a very busy man you know."

"Oh, it's no trouble ladies. Miss Susan, you enjoy your lunch," interjected David.

"Don't be silly, boy. Miss Susan, Mr. Drahtman wants to know if you saw his secretary, Dana down here earlier."

"Dana? Girl that looks like a rolling pin? Always got a face on like she got a pickle in her purse, that one."

"Miss Susan!"

"Oh stop it, Miss Marie," said Susan, waving her hands and squinting her eyes. She took another nibble of what looked like turkey, chewed and swallowed. Before she could go on, Marie started.

"Didn't I see her out front with Mr. Jay? I was helping the young gentlemen find his earphones under the desk, thought I saw her out front—*smoking*."

"Nasty habit, that is," said Susan, and the two women nodded to one another severely. David felt he was losing control of the conversation and quickly jumped back in.

"Who is Mr. Jay?"

"Well, Jay is his last name, I suppose. 'Course it could be

the first. Hell, could be initials, whatcha want from me. He's a friend of Mr. Shank's I reckon. And a smoker"

"Filthy, disgusting habit!" They nodded and shook their round faces at the mere mention of it.

"Yes. Terrible," said David, "And you saw them talking then as well Susan."

"I sure did. She came down asking about some package and I said 'Listen here swizzle stick, there ain't been no package delivered for Mr. Drahtman, and I woulda called myself if it was."

"And then?"

"She got all huffy and stormed out the door, near ran over Mr. Jay out front. And from what I saw they had themselves a little chat."

"And a cigarette," added Miss Marie.

"And a cigarette indeed! They looked pretty comfortable if you ask me."

"And what did she do when she came back?"

"She didn't"

"She didn't? She left?"

"I suppose so if you ain't seen her upstairs and we ain't seen her come back!"

"Did this, Mr. Jay, come back in?"

"Don't you listen? He was coming in when that vanilla bean ran him over. 'Course he came back in. He had lunch with Mr. Shank, didn't he?"

David had a vague moment of recollection and then lost it.

"Well, I'm sure she just left early for the day. I expect we'll see her tomorrow morning."

"Wonderful," the two ladies said sarcastically, in tandem. Smiling, he waved his left hand to them both and bade them a good night. David had a dinner engagement with Reynaldo Melendez, and he did not want to be late.

David had never been inside this restaurant, but had heard of it from some co-workers who had used it as a fine tool for plying potential clients with its impressive location and ritzy décor. Traîtrise opened at the west to glorious views of Central Park and the inside was no less impressive. It was a glassy, translucent sort of place that reflected sunlight in every direction, somehow managing to avoid putting out one's eyes with a sunbeam on the hottest of days, which this day in particular would no doubt qualify as.

The tables themselves were impeccably designed, dressed in crisp linen, and fresh flowers in crystal vases and the chairs were high-backed yet simple. Clean white-gold lines that curled and coiled in the appropriate places. It was the perfect place to snare a victim. The splendor of the place would surely conjure images of wealth and importance, a quality not to be overlooked in the business of negotiation. David knew that his ability to pull this deal off would count heavily on his ability to convince Melendez that his family would dine in restaurants like these morning, noon, and night after signing on the dotted line with David.

Reynaldo was late, but not by much. David found it easy

to pick him out by the color of his skin and the state of his dress. Reynaldo Melendez, whose skin was not dark but the color of terra-cotta pottery or worn khakis, was wearing a smart, if a bit over-worked, black suit. His tie was knotted in a way that made clear he was a man who was not often asked to tie ties. A jumbled, sloppy ball bobbed before an open collar, and the thin end of the blue-gray tie peeked out from behind its fatter end. He was a restaurant manager and a chef; professions which did not lend themselves to high-gloss footwear and starched collars.

Reynaldo stopped for a moment by the desk and had a brief conversation which concluded with the host pointing to David's smiling, hand-waving visage. Drahtman stood and the two men shook. David thought he smelled cooking onions.

"I do apologize, Mr. Drahtman, for my appearance. We were very busy and I didn't have very long to change. I hope you don't mind."

"Oh don't be crazy Mr. Melendez, please sit."

Reynaldo Melendez was, despite the ragged dress, an impressive figure. Tall, cut like a monument, Reynaldo might have had a career in modeling if he had avoided the beans and beef that took hold of him in later life. He was probably in the area of forty, but looked fifteen years younger and, outside of a dusting of stubbly black hairs interspersed with an occasional gray sprout, the ridiculous knot in his tie, and lilting scent of cooking onion, he was every bit an imposing figure. Most striking, to David, was his smile. It was one of confidence, cool, and calm. It struck David as odd, if only for the reason that it

157

didn't quite match the defeated sounding voice he had heard earlier. For that matter, the voices didn't quite match either. This version of Reynaldo seemed far more relaxed, assured, and dare he say, happy.

"Call me Rey."

"Okay then Rey. I've already gotten myself a drink," said David, swishing a clear drink in front of his face, "so feel free to get yourself something when the waiter comes back."

"Great. Is this a restaurant you are familiar with? I've heard great things but have never had a chance to come."

"Oh I've been here many, many times. It's beautiful, no?"

"Gorgeous. I love the glass everywhere, it feels like church. I'm sure the food will be just as heavenly," finished Rey, smiling at David before turning his big eyes on the on-coming waiter, who bowed and opened his mouth as if to speak. Rey answered before he could utter a word, "Just water, please. Thank you."

"Water? Well, don't mind me for indulging, please," said David as he took another slug from his rocks glass. David, ever the master of conversational manipulation, was trying to match tones with Rey, trying to balance his air of confidence with Rey's, trying to seem as downright jubilant as Melendez did.

"Actually I love a good drink or two with dinner, but I have to be back in the kitchen tonight and knives don't mix well with wine"

"Oh of course! Me – ya know, I never-"

"I will tell you that I am quite excited to eat something

158

that doesn't have sofrito in it. It's been so long since I've had a chance to get out to eat anything my family didn't cook." He laughed again and bared brilliant white teeth.

"Sure, sure. I understand. But I have to say that I would just kill for some Mexican right now. My wife couldn't tell a chalupa from a gordita!" David was now the only one laughing.

"I don't know much about Mexican food, Mr. Drahtman," said Melendez sternly, "but one thing I do know is that both the *chalupa* and *gordita*, as produced by Taco Bell, as I assume these are the recipes you are referring to, are nothing like their actual Mexican counterparts. In fact my daughter once came home from dinner at one with a friend from school and asked me what her meal's name meant in Spanish." Desperately trying to avoid being seen as a fraud for not knowing that Reynaldo Melendez and his family were in fact Puerto Rican and not Mexican, David eagerly egged for a conclusion to Rey's story by nodding frantically

"I read the label and told her what it said."

"Yeah? And?" sputtered David, smiling.

"I told her she was eating 'A small fat girl with cheesy party potatoes.'" David forced a laugh and slapped the table in the face, as if he were convulsing with overwhelming hilarity

"So am I to understand that you and your colleagues were under the impression that I am a Mexican?" David needed to cut his losses.

"Mr. Melendez—Rey—I am so sorry—you must understand. I'm really not a very important man in the business, and my superiors told me that you were, in fact, Mexican. I do hope you aren't terribly insulted?"

"If I were to tell you that this was the first time my Puerto Rican heritage was mistaken for Mexican I would be lying. No harm done, Mr. Drahtman." Rey offered his hand again to David to shake. This was a relief to Drahtman, but it again raised concerns as to the demeanor of Mr. Melendez. Earlier that day he had seemed absolutely offended by David's attempt at Spanish and now he had actually mistaken the nation of the man's birth. It was like someone had taken David for a Ukrainian simply because they both had white skin. The problem was that Rey seemed nonchalant, as if he hadn't a care in the world. David Drahtman, however, knew better. And this contrast irked him. He liked to be in control. David decided the next best move was to appear as docile and harmless as possible. He thought he should admit his ignorance and hopefully appear genuinely interested by asking all about Puerto Rican cuisine. Before he could speak the waiter returned.

"Et que voudriez-vous pour le plat principal, monsieur?"

As far as David was concerned, this man was speaking Elvish. To his even greater surprise, Rey answered him perfectly.

"Coq au vin, s'il vous plait."

"Un choix excellent." The waiter turned to David, "Et pour vous, monsieur?" David's eyebrows joined his hairline and he experienced an entirely unheard-of-for-him moment of speechlessness.

"Um. I'll have what he's having."

"Excusez-moi?" said the waiter, confused by David's use of the King's English. There was a period of silence, intersprinkled with a few more "ums" and "ers" until Reynaldo, whose eyebrows were perched equally high on his tawny brow interjected.

"Mr. Drahtman. He's speaking French."

"Oh—yes of course."

"I thought you said you took French in high school," he said warily.

"Yes, well—I did, I did. It's just, well—It's been years you know." Reynaldo turned up to the waiter, and in seamless French ordered David the same dish that he had asked for himself.

The server bowed slightly again, turned away from them and Reynaldo looked gravely at David and sipped his lemoned water before speaking.

"So who normally orders your meals for you, Mr. Drahtman?"

"Call me David?" he said with a hopeful grin.

"So who normally orders your meals for you, David?"

"What do you mean?"

"Well, I mean that you said you have come to this particular restaurant many, many times. And I can't imagine eating here even once without some basic language skills."

"Oh, yes, that would seem odd. My wife, perfect French, spent some time there as a child. Her father was a diplomat of sorts." The latter half of this sentence was actually true.

"Really? That's how I picked up my French. My father sent me to culinary school at sixteen. Insisted I know more about cooking than adobo and plantanos." Reynaldo finished the sentence with a chuckle. Once again, David was at a loss for what either adobo or plantanos were. He got the sense that Reynaldo was aware of this, and did not like it one bit. Underneath skin pinker than his wife's Hummer (which David had parked three blocks away to avoid being spotted), David began to simmer with subtle yet ever-present anger. It was a slow roll; not a full boil. It was, however, most definitely starting to bubble. He choked this lathering pasta water back and continued on. Under no circumstances could he lose this one. His job could be at risk. Perhaps worse, his pride.

"So, Rey, tell me a little bit about Puerto Rican food."

Rey smiled and tore a heel of bread from a basket between them.

"My restaurant, Cocina Criolla, is based on traditional Puerto Rican foods. It has its roots in Taíno culture with lots of local ingredients, most especially produce. The fruit you will find on my home island will dazzle you, Mr. Drahtman."

"Please Rey, call me David"

"No, that's fine. Anyway, as many new foods, namely proteins like beef and pork, were introduced to the island by Europeans we began a great love of the open fire and its applications on these new meats. Modern Puerto Rican food is a blend of old and new. Indigenous, home-grown foods used to bring out the best in whatever we have available. Our real genius is in soups and stews, but you may be more familiar with the Americanized *pastelon de carne*. Meat pies. They've great popularity in New York." David wouldn't eat something called a "meat pie" if it was made of ground-up bits of his wife.

"Oh of course—of course! My kids love them"

"Yes, I would think so, young people love Puerto Rican food. Much of it is easy to carry and if I don't say so myself, is flat-out delicious. Or as they say in French, 'délicieux!'" He gave a teasing wink and grinned to David, whose belly began to froth and fizzle.

"Very nice," said David bitterly and drained his glass. Half sweated-out cubes of ice jangled against his teeth. David let one slide into his mouth and crushed it to watery crumbles.

He was tired of the pleasantries, and if this man continued to poke at him and question his validity on the things that came out of his mouth, David was about to go Bruce Banner on the guy.

Calming himself as best he could, David set his line in the water.

"So Rey, let me tell you what my company would like to do for you."

"Ah, yes, the business," said Rey ruefully, macerating a hunk of baguette in his gum.

"Yes. Well—to get straight to the point—I had an opportunity to speak with my superiors about your situation. I let them know that you were experiencing some private family issues. They were very concerned Rey—very concerned—and they actually upped the offer for the restaurant."

"And…"

"Well—Rey—we would like to offer you three and a half million for the space." Reynaldo, amazingly, seemed unimpressed. David knew very well that the building itself was worth less than a third of the offer. Further, three million would have been plenty enough to put his son in the best hospital on earth until a time when an organ became available for donation.

"The space?"

"Excuse me?"

"You called it, 'the space'," said Rey rather distractedly, picking at the crust of his bread.

"Yes, well, the restaurant."

"And what is your plan for the 'space'? Will the restaurant remain open? Or do you plan to just pave over it."

"Oh, well, we will all, yourself included, have a sit-down discussion about that once the financials have been set in place. You can be assured I will back you in any plan to keep Cocina Criolla open as it is."

"And what about keeping me. The health plan you mentioned?"

"Again, that is something for board members, yourself, and I to discuss." David was trying with every syllable to regain control of the conversation. He wanted, as he had planned all along, to appear as a last resort for a man in need of assistance. It seemed, by the rather whimsical way in which Reynaldo dabbed and swiped his bread in a pat of butter that he was, at least at this

164

juncture, not being very successful. Before he could continue, the waiter returned with their dishes.

He placed them before each man and pointed to David's empty glass. Using all the French he knew, David nodded at him.

"Looks excellent doesn't it" said Rey, who seemed thrilled by the look of the plate and the scents that spiraled visibly from the heart of the dish—half of a perfectly roasted bird—in thick, tight coils.

"Yes it does," said David, not so much as glancing down at his plate. "Rey, I am wondering how the deal sits with you." The way David saw it, Mr. Melendez didn't have a choice in the matter, and he was quite perplexed as to why the man wasn't leaping out of his *pantalones* to sign his name on the dotted line. Inside him, David's crucible of spitting rage was quelled momentarily by this fleeting speck of humor. *Pantalones. HA!* "Well, to be honest…" he broke off for a second to pop a moist, steaming piece of bird into his mouth. He smiled and closed his eyes, then swallowed. "To be truly honest, Mr. Drahtman, I am not impressed."

Now David was visibly pissed off. "Not impressed?! Mr. Melendez, I assure you, you will find no better offer for your restaurant—the space is just—"

"Don't be so sure, Mr. Drahtman. And don't get so upset. Please, eat." He pointed a fork at David's cooling chicken.

"I'm not hungry. And don't be sure of what *Reynaldo*? What exactly are you going to do in a few months when your son can't eat his Cheerios without needing dialysis? You need this

165

money, pal, and…" Now David had made a mistake; he shouldn't have known anything at all about the younger Melendez. Rey slammed down his utensils, any trace of whimsy gone from his face and pointed a finger not a foot from David's face.

"How *dare* you so much as mention my son? Is that what this is about *David?* You thought because my son is ill you could ply me with cash, force me to sell my restaurant. You'll never get it. Ever! I know your type and I knew this would happen. For your information *monsieur*, I have been tendered an offer by Wetra International that not only provides me, in writing, control of my restaurant, but also affords me a SOLUTION to my problems. Rather than throwing cash at the problem, the company has a way to save my son's life. And I, being a *MAN,* came to this meal to fill my obligation to you and give you the respect I would expect from any man. But apparently a courteous meal was not the motivation for this meeting."

David, flabbergasted, stood.

"How exactly are they gonna do that you tough guy?! Short of cutting open a homeless guy and stealing his kidney it's not gonna happen. Your son's gonna die and the rest of you will be homeless because you're too fucking thick-headed to take a good deal when it stares you in the face. You were lied to Mr. Melendez, and now the deal's off the fucking table." David turned as if to leave but he didn't make it very far because Rey Melendez put his fist through David's nose. He flew back onto the table and the steaming chicken, smashed through the table

166

and watched as cut glass and fresh flowers cascaded down upon him.

Reynaldo Melendez, being the gentlemen he was, paid the check and left just as the waiter had returned with David's last drink.

<u>16</u>

As Thomas Jones wound his rusty, tinkering tin can through the twisty wormholes that comprise service roads beside the New Jersey Turnpike he began to consider how he was going to be able to keep this drive up on a daily basis. It was his first day of work and he was already dreading the commute.

As we have already seen, Thomas is no NASCAR driver. Timid, cautious, and hesitant in every turn of the wheel, his driving chops did not quite translate to two hours on the honking, foggy, stink of a possum fart that is the Jersey highway system. He was, in fact, petrified of the six-lane leviathan and had switched to service roads twenty minutes into the ride. Thomas was now going to be late. This prospect, however, was an easy trade-off to being crushed like a can of Miller against a fraternity president's forehead rather than beneath the wheels of hordes of eighteen-wheelers which coursed this terrain. Truth be told, he probably should have been driving over 45 mph. Regardless, Thomas had already upped his salt-ratio in the last few days and was making steps in the right direction. Moving violations would be sure to follow if he only stayed the course.

As the trip lengthened and the Jersey air thickened around him, Thomas became convinced there was no way he was going to be able to keep up this sort of travel schedule. Selling his

family's home was becoming a more and more real possibility
with every mile. The good Lord knew Thomas Jones could do
without Wildwood. He imagined a world without drunken
teenagers screaming in (and on) ecstasy in his mother's azaleas. A
world without boardwalks and tourists, without the constant,
omnipresent fear of his family knocking on his door. Most
importantly at the present moment: a world without having to
drive through the armpit of the nation to reach his job. Between
his family history and his new job, Thomas had already made up
his mind. And he hadn't even punched in yet.

     The directions he had been given were leading him ever
northward toward the town of Thistlestick River, New Jersey.
While Thomas had been told he would be assisting in the
management of a factory in northern New Jersey, he had no clue
that there the closest thing resembling a factory in this
particularly affluent community was a gas station.

     When he finally arrived in the area at well after ten in the
morning he truly thought that he had made a terrible mistake.
Thistlestick River is the second-most-affluent community in the
state, behind only the richiest of riches, Mantoloking, a sandy
skirt of beach-houses on the coastlines, where only four hundred
people lived. When you multiply its population by their per capita
income, the residents of Mantoloking could have purchased an
NFL franchise that played home games on a floating stadium in
the Atlantic. Thistlestick River, always the more modest of the
two, perhaps could have purchased a professional hockey team
and housed them in a gymnasium. Where Mantoloking was

luxurious and tasted like salt water, Thistlestick River was fresh, wooded, smelling of pine needles and deer musk. Surrounding its eponymous waterway, the community of Thistlestick River was sparsely populated for its size. Most buildings were imposing residential structures laid gently amongst sloping tree-speckled hills. Some of the richest of men lived in Thistlestick River, the sort that you never hear about on television. Not the all-star shortstops and point guards, but the wizards of technology, finance, and big business—a far more dangerous breed.

As Thomas crooked and curled through one-lane forested roads, each of which was clearly outlined in his directions, his always churning brain began to imagine that this had all been a joke. Or worse, perhaps Jameson had intended to have him drive out into the middle of nowhere with the expressed intent to put a bullet through head. Thomas was flattering himself.

Finally, car creaking and whining all the way, he began to pass gold lettered numbers ensconced on humble piles of gray stone. Slowly enough, the numbers which would precede the location of the "factory" rolled passed him to his left. 869, 871, 873...875 Wolf's Hill Road. Thomas Jones put on his left turn signal and slowed to a stop in front of the small pillar of stone whose face was emblazoned with the wrought metal, gold-painted numbers "8-7-5." Thomas rolled down the window, checked his blind spot and pulled up and into the gravely driveway which climbed through a tree-lined hill. His tires skiddled and scrabbled through thousands of baby stones until it finally reached the breast of a hill when the factory came into plain view.

Stretching high into the mid-morning's denim blue sky, a great wooden structure stood stiffly as if at attention. It was enormous.

Primarily a faded shade of red, which gave it the appearance of a centuries old barn on anabolic steroids, the building was less factory and more little house on the prairie. Correction: huge mother-fucking house on the prairie is the better descriptive term for the situation. Great, ridiculous towers the same shade of paint and state of disrepair rose from the structure's two rear corners. Its center was a massive, dramatically angular rooftop whose own shade was entombed in thick bracken of ivy and moss. The building's face was two colossal white doors which stood like front teeth over a long, bare, wooden tongue of stilted stairs. Like the building was forever biting its tongue at some wildly funny inside joke.

Just beneath the roof's lip, where the vines hung thick on its forehead like bangs on a sea-monster, two large single pane windows that looked like they were made of black glass were flickering. The factory was either home to a family of tarantula-sized fireflies or there was work being done within.

Thomas parked beside six or seven other unimpressive vehicles and got out. The first thing he noticed was the air. Unlike the voyage up here, and further unlike his mental image of a "factory job," the air was clear, thin, and smelled like fresh water and wood smoke. Thomas heard what he thought were barking dogs, and also could have sworn he heard that most classic of barnyard sound bites—the gentle cry of *animalia chordata mammalian artiodactlya bovidae bovinae bos taurus*: the cow, mooing happily on a summer's morn. There were farms in the area, and the idea of being so far removed from homemade Thomas's insides squeal with glee. While it was not likely that Jameson was running a cattle farm, at the very least - whatever task he was going to be assigned would be in far closer proximity to nature than he had ever been in his life. Unless you count rats in a restaurant. And Thomas Jones most certainly did not.

As Thomas moved from where the cars were parked, he walked along a high white fence which scaled at least ten feet from the ground. It met the red-faced home at its ear and finished in the edges of the house's sandalwood tongue. Just as he had put one tentative foot on the sprawling, raw-white lumber welcome mat he saw that one of the black window eye's sparking lights had gone out. Now the house was winking at him.

Not a moment later that black glass was thrown up and the head and shoulders of a man fell out of it and looked down on him. The man, dark as the window's glass, was clean shaven with close cropped black hair. His white shirt seemed impeccably fresh and starched for working in a factory, as Thomas had assumed that at the very least, the sparkling-eyed rooms must have been the depository of the company's industrial elements. The man cocked an eyebrow at Thomas and yelled down at him. "Jones?" It took a moment for Thomas to realize he was being spoken to. He absolutely loved when people called him by his last name, like he was in the FBI, but since no one ever did; he gave a glance over his shoulder before yelling back.

"Yes sir!" Thomas was excited.

"Late." This being barely a sentence, we can forgive Thomas Jones for not immediately responding and offering his new colleague another moment with which to furnish a complete and cogent subject-predicate agreement. When Thomas came to the conclusion that no such grammar was to descend upon this conversation, he apologized.

As he was coming to be aware, Melvin Wilson was a man of very, very, very few words. One occasionally gets the impression that Melvin is playing some strange game in which he is to hold entire conversations without ever venturing beyond the constraints of monosyllabicism.

"All right," said Melvin once Thomas had finished a four-minute monologue on his soul-rending fear of superhighways. "Come in," finished Melvin before snapping shut the windowpane. The house stopped winking as a thousand sparklers went on within.

After about two minutes in which Thomas Jones sat in the same spot he had been at the onset of his conversation with the man who he still did not know was Melvin, the man he was to work for here at Keepwater, the tooth-white doors opened at their center.

"Melvin," said Melvin, pointing to his beefy chest. Melvin was about five foot in heels and wider than he was tall, but he dressed impeccably. His shoes were some form of reptile, and his slacks and shirt couldn't have been cleaner if he was a client of a laundromat staffed by Snuggles the Bear. His collar was so sharp you could cut a steak on it.

"Oh, hello Melvin. I am Thomas Jones."

"Yup. Come on." He waved Thomas up the sandy stairway and between the double doors. The main floor opened before him. It was clear that there had been many modifications made to the building since it was taken over by Keepwater. Where there surely would have been walls and partitioned rooms there seemed to be none. The first space was wide and open from wall to wall and was filled with hundreds of workstations where workers leaned over desks doing what looked very much like needlework. Glancing around he noticed one of the workers had a pile of product next to her, which seemed from a distance to be handbags. There was an upbeat, keyboard-heavy tune playing over loudspeakers and great steel fans which cooled the employees in a room which had decidedly poor ventilation. There was also a good deal of laughter and he noticed two employees chasing one another between the desks, one brandishing a handbag and swinging it wildly.

The back of the room proved Thomas's original suspicion wrong. There was a wall with four doors on it which cut the great room off. Consequently, there were no views through to the back of the structure. And in either corner there were spiraling stairwells which he assumed were the base of the rear towers. The right side of the room had a door in its center and one large window. He could see some scholarly sort of activity going on in this room, with white coated scientist-types mulling about inside.

The floors were a sort of kitcheny linoleum with orange corners. And although it was a bit stuffy inside, the room smelled like fresh linen and chrysanthemums. Thomas felt at home.

"A bit behind schedule today, Tommy-boy?" Thomas jerked around and found Jameson with his arm around Melvin, smiling. He had to hunch a bit to reach the man's shoulder but it didn't look like it was too uncomfortable. Melvin was smiling too. The men clearly thought fondly of each other.

"I'm so sorry Jameson, I had no idea how far the trip was. I'm not the best driver and…" As if the voice had been plucked with two fingers from his windpipe, Jameson raised his palm and smiled again.

"Thomas, please, don't worry about it. You're coming a long way. I think I might be able to help you with a new place if you'd be interested?"

"I was just thinking that on the way up. If I sold the house in Wildwood—"

"We'll get to that later. I doubt you'll have to sell the house—we own a few local spots which could probably do for a living space, but like I said—later." As Jameson lit a cigarette, Thomas glanced around the room again.

"Not too shabby right? I know it's not much to look at from the front, but I believe you'll find the inside of this place to be quite impressive," said Jameson in a mumbled sort of way over his cigarette butt. Melvin laughed.

"Anyway, Melvin, why don't you head back up top, I

think it's best to keep an eye on the operations up there. I'll show our new guy around." Jameson patted Melvin on the back and he responded with a grin, a nod, and nothing more.

"So, they're making handbags," said Thomas waving indiscriminately at the workstations before him.

"Today they are. Generally this room handles leather work of all varieties. I've got a connection for some stuff you wouldn't believe. This room houses Tafas Leathergoods, one of the companies which we hold under the umbrella of Keepwater. Today, as you have so astutely observed, we are making handbags. You would not believe how much some ladies will pay for these things," he said twirling one on his middle finger, "But we should move on because I really shouldn't be smoking in this area. Flammable chemicals, et cetera."

Jameson led Thomas with a palm between his shoulder blades toward the western wall. "What's through there?" asked Thomas pointing at the window through which the men who looked like rocket scientists or brain surgeons were engaged in some sort of work.

"Ah, The White Room. Lots of things," he said smiling, "as I'm sure you can imagine the business of working with leather requires a bit of mess which needs to be addressed in a sanitary way. But that is hardly the sum of what goes on in there. All of the more important activities we engage in which require a certain level of hygienic consideration goes on in there. Nothing you need to worry about."

As they passed the window one of the men in white coats

waved at Jameson and after taking a look at Thomas pulled a cord as internal blinds dropped over the window. Jameson noticed his rather affronted look and reassured him.

"Don't worry Thomas, they're very private guys. Nothing personal."

The pair made a path along the right wall of the building, took a left past the stairwell and began to walk along the wall with four doors. Before Thomas could ask, Jameson answered.

"These rooms are used primarily for training purposes for some of the service-related industries we engage in. Here," he said knocking a knuckle on the first door, "we have a form of art class, its complex, but we'll get you in there later. Next," knocking again on a second door "is another class for a different sort of employees who deal quite personally with their clients. Kinda stuff you'd see in a day spa. Next we have an office for employees who manage the activities which go on in the back. And the fourth door. Well, the fourth door. The fourth door we'll tell you about when you're all grownup." Jameson smiled audibly.

Thomas noticed there was no knob on the last door. He had never wanted to open a door more; and there it was, knobless.

As they approached the eastern stairwell, Thomas got the feeling that he was on a need to know basis with everything in the building. He wondered when he was going to be allowed to open a door. How the hell was he supposed to manage anything from behind a door? Morse code?

"Sir—""Jameson."

"Jameson, sir, I was wondering what exactly you had in mind for me here. There seems to be a whole lot going on here, but I can't say it will be very easy to manage much of anything without being allowed in a room." Jameson stopped suddenly, turned and put a hand on Thomas's shoulder.

"Thomas, we are just now coming to the place where I have confidence you will be of use. With the exception of the fourth door in the eastern corner and the White Room, you are more than welcome to investigate wherever you please. Further if you have any questions I would be happy to answer them"

"Okay—what kind of art class—"

"—at the conclusion of our tour." Jameson laughed, shook his head and beckoned Thomas to follow him. "The second floor, which we are passing now, is full of all sorts of goodies that we can get into a bit later, but before I get to my job for you, I'd like to show you the third floor."

They reached a landing where a large mahogany door was shut snugly in its frame. By the sputtering orange lights under the doorjamb and around the frame, Thomas knew where he was in relation to his view from the front. Jameson placed his hand on the knob, paused and removed it just as quickly.

"I understand that Cleo gave you an idea of what this factory does." He waited for a response.

"Um, luxury, she said."

"Correct. This building deals with objects and services which are of primary interest to the wealthiest of wealthy. We here in this division are set with the task of creating new ways to impress the rich. There is no income like disposable income, Thomas, and the more witless and crude the affluent in our society continue to be with their surplus booty, the better for us. Keepwater is not interested in ripping off the poor, the working class, and the struggling. This is why we don't make handbags for K-Marts in Weehawken. We make them for Beverly Hills. We do so for good reason. Follow?" Thomas didn't quite understand how handbags and art class had anything to do with Jameson's speech, but he was more interested in what was behind the door than he was in asking more questions.

"Finally, Thomas Jones, you do recall our conversation in my offices in New York in which I outlined the possibility of you seeing things which may seem to you to be unethical?"

"Yes sir." Jameson raised his brow and smiled before Thomas corrected, "Jameson."

"I do appreciate it, Thomas; I hate the 'sir' thing."

"Sure thing. I apologize."

"It's cool, my friend. Anyway, what I am about to show you is nearly operational but not yet, so don't mind the mess. We hope to get it humming today, or at least tomorrow. Also, Thomas, you may need to use your imagination a bit here so be prepared." Thomas's interest was officially piqued.

"So, I give you Keepwater's newest acquisition, something I have so cleverly named "Supply & Diamond." Jameson swung the door open and the spitting white-orange fireflies died as Jameson clicked on a switch.

In the center of a room, as large and open as the handbag floor, was a massive metallic structure the size of the USS Enterprise. It was conical, coming to a point at its base, widening and thickening to its flat, beveled top. It looked like an ice cream cone for a Transformer. Around the structure were six or seven individuals all staring blankly at Jameson and Thomas through welding masks. The shortest of the figures snapped open his mask.

"What?" said Melvin.

"Everybody take a break," said Jameson to nobody in particular, "And Doc if you could, hang back for a sec," Jameson was addressing a tall, wispy fellow on the latter end of his seventies, who was wearing a stiff black apron. He took off his mask and laid it down on a desk before walking rather slowly up to the pair.

"What can I do for you, Jameson?"

"I was hoping you could explain what's going on here to our newest employee, Mr. Thomas Jones." Jameson opened his arm to Thomas, displaying him with pride like Vanna White with her letter-board.

"Well, Tom—"

"Thomas," said Jameson, cutting the doctor off expertly, "he prefers Thomas."

"I'm sorry, Thomas," the doctor said very genially, and truly no harm had been done. "Anyway, my name is Dr. Clark Carter, and what you see behind me is the result of years of research. To put it bluntly, this machine makes diamonds."

Thomas reached far and deep into his mind to pull up his mental file of how diamonds were made and found, as he suspected, a discrepancy in the numbers.

"I thought it took thousands of years to make diamonds. Don't they come from charcoal or something?"

"Carbon, under intense, mind-bending pressure and heat makes diamonds." Thomas could tell that Carter loved his job by the excessive hand-wringing and lip-licking that was taking place. "The only reason they take so long to make is because the Earth itself is a very slow- moving beast. Science has easily outstripped nature now, and it's really quite a simple process. You see, carbon, in graphite form, is mixed with a metal flux in a cylindrical shape. An infinitesimally small seed diamond is placed at the bottom of the cylinder. The metal and graphite are subjected to extreme pressure, more than 800,000 pounds per square inch, and a temperature of 3000 degrees Fahrenheit. During the period, the carbon atoms within the molten metal crystallize on top of the seed diamond—"

Jameson had to cut him off before the foam collecting in the corners of his mouth spilled over on to the floor. "Easy doc, easy. Let's get to the good part." He turned to Thomas, "Where a three carat yellow diamond once took several thousand years, we can now create the same size and quality gemstone in—" he opened his hand, palm up to the doctor and asked him wordlessly to finish his sentence.

"About four days."

"Four days?! But that's crazy—you must—" Thomas's

voice descended into a blabbering froth of spit and syllable. Melvin was laughing, and so was Jameson.

"Impressive, yes?"

"I'd say so!" Thomas began to imagine, using relatively poor math skills, how much diamond a man could produce in such a massive machine with that sort of ability. Then he realized that there had to be a way to detect the difference between the millennia-old stones and the weekend variety. Further, how is it possible that no one else was doing this? "Jameson, is anyone else doing the same thing?"

"Sure, but the products of the process are being used for science, and not the decidedly more lucrative market of jewelry. Besides it's a very expensive process to do pull off on this scale and most people are concerned that the diamonds produced here wouldn't be of the same quality and would be easily detected as fraudulent.

"One way we avoid speculation is that we won't be selling them to professionals and geologists. We're not even going to be making traditional jewelry. You'd be astonished at the sorts of things that people want to put diamonds on. Cell-phones, belt buckles, sun-glasses—"

"Handbags!" offered Thomas.

"Handbags indeed, Thomas! Wealthy socialites will send us their toilet seats to be covered in diamonds and we will comply. And we just don't think the risk of them taking the products to a professional is very high. Especially since most people cover their crap in diamonds for the look of opulence, and not the geological character of the stone." He paused and looked warmly at Thomas, "See… you're already taking to our style of business."

And he was. Thomas Jones was so taken with the brilliance of this particular idea that it seemed to matter little to him that this was a far below legal venture. He did not realize it at the moment, but by the virtue of the careless nature with which he glossed over the felonious character of Supply & Diamond, Thomas Jones had just salted himself considerably.

He came back to Earth suddenly however, when he realized that this was not to be his specific position. Jameson seemed to read this.

"You can have all the diamonds you want when the machine's up and running, but for now it's best to leave this to the brains."

"Oh yeah, sure."

"Let's get to where I am going to ask you to start." Excited, but quite sure that nothing was going to outdo a spaceship that shits diamonds, Thomas followed Jameson out on to the landing and back up the stairs. As they climbed, it became clear that they were now within the tower and beyond the main structure. The sounds of the surrounding landscape became clearer as the walls thinned. Thomas could still hear the sporadic *moo* and *bark* of animals no doubt spread throughout the Thistlestick River community. Thomas felt like Old MacDonald.

The spiraling trip to what Thomas assumed would be the top of the rear tower reminded him of a trip he took with his mother to see the Statue of Liberty when he was a boy. The trip up through the bowels of the iron lady was an authentically horrifying experience for Thomas. On a busy summer day the inside of lady liberty stunk like sweat, copper, and dirty-water dogs. Tourist-flesh, damp, sticky and exposed due to the season was pressed into a mass that wound and coiled around the spiraled staircase to her crowned dome like a piping tube of fish sausage. Thomas remembered vividly being inches from the back of a humongous, sweaty leg that smelled like over-boiled ham. This climb, to the contrary, smelled like cedar and despite a lack of windows, the air within was cool and comfortable. Not to mention that rather than a porky knee-back, he was staring at Jameson's backside. This, all things considered, was an improvement.

"Jameson, can I ask you a question?" asked Thomas quite confidently into his new employer's ass as they walked

"Course Thomas, what's on your mind?"

"I was wondering how you got a guy like Dr. Carter to work here. I mean, can't a genius like that get a job in a government lab or something?" Jameson laughed.

"Well, first of all, I'd like to think he's got a better gig with us then with the suits in the government, but that's subjective I suppose. Nevertheless, the main reason it was easy for us to retain his services is that he is an alcoholic, and no one will hire him elsewhere."

"Oh my—really?" responded Thomas who was surprised Jameson has told him such sensitive stuff about the doctor.

"Yes sir. Real boozer. Last place he worked—he showed up one day in a shirt, tie, suit jacket and no pants. Shoes, and black socks, but no pants. How funny is that?" Thomas did laugh.

"Ha! Well, he doesn't do that here?"

"We keep him in check, and that's kinda your job as well—keep him away from the liquor."

"Well how do you keep him clean?"

"Pot. Lots of pot."

"Drugs?! But doesn't that seem a bit pointless—"

"Thomas, marijuana grows in the ground and has unlimited medicinal applications. One of which is that it serves as an excellent supplement for subjects of abuse, without the addictive properties. We keep him good and stoned every night and he doesn't go out drinking and trolling for ass. It's a good thing. Trust me."

Thomas had no argument for this. He smoked weed once in his life and didn't remember doing it the next day. The only way he knew it had happened was a Polaroid his friend Ben had taken of Thomas standing on a chair with his mouth attached to the business end of a six-foot-tall green plastic bong. He had awoken the next day in someone's garden shed using a lawn mower for a pillow, with a penis drawn in blue lipstick on his forehead.

After what felt like ten minutes, Jameson opened a hatch above them and climbed out into morning. Thomas followed. They were on a large, fenced-in roof which formed the top of the rear tower. Maybe two hundred feet from the main building's roof, it seemed that this would serve as an excellent look-out post if one had a need to be on the look-out for anything in particular.

As his eyes adjusted to the bright noontime sunshine, he saw they were not alone. Sitting in a cloth-covered folding chair, with his feet up on a cooler and eyes pressed to binoculars was a man Thomas did not know.

"Mike!" hollered Jameson at the back of the man's head, from which sprouted a decent length of black hair tied up in a ponytail. The man named Mike stood, shielding his eyes from the sun and smiled.

"Jameson, how we doin'?"

"Great. This is Thomas Jones, the new guy I got for you; he'll be working with you for the foreseeable future."

But Thomas Jones wasn't paying attention to the conversation. He had reached the edge of the tower and was looking down an enormous, sprawling landscape that spread out into hills and wooded area just within the reach of his eyesight. And before the house, on what Thomas could only describe as a "back yard," was what Jameson had planned for him.

Two vast, fenced-in enclosures on the property held two very different charges. In the larger of the two were several hundred dogs of all breeds, colors, and sizes. Even from here, Thomas could tell that these were pets. They all were collared and were far too well-groomed to be strays. Beyond that fence to the west was another enclosure which was filled with about fifty solid black beasts that Thomas immediately identified as cows.

"Gorgeous, aren't they?" said Jameson, breaking Thomas's concentration. "The cows, I mean. Of course the dogs aren't bad either but we just watch them—those cows are some of my most precious babies."

"What the hell is this?" asked Thomas with a tone that was soaked with incredulity. A farmer, Thomas Jones was not.

Before Jameson could answer, the man with the ponytail handed him a brochure whose cover read *Total Immersion Doggy Day Care.*

TOTAL IMMERSION DOGGY DAY CARE

Do you have no time to chase around your darling animals?

Do you want your beloved pet to have the very best care money can buy?

Are you a discriminating consumer who only wants the highest class service for your dollar?

Then you need Total Immersion Doggy Day Care!

Founded in 2003, Total Immersion Doggy Day Care is the very best in high-end, luxury animal maintenance. Imagine your family pet spending its days in the sprawling wilderness of secluded, first-class THISTLESTICK RIVER!

Imagine them dining on the very finest foods—meals most middle-class families couldn't pronounce, let alone appreciate!!

What separates T.I.D.D.C.from other Doggy Day Care services is special, one-on-one consideration no one else can provide. Our specially trained handlers are skilled in dog-psychology (dogcology) and are able to serve the emotional and spiritual needs of your animals. Each day, through personal reflection time, acupuncture and hypnosis, your animals will become more in touch with their inner-dog. By spending eight hours a day in a TOTALLY IMMERSIVE environment in which their every need is met by their own personal dogcologist, the animals receive constant, overwhelming attention and love the likes of which even the most dedicated of owners can hardly provide.

CALL TODAY!!

Please be advised T.I.D.D.C reserves the right to deny undesirable dogs or dog-owners

"It's actually quite brilliant. Many wealthy individuals purchase these animals for nothing more than show-pieces. It's incredible how surprised they are when they realize they have to feed and walk them. So a market sprang up in the last decade for doggy day care." Thomas repeated the words "doggy day care" like he couldn't believe it was possible, "and much like anything else the upper-class wants, they want it one better than their neighbor. So Mike here, who is our resident copywriter," Mike nodded and smiled, "came up with a brilliant brochure which highlighted why our day care is the very best money can buy."

"And why is that?"

"Because we charge more than anyone else," Jameson replied simply.

"How much?"

"A thousand dollars a day."

"What?!"

"Amazing, huh? You see we've come to realize that when it comes to the upscale consumer, the only factor that matters is that it's expensive. So we make things expensive."

"And all this stuff about 'dogcology' and 'the finest food money can buy'"? Thomas asked, since the picture on the brochure had one dog playing fetch with one person, and this backyard had over three hundred dogs playing, albeit happily, with one another and a sparse crop of handlers in the great outdoors.

"Well, obviously a lot of it is bullshit, like the price. But how can you hate a $200,000 a day income to use your backyard. This thing is a golden goose. One thing that is true is the thing about the food. They eat well indeed. That's where the cows come in."

"THEY KILL AND EAT THE COWS!?"

Mike and Jameson exploded in laughter at this. After a few minutes of thigh-slapping and breath-catching, Jameson composed himself.

"No, no, no. I mean, they do eat the cows, but they don't kill them. That would be disgusting. Those cows are the second part of our outdoor operations here at Keepwater that you and Mike here will be overseeing."

"So now I'm a cowboy?"

"Ha! Hardly," blurted Jameson.

189

"A butcher?! There's no way I'm working in a slaughterhouse."

"Calm down, Thomas," he said rather severely. "We don't do any slaughtering here—it damages the meat."

"What? I am so confused. I—"

"Then allow me to explain. Those right there are the happiest cows on the face of the earth. They begin their mornings with a two-hour massage while drinking warm malt beer. They spend the rest of their day roaming free over the land and grazing as they please. They eat when they wish, mate when they want, and each night before they sleep they are massaged again, this time with cocoa butter. When you compare this to the life of the average domesticate American cow, whose life is spent in bare iron cages, feeding on the ground-up bones of its uncles, and you can see why the end product of this process is the fattiest, most tender, most sublimely delicious beef on the planet. These cows go for $40,000 a head."

"So you sell the beef and use the leather for the handbags?" Thomas thought he was tying up the loose ends of this mystery.

"Oh no." said Jameson simply, "Definitely not."

"But—"

"Thomas, I have to be going, I have a meeting that I am going to be quite late for if I do not get my act in gear. Mike here will show you the ropes." Jameson patted Thomas on his stunned and bewildered back and smiled before turning and walking back towards the hatch. When Thomas turned to watch him off he realized that Jameson wasn't going to the hatch but up a small set of stairs descending off of the tower's top to another structure which was hidden from view to someone viewing the house from the front. It was a helipad. Just as Thomas was about to ask another round of questions, the chopper started and all sound outside the whirring, punching throttle of the propellers ceased to exist.

<u>17</u>

David Drahtman was having a nightmare. He dreamt that he had been punched in the face by a steaming chicken thigh, and that his secretary had squeezed his testicles so many times that his penis was now the size of telephone pole. Only it was no longer Dana, but rather Alastor Shank, who was now driving off in a pink hummer, laughing. Minutes later he was being chased by his wife's dogs, one of whom wanted to mount him, the other eat his scrotum (which had turned into two balls of fresh mozzarella). They hounded him into a corner where his twin boys were playing the triangle wildly, both of them ding-donging so loudly that it woke him up.

That clamorous tune was being played not by his sons but by his own doorbell. David woke with a start and grimaced at the sudden pain that bound like a belt across the bridge of his nose. Melendez had rapped him square in the shnozz.

Sore in all sorts of places, David got his balance, poking and scraping sleep from his eyes, and began to waddle out of his bedroom towards the repeated ding-dong-ding-dong-ding-dong of a very impatient houseguest.

As he navigated the stairs he heard his daughter cursing and screaming indiscriminately at him from beneath her comforters. He thought he could make out "cocksucker," but he couldn't be entirely sure.

Behind the glass of his front windows and white curtains David saw lights flashing and momentarily was under the impression it was Christmas. When he opened the door there was a tall police officer standing with his left elbow resting on the frame, one eyebrow cocked at him and a smirk pasted across his jaw. With his right thumb he pointed behind him and asked David, "You the owner of the S.S Douchebag?" David hadn't a clue what this man was talking about. He blinked a few times and took two steps barefoot onto his porch.

With its ass end hanging four feet off the driveway from a thick steel chain pulled taut by a tow truck, David's Lamborghini had seen better days. All four tires were gone, the roof had been torn off, and in yellow-spray paint across the driver side door (the passenger side door was missing), and it read: "S.S Douchebag." The car was beginning to rust because it was soaking wet. The seat-backs looked like briny sponges and there was seaweed clumped and caught under the hood's clasp.

"What—the fuck—" stammered David, eyeballs swirling in their sockets.

"Couple kids, we guess, found it and decided to make a boat out of it."

"Evidently!" David was positively flummoxed. And if he wasn't mistaken, the cop seemed to be enjoying himself.

"It—the car was like a mile from the beach."

"Oh, I dunno where you left it, but it turned up in Staten

193

Island."

"Staten Island?"

"Yup," the cop said, grinning wildly. "Pretty incredible huh?"

"What do you mean incredible?! Do you know how much that car's worth?"

"A lot," said the officer, nodding and smiling. "You know, we're sorry and all, but you probably shouldn't have left it wherever you did." He was stifling a furious fit of giggles. The tow truck driver was laughing shamelessly, at the top of his lungs, from within the cab of the truck.

"Well I want to press charges!" David was livid, but now the tall cop couldn't contain himself, he laughed briefly and shook his head.

"Sure sir, I'll go get my handcuffs here," he reached behind him and grabbed the cuffs from his batman utility belt, "And now I'll go arrest the Atlantic Ocean!" He walked off like he was doing improvisational comedy in Los Angeles. The tow truck driver gave a sustained fifteen seconds of pealing cackle. "You know sir, I can't see his wrists." he looked seriously back up the stairs at David. "Do you?"

"Are you fucking kidding me?"

"I wish I was, sir."

"What do you mean? Quit fucking around, I want you assholes to find who did this!"

"Sure thing sir, we'll let you know if we find anything." the cop tipped his hat and blushed back another giggle.

"I'm not kidding!"

"Of course, of course, you leave a six-figure Italian sports car unlocked on the side of a freeway for half a week and want us to find the person who might have motive to take it."

"Are you being sarcastic?" gasped David, mortified.

"Unless of course the kids who took this car assaulted you personally?"

"No, but they—"

"You sure sir? Because you look like you got the piss kicked out of you."

the truck driver was doing something between a howl and a screech and David thought he saw him slap the steering wheel repeatedly, then grab the dashboard for support.

"Excuse me?!"

"You can tell me, sir. We'll find the bastards. I mean, you probably shouldn't have left the keys in it either. I mean, I guess we're lucky they didn't just steal it outright. But I suppose this has its merits."

"Merits?"

"Well, it—is—*hilarious*"

"What?"

"I mean…S.S Douchebag? C'mon, that is just *gold!*"

"You think you're fucking funny, do you, big man?" The cop showed David his hands, shook his head and tried to keep from laughing, "You think this is a big joke. What kind of a police force lets things like this go on?"

"Well, you are aware you live in the Hamptons and on

195

any given night there are several thousand twenty-year-olds tearing through this place like a tornado. I mean, if there was any time of year to leave a Ferrari lying around with the keys in it—"

"It's a Lamborghini!" The cop smiled and paused for a full minute, before arching his brows and shrugging his shoulders.

"Does it really matter now? I mean—look at it—"

"Yes, it fucking matters and I don't care if Pope-goddamned-Benedict the mother-fucking-eighteenth is dee-jaying at the Boardy Barn, I want the people who did this punished!"

"Oh that's not nice to say about the Holy Father now is it?"

"I'm not joking around, gentlemen! I want this taken care of!"

"Oh, no, of course not. Neither are we sir."

"I want your goddamned names. Right now!"

"Sure thing cap, mine's Rooney." Lacking paper and pen, David gave the look of someone trying to commit something to memory.

"Yeah—," like his CPU had alerted him of the file's successful save. "And his?"

"Who?"

"Mr. Funny Pants in the truck!"

"He's a tow-truck driver sir; I don't think you'll need his."

"But I want it"

"And I want to get home and catch the Mets game. You have a good day, sir. Oh, here's the keys—" He paused for another few seconds before finishing, "to the S.S Douchebag." At this the driver of the truck lost all control and began kicking the windshield and broke into a cackling, snorting, tittering meltdown.

Two minutes later the driver pulled a lever in the truck and the back end of the powder blue dragon smashed to the ground with a clattering bang and jangle of parts that no longer worked. A dead fish fell out from the undercarriage with a decisive, squelchy flop.

Hours passed, and David found himself behind his desk at Ohmco. Gently massaging the blue-black ridges that framed his busted gonzo, while taking care not to run roughshod over the bloated, crusty crests of over-ripened skin and pink flesh, David made careful work of calming and softening the edges of his condition. His face was a minefield, and his fingers the ginger toes of refugees working their way to the water.

As the medicine on his face went to work, David occupied himself as best he could. Trying to suppress the desire to run to the car and drive it through Cocina Criolla, he checked his email. There was a memo about new bathrooms, a request from a tech intern requesting he update his contact information, and a forwarded link from Bobby Collins which led David to a video of an Asian woman giving a hand job to a pig. He deleted the first, replied to the second, and watched the first few seconds of the third before becoming disgusted with himself and closing the browser.

Not even the depths of Bobby Collins's brazen and

shameless depravity could distract David any longer. He needed a plan. Barring David arriving to dinner in a man-sized taco costume, he couldn't have possibly offended the sensibilities of his target more. Now, however, was not the moment for regret. He had made his bed, albeit one constructed of six-inch nails and blackberry brambles, and now had to do the proverbial lie-in.

He was pretty sure that he was the only one aware of his mistake and this afforded him an opportunity to cover his tracks. He needed a plan which would not only cover the incident at the restaurant, but would also deliver him the property. Stealing real estate right from under the nose of its owner is quite a task, and notwithstanding David borrowing Gulliver's trench coat, stuffing the restaurant in its pockets and stealing off in to the night, he had very little to work with.

Resolved that he thought better with food in his stomach, David decided to order out for lunch, but just as his middle finger descended on the speakerphone button he remembered the ever-present fact that he still had no secretary. This wouldn't be an issue for your average businessman, as David too knew how to manage the operations of a fax machine and telephone like any chimpanzee can. It's just that David thought it was beneath him.

While David could certainly wrangle a fax, he hadn't the foggiest clue as to how he was to order himself a meal. Did she know the numbers to local delis and restaurants off-hand? Did she go there and pick it up or did they deliver? He strode from his office and made his way to Dana's empty desk. It looked as if she had just gone to the bathroom rather than whatever did happen to her.

Her desk was a cluttered jumble of paper clips and manila folders decorated like a Native American head-dress made out of multi-colored post-it notes. Her computer monitor itself had so many different tinted post-it notes framing it that it looked like the ass end of a peacock. Pulling and rifling through papers and drawers and growing ever more frustrated by the moment, David's fingers finally found pay dirt. At the back of one of her cavernous steel drawers was a small rubber-banded package of menus to local restaurants. Grinning as wide as his punched-in and sun-scorched face could manage, David snapped the rubber tie off the menu and began shuffling through the menus. Greek, Korean, Mexican—no, definitely not Mexican—Italian, BBQ…as David searched for something to fill his empty shriveling stomach; he felt a shadow behind him. It was Collins.

"Damnit, Collins, you scared me. What's going on?" David asked, although he could care less, as he sifted through the menus in search of something remotely appealing. He had a vague idea of what he wanted—it smelled like lamp chops—but he couldn't place it. So accustomed as he was to the sound of Collins's overbearing, swear-tongued litanies that it struck him as strange when the response he got to his question was not a string of swear words like roped pearls, but rather—

"Been better." This was without a doubt the shortest sentence Bobby Collins had ever let slip from his sweat-dappled lips. Running a big clam-chowder paw through a thinning bristle of blonde, he went on, "Been better, Davey"

Honestly concerned, David turned away from a pink menu with a photograph of a veal parmigiana sandwich, and looked into Collins long, sad, horse-like face.

Still soggy and drawn out in the jaw and nose, this version of Collins was far more severe. Rather than running in rippling rivers down his brow, the sweat now pooled in the ridges of a forehead so deeply creviced it looked as if it had been raked with razors. His eyes were heavy, pink and padded like pieces of beef were super-glued to the bottom of his eyeballs. Most strikingly, his mouth was closed, turned even, in what appeared to resemble a frown. A non-purple, non-burger-pinching, grimace.

"Collins? What the fuck happened?" asked David, wide-eyed at the majesty of an inoffensive Collins. His colleague sighed long and breathy.

"Just been better Davey. Rough night." Collins frowned again, laid a palm so swampy it soaked through David's jacket sleeves on his arm. He squeezed, soaking David's shoulder in a sort of tepid tea, and released. Frowning once more, Collins turned and began to walk away with a folder he had just lifted from Dana's desk.

"Hey Collins!" hollered David. His fellow businessman turned slowly, still frowning like a sad clown and raised his eyebrows, not even taking the opportunity to throw in a casual, "What the fuck do *you* want?" though David gave him a full ten seconds to employ whatever nastiness he saw fit. When none arrived David asked, "Any clue what happened to *this* bitch?" On that last pair of words, he swung a thumb over his shoulder and hung one eyebrow on his earlobe. Hoping to goad a smile and a swear-word from Collins, he finished the ensemble with a half-hearted wink. For a moment, at the sight of his colleague's half-raised brow and half-open mouth, David thought he had succeeded. He hadn't.

"Took a new job I suppose, no?"

"Huh? Where did you hear that?"

"Didn't hear it." At this he looked puzzled. "I mean the note."

"What note?" now Collins looked surprised.

"The one on her desk, Davey, I just assumed you were cleaning up her stuff now."

"What? Cleaning? No. Lunch. What note—where?" David sidled around the desk and couldn't believe he missed it. The note, a purple post-it right where the peacock's asshole would have been was pasted right at the tippy top of her monitor's frame.

I quit. Got a new job.

Picking my shit up in a couple days.

-Dana

P.S. David has to squeeze his nuts to get it up.

David, flustered, tore the piece of paper from the screen and crumpled, smashed and smushed it. Collins, in an attempt to ease his friend's embarrassment, "Don't worry, Davey, I can't get it up without the pills." after a pause, "I was wondering why you didn't take that down." another pause and a near chuckle. "Well,

I gotta be going."

The very fact that Bobby Collins did not punch David in the shoulder, laugh and scream obscenities from the lips of his lungs was a testament to the fact that he had most definitely *not* had a very pleasant evening. Whatever it was could not compare to what David Drahtman was going through at this moment. He thought he heard snickering coming from an anonymous cubicle. He punched the desk and stalked back to his desk. Just as his hand had crunched around the handle, he heard another door open with a forceful swing behind him.

"For the love of all that is holy Mr. Drahtman you get in my office this INSTANT!"

It was Mr. Prewitt, who had evidently just discovered that David had met a client for lunch and convinced him, rather than selling to Ohmco, to punch David dead in the nostrils. It was a minor miracle that Prewitt didn't snatch David by his earlobe and drag him into the office like an arithmetic teacher who just caught him sticking gum under the desk. Instead, Prewitt pressed three crinkly fingers in the small of his back and directed him, like a steer, between the frames of his own doorway. David, not unlike livestock, dispensed with all dignity, bowed his head and galumphed over the threshold like a spoiled five-year-old girl with a busted Barbie.

Prewitt slashed the door close with as much force as a man of his year and condition could. On the mere winds of his fury, the door still gave a considerable clap as it shut. A larger and younger man might have blasted the thick bolt of wood through the frame and sent it whirling off its hinges down the hallways, disarticulating heads from shoulders all the way to the windows. (It might, if the air were thin enough, have spun straight out the window in a tight rope, wind curling in a thin column of smoke behind it, and walloped its way through a passenger jet, leaving two door-shaped blow-holes in the sides of a Boeing – soon to drop from the sky like a sack of screaming, dead potatoes.)

"Have you any idea? Any IDEA what you've done?!" Prewitt spat through his kissy, cockled lips. A cool mist of stippling splatter pattered David's face. Assuming that Prewitt either didn't realize he had just washed his breath on David's cheekbone washboard, or he was well aware and the gesture was intended. Either way, Alexander Prewitt was waiting for David to speak. Being highly and seamlessly skilled in this regard, David knew that no matter how sure he was that he was correct in his assumption of what Prewitt was referring to, that is, being punched in the honker by a potential client, he had to play it safe. He had been guilty of far worse and was not yet too proud to play the fool.

"I'm sorry sir, what do you mean? What happened? I've very confu—"

"Confused!" Prewitt said in a near whinny. "Confused!? You engaged in FISTICUFFS with a man we are trying to do business with!"

"Well, I don't know about *fisticuffs*…I mean, this wasn't ice hockey. It—"

"Do you think you're FUNNY?" Prewitt's entire head

203

was the color of a keg cup and it was shaking like a wet dog with Parkinson's in winter. "DO YOU?"

David was legitimately frightened. Prewitt's knobby, wrinkled, vulture-egg head looked loose and rickety—like it was going to just roll off his shoulders any moment.

"Mr. Prewitt—"

"By the LOOK on your face, Mr. DRAHTMAN, you CLEARLY induced a potential partner in our business to SOCK YOU IN YOUR BLASTED FACE!" David could have sworn his boss was so angry he was crying. His fists were bobbling and wiggling on the end of his arms and his whole body was oscillating with pure, furious apoplexy. There was a whistle of steam in his wispy white ears and a fog of ground molar dust pulsed and pumped with each wheezy pant.

"Mr. Prewitt. I think you need to calm down." He was serious. The man was fluorescent red and he shuddering like Howdy Doody on a blow binge.

"MR. DRAHTMAN! You do NOT understand—If Mr. Shank hears that this has happened—you will have cost BOTH OF us OUR JOBS DAMMIT…" His voice was wavering in and out of earshot. He was yelling, and then whispering, breathing then screaming, "We—as in you and I—were the only ones to know about the Melendez problem. He set me personally to ensure your success in its endeavor."

"Oh god—"

"MR. DRAHTMAN. We will lose everything—we will."

"MR. PREWITT. I am very sorry sir, but you must

understand the situation…" David turned his eyes to the carpet and began to cobble together some sort of explanation. "He was being, in-in-insensible. The—the—man has no ability to understand the way business works. We can fix this I assure you…" With the last syllable, David's down-turned eyes flashed upwards at the sound of a creaky, wood meets plastic, *thud*. When his eyes caught the air which Prewitt's violent, trembling head had just filled, he found a window. Behind his desk, Alexander Prewitt had just collapsed. His eyes were closed and he wasn't breathing.

David peed a little in his pants and slapped his palms on his cheeks like Macaulay Culkin on Christmas day.

<u>18</u>

Thomas put two hands on the fence at the edge of the southwestern tower that leaned over on his new charges. He could see another twenty or so men walking amongst the dogs and another five or so tending to the cows. Behind him he heard Mike strolling up beside him. He had a massive rifle over his shoulder and it scared Thomas out of his tightie-whities. He gasped, and trying to cover his shock, coughed. Mike smiled at him.

"Beauty, ain't she?"

"Gorgeous," said Thomas, as seriously as he could manage.

"Just a tranquilizer 'course. Case the dogs get stupid."

"So you just oversee? What am I supposed to be doing?"

"Just keep your eyes open. We just make sure nothing gets too out of hand, which it never really does."

"What do you mean 'out of hand'?"

"Well, there's really only two rules: no fighting and no fucking. We can't have them ripping each other's ears off. And we certainly can't send $10,000 pure-bred shit-zus home pregnant with a Rottweiler's puppies, you know?"

"Sure. Sure."

"It's usually pretty quiet, but if one of the bigger dogs gets a little pissy and starts chasing an ankle biter around and the guys downstairs can't do anything, then I can take him down from up here," Mike finished, tapping the rifle with his right hand.

"Have you ever used it?"

"Oh yeah, but I've used it more often to shoot one of those jackasses with it as a joke than I do on the dogs."

"Holy shit! Does it knock them out?"

"No, but they look like they drank a barrel of Beam for the rest of the day." Both men laughed at this. "Regardless it's not a hard job we have, we look after the yard in case they need real help and basically we just handle communications." He waved his hand over a portable phone which was set up next to a laptop on an aluminum folding chair beside the cloth one Mike had been using. "I suppose you were hired 'cuz you've been in a managerial role before, and that's all you really have to do—answer phone calls from customers to either the beef end or the dog end. If there's ever a problem, you'll also have to make phone calls to customers."

"What kinda problems?"

"No problems," Mike smiled and shook his head. "Like I said, our job is pretty easy. The real trick is the smaller dogs. It's so fucking popular now for these morons to have dogs they can hardly see. They keep 'em in their pocketbooks."

"Ha—"

"Yeah, so keep your eyes peeled 'cuz sometimes you'll see one of the bigger guys running around and you'll think he's chasin' a mouse, but it's actually Mrs. Cavendish's prized Border terrier."

"Ah. I see."

"Anyway, it's probably smart for you to spend some time working with the animals just in case you ever have to deal with it, so Jameson told me to have you downstairs for a few hours this morning."

"Oh." Mike seemed to sense Thomas's disappointment.

"Yeah you'll be shoveling shit for a few hours, but it won't last forever. I need another pair of eyes up here—business is booming and I can't keep track of all the dogs. You're gonna get your own tower eventually." Mike smiled and pointed a finger on his right hand to the other tower. Thomas had never been more excited in his life about anything.

"What? Really? That's great!"

"Yeah man, soon enough."

"Do I get—um—one of those?" Thomas pointed cautiously at the rifle. Mike's smile turned severe.

"We'll work on that later, for now you get this," and he handed him a walkie-talkie. This was still pretty cool to Thomas who had owned a pair as a child but never had a friend to use the other one (though he certainly wore them out by himself pretending). He immediately snatched it from Mike, depressed the button and said, "Roger that, five-niner, over and out," and smiled. Mike picked his up and played along.

208

"Roger soldier." The two men laughed with a seven-year-old snort of satisfaction. Thomas took his walkie-talkie and a black vest which Mike handed him and made his way back towards the tubular stairway which descended down to the ground and out to the yard.

"Second door on the left and out back. Tell Beulah I sent you."

"Beulah?"

"That's her name. And be sure to speak up." Mike pointed his non-rifle hand to his ear. Thomas had never met anyone named Beulah and was afraid she wouldn't speak English. Her name sounded like a type of fish to him.

When Thomas had reached the floor, he passed the first door on his left which was the black door with no knob. He cursed silently. When he opened the second door, an office came into view whose back wall was a single pane of glass with a door in the center. Through the glass one could see the rolling, hilly range on which the dogs yapped and yipped happily. Out of the corner of the glass you could just make out the cow territory. His eyes having been drawn so quickly to the beautiful view beyond the office's contents, he missed entirely the woman sitting behind a desk in the office who was staring plainly up at him.

If she wasn't blinking, he would have taken her for a corpse. She looked to be in excess of ninety, darker than midnight in the desert, and so crinkled and folded she resembled a five foot raisin. As dark as she was, her hair was whiter than a snowman's smile. She blinked furiously, eyes enlarged to the size of cue balls behind spectacles so thick they looked like hockey pucks made of glass. She stood stiff, and plainly had no clue who Thomas was. Finally her tightly rumpled lips spread and she spoke in a yell with the voice of a thousand men.

"WHO YOU?!" She was deafer than Russell Simmon's Comedy Jam. Thomas couldn't initially respond because he was taken aback by the fact that this tiny prune of a thing had the voice of a hundred angry gods on Olympus. There was not a drop of femininity in it. She sounded like a cigar-smoking construction worker. Like a Viking warrior and his conch.

"Umm. I'm Thomas, Thomas Jo—"

"PROMISE? I AINT PROMISE NUFFIN! WHO YOU I SAYS!"

"No, no. Thomas…THOMAS!"

"THOMAS? WHO THOMAS?"

"Er, me—I'm Thomas"

"SPEAK UP NOW BOY!"

"I'M THOMAS. THOMAS JO—"

"THOMAS! FOW DA DOGS?" she pointed at his vest and walkie-talkie apparatus.

"Yes! Yes. Mike told me to tell you that he sent—"

"YES. YES, THOMAS. I LIKE YOU TOO. NOW GO THOO THE DOW!" She pointed a rickety arm at the glass door. Thinking he needed to explain that Mike had sent him, Thomas insisted.

"No no. MIKE sent me. Mike with the ponytail," he said louder, gesturing with his hand behind his head, trying to drawn an invisible ponytail with his fingers.

"WHAT WRONG WICHOO?" she said arching and bending white eyebrows and scrunching up her little brown mouth. Thomas thought it was better left alone and walked towards the glass door. He left Beulah to her work.

As he crossed in front of her desk he noticed she had no computer, only a rotary phone and a few picture frames whose back ends were to Thomas. She had already forgotten he was there and was now scrawling tiny notes in pencil on a legal pad with her white cotton head mere inches from the page. There were boxes of old files littered through the room and he navigated his way through them to the next door.

As he shut the door behind him the full sound of the acreage surrounded him. Happy *arfs* and plaintive *moos* swung about and around him. It smelled like sweet grass with an only appropriate hint of animal doody wafting on the back end. As he began to walk he noticed two other men dressed very similar to himself were walking towards him waving. They were both Hispanic and had great black moustaches. They were smiling.

As Thomas went to raise his hand and return the gesture he heard a whiz and *pop* and felt a thin, quick burst of wind whip at his back. In the ground behind him was a prodigious tranquilizer dart with a bright red feathery back end. Thomas heard someone laughing wildly on top of a tower. He laughed back. And so did the two men who had just now arrived behind him. The taller and thinner of the two put out his hand.

"Don' worry bout him amigo, he does it to all da new

guys." Thomas gave a sort of grunt that he wrapped in a squinting grin. "My name's Pedro. Joo mus' be Tomas." He spoke a fluid and beautiful form of English with a heavy accent that sizzled in a way that made Thomas wish he was born in Mexico. Which is where these men, by their matching national flags on their bare arms, were clearly from. They wore no shirts, only the black vest and both had tan baseball caps on. The shorter and wider of the two was introduced as his brother Pablo. Thomas shook the second man's hand vigorously.

"So what can I help you guys with?" Thomas said eagerly.

"Okay, Miguel say joo gonna be up on da tower yeah?"

"That's what he said."

"Said joo gonna be da big boss man!"

"Well I dunno about—"

"Yeaaaaah, joo got alotta sperience ways I heard from him. But out here on da ground is Pedro's boss-man time. Okay?"

"You got it, Pedro." Thomas saluted. The brothers loved this and smiled with open mouths and both patted him on opposite shoulders.

"We gonna have lossa fun, Okay?" said Pablo happily.

"Okay!" responded Thomas.

For the next two hours, Thomas followed Pedro and Pablo around the dog-pen and talked about dogs. The two men were infinitely skilled with canines and when one or the other said "Sit" about thirty dogs parked their behinds and waved tongues in a snap. There were a good deal more people working in the fields, most of them cleaning up after the dogs. These packs of shit-shovelers were dressed much like Thomas and the brothers, but instead of walkie-talkies they carried poop-stained shovels. They looked like college students. Every one of them was young, white, and seemed to be happier than a pig in dogshit. Thomas was correct. They were all students at one of many universities in the area and worked here for summer cash. They appeared to be having the time of their lives and listened like good little crap-cradling soldiers whenever Pedro said anything to them. Pablo was more the silent leader. He worked with the dogs better it seemed and Pedro made sure the kids didn't start flinging dookie at one another.

"Ay mang. Cut da shit rye now!" he yelled at a pair of kids who were evidently planning to do just that. A short skinny boy in shorts and a vest was hiding behind a massive Saint Bernard while another flung turd grenades off the end of his shovel. When Pedro hollered they both stopped immediately and tried to cover by whistling and looking in opposite directions.

"Fuggin gringos," Pedro muttered to himself.

As they walked on, Pedro explained the finer points of doggy day care. It was clear he treated the task with great reverence.

"Joo know—more dan anyting joo gotta make sure dey don do no fuggin'." At this Pablo gave a sigh and shook his head.

"Yeah, nooo fuggin'," agreed the brother.

"Joo see if dey go home with da puppies den da owner gonna know something's up. Dey supposed to geta one on one

tree-ment, joo know? Not a one on one tree-ment of a fuggin'
udder dog."

Thoroughly entranced by the complexity of the task,
Thomas inquired, "And has that ever happened? A dog getting
pregnant, I mean."

"Oh yeaaaah, Lossa times. One time dis lady, she love
Jesus sooo much and she think da dog had a version birth. Like
the version Mary!" The two men laughed and pointed at each
other with fingers of remembrance. Thomas laughed
too—religion was certainly hilarious sometimes.

After about an hour in which Thomas broke up three
relatively unserious dog skirmishes and had turned his sneakers
into galoshes made of dog feces, Pedro told him to meet his
brother Paco by the cow pen.

"How many brothers do you have?"

"Der's seben of us. And dey all work here."

"Oh yeah? Will I get to meet them all?"

"Yeaaah. One work inside wit da leathers, two work
downstairs in da kishins, and ders tree of us here."

"But—that's only six."

"Yeah?" Pedro looked confused. He glanced at Pablo
who also looked confused. They started counting on their fingers,
"Pedro, Pablo, Paco, Pancho, Placido, Pepillo, y…y…y…OH!"
they said together, "Pepe." They said his name with a kind of
disapproval.

"What's wrong with Pepe?"

"Pepe no like to work. Pepe only like the senioritas."

"So he doesn't work here?"

"Oh yeah he here but he don't do no work. He teachin' peoples to rub on da chicas all day. Jameson call it *massage*," they mouthed this last word in as American a way possible. His lips danced on it.

Pablo seemed more offended than Pedro by his brother's wily ways.

"Pepe don' even do *massage*," he struggled with the word too. "He scratches da back. Like crazy he scratches da back."

"Yeah! Yeah he does! Jameson say das what he wans 'cuz you gotta go to school to do *massage*, so instead he scratch da back. All day scratch da back."

Thomas was mildly confused by all this, but convinced himself that they were mixing up the details or that some element of what was going on was being lost in translation. When he finally extricated himself from the conversation and made his way down a slope towards the cow-pen fence, he took a few minutes to mimic the way the brothers talked. He loved when they said "you." It made him feel like a bull-fighter.

When he had gotten a bit closer to the pen he saw Paco sitting on a fence post, looking serenely out over the field. He was holding a beer in one canvas-gloved hand which was sweating worse than he was in the blistering heat. Paco also wore a black moustache and appeared to be an even shorter and further widened version of his brothers. It was almost as if they were made like Russian dolls. Like Paco fit inside Pablo and Pablo fit inside Pedro (The lord only knows who fit inside Pancho, Placido and Pepe). He was also wearing a wide-brimmed khaki hat and sunglasses.

He stood behind the cow-herder for a moment, not wanting to interrupt his enjoyment of the beautiful view and his frosty ale. After another moment of uncomfortable standing around, Thomas spoke up.

"Excuse me." Paco leapt off the fence, rotated in mid-air and landed in the squashy mud behind the fence with two fists up, one of which was wrapped around a beer bottle. Paco was amazingly agile for a person shaped like a beach ball. He scrunched up his face in suspicion.

"Ooo is joo?"

"My name is Thomas. Pedro sent me to help. I'm new." This relaxed Paco considerably, as he then smiled.

"Ohh jes. Pedro is tellin' me bout joo. You work wit Miguel no?"

"Sí. Er, I mean yes. Yes I do." Thomas was learning Spanish by osmosis.

"OK. Joo come. We meet cows." Paco waddled ahead, taking a long pull from his brown bottle. Thomas followed.

Jameson and Mike were certainly not lying when they said that these were the finest cattle on earth. Not that Thomas had ever before been this close to one, but these cows looked absolutely delicious. They were fat, shiny, and friendly. As humans represented food, warm beer and twice daily brush massages, they were quite fond of primates in general. Strangely, Thomas took to this rather easily, going so far as to pet one who was sniffing at his crotch. Paco found this amusing.

"Oh jes, jes, dey loves to smell joo pennis." (He tried to pronounce "penis" in English, but it came out like it rhymed with tennis). "They think joo pennis is smelling good. Like breffest time." He chuckled. Paco clearly was dead set on learning as much English as possible, pronunciation be damned.

"So now is time to milk da cow," Paco said as he reached a paddock where three or four lazy beasts were splayed out on their side, as if to tease Thomas with the promise of a steak that would cook by sunlight. Paco passed the tent and opened the door to a small shed. The cows responded to the sound of the door's clasp and all scurried over behind the diminutive Mexican cowboy.

Though Thomas couldn't quite see what he was doing, when he turned it was a bit plainer. Paco laid three large metal bowls out on the grass and filled each with one of three brown bottles he had under his arm. They looked identical to the one Paco had recently emptied.

"They is like the beer hot. No know why. I tink dey is crazy. I like my beer ickey cold." It took Thomas a full two minutes to realize Paco was trying to say "ice cold."
As the cows nuzzled their noses and lips into the frothy brown beer bowls Paco set up two stools between a pair of cows. Thomas hesitated.

"Don' worry, Tomas. They is like to have you pull on dey tits." That last word was perfectly clear, though he likely was trying to say "teats," the meaning was the same.

Thomas Jones sat down on a stool and took a nipple-

217

yanking lesson from a Mexican. He took a good deal of the stuff on the face and shirt due to improper tit handling. Thinking he was dealing with supermarket-ready chilled whole milk he made the mistake of licking his lips. Having just exited the belly of a living mammal, the milk was hot and stunk like the inside of a cow's tit. It was bitter, thick, and sticky.

While Thomas was rubbing his face and chest in the grass like some sad sort of a break-dancing to the beat of Paco's high-pitched laughter, they and the cows had their attention diverted by sound of two or three shots from what was no doubt Mike's rifle. The three, quick *cracks* were followed by some barking and yelling. Thomas got up to go look but Paco put his hand on his chest and told him to wait. The cowboy then scrambled up the nearest post and stood on its top on his tippiest of toes.

"Oh is no prollem. Dey gots it under control. Pedro and Pablo not running around like dead chicken with its head on." Paco clearly had trouble with idiomatic expressions as well. "Dey would call me if dey needs help. Don' worry Tomas. Joo still got leche on joo shirt amigo." Paco snickered to himself and wiped the sweat from his brow with the back of his glove.

Around four in the afternoon. Paco's walkie-talkie awoke with the voice of Mike blaring out of it as Thomas was getting his first cow massage lesson. Paco pronounced that word even worse than his brothers. It sounded like it rhymed with "roughage."

"Hey amigo, tell Thomas to meet me over in the main pen."

"OK Miguel. Joo got it." He turned to Thomas, "Joo

hears him. Go 'head."

"Well, thanks for all your help, Paco, it was nice meeting you."

"Jes, jes, nice is meeting joo too, Tomas."

When he reached the main pen again he saw that Mike had come down, rifle still over his shoulder, and was talking to Pedro and Pablo, both of whom seemed to be shrugging their shoulders.

"Hey man, how's your day been?"

"Great. You know…little milk in my face and shit on my shoes, but all in a day's work."

"That's the spirit," Mike slapped his shoulder with his non-rifle hand.

"Yeah so what happened over here? We heard some shots. Paco said nothing was up but it sounded like Vietnam." Thomas thought this was funny, and apparently Mike agreed. For some reason they were taking nicely to one another.

"Oh nothing much, I saw a bit of a skirmish in the northwest corner with a bull mastiff and a few smaller dogs. Pedro and Pablo normally can handle it but they were chasing a stray cat out of the pen before the dogs saw it and started a riot. One of the kids tried to help but he just sorta jumped on the mastiff's back like a miniature pony. Had to make sure the dog wasn't hurting any of the little guys so I took a shot and missed. Took another.

"Missed?" offered Thomas. Mike smiled and pointed at him.

"No, I hit something, but it was Jarred, the kid on his back. The third shot got Grawp."

"Grawp?"

"The mastiff."

"Strange name."

"We've got a poodle named Whirlpool, so Grawp's pretty standard."

"Whirlpool?"

"Long story, dog likes the rinse cycle. Yada yada yada. Anyway we don't think anything happened as we didn't find a half-eaten Collie. So we should be okay."

"Ok. So how can I help?"

"Well, seeing as how Jarred walked off into the woods claiming he was going unicorn hunting, we're one short on the cleaning crew. You up to pitch in?"

"Sure, what's a little more shit?"

"Great. Pedro and Pablo are gonna start moving the dogs back to the east pen to clean 'em all up and get 'em ready to go home. The rest of us are gonna just start getting some shit shoveled." Mike handed him a tall metal shovel, "Just make a pile with whatever is around you and we'll come around with the truck to get it all."

"You keep it?"

"Best fertilizer on earth. We sell our customers back their own dog shit for gardening." Thomas thought this was frigging brilliant.

Thomas and the remaining, non-hallucinating college

students spread out over the area and got to work. It wasn't five minutes before Thomas was sweating like a horse and panting. He began to fling shit over his shoulder without looking and was getting more on himself than in the pile. After he had cleared up one corner, he looked around and saw a small mound in a relatively clean area. When he reached it, Thomas saw the most perfectly coiled, nasty brown dookie snake on the ground. Like chocolate soft-serve it came to a peak and curled back on itself. Amused, Thomas got his shovel under it and lifted. It felt heavy. Really heavy.

Thomas turned his shovel over and dropped the poop eel back on the grass.

There, caked and smeared with feces, Thomas could swear he saw a tiny glint. A sparkle even. Reaching down, Thomas used a gloved hand to pick through the crap and find the source of the shimmer.

Thomas pulled out a long black leather collar that was studded with diamonds. It caught on something in the shit-pile. He gave it a hard tug and the center of the collar—the tag— popped out.

A massive, diamond letter "G" was bobbing off the center of the collar, smeared in dog doody. It was the shittiest diamond Thomas Jones had ever seen. It was, however, impossibly tremendous. And real.

19

As David Drahtman weaved in and out of Manhattan city street traffic in a hot pink school bus he realized he would not be getting lunch anytime soon. Desperately trying to keep pace with an ambulance which might or might not contain the dead body of his employer, he blew red light after red light, hoping beyond hope that there was still a breath to be breathed in that insufferable windbag. It was possible, nay probable, that someone in his office, in a frantic attempt to gain favor in the company, would outright accuse him of murdering the man. Anyone with hearing and half a hemisphere could tell that Prewitt was last seen berating Drahtman on their way into his private office. They all heard nothing but screaming and the audible *thwack* of old man on carpet. The next thing they saw was David tear out of the room screaming. Who's to tell *what* happened in that office?

At the image of his being indicted on manslaughter charges against his employer, David nearly ran over a bike messenger. We can hardly blame him, for from behind the wheel of a little girl's Hot Wheels he couldn't see very much around him. It was like driving a nuclear submarine. A nuclear submarine full of cotton candy and rainbows.

Remarkably, he was able to keep the thing in his sights and pull in not ten seconds behind the ambulance. David caught sight of the stretcher entering through massive sliding glass doors. He noticed, praise be to God, that there wasn't a sheet over the old bastard's face. Rather, there was an oxygen mask and a number of hands snaking all over his body in an effort to keep it from pickling on the spot. Prewitt's shirt and tie had been cut right up the center and his thin, livery skin looked ready to split, it was pinched so tightly within every ridge betwixt every rib. There were brown splotches like gravy stains every six inches across his chest and the occasional thick white hair fell tired against a trunk the color of a spoonful of mayonnaise left in the sun.

To make a long simile short: He didn't look so hot. As the doors slid shut with the *thhhwup* of rubber sucking rubber in front of his face, David nearly swallowed his tongue. The stretcher had been met by six doctors and nurses, one of whom had immediately mounted Prewitt like he was giving him a lap dance. As much as David wanted to believe that the nurse was just feeling him up, it was clear that his employer was now being administered CPR.

Running like every dollar he had depended on it, David flailed his arms and kicked his legs wildly behind him, dodging and ducking around hospital employees, wheelchairs, and kids on crutches—trying to catch up to Prewitt's swiftly departing soul, maybe thinking he could shove it back into the old man like a coin in its slot.

Finally, he turned a corner he was sure had to be the last and ran straight into a pair of breasts the size and shape of a sofa. They literarily knocked the wind out of David who wheezed and dropped to his knees. The sofa-breasts were attached to a short, portly woman with stringy white-blonde hair. By her dress, it was plain she was a nurse of some variety. She even wore the little hat which David could swear none of the other others were wearing.

"Can I help you?" said the nurse, looking down at David who looked like he should be using some form of inhaler.

"Yes, please, Alexander Prewitt. Where is he?" asked David while struggling to his feet. He nearly clonked the back of his head on a shelf the woman's breasts made from when standing. They appeared to reach her kneecaps.

"I'm sorry, but he is still in the ER with doctors. You're going to have to wait."

"He's in there though, right?" asked David with a puppy-dog face on, pointing at a room just behind the nurse.

"Yes he is, but you are not to enter unless you also wish to require medical attention." David was petrified of the woman and nodded obediently.

"Are you family?"

"No—YES. Yes, I am... I'm his nephew. His nephew...in-law."

"His nephew-in-law?"

"Er, yes. Mother's side—his sister is my—"

"Sit here... nephew-in-law, and I will let you know how things go." She pointed a short, chicken sausage finger at a green metal bench near the two. "And please do not go in that room."

"Yes, ma'am." David was about to salute her but thought

224

better.

He spent the next three hours trying to figure out how the term "nephew-in-law" really worked while intermittently pacing and attempting a peek behind the door holding his employer. Eventually, Prewitt's room opened and two male doctors exited. David stood swiftly, and stared anxiously at the doctors like Alexander Prewitt was his pregnant wife.

"Waiting on news about Mr. Prewitt?" said one, with a bit of caution in his voice.

"Yes sir! I'm his nephew-in-law."

"His nephew-in…" said the other doctor with his eyes squinting quizzically.

"Forget it," said the first, taller doctor, cutting the second off. "He's going to be fine. It seems as if he had a mild stroke but we won't know for sure until we get some tests done. He's going to need to stay here for a few days and I'm unsure of what lingering affects it might have." David had the sudden mental image of having to teach Prewitt how to put his pants on and screeched.

"Oh God! What affects? Lingering? What lingering effects?"

"Relax sir, it likely won't be anything too serious, he is already talking and alert, but if things start to seem strange let us know. Normally a nervous tick, a tremor, or some slurring of speech may occur. But for a guy who's just been through what he's been through, he appears to be in good spirits. Would you like to see him?"

"Yes, please. I would." said David, still hyper-ventilating.

"Whenever you're ready you can go in, just don't stay too long, he needs rest."

When David crept in to the room, sliding his body through the thinnest possible crack of the door, he saw Prewitt lying on his back in the bed, eyes wide open and staring into the neon-lit ceiling.

"M-Mister Prewitt, sir?"

"Yes?" responded Prewitt nonchalantly without averting his eyes, like he was lying in an invisible tanning bed.

"Oh, thank God you're all right. I'm so sorry for everything. You just can't imag—"

"Shut up, Mr. Drahtman," said Prewitt, cutting him off.

"Do you want me to leave? I can, I just wanted to be sure you didn't—well, that you were—"

"Alive?"

"Well—"

'Never mind, Mr. Drahtman. Come and sit," he said, slowly and evenly, pointing to a chair against the wall near his bedside table. He still hadn't so much as peeked at David. When he had sat down, Prewitt's head finally revolved to its right so that his watery, blood-laced eyeballs were staring through David's own pair of clogged toilets.

"You look great," said David optimistically, though in reality his boss resembled a month-old corpse that had just been pulled from the bottom of a lake. Prewitt ignored the compliment entirely.

"Mr. Drahtman, I am quite famished. I would like you to page the nurse and get me something hot, some broth perhaps. A thin soup." His voice was frail and quivery. He seemed to take a breath between every word.

"Are you sure you should be eating so soon. Is that healthy?"

"Mister Drahtman," he labored over every word, this time not with exhaustion, but frustration, "I am quite sure it is all right for me to be eating"

"But sir, you've just had a stroke."

"I always take broth after a stroke." David's response to this was less a sentence and more a grunting hoot of inquiry. "This is my fourth. Now bring me something hot!"

"Um—okay then." David scurried outside and nearly took the very same loveseat to the sternum before catching himself and pulling up on his heels. "Oh nurse. Thank goodness, Mr. Prewitt would like some soup."

"I think we may be able to manage that. Be careful sir, you'll get yourself hurt running around a hospital like that."

"Yes ma'am. I'm very sorry; just want my uncle to be comfortable, that's all."
"In-law?"

"Uncle-in-law, yes. Of course." David waited until the nurse had toddled around the corner, spine hunched like a question mark at the weight of the futon she had hung from her clavicle.

When she had passed from view David made his way

back into the room and sat down next to Prewitt, whose head was still flat against the pillow, bloody eyeballs staring off into space. A few minutes passed in silence, with David waiting for his boss to gum his tongue, to show some sign of consciousness other than a lunch order. As they stared awkwardly off into different corners of the room, David wondered whether or not Prewitt's habit of chewing his tongue and pursing his crusty lips weren't a result of one of his three prior lapses in brain to body communication.

"Mr. Drahtman." Prewitt's words cut through David's imagination like a chainsaw through ricotta cheese.

"Yes?"

"An idea has just come to me."

"An idea? What sort of idea?"

"An idea as to how we may be able to fix the problem with Senior Melendez." he pronounced the man's last name in a spitting hiss. As David opened his mouth to ask the obvious question, a nurse who did not have a sectional in her blouse entered with a plastic tray and a bowl.

David took the tray from an Asian nurse who gave a sort of nod before turning and leaving. The textured tan plastic tray had a cup of green Jell-O, a bowl of yellowish broth and a spoon on it. Tiny bits of pasta clumped in the basin's bottom. Maybe alphabet soup would be helpful if Prewitt forget how to read, David thought humorously to himself.

"Mr. Drahtman," said Prewitt expectantly with both hands extended towards the tray. He was now sitting upright in the bed, paper gown clinging to his clammy body. The skin hung loose from his bare arms like a warlock's shirtsleeves. David, realizing he had been daydreaming over the man's soup, handed it over.

As Prewitt settled the tray on his lap and removed his disposable spoon from its plastic wrapping he answered a question David had yet to ask.

"It is clear, Mr. Drahtman, that Mr. Melendez will not be selling us his restaurant. Would that be an accurate appraisal of our current predicament?" he asked, stirring the pasta scraps about in his steaming broth.

"I would say so. He seems to have had enough of me. Perhaps Collins could talk to him."

"While I intend for Mr. Collins to assist you, I don't think talking will do. We need to be more aggressive and resolve this before Mr. Shank gets wind of it and fires us all."

"So, what do you have in mind?"

"I would like you to attack this situation in a not dissimilar way to the manner in which you resolved the situation in Patience, Mississippi. Do you recall that event?" said Prewitt, holding a spoonful of broth six inches from his lips.

"I do sir, but I don't know if Japanese hornets will go over as well in Manhattan. Plus, they eat bees—not concrete—and…" just as David was trying to remind his boss that the hornets would not be much good at negotiating real estate purchases, it became quite clear what lingering effects would plague Mr. Prewitt. He had struck himself in the eyeball with the spoon.

"Blast! Damned plastic cutlery!" Prewitt shook some soup off his folded face and tried again, this time poking himself directly in the nose. The third attempt resulted in him punching himself in the forehead. Alexander Prewitt was going to have to re-learn how to use silverware.

After another few attempts which ended with him sloshing chicken broth all over his pillow and paper-gown, Prewitt gave up and tossed the entire tray and contents on the floor. He broke the spoon in his weathered, knobby hands. Taking a deep breath with his eyes closed he turned and looked at David. The eye he had taken the soup-spoon in was the color of raspberry jam. Despite his ridiculous appearance and newly found handicap, Prewitt spoke calmly and slowly.

"I was not referring to hornets. I do not care how you handle the situation, but I think you might do well to consider an animal which, when present in a restaurant, can wreak specific hazard. Then, you might if you were so inclined, call local authorities and report the establishment for glaring health code violations. Are you following me?"

"Yes." David loved this idea. "And if we can do enough damage, then the place will be condemned. They won't be able to pay the fines and the place will go to foreclosure. And then we can just buy it at auction!"

"And Mr. Shank will be none the wiser."

"Brilliant!"

"Yes, I thought so. Mr. Collins will be able to assist so I

suggest contacting him before beginning."

"Great. I'll call him when I leave."

"Fine. But for now, feed me that Jell-O."

About an hour later, David was demoralized and humiliated. He had just fed his eighty-year-old employer like his wife had once done their children. The only thing that was missing was the "Here comes the airplane! Vroooom!"

As he was walking through the sliding glass doors at the emergency room's entrance, David flipped out his cell phone to call Collins when the face of the phone lit up and the sound of John Williams's "The Imperial March," began playing loudly from his phone's speakers. Not a second later a picture of his wife appeared in the display. He closed the phone and muttered under his breath.

Hurling himself four feet off the ground and into his wife's armored vehicle, David winced as his phone rang again, conjuring for the second time images of black-hooded space villains. He assumed she needed help figuring out how to tie her shoes or use a doorknob or something else about two shades short of being adorable.

David ignored her and started driving. When the phone stopped, he cycled to Collins's name in the phonebook and dialed. As David tried to explain the situation to Collins as quickly as possible (so he wouldn't be pulled over for using the phone while driving), his wife called at least three more times, incessantly *beeping* into his conversation with Collins. She was nothing if not mind-numbingly annoying.

Collins gave David a number for a friend who might be able to help with the proper wildlife application. David had met the man before; he was an exterminator in the city and was known to be helpful in delicate situations like these. His name was Crabbitch and he was a disgusting human being. For David, however, it took one to know one.

Once David had punched Crabbitch's address into his wife's glittery pink GPS system and put his phone on vibrate so the next twelve calls would bother no one but the internal plastic of the middle console, David relaxed a bit and settled in for the drive.

The last time the two men had met, David needed someone who could be plied with cash to ignore an infestation of termites at a factory the company ran in the Bronx. While he was aware that Crabbitch was unscrupulous as one could be, he was not aware that Crabbitch was an insect-enamored paradox.

Despite smelling and looking like a pasty sack of spider eggs, Crabbitch was both murderer and care-giver. When he wasn't being paid to smite entire civilizations of red ants with chemical warfare, he was home letting them traverse the prickly thickets of his arm hair. He loved parasites of all varieties far more than he had ever loved another person, and according to Collins, would be able to provide David with some assistance. The last time they had met was on-site. This time, however, David was being given the austere pleasure of visiting the home of Stanley Crabbitch himself.

Crabbitch lived in a terrible neighborhood in Queens,

which, technically speaking was on David's way home, so it wasn't out of the way.

When his GPS gave its final digitally-voiced instruction, David pulled into a thin grass driveway. The home to which it belonged was tall and skinny, like most homes in the area where people and pets and places of business were packed as tightly as possible in every available inch of land. In the late afternoon's fading light, the house looked brownish and worn. Although the color could just as easily have been the result of complete and total neglect, it certainly smelled like a landfill.

Just as he reached the tiny porch, the door whipped open and Stanley Crabbitch stood in the frame. He had the body of an eggplant, wide around the middle with slight, stick-thin arms and legs. He face was smattered with brown hair and sweat and he was still wearing his work overalls: a dark blue denim number with a patch featuring a cockroach with "X's" where eyes should be. He wore thick glasses and a matching blue hat covered in white blots which were the salt from sweat stains of yesteryear. David was utterly repulsed by the sight of the man.

"Hey David," said Crabbitch, like the two had only yesterday had a beer and watched the game.

"Hello Crabbitch." David's face could not have more obviously displayed repugnance, but Stanley got this all the time, so for all he knew David was hitting on him.

"Come in," said Crabbitch waving an arm into the dark room behind him. David would have more quickly accepted an invitation for a shower from a Nazi, but business being business, he entered.

Like every horror film ever made had been filmed on location in Stanley Crabbitch's living room, it literally crawled with insect and rodent-kind. Amazed that he showed no embarrassment at the sight of the place, David stepped over a festering mound of roach and ant that was feasting on something else that had once called this hovel home. It stunk of sewer-mouths, tooth-rot, and feces. Just as David was considering the stench and wrapping his tie around his face like a bank robber in 1830, Stanley Crabbitch drew a deep breath through his pimpled nose as if the room was blooming with tulips and lilies and spoke.

"So Bobby says you need something for a restaurant, eh?" said Crabbitch squinting behind his glasses and showing a row of snotty brown teeth.

"Yes Stanley," mumbled David from behind his silk-tie face-mask.

"Rats, I suppose, no?"

"Sure, whatever you think will do best"

"Yeah, rats. But you'll need a bunch. And not knowin' the size of the place, I'm a little nervous about it. Might be too few. Too many. Maybe it—"

"JUST GET EM'," said David, waving at a yellow fog that had fallen between them. He didn't care if Crabbitch gave him a giraffe, so long as he got the hell out of this giant, wooden rectum.

Crabbitch however, insisted, "I'm just sayin' Dave, too many rats is no good, they turn on each other. You need the perfect number."

"GET THE RATS, STANLEY!" Stanley shrugged and turned down into a hallway. David heard a door open and then the sound of thousands of tiny animals squealing and scratching. For a second he thought Crabbitch just had a closet full of rodents, but then he heard footsteps and realized he was heading to a basement.

It wasn't five minutes before Crabbitch returned with six immense crates on a hand-truck.   Each box was jittering and screaming.

"You gotta get them in the restaurant tonight, or they'll just rip each other's heads off in the box."

"Fine. Fine." he said quickly, throwing a few hundred dollar bills on the floor. David grabbed the handles of the hand truck and rolled as fast as he could out the door. He tossed each box into the back seat, wiping his hands on his pants between each throw, and kicked the hand-truck out of the way. For a moment he saw the true size of the vehicle and realized he was being conservative. Re-wrapping his face, he went back to the door which was still open and yelled in.

"Crabbitch!"

"Yeah," said Stanley from behind his refrigerator door. David thought the room smelled even worse with that lightless box opened.

"Gimme six more."

"No. No way. It's too much" Crabbitch said with the air of a doctor prescribing antibiotics.

"I'll give you a thousand bucks for six more boxes."
Stanley didn't He say a word. Closed the fridge door and went
back to the basement.

With nearly a thousand rodents squirming and screeching
in his wife's car, David pulled out of the driveway and began
making his way home. It was nearly 8 o'clock. He had left the
hospital over an hour ago. The thought that he had spent that
much time with Stanley Crabbitch made him vomit a little in his
mouth.

Thinking he should call Collins and update him, David
reached in the console for his phone and saw that he had thirty-
four missed calls. Every single one of them from Anakin
Skywalker.

Believing there was no possible good reason for such
behavior, David sped off home. He couldn't plant the rats while
the restaurant was still open, obviously. He would go home and
find out what in the name of all that is holy was going on there,
and then he would start back towards the city. The phone rang
again, and this time he picked it up.

20

"So I think we have a problem," said Thomas, loud enough for a few of his co-workers to hear as he held a ten-thousand-dollar diamond necklace for a Chihuahua in the air between two pinched, poopy fingers.

"What's going on Tomas, erryting okay, amigo?" said the approaching voice of Pedro who was coming to see what the gringo was whining about. "It's gonna be okay, is only some shit—you just gotta—SANTA MARIA JESUS CRISTO!" screamed Pedro at the sight of the massive, gaudy ice cube. Pedro continued screaming in Spanish, which sounded as if he was identifying every saint and angel in the heavens by name. It appeared, as several baffled white guys and a few Mexicans stared at the rock, that Grawp had indeed been trying to find himself a moveable feast and had succeeded. So successful was he, that he had also by the time Thomas arrived on the scene, digested the little dog and spat out the undesirables from his doo-doo shooter. In this case, the undesirable was a jewel heist worth of gemstone. A veritable bowtie of bling.

It also appeared that whichever pooch had suffered such a terrible fate was known to its owner by a name that began with the letter "G."

"Maybe Grawp ate his own collar?" said Thomas hopefully.

"No, whatever dog that belonged to had a neck the size of a drinking straw. It's a smaller dog, and I doubt another dog picked his pocket and ate his collar," said Mike who had just arrived to the scene.

"That's pretty fuckin' big, no?" said Mike, who was clearly no diamond expert.

"I'd say so. I mean—that's big. For a collar…yeah, definitely," replied an even less credible diamond expert in Thomas. "Though we should probably give it to that guy inside."

"Who, Carter? I guess. It is his thing, right? I'll see if I can't get him down here." Mike finished and turned his back to Thomas, who was holding the collar in the sun and inquiring via radio as to the location of one Dr. Clark Carter.

While they waited for the ace of diamonds, Mike noticed an engraving on the diamond's steel backing. Thomas transcribed a phone number by scrawling it with a stick in a slick of dogshit.

"Looks like the name is Drahtman—Drahtman? That's a shitty name." Despite practically swimming in fecal matter, none of these men could muster the ability to resist the making of shit-jokes. It just wasn't gonna happen.

Mike was unable to unclasp the brass fasteners on his left breast pocket where he kept the portable phone before Carter had meandered his way through the few grassy enclaves which dotted the field like oases for refugee loafers.

"What've you got, gentlemen?" said Carter with the look

of a man expecting to be handed an engagement ring, nothing for a man of his gemstone-pedigree to be impressed with. But even Clark Carter had to pop his brow at this beauty. His mind churning brain-butter at an alarming rate, Carter skated over the idea of expressing approval of the stone and said far too quickly to be considered innocent, "You say the dog this belongs to was eaten? It's dead?"

"Well—yeah—Why do you have that look on your face?" asked Mike.

Carter had started sweating and his eyes were inching out of their sockets, bloody belt lines barely able to keep their lips around bubbles of cream.

"Um. Well, Michael, the thing is that we are quite ready to start the machine, and all we have been concerned with for the last day or so has been choosing our seed diamond."

"Seed? What?" Mike didn't seem to have a clue what he was talking about. Thomas did, sorta.

"You see, Mike," started Thomas, channeling the spirit of Carter, "a tiny seed diamond is placed at the bottom of the cylinder. The metal and graphite are subjected to extreme pressure—"

"Very good!" cut in Carter, still sweating in sheets over his bushy white brows, "Michael, we built the machine as large as we did under the premise that the same baby diamond sliver would coat the entire surface of the cylinder, creating millions and millions of dollars of stone. We—I mean I—just never considered what would take place if we tossed something the size of a golf ball in the thing. It might actually *fill* it, like a cup, a bucket, a blessed dumpster worth—"

"A dumpster full of diamonds?" Thomas stammered.

"Just about." Carter stopped breathing with his mouth open and looked around, taking stock of his colleague's opinion on the matter. When he saw no objection, he went on. "We need to call Jameson immediately."

"Who we *need* to call is…" Thomas interjected before pausing to look at the filthy metal backing again, "Staci Drahtman." He stalled again, "She spells her first name with an 'i' at the end?"

"Oh, that's awful," said an offended Mike, "but he's right. This lady's dog got eaten."

"Das Gabbana collar," said a small voice from the back of the crowd, where several more men had arrived at the posse from packing up the survivors and sending them back home in limos.

"Who? What?" said Mike.

"Gabbana, das his collar," said Pablo, stepping out from between a few college students' kneecaps.

"Okay," said Mike, sounding unsure of why it mattered at this juncture. Pablo waited a minute, and sensing Mike's point, continued.

"He gotta hermano."

"Oh. Oh! You mean there's another collar?" entered Carter.

"Oh, for the love of god Carter…The problem is that

there is a matching DOG that is on its way back to its owner without its brother. We have to call this woman now." There was a pause as Mike's eyes swept over them all, the three brothers and some of the college kids laughed into one another's armpits at the idea of one of them calling her. Finally, and most predictably, Mike's big brown eyes fell on Thomas Jones.

A week ago, Thomas would have preferred to have screwdrivers driven through his eyes and ears then make this phone call. But now, calmed and cooled, softened and salted, Thomas felt more collected and confident than he had in his entire life. And without another moment's hesitation, he took the phone from Mike's hand. After all, sounding like the boss was what he did best. He may not be the best boss, but he sure as the shit on his shoes looked and sounded like one.

Somewhere far away, David Drahtman was hanging up on his wife. She had said something hysterical about one of the dogs. All three of his children were screaming in the background, although none of that screaming appeared to have anything to do with the dogs. It seemed that in the midst of their mother's fervor, the three junior Drahtmans, smelling blood in the water, had responded like ravenous piranhas in search of new cars, paintball guns, and replacement Chihuahuas.

David further depressed the gas pedal and zoomed on

forward in a blind rage. He didn't need this. As if he hadn't had enough on his plate already. His face was still in a jungle-print, he had three hundred pounds of shrieking, squeaking, humping, murdering rodents in the backseat of the fluorescent pink truck he was being forced to drive. He had been punched in the nose by a client only yesterday, and just this morning had nearly caused his employer's brain to turn off at the sight of him. And now, for the love of all things good and holy, he could not discern why anyone would want to cause the pack of rabid wolves he called family to collapse in on itself and produce the crying-wife, whining-daughter, animal-abusing children cell phone holocaust within which he now smoked and stewed. He choked the life out of his wife's fluffy-pink steering wheel cover.

In Jersey, Thomas Jones was now dialing another number. When he finished dialing it Mike grabbed the phone and pressed the speaker button so they could all hear the voice on the other end of the line.

"Yello," croaked Jameson from wherever he was at the moment.

"Jameson, its Thomas."

"Speak of the devil, Tommy-boy, I was just talking about you."

"To whom?" Thomas was actually kind of excited that

anyone was talking about him, and then he considered that Jameson may not be saying anything positive.

"Never mind that, suffice it to say an old friend, but you called me, Thomas. How is the first day going?"

"Well, good, but we have a small issue," he started carefully.

"You have two issues. The first is why am I on speakerphone?"

"Well I'm with Mike and Pedro and Pablo and Carter and we all need to ask you a question." Thomas hadn't even considered that Jameson would take issue with this but he kinda thought it was cool. Like he was used to having his phone tapped. Thomas resolved privately to ask his sister that question the next time she called him. Even if she wasn't using the speakerphone. Just to see what she said.

"Well, how the hell is everyone?" yelled Jameson as his gaggle of employees all hollered different salutations at him.

"Wonderful, so what's up guys?"

"A dog got eaten." There was a long pause. It sounded like Jameson was saying the next words into his shoulder. They were muffled.

"One of our dogs got eaten by another dog?"

"Yes."

"Well that's no good at all." said Jameson flatly, this time at full volume with a tone of humor in his voice which calmed everyone in the dog-pen, "Did you alert the owner?"

"We have. She was pretty hysterical, kinda lost her mind."

"Did she sound like she was going to sue or otherwise take action against us?"

"I don't think so but she kinda sounded like she wasn't the sharpest knife in the drawer." Jameson laughed at this.

"I want you to call her back and offer her some cash. Say five large, and see if that makes her feel any better about the situation. I don't think this will be too serious. What's the name?"

"Drahtman"

There was a long pause.

"Well then. Go ahead with the call. See if we can't get Staci to help us out of this."

"You got it.," said Thomas, nodding with all the others in attendance at this directive.

"Let me know if anything else happens. I'll be in the office."

"Well, there was another thing," added Thomas.

"Yes?" asked Jameson with a vague touch of impatience. At this Carter interjected and began to explain to situation to him. About a minute into his speech Jameson cut him off and told him to take the phone and turn off the speaker. He wasn't surprised as there were several twenty-year old English lit majors with wide-eyes at the words "diamond machine" and "on the third floor."

Pedro seemed to notice the piqued interest and immediately sent them off with a coil of yellow rope to find and bring back Jarred, who was no doubt half-conscious under a tree somewhere playing pinochle with imaginary spider monkeys.

They obeyed with a minimum of moans and throwing of hands.

When Dr. Carter had hung up the phone and handed it back to Thomas he pocketed the diamond and made his way back in to the house with a canter that was as close as he could muster to a jog. It was clear that the boss had agreed with Carter's little scheme and that it was being implemented at this very moment.

Wholly agreeing with the idea, Thomas read the number to the Drahtman house off the shit-slick and just as he was about to dial it, the phone's LED lit up with the very same number Thomas was preparing to dial. For just one second, that strange, stupid jolt of elation we all get when the person who we are about to call calls us zagged through Thomas. And then it quickly faded.

The phone rang and rang. It ringed, it ranged, it rung and rung again and again but there was no way on earth David Drahtman was going to hang it up. No possible way in the vastness of the universe that David was going to let this go.

Staring at his own reflection in the kitchen linoleum, David caught sight of the thing his hearing had learned to ignore, a mob behind him who couldn't seem more prepared to cut his throat if they were carrying pitchforks and standing outside a medieval castle.

His two sons Leo and Theo were holding a hammer in

each hand and had the entire top of their heads shaved clean.
Inverted Mohawks. They had the hair-dos of a forty-five year old
deli manager. They were screaming and crying indiscriminately,
and David wasn't even sure they were speaking English. His
daughter, dressed for a night on the town (which meant barely
dressed at all) was holding the electric hair buzzer (which was still
on) in her right hand and in her open, upturned left palm she had
the remains of a pink cell phone. There were rhinestones all over
the floor and the shattered fragments in her hands were no bigger
than the top she was wearing—which, amazingly, was smaller
than her earrings.

And worst of all, his wife Staci was lying on the floor
crying hysterically, rivers of snot and mascara pooling in her
trembling bottom lip. Desperately clutched to her chest was her
only remaining dog, Dolce, who was too busy trying to mount
her right breast to notice all the commotion.

And still…no one would pick up the goddamned phone.
Waiting, ever so patiently, for someone to answer the phone at
Total Immersion Doggy Day Care he flipped through the brochure.
He considered the nobility in suicide by paper cut, and then
someone, thankfully, answered the phone.

"Total Immersion Doggy Day Care, this is Thomas Jones
speaking."

"Hello, Thomas Jones, my name is David Drahtman,"
said David in a voice that barely coated a brimming, broiling
venom pot, ready to explode all over Thomas Jones' left ear. He
hated the way this asshole used his first and last name…Thomas

Jones…who the hell does this guy think he is?

"Hello, Mr. Drahtman. How can I help you, sir?" asked Thomas, playing the fool.

"Oh I don't know, *Thomas Jones,* maybe you can tell me why my wife is weeping uncontrollably on my kitchen floor while she gets TITTY-FUCKED by the only dog she's GOT LEFT?"

"Ah. Mr. Drrrrahtman," Thomas said like he dealt everyday with lots of names that sounded just like Drahtman. "Yes sir, I am very sorry about that. It was an absolute tragedy, I hope you understand that we too—"

"You what?! You feel bad? DO YOU HEAR THIS?" David held out the receiver into his mosh-pit kitchen for ten seconds, "DO YOU? What the FUCK happened to this animal?"

"Well, Gabbana, being a very small animal, we suppose was mistaken for another mammal and was eaten by a predator."

"What predator?"

"An owl…a…a big owl." This was the best Thomas, Mike and the brothers could come up with in the twenty seconds they had while the phone was ringing to decide how to explain that there was no dog body to provide them with. Their advertisements being what they were, they couldn't just say it was eaten by a dog seventy times its size which he was sharing a pen with. That plus the fact that they had no intention of returning the collar.

"AN OWL?" he yelled with absolute incredulity. "A FUCKING OWL?!"

"Um, that's right sir, a big owl. Huge really. You know, we have them out here enjoying themselves in the wilderness with skilled handlers but—you know—it was a really big owl. And well, we can't fly—so…"

"Well, THOMAS JONES, you better go get your boots on 'cuz you and I are going OWL-HUNTING. There was 10g's in diamonds hanging off that fucking rodent's neck and if you think I'm letting you hippy-dippy, tree-fucking faggots off the hook you're out of your goddamned mind."

"Now, now sir. Please relax; there really isn't much we can do in a situation like this." Thomas was now trying to put out the fire using seamless assistant managerial vernacular, "As you signed the insurance waiver, we cannot be held liable for—"
"Oh you must be out of your fucking skull, there is absolutely no way you're saying this to me. I'm coming out there, TOMMORROW, and we'll see just how funny you are then."

"Mr. Drahtman, we would be happy to pay for the collar. My superiors have authorized me to compensate you for your loss." Thomas was doing well, but was dealing with an entirely different sort of human being.
"You listen to me, you pathetic little son of a bitch. I don't give a shit about the goddamned diamond. I can buy all the diamonds I want you little prick, it's about the principle. You ruined my fucking night, and now I've got two bald seven year old sons, a prostitute for a daughter and a wife who is cheating on me with a Chihuahua. This is your fucking fault, and I'm coming out there to see just how TOTALLY FUCKING IMMERSIVE your little business is that you can allow my dog to be

eaten—by—a—fuck—ing—OWL!"

"It was humongous," said Thomas laughing. After all, Drahtman had no idea where they were located. Everyone in the group was laughing at this last remark, and by the time they had caught their breath, David had hung up.

Just as they were about to finish up the day's speed shoveling, they all turned to the sky at the familiar sound of machine-gun-like propellers slicing and dicing the air over the tree-tops. Jameson's black chopper made its way over their heads, sending mud and crap into their faces, and landed on the helipad.

When he reached Mike and Thomas, Jameson, followed closely by Jonathan, seemed purposeful, like he was mildly concerned with something. This was a side of Jameson with which Thomas was not yet familiar.

"So what happened with Drahtman? He taking the money?" said Jameson before even shaking a hand. Mike answered him.

"No I don't think so, he—"

"He wasn't very happy," said Thomas, realizing Mike was trying to cover for the new guy. "He said he was coming here tomorrow to—um—see just how totally immersive—we are." At this, Jameson's eyes opened a bit wider before squinting.

"He's coming, *here?*"

"Well how would he know where the place is?" asked Mike, sensing Jameson's concern.

"Well, by the sound of his use of 'Total Immersion' he

has the brochure. And if he has the brochure then he knows where we are."

"What? I didn't put the address on the brochure"

"Nooo. But I did. I put this business here for the address. We are taking people's animals from them and I don't think we would have had so many customers were it not for the ritzy address a home in Thistlestick River provides us."

Jameson rubbed his temples as Mike and Thomas flipped through the brochures and found the address. "I also never suspected of all the business we do that this would be the one to cause us trouble. You know this was supposed to be like fifty dogs a day, how the hell are you guys supposed to keep track of three hundred dogs? I knew this would happen. Stupid. Stupid." Jameson was teaching a clinic in management: take responsibility, admit mistakes, and find solutions. He was just getting to this last one as many of the co-workers were getting nervous about the idea of some maniac coming to a building full of cows, dog-crap, and a diamond-pissing spaceship.

"Everybody calm down. Pedro, you know the drill – go and lower the signage." at this, Pedro ran off towards the house. "Everyone else listen up. This guy is a world-class villain, he *will* try to come here tomorrow and if he finds anything strange he *is* going to do everything in his power to put us all out of business and if possible in jail."

"We are going to our 'emergency plan', which Pedro will handle the bulk of. Jonathan—" He turned to the tall, ginger-haired super-spy who had come with him in the helicopter, "I need you to go to the White Room, pick up the package for tomorrow, and let them know what the situation is with this Drahtman guy. The rest of the building is going to operate as normal. Handbags, art & massage class…nothing strange. We do, however; have two last problems that need to be taken care of immediately. Firstly…" he turned to Paco and put both hands on his shoulders, "My friend, we cannot have a backyard full of cows. It looks too strange and suspicious."

"I understand Jameson, but what can we do wit dem?"

"We're going to release them into the woods. We're gonna create our own species of wild forest cows. It's evolution baby. Come back in two lifetimes and they'll be swinging from trees and talking Chinese." Jameson was trying to lighten the situation as delicately as possible, but Paco's eyes still began to glaze.

"Jes sir. I will go move dem now."

"I owe you much my friend. And I thank you." With that, Paco walked slowly towards the cow-pen. Jameson turned back to the rest of them like he wasn't even close to done speaking.

"And then—there is the issue of a twelve ton steel martini glass on the third floor. There is no way that can stay here. While it is unlikely Drahtman will go looking on the third floor for his or other peoples' dogs—we cannot take the chance. Further complicating things is the fact that about twenty minutes ago that machine became operational. Turning it off or damaging it in anyway could cause irreversible damage and cost us years of development. It needs to stay on for the next 72 hours so it can produce what should be a pretty enormous load of ice." he paused for a moment and looked around, "Any ideas on where we could stash this thing? Somewhere far removed from here?" now he was only looking at Thomas, "Like an empty house like an hour south of here..."

"What about my house?"

"THAT's the spirit!" said Jameson, just on the heels of Thomas's offer. "Thomas, you Mike, Carter, Paco and Pablo are going to get that thing into an eighteen wheeler I'm going to have moved here from a factory in Trenton within the hour. The rest of you," he now turned to his employees white and brown alike, "Help move that fucking machine and then go home. We won't be shoveling shit for some time my friends. Only those of us who work in Murals, Massage, or Leather will be asked to stay. Speak to NO ONE about any of this. As of tonight, this is the Thistlestick River Technical College. Go, friends! I will be in touch."

With that, most of the people dispersed, heading no doubt to begin discerning how they were going to get the diamond machine out of the house. The only people who remained were Mike and Thomas, with whom Jameson, now in a much softer voice, directed his attention.

"Mike. Thomas. Take the machine to Wildwood and get it in the house or yard—somehow. Tarp it. Whatever you have to do. Tell the neighbors it's a pool. I don't care. We just need it away from here until we can divert Mr. Drahtman's attention from us. I tell you now boys, that this man is dangerous. If I am not mistaken, he has found a new enemy in Mr. Thomas Jones. For that reason I am moving both of you to God's Demand LLC in Manhattan for the foreseeable future. Mike knows where it is. Drop off the machine, and bring everyone back to Manhattan. Melvin will stay here with Pedro and work the decoy 'technical college'."

Without question, both men nodded.

"I will be in touch all throughout tomorrow. Expect a call at the factory. Help however you can and keep low. If Drahtman finds out about the day care, the machine, or any of our businesses this entire thing will unravel. Thomas, I know it's your first day, but I chose you for a reason, and I believe you, with Mike, can be of service. Now go! Get the machine to Wildwood and meet everyone back at God's Demand in the morning."

"Now?" they said together.

"GO!"

<u>21</u>

After David hung up on his new worst enemy, Thomas Jones, he turned around and stared at his fundamentally ridiculous family. At some point in the next few days he was going to have to buy his daughter a new cellphone, his-seven-year old sons a pair of matching toupees, and somehow, someway, fix his broken wife.

Staci had clearly cried herself out, as she was now curled in a ball under the kitchen counter, next to her sleeping Chihuahua who had most likely just ejaculated on her pajamas.

Still not having so much as acknowledged any of their presences since entering the house, David's insides began to crank. In his mind a set of scales appeared. In one bronze dish was his family. In the other, a thousand black rats. David Drahtman walked out of the kitchen, out of the house, and back to work.

When he opened the driver's side door to his wife's truck, it had the effect of turning on the stereo at the highest possible volume to a radio station that exclusively featured songs about rodents raping and murdering one another. Wincing, David screamed obscenities at them. Surprisingly, this had no effect on their behavior.

Quite plainly the rats were becoming less and less pleased
with each other. David looked back for a moment at his home,
shook his head, and hurled himself into the vehicle. He closed
the door with a smash, and then wrenched it back open with
both hands at the foul stench that had formed like a fog of death
in the car. Outside again now, taking deep lungfuls of clean air,
he would never have thought the animals could do so much
damage to the Hummer in the short time they had called it home.
Unfortunately for David, there was no choice in the matter. He
reached in to turn the key and with four fingers lowered each
immense window at once. Removing his necktie entirely, David
tied an all-to-familiar mask over his nose and mouth and got back
in the truck. The restaurant would be closing around now and he
still needed to call and pick up Collins, as well as call the
inspector to lodge a complaint about a minor rodent problem.
Over the din of whipping wind and the cries of rodent-kind,
David dialed his colleague's cell.
"Hello?"

"COLLINS!" he was going to need to yell if he wanted to
be heard with four windows the size of the windshield on a
passenger jet open on the highway.

"Jesus, Davey where the hell are ya?"

"I'M COMING TO GET YOU. BE OUTSIDE IN
FIFTEEN!"

"Huh? What do you mean? David, where the fuck are you
right now? Sounds like you're in the middle of a fuckin
hurricane."

"ON THE ROAD! SAW CRABBITCH! GOTTA DO THIS TONIGHT."

"Okay, Okay. Cool your fuckin' heels Davey, where are you now?"

"COUPLE EXITS FROM YOUR HOUSE! JUST GET OUTSIDE!"

"Well—I'm not there Dave. I'm close though."

"DAMMIT COLLINS, WHERE ARE YOU?"

"Um—well, I'm at the Econo Lodge at the next exit on the expressway." David's response to this would have been a yell, even if he didn't have to make himself heard over his adorable little passengers.

"WHAT THE HELL ARE YOU DOING AT AN *ECONO LODGE?*"

"Long story, I'll explain when you get here. Room 107."

David hung up without saying goodbye.

As soon as he had parked in the lot behind the Econo Lodge, David leapt from the car and breathed deeply the salty night air. The hotel was the color of a pissed-on snowball. Faded and elderly, the place looked like it had been sent via time machine back from the early seventies to make every other hotel look better. It was the color of the scum under the lip of a public toilet. To the left of the parking lot was a tiny pool, filled to choking with last year's leaves. David thought he heard frogs croaking in the water, as though the pool of stagnant fluid had been so long neglected that an entire ecosystem had sprung up around it.

By the light of one dim, fluttering streetlamp David found his way to room 107 and knocked twice.

Bobby Collins answered the door, still in his work-clothes and looking no better than David. He smelled of booze although his voice was more stammer than slur. Like he had been planning a world-class binge but had only made it four or five drinks in to the evening. "Hey Davey! Can I fix you a drink?" said Collins, shaking the ice at the bottom of a small plastic cup like a single maraca.

"Nooo, I don't think so Collins. And I think you've had plenty yourself. We have work to do." David said to his co-worker whose suit was rumpled and smelly. His hair looked like he had been given a noogie by a mountain troll. The whole package was quite a sight. He seemed to be in better spirits than earlier that day, but had gone from the successful vice president with a palatial estate in the Hamptons to the sloshed hobo in room 107 in a matter of hours. Collins had yet to argue with David's insistence that he pull himself together. he was still shaking the plastic cup and staring mournfully into the disappearing ice cubes.

"Why are you here, Bobby?" David was concerned. A minor haze of boozy indifference was one thing, but the man looked bonkers—like he had at some point in the last day or so stepped over some irreparable precipice. Like the palm tree that broke the camel's back.

"Ohhh nothing Davey," and then turning his eyes up to Drahtman's, "problems with the wife. Strangest fucking thing…"

Collins's voice trailed off and he put the cup on a dresser behind him before walking out and closing the door behind him. "Let's get a move on."

Collins started walking towards the car as David watched. Whatever his problem was David still needed to make a phone call before he got back into the vehicle.

David called the number to the local office of the New York State Department of Health. He pretended to be a concerned family man who had eaten with his children at the restaurant not two hours before. According to John Q. Citizen, he noticed, while indulging in a *pastelone de carne* (a phrase that died like a racist joke in his mouth), several rats running around in the kitchen, and that when he went home later in the evening both of his children experienced flood-like, fluorescent vomiting and intense, explosive diarrhea the likes of which could only be described by broken levees once used to hold back an irrepressible torrent of turd. He used his most angry and severe of tones when he threatened class action lawsuits against both the restaurant and the state D.O.H. In fact, he added that a call to his attorneys was to be placed immediately following the conclusion of this message. As David Drahtman waxed Shakespearian from the door of room 107, he watched as his fellow employee walked to the middle of the parking lot and began spinning in a circle like an eight-year old discovering centrifugal force.

When David was under the impression that he had sufficiently lambasted the state government into submission and had ensured that a safety inspector would be on the premises the next morning, he walked deliberately up to Collins and with two hands brought him to a complete stop. His head rolled on his shoulders for a few seconds and then he shook it, blinked, and looked directly at David. At the very least, he was now smiling.

"Fucking shit! Forgot how much fun that was." David sighed contentedly at the sound of swear-words working their way out of Collins' lips. If he descended into suicidal depression in the future, David would, he thought, spin him in a circle a few times to sort him out.

The drive into the city was unrelentingly brutal; the foul stench and mind-tearing sound of the rats quickly sobered and straightened the brain of Bobby Collins, whose head was obscured by the bottom half of his untucked shirt, which he had pulled front ways over his head and face. He also had two palms sealing his ears despite hanging out of the window to his waist. He looked like a dog that was so excited about being in the car that he had to suffocate himself with his owner's work shirt to calm himself down. David still had the Great Train Robbery mask tightly pulled over his oral and nasal cavities. He was getting better at it. If he did get fired he might have a future as an expansion era outlaw.

When they parked, Collins forced his way through the door of the car, pulled his shirt off his head and gasped for breath. He was cursing so furiously that he was able to squeeze in a few "fucks" and "shits" while breathing *in*.

"FUCK! David, oh fuck fuck. What the fuck—," David leapt out of the Hummer, ran around it (which felt like it took fifteen minutes) and grabbed him by his collar.

"Shut the fuck up! Shut up! Shut up! Shut up! BE QUIET!" David screamed on the frazzled edges of an angry whisper, "Shut up and help! We've got to find a way in the place first. Come on."

Collins calmed down a bit, pulled his shirt back over his head and followed David around the back of *Cocina Criolla*. The restaurant's exterior was truly beautiful, despite its antiquity. Its walls were composed of bricks more pink than red and the windows were framed in white wood that chipped and peeled in an almost intentional way; like blue jeans purchased with a hole in each knee.

The rear was not unlike what one would expect from a foodservice establishment. Its major feature was a black-green dumpster that stunk of yesterday's poultry, fruit rind, and black plastic. This smell was, of course, altogether preferable to the display in the rear of Staci Drahtman's Hummer, so they took no real notice of it.

Behind the dumpster they found the back door to the restaurant and a dingy, small square window. Surprisingly, there was also a quaint, enclosed garden on the opposite side of the door from the dumpster. Moonlight fell fat and white on the cheeks of tomatoes. A firefly, green ass all aglow, launched himself into the midnight.

It was clear to both men that the building itself would not prove much an obstacle in the business of breaking and entering. Being a neighborhood landmark, beloved by both children and the elderly alike for a century, it was no doubt unthinkable to the

Melendez family that anyone would attempt to sabotage their enterprise. Any form of electronic surveillance or monitoring system would appear to be superfluous. Furthermore, restaurant managers leave for the night with the day's totals on their persons. There was little to steal that wasn't edible. Perhaps an especially famished burglar might make an attempt, but they considered the idea improbable at best.

On the night in question, however, this decision by the family Melendez would appear to have been a mistake. On this night, they would be dealing with an entirely different breed of criminal. Not mere thieves, but a plague—salesmen of warfare in a battle for the daily bread.

The two men's first instinct was to dump the whole load through the small window, but this seemed risky. David wanted to be sure he wasn't unloading his precious cargo into a bathroom. He wanted to drape the structure's insides with black rats—to paint it in fur and brown blood.

Collins kept watch as best he could while David put his left foot through the back door. His heel struck the knob perfectly and the lock split to the wood. It swung open on the night's next strong breeze. Like a yawning mouth, the blackness within grew with the rush of the warm august wind.

Slapping and dragging a palm across the walls, David finally stumbled over the small plastic nub that would let light into the world.

Rey Melendez's kitchen was immaculate in every sense of the word, and that included multiplicitous images of the Virgin

Mary which stared out from every conceivable surface. The Mother of God apparently kept watch over each pot and pan in the building. She took great interest in the chopping of vegetables, the dazzling crackle of sofrito, the simmering marriage of bird and oil.

Tonight, however, the blessed virgin watched great treachery unfold under her sexless nose. And though in each portrait her eyes were turned away, often to the heavens, David had the feeling that each time his back was to her, she was stealing glances at the two men and plotting heavenly retribution from beneath her bluebell head-dress.

Outside of the extent churchliness of the kitchen, it was remarkably clean. Everything was made of stainless steel and the effect was to bounce images of the two disheveled businessmen all across the restaurant like a hall of mirrors. You could have used the floor as a cutting board and not felt bad about serving the results to your mother.

Set in the opposite wall of the kitchen were two swinging steel doors with small spider-glass squares at their center. David approached and looked out one of the cubes onto a cozy corner of small wooden tables. The kitchen was no doubt twice the size of the dining room, but as David knew from Melendez's business records the only time of day that they were empty were right now, in the middle of the night. Drahtman had to push hard against one of the heavy steel doors to make his way through the frame.

The floors were a dark leathery hardwood that looked

sanded smooth by the grit and gravel of the shoe-soles of a century. There were great bay windows in the building's front end which were dressed in thin linen sheets the color of fresh spinach and swamp water; a green deeper than and blacker than the bottom of a sea-monster's belly. They were shut at the moment, but David could tell that in the day they would have been pulled back to reveal what would surely have been a powerful eastern sunrise. There were also at least three other images of a woman known as both *White Lily of the Trinity and Vermilion Rose of the Heavens* to some nationalities and equally as *Our Lady of Prompt Succor* (which just sounds inappropriate).

David unlocked the front door from within and walked back to find Collins in the kitchen with his head swung flat back and a bottle of marsala cooking wine held completely upside down over his open mouth. David, realizing the argument would be futile simply snatched the bottle away and ordered him to follow.

It took nearly an hour to get the twelve crates of black sewer rats into the restaurant. They were, by the moment, becoming more loud, vicious, and smelly. Each box was carried with one hand on either side, arms extended out in front of the body. They each returned to the habit of face-masking. This made it quite difficult for Collins—with a button-down shirt wrapped backwards over his head—to walk anywhere very well. He hit a few falls and if you weren't lying you'd admit a few of the rats were laughing.

Finally, with twelve white plastic crates of rat on the floor of the kitchen, the two middle-aged businessmen stood on two chairs from the dining room and opened each door as fast as possible while whimpering and cursing through facemasks.

The effect on the kitchen was immediate. Like time-lapse photography, the beasts swarmed every clean surface, blacking mirrors and fogging the air with shadows, stench, and screams. They were tiny things, like fur-covered stomachs with tails and teeth; but en masse they were primally frightening. It was not five minutes of utter horror before Collins saw one actually tear another's nose and eyes out. War had erupted. Both men ran from the kitchen in screams out the broken back door. David stopped for a moment to smash a metal basket filled with dirty aprons and dish-towels up against the door before scampering off after squealing Bobby Collins through the garden, murdering a copse of green tomato in his wake. A plump, elderly tomatillo wept into her leaves.

David jumped into the front seat of the Hummer and squealed off into the early morning. By the volume of his frantic howling, Collins had likely woken at least one neighbor in the densely populated area. It was also likely to assume that any neighbor who saw an enormous fluorescent-pink monster truck with tinted windows and big red hearts for hubcaps being jumped in by two screaming middle-aged men—one of whom had his shirt over his head, crying and the other with a tie around his mouth and nose like a cowboy—might take issue with the scene and consider inquiring further.

Drahtman knew they would have to return, but it made

sense to get away for a few minutes and let any surprised locals get back to sleep. The car still stunk of rat-pussy and wet fur, so they drove with the windows down.

"Oh my god, take me the fuck home!" yelled Collins through his shirt-buttons.

"No one's going home Collins, we're waiting this out. Just relax."

"Wait…what? Fuck waiting—for what?" sputtered a baffled Bobby Collins.

"Well…" started David with an air of life-threatening impatience, "Because I am going to watch this go down. First, when the spick shows—I'm gonna call him out right on the street and tell him I can call off the inspector—"

"You can't call off a food safety inspection, you gotta—"

"I KNOW, Collins. But I'm gonna tell him I can and if he sells now I will make it all go away. He'll get a lot more from us than he will once it's condemned. Then if this asshole still doesn't wanna play ball I'm just gonna wait for the inspection and watch him tell his kids that they won't be able to afford a Christmas tree this year."

"That's fucking—"

"THEN, I'm gonna laugh in his face all the way to the bank. And then in December, I'm gonna send him a Christmas card with a picture of the hole in the ground that's left of his daddy's restaurant. How's that sound?" David spat, red-faced, sweat running the rim of swollen vein on his forehead.

"Wow."

"WOW IS FUCKING RIGHT," David yelled this last line while literally strangling his wife's steering wheel cover to death. It reminded him of his wife, which reminded him of the dogs, which reminded him of Thomas Jones. The very thought of his simpering little chuckle from earlier made the fluid in David's brain bubble and cook. His eyes were glazed and unfocused. If he didn't care more about his job than he did anything else, he would have driven to the address on the brochure in his back pocket and burned it to the ground. On the contrary, however, David altogether needed to return to Cocina Criolla and wait till morning, which was approaching evermore swiftly.

When he pulled back up, David shut the lights and pulled back to the same parking spot across the street. He wanted to be an inconspicuous as a pink house on wheels can be at three in the morning. Collins fell asleep within the first ten minutes of parking like a six-year-old who had had too much excitement for one day. He drooled boozy spittle that stunk of chicken marsala into his shirt sleeve and snored like a crocodile.

It certainly wouldn't be an easy task for David to stay awake after *his* day, but he was going to put everything he had into it. He saw the light at the end of the tunnel that had comprised this past week. His penis, amazingly, was fully and wildly erect at the very thought of what he was about to do. If he didn't know better he would have fucked his shoe right then and there.

And indeed David did survive the night for many hours. On three different occasions he had to get out of the car and pace back and forth and slap himself around a little, but he made it into sunrise. The yellow of morning leaked over a dissolving moon. He had to squint to adjust his eyes. The squinting became blinking which slowly became a pair of shuttered eyelids.

It was in the opening moments of a dream about being a policeman on a stakeout at a suspected murderer's place of residence that his partner, Patrolman Bobby Collins said, "Who the fuck is that?"

"Huh—wha?" said David, sitting upright with a start, shaking his head in all directions. When he got a grip on himself he saw a young woman of no more than twenty-five walking to the front door of Cocina Criolla. David checked his watch. It was six o'clock, perfect. This woman must be opening the restaurant. The woman, unfortunately, had no such plans. Rather than reach in her pocket for keys, she pulled a folded piece of paper and some tape from her jacket. She affixed a small, single sheet of printer paper to the front glass and walked off, staring strangely at the hot-pink Hummer and its two bruised, smelly, and confused inhabitants. David was still too freshly awakened to chase her down and insult her. Besides, he was bewildered by what had just happened. When her little blue Toyota had turned the corner, David whipped open the door of the car and ran to the front of the building. It took him a moment to find it, because the message was written in a big font in Spanish, and in smaller type below it, in English:

We are sorry but Cocina Criolla will be closed from Friday,
August 4 to Monday, August 8 for personal leave.
We apologize for any inconvenience and look forward to
serving you when we get back.

-Management-

This was not good. Firstly, he did not know what those animals would do with four days of time. He already was sure that there were far too many rats in the building, but he assumed they would spread themselves out through the dining room, the basement, and anywhere else they smelled food. Resolving that there was no way he was going back in the place to release some of them, and that the more damage done to the restaurant the better, he walked back to the car.

The more pressing issue for David was that he had worked very hard to get a D.O.H inspector to agree to a visit and now there was no restaurant to inspect and no owners to report poorly upon.

David waited another two hours for the inspector to show. The plan was simple: David was going to pretend to be the owner, and let them in by going into the restaurant himself through the back and receive the fines and levies and documents which were sure to be provided by a disgusted health inspector. He could not, however, do that today. He hadn't showered in more than a day and smelled like rat-shit. He looked awful. All he needed to do was take whatever notice the inspector left behind and call him back a day before the Melendez's would arrive back and have the inspector come in early. It was brilliant and David knew it. Most importantly, he had another destination in mind for the remainder of his day.

At 9:30 a tan Oldsmobile rolled up behind the Hummer. Giving a nauseated expression at the sight of Staci's car, David watched a thin, wiry man with no hair and thick glasses walk toward the restaurant with a clipboard. He was wearing a navy blue suit with some ridiculous badge hanging off the breast pocket. The man looked smug and self-important and Drahtman thought it a shame he was going to have to fool him.

Just as David had hoped, the man read the sign (squinting and bending over to read the English) and left a business card before leaving. He gave another look of astonishment at the vehicle and its two occupants, only one of whom was conscious, before he passed out of sight.

Thirty seconds later David had placed the business card in one pocket and then placed the same hand in another pocket and pulled out a folded piece of glossy paper that read *Total Immersion Doggy Day Care*. He read something off its back before turning over the ignition.

22

Moving the diamond machine down three flights of stairs was not going to be easy. It was built and stitched together with the intention of it remaining indoors for the duration of its use, and although it was simple enough to take apart, it couldn't be done while the machine was working. Since the electricity required of such a monstrosity would have been infeasible to get from a normal outlet, the seven generators in the room would also have to make the trip to Wildwood, never to be detached from the mother-ship. She was a mechanized spider-crab with steel spaghetti legs and washing machines for feet.

The coiled, rust-red iron stairwells that connected the complex's floors were also not going to permit the passage of something roughly the size of an above-ground swimming pool through its bends and turns. Thankfully, there was a solution to this most vexing question. As some of the men stood around perplexed, obviously concerned with the same questions, Dr. Carter walked to the room's far corner and pulled a lever against the wall.

The building's face, its winking eyeballs, began to fold mechanically outwards like a garage door opener from the year 6000. When the slat of wall and wood reached a forty-five degree angle to the ground below it folded out twice more until there was a ramp of steel wrapped in faded red wood marking the pass over the stairs to the front lawn.

"We used to keep cars up here, on the third floor, so that any neighbors wouldn't wonder why there were sixty-five cars parked on the lawn everyday," said Mike, explaining the ramp.

"And where do you keep all the cars now?"

"Well, a few of us who don't live here keep a car out front, where you parked, but Jameson turned the second floor into a kinda dormitory. It's pretty sweet actually. We've also got beds and kitchens in the basement which is primarily why we didn't build the machine down there."

"People live here?"

"Sure do. It's pretty nice, everybody's got plenty of space, and most of the workers are either family or classmates so it runs pretty smooth. I normally live in Queens myself, but I tend to spend summers here to get away from the hustle and bustle."

"Wow."

"Yeah, it's not too bad"

As Thomas looked around at the enormous machine and its seven electrical generators, each of which would require two men to move, his back and shoulders began to wince and crack in apprehension. He hadn't spent so much time doing manual labor in years, and all the turd-shoveling in collusion with a cracked rib was taking their toll on Thomas Jones. He excused himself to the downstairs bathroom while they waited for the truck and took two Vicodin. He was trying his best to be more conservative in his dosing after having a pill-drunk fit at his grandfather's funeral.

When he returned, Mike was yelling through cupped hands out of the rectangular hole in the building, apparently assisting in the parking of a large vehicle by giving directions.

"LITTLE TO THE LEFT…NO, NO, BACK THE OTHER WAY. LITTLE MORE…"

Beside where Thomas had just pulled up to watch the parking job, sitting on a crate with his head in his hands was Dr. Carter.

"What's up ,doc?" asked Thomas, thrilled by his Bugs Bunny imitation.

"Oh…Thomas," said the scientist, looking up. "I'm quite fine, just a bit nervous about moving her when she's—you know—pregnant," finished the doctor before stuffing his head back in his palms. Long white hair whirled and danced in the wind of the open third-story wall window. It was plain, in the loving and near desperate manner in which Carter addressed the machine as a "she," that Thomas saw why pot would benefit a man like this.

"I think it'll be all right, Dr. Carter, we've got plenty of bodies to make sure nothing happens."

"Understand—I'll need to ride with her, to be able to keep my eyes out for any complications."

"Of course."

"You do realize that one pot-hole, one short-stop could irreparably harm her delicate internal parts. It would be…"

"BIT MORE TO THE RIGHT! THAT'S IT. KEEP

COMING!" yelled Mike, overwhelming the last words of Carter's sentence. Thomas pretended he heard it all and nodded severely.

"I promise we'll take every precaution, and once we get to Wildwood you will be able to stay with her until the—er…birth." Thomas heard Carter mumble something under his breath and nod. He resolved to be sure they didn't find themselves making any pit stops at liquor stores on the way down to Wildwood.

"RIGHT THERE! RIGHT THERE! STOP! PERFECT!" finished Mike clapping his hands together as Thomas walked up beside him.

Below them, with its ass-end lined up with the ramp, was an open-bed eighteen-wheel trailer truck. The cabin up front was purple and had black flames painted on it, while the remainder of the vehicle was one long, wooden flatbed. There was no housing, just tarp, ropes, chain, and a great orange vinyl sign that read "OVERSIZED LOAD"

It took Thomas, Mike, Pablo, Carter, and about twenty college students close to an hour to slowly inch the machine down the ramp and on the back of the machine with Carter squealing and crying at every bump and wobble. Trailing behind them another dozen students were edging their way down with the generators, two to each.

Finally when the machine itself and its generators were on the center of the bed, covered in tarps and ropes, Carter climbed up on to the truck and disappeared within the green plastic drapery. Clearly, the possibility of falling to his death on the Jersey Turnpike was not going to deter the good doctor from protecting his precious cargo.

"You Thomas Jones?" said a voice behind Thomas Jones. When he turned around, Thomas found a skinny little man with sunglasses and a blue baseball cap emblazoned with the logo of a gas station. He was wearing a red and green flannel shirt which was tucked into snug blue jeans which looked like they could have fit a nine-year-old ballerina. The man's face was deeply lined and he smelled distinctly of tobacco smoke. Around the rim of his cap dark brown hair fell in messy chunks around his ears. He could have been thirty, or he could have been sixty.

"Yes?" said Thomas, coughing a bit at the overpowering haze of Marlboro smoke.

"Guy der say you the boss?" the man's voice even sounded like the sizzle of a cigarette's head. He had an unmistakable, deep, chicken-fried Southern accent.

"Name's Reg, I'm yer driver." the man held out a hand and squeezed Thomas's like he was trying to crush a ferret to death and smiled, sharing with Thomas his checkered dental history.

"Now listen 'ere – I don' care none bouts whatcha hawlin', just like to be paid up front so longs it's good by you. Fair?" Thomas nodded although he didn't quite make out every word of the man's statement. The one word he did hear clearly was 'paid'. Thomas signed a clipboard the man had under his arm and took this to mean that he had satisfied the one named Reg.

Thomas, Pablo, and Mike squeezed in to the front of the cab with the driver, who took up very little space. Carter remained behind in radio contact with Mike should something seem to be going awry. And off they went.

The first hour of the drive consisted of little else besides Reginald Jefferson Davis IV, recounting his life's history with the men. A man who spends seventy-five percent of the year on the road hauling various products of all sizes and descriptions from toilet paper to, most recently, ostrich eggs, certainly was thrilled at the opportunity to communicate with someone other than himself and the occasional truck-stop prostitute. Truth be told, even some of the hookers were beginning to avoid him because he just wouldn't shut up all through the process, constantly going on about the pecans and toothpaste and toaster ovens and whatever else he was hauling that week. At this moment, Thomas Jones would have preferred anything else on the planet rather than listen to this dissertation, including giving hand jobs at a truck stop in Winston-Salem.

"See, deese arstrich eggs—Boy, you just dunno! Woo! Them things isso big, they like daggum soffballs. Like two hunerd thousand soffballs—an' I'm hawlin 'nem sumbitches to Yazoo City! Woo!" Reg went on and on and on and on about ostrich eggs with nary an interruption, laughing and "woo"ing all the way.

It was with great initial relief that Thomas heard the soft beep which alerted Mike that his radio was receiving a signal. Mike turned a dial and the voice of Dr. Clarke Carter came blaring through the speaker. The wind roaring about him like invisible lions made it very difficult to hear.

"JEWS MUST GAS A POOPER!" he screamed over the ripping wind.

"Jews must—what the—" started Mike to no one, and then, depressing the button on the radio, to Carter, "WHAT THE HELL DID YOU JUST SAY?"

"YOU JUST PASSED A—"

And the sentence was cut off by the sound of blaring, whining sirens behind them, Thomas finished Carter's sentence for him, "Trooper…we just passed a trooper."

"So?" said Mike.

"Well, we are," said Thomas, leaning over Reg's shoulder, "going 95 miles per hour."

"Oh that might do it," said Mike, opening his mouth to say something to Reg, but he was already cursing loud enough for them all to realize he had hear the sirens.

"Guldarned Yankee polees. I sway to da lowd above! Damnabbit! I tole Jameson I done wan no mow nonsense!"

"Calm down Reg, just calm down, everything's okay, it's gonna be—"

"Stankin' union troopers! I'll show dem boys, I sway I show dem!"

"No—no! Don't show dem. Please don't show dem," said Thomas quickly trying to calm him down as he pulled the big rig over to the side of the turnpike with a jerk. His small body flung nearly onto Thomas's lap before leaping in one motion out the other direction and through the door of the cab onto the dusty shoulder.

Still in shock, the three men in the one passenger seat looked at each other in horror. Then they saw Reg stomping off with one finger pointed towards what was no doubt a police officer, screaming at the top of his little confederate lungs.

"Na you lissen 'ear strawfoot, see I ain't donuthin but drive ma rig—I dun care what yo little speed-o-meeter say boy! Done cay inna leest!"

There were other angry voices, but no clear words could be heard over the voice of Reginald, squeaking and scratching like nails through gravel in the muggy summer night. The state trooper's lights swirled and whipped through side-view mirrors fogged out entirely like they were driving through a hot shower.

Sensing trouble, and no doubt an opportunity to prove himself, Thomas Jones followed Reg through the driver-side door. Through the obnoxious flashing and whooping of the horn and light display atop the patrolmen's vehicle, Thomas could discern Reginald's sprite-like body splayed chest down on the hood of the cruiser. He was spitting and hollering all over the paint-job, legs kicking and flailing in complete circles, and his hat was spinning in the dirt. He really did have an amazing head of hair for a man with who had wrinkles cut deeper than crop-circles coursing his leathery face.

He washed his hands in tobacco juice, but his hair smelled like coconuts and looked like loomed flax.

"Sir...excuse me?...sir?" Thomas Jones said at increasing volume, attempting to get their attention off the demon from Dixie who was, by now, smashing his forehead repeatedly into the hood of the patrol car.

While they may have lost their driver, at the very least Dr. Carter had not run screaming out from under the tarp, like some strange sort of human trafficking that exported old men into Pennsylvania.

More importantly, of course, than Dr. Clarke Carter was the ever-expanding swathe of diamond that was slowly enrobing the guts of a four-ton stainless steel Dixie cup on the back of their driver's truck bed.

Even when they had successfully forced Reginald into the back of the squad car, he buzzed around the inside like a wasp under a shot glass, screaming and kicking and spitting on the windows.

"Sir, I need you to put your hands in the air for me, okay?"

"Yes sir!" Thomas had his nuts dissolved by the threat of criminal arrest, "Yes sir—sir I am very sorry, sir."

"Just shut it," said the cop who snagged Thomas's arms and cinched them quickly in his cuffs. Thomas peed a little in his underwear.

"Oh god—oh god—sir you've got it all wrong," he stammered gushingly. The cop turned him around and propped him up against the car. The impact made his rib squeal in agony. Two Vicodin really weren't cutting it.

"Now, you're not under arrest, son, I just need to know why this man is having a—" the officer was cut off by the sound of repeated knocking of knuckle on glass. Reg had ceased his epileptic fit and was now knocking, rather politely, on the window like he was a girl scout selling thin mints. The officer, impressed by the man's calm, walked over and opened the door a half an inch.

"Need ter use da ressroom, offser."

"You can either hold it or you can piss your pants," the officer spat and shut the door with a snap before walking back up to Thomas, "So what are you all hauling this evening?" said the trooper, pointing aimlessly toward the tarp. "That's an awful large somethin' or other."

"Well, sir, you see—he's a new driver, and I'm sorry bout the speeding."

"Son, you don't look like a trucker."

"Well, thank you—but that's cus—"

"And you stink to high heaven boy! Is that shit on your shoes?!"

"Um, well—yes sir. It does happen to be shit. Dog-shit actually. See that's what we're carrying. A—um—a dog shit dumpster. New invention really, keeps the smell down.

"Hmmm. Sound like you'd need a helluva lotta dogs to fill that thing, no?"

"Well it's a—um—it's a prototype, see—we're bringing it to Philly for more testing."

"Well, I tell you what son, I'm gonna let you go on your way, Lord knows I don't need no dog crap on my nice uniform, but Mr. Lynyrd Skynyrd over here is coming with me. Can't resist. Sure you understand. You give your superiors this card," he said, handing Thomas a business card, "and you tell them the Southern Man is gonna be up North for a while."

"Um, yes sir. Sure thing, sir," Thomas did not have any idea how to drive an eighteen-wheeler and he assumed neither of his companions did, but as long as this cop took him for a trucker and didn't pull down the tarp, he wasn't going to argue. As he made his way back to the truck's cabin he heard the door of the police-car open again and the officer exclaim.

"Good lord! What? What'd you do, you crazy old bastard? You pissed on my seats!"

"Got whatcher assed fer dint cha? You's the one who says to piss ma shorts. Got what you asked for, ya yer bluebellied S.O.B!"

They heard another door slam and the cop car sped around them and out of sight into the night. Thomas waited a full ten minutes before starting again just to make sure there was no way the cop was going to see what was undoubtedly going to be a rough initial mile. None of the individuals had ever driven an eighteen-wheeler—Pablo had never driven a car—and with Mike trying to calm Carter down via radio—it fell to Thomas Jones to master the beast.

They were about thirty miles from Wildwood, but it took three hours to get there. They stalled fourteen times, Thomas wasn't able to get out of second gear, and they only realized there was a double clutch when they were turning onto his block. When they finally got the back end of the truck on to Thomas's lawn (which took a half-hour on its own), Carter sprinted from the tarp with the speed of a much younger man and fell to the lawn panting. He had stripped down to his pants and undershirt and his glasses were missing.

"You OK doc?" said Mike, genuinely concerned.

"SWEET GOD, I CERTAINLY AM NOT."

"Doc, you don't have to yell anymore."

"Oh my god—my glasses—ripped off my head the second we hit the freeway. Its ten thousand degrees under that tarp—hardly breathe—oh my lord—oh my sweet Jesus."

"You're okay, we're gonna get you inside, get you a glass of water and a nice bed."

"WHY THE HELL DID IT TAKE SO LONG?" panted Carter.

"Doc, please, don't yell. The neighbors are gonna find this strange enough without a half-dressed geologist screaming on his belly."

"Oh God, I don't understand—it's two hours, tops, to Wildwood. Are we in Atlanta? I swear to God we could've driven to Tallahassee in the time it took—oh God."

Pablo helped Carter to his feet and walked him into the house while Thomas and Mike began to consider their options.

They decided that Jameson's initial suggestion was the only one that was going to work. Lacking a retractable wall on his ancestral home, Thomas only had one spot large enough to hold the machine, and that was his backyard. They would have to remove the fence to get it behind the house, but that's what one o'clock in the morning is for.

Since the thing wasn't going to levitate into the yard on its own and they were going to take down the fence anyway, the men decided back the truck right over the fence so that they had only to drop the machine and its generators on the ground, tarp it again and prop the whatever was left of the fence back up to avoid prying eyes.

Needless to say the sound of a big rig crushing a thirty-year-old fence is enough on its own to invoke the peeping tom in any normal neighbor. This, however, is Wildwood, New Jersey, and at this moment, Thomas's neighbors on both sides were three dozen seventeen-year-olds who were all at the Boardwalk boozing illicitly or otherwise had already by this time of the evening drunk enough to create an alcohol-induced coma from which not even the landing of the diamond-pissing space-ship could rouse them.

It took another hour to get each generator and the machine on the back lawn. Once it was tarped and the shreds of fence piled in something that resembled a property boundary, the three men sat in the grass and relaxed, listening to the sounds of carnival attractions, smashing bottle-glass, and teenaged orgasms.

"Sure could use a drink," said Mike suggestively.

"Jes, Jes! Dassa good idea." Pablo was excited.

"Um, yeah? You guys wanna go out?"

"Jes sir!"

"Yeah man. Why don't you show us around your hometown? Sure looks like some people are having a good time. Mike was pointing to a group of kids who were passing the front of the house doing cartwheels in their underwear down the street. Thomas had spent less time on that boardwalk than he had sucking on toes; he had all his life been phobic of that place. To him, it was the valley of evil. The Black Land. Mordor. Lord Voldemort's walk-in closet.

"Sure thing, guys. Let's do it up," said Thomas a bit more confidently than he had intended. What did he have to lose? He was with two cool guys and they had worked hard for nearly twelve hours. He had earned a drink.

In reality, the boardwalk at Wildwood is no different from most other summer-time beach attractions. It's made of wood, and features various establishments serving a wealth of frozen concoctions in many shades of blue, pink, and purple. There are games and goofy shit at every turn, and food that some considered the very worst and best dietary innovation. Like French-fry pizza. The draw—in Wildwood—is ethereal. No one knows why, but every year the migrating flocks arrive and do not leave till September. Maybe it's the lack of reasonable law enforcement. Maybe it's the fact that so few people above the legal drinking age live here year round, so that the town itself is literally run by class presidents and cheerleaders in the summer. Some people think it's the name. No one truly knew, but as for Pablo, Mike, and Thomas Jones, they couldn't care less.

They were laughed out of the first bar they stopped at when Thomas ordered a Shirley Temple. Pablo didn't stop laughing for twenty minutes, while Mike was a bit sweeter about it.

"Yeah man, you don't wanna order Shirley Temples."

"Yeah, I just thought I would start with something light. To uh—you know—um get the night started."

"Then try a bud light. But don't order another Shirley Temple unless you're wearing a skirt…You know what, even then—don't order a Shirley Temple."

Thomas was mortified. Mike did the drink ordering for him for the rest of the evening.

And what an evening it was. Before the sun had pulled itself over the horizon with its many fiery hands, all three men would be flat-out snockered. So absolutely plowed were these three men that they were practically anesthetized by morning. At some point Mike and Thomas lost Pablo, only to find him sitting on the beach singing in Spanish and playing an air-mandolin, surrounded by two dozen empty cans of Tecate. Mike taught Thomas how to do Irish Car Bombs, and Thomas won an enormous stuffed elephant by shooting a clown in the mouth with a water gun. Sometime around four in the morning, Thomas was pushed into a photo-booth and sexually assaulted by an eighteen -year -old girl who was in excess of two hundred and fifty pounds and had what tasted like hot dog pieces stuck in her braces. Thomas stumbled out of the booth with a bloody lip and the wrong drink (something with an umbrella in it). Mike kept the photos, laughing until he couldn't breathe. The three men watched the sun rise while smoking a cigar that they emptied of tobacco and filled with the marijuana that Mike was carrying for Carter. They laughed for an hour at a seagull that was chasing a hermit crab before falling asleep on the stuffed elephant.

They didn't stay asleep long, as a beach cop on a bike took the trio for homeless men and woke them around 9a.m. and told them move along.

Viciously hung over and dehydrated they walked, slowly, back to the house on Sandy Circle. Pablo stopped to drink from someone's sprinkler and was chased off the lawn with a broom. Thomas couldn't help but think of his dear old mother.

When they arrived, Carter was out back fiddling with the external features of the diamond machine. He seemed to be talking to himself, and was agitated about something. He was also wearing a massive pair of red glasses which had once belonged to Thomas's mother. They were big, plastic and winged so that they resembled a masquerade mask more than reading glasses. All three men ignored him and walked directly to the couches and collapsed. Perhaps thirty seconds elapsed before the house phone rang.

Thomas lurched from the couch, tried to straighten his spinal column out and shook beach sand from his hair before lifting the receiver.

"Good morning, sunshine!" blared Jameson into the receiver. Thomas cringed at the earsplitting sound of Jameson yelling over his helicopter's throttle through the phone. His head had a heartbeat, it hurt so badly.

"Morning, Jameson"

"My goodness, you sound like SHIT!"

"Uh yeah...Feel like it too."

"We weren't drinking on the job now, were we?" Jameson asked with an audible smile in his voice. Thomas missed it.

"Oh no sir. Not at all, sir—I mean, Jameson—sir, Jameson."

"Music to my ears! Listen, Thomas, we, as in I, have a question and a problem that are quite inter-related: Firstly, how on earth did you drive that thing without Reg?"

"Oh—um, well it wasn't easy"

"I wouldn't imagine it was! And that's the problem—I've paid his bail but I'm going to need you guys to get him, as that truck is his home and financial blood-line and he is a dear friend of mine. Have him drop you and everyone off at God's Demand, all right?"

"You got it."

"And when I say everyone I mean everyone except Dr. Carter who will need to stay with our little machine—hold on Thomas, I am sorry—Lo dejó allí. Más rápido, señor. ver la cornisa, I apologize Thomas—as I was saying; Dr. Carter will need to remain in the house for the next few days until the machine has completed its cycle. I expect that's cool by you?"

"Uh, sure—sure thing."

"Great! You and Mike are going to head, right now, back into Manhattan and meet at the small establishment I mentioned yesterday. Help out in whatever way you can and when I return in two days' time we will be having a big meeting in my office downtown. I'm counting on you, Thomas!"

"Yes sir!" There was a long pause. "Err, yes, Jameson"

"Thank you so very much, Thomas."

"You're wel—" and the line went dead.

23

David Drahtman slapped the chest of Bobby Collins with the back of his right hand to wake him. He struggled out of his shirt-mask, wiped a wedge of drool from his face with his forearm and blurted something incoherent that sounded like, "Time in pie mace!" David thought a mace that was scented like apple pie wouldn't make a very effective deterrent to criminal activities.

"Huh? Jesus Christ Collins—wake up, we're here."

When Bobby Collins had peeled apart his eyelids, he found before him an immense, strange-looking red building. Above white double doors and between two black glass windows was a large wooden sign with words routed into it:

THISTLESTICK RIVER TECHNICAL COLLEGE

'Where Everybody's a somebody!'

Est. 2003

David hadn't even read the sign until Collins had read it aloud. He was busy checking himself in the mirror when he heard what the sign said. David slapped up the visor with a start and squinted to see the sign for himself.

"What in the? That's not right, the brochure—" David leaned his rear off of the seat and pulled out the increasingly crumpled brochure, "875 Wolf's Hill Road." David looked up again over the brochure and read the same numbers from above the white doors. "875! What the hell is this?"

"Well, Dave, a technical college is a school where special skills are—"

"Oh, just shut it Collins! I know what a technical college is," David lied. Collins only knew because he had a brother who had spent time in prison and attended a technical college after being released.

"Well, the brochure says that this is where the day care is. This is the place. Something fishy is going on Collins, I can smell it."

"Me too. And it smells like shit," observed Collins.

"It sure does, Bobby... it sure as hell does," said David like a detective on the brink of the big break in the case. David pulled the Hummer beside six or seven other cars parked alongside the left fence-line and the two men got out.

"What the fuck is with the towers?" Collins pointed to the two cylinders rising high above the building.

"I have no idea, probably where they keep all the dogs, locked away like our little friends in Stanley's basement. Or maybe that's where they keep the owls that ate my wife's fucking dog."

"An owl?!"

"A god-damned-OWL."

"Dave what the—"

"I don't wanna talk about it."

"An OWL?!"

"Bobby! If I have to go over it again I'm going to have a coronary, please let's just find this *THOMAS JONES* and inform him that he and his little *business* are up a fucking creek."

"Well, what're we gonna do Dave?"

"I don't know yet, but it's gonna hurt.," said David as he rapped three times on the door, "and if I find out he's got a pet I'm going to put it in an oven and eat it for lunch.," They heard movement behind the door and David finished briskly, "Just follow my lead."

The doors opened at their center and a small black man with close-cropped white hair stood before them. Behind him a room full of bodies behind small desks worked over sewing machines. There was a short Hispanic man walking between the rows, giving pointers and helping the individuals with their work.

"Yeah?" said Melvin in his most loquacious possible manner.

"Yeah, um, I'm looking for Thomas Jones."

"Thomas Jones?" said a taller Hispanic looking man who stepped out from behind the door and stood beside Melvin, "I don't know no Thomas Jones? You Melvin?"

"Nope."

"Sorry, can't help you sir," Pedro said with a smile as he began to close the door in their face.

"Hold on a second, pal" said David, holding the door

open with his left hand and pulling the brochure back from his pocket with his right. "I'm looking for THOMAS JONES." He mouthed this loudly and carefully for Pedro. "He works here," holding the brochure before their faces. "And somehow, he managed to feed my wife's dog to a nocturnal bird of prey"

"Oh! Jes, joo not da first person to be lookin' here for dogs. Dat bro-chore got da wrong address on it. I dunno where dis place is dat joo looking for. Very sorry!" Pedro tried again to close the door but was once again rebuffed by the hand of David Drahtman.

"So!" he started with a smile, "this place…this is a *technical* college, is it?"

"Jes sir! Thistlestick River Technical College"

"And what do you teach here at Thistlestick River Technical College, Mr.…."

"I am Professor Peligro and this is the chair-mang, Professor Willy-ams," Pedro indicated to Melvin, "We teach lossa stuff here, joo know, like a sewiiiiing, and a paaaintiiiiing, and a massaaaaggees."

"And there's no dogs in this building?" asked David hurriedly, missing something quite important.

"No dogs!"

"You're sure?"

"No dogs" said Melvin this time, a bit more forceful.

"So you wouldn't mind if I had a look around? I mean, you must understand, my poor little dog is missing and apparently dead. And according to Mr. Thomas Jones and his lovely little *brochure,* my dear little Gabbana was last seen at this address."

"Sirs I been telling joo – ders no dogs heer, that doggy place maybe somewhere close, because people always be looking for the dogs here. No dogs! Maybe cross da street? Maybe you go to da zoo, you find doggies at da zoo."

"The zoo?"

"Jes… issa place wit a lotta animals. Dey gotta da elephanteeees, dey gotta de monkeeeeys, dey gotta de…what else dey got Chair-mang Willy-ams?"

"Hippos"

"Jes! Dey gotta hippopotamaaaaaas" said Pedro excitedly. David's internal organs were being microwaved by the sheer force of his rage for anyone of Hispanic descent. Strangely, David was able to handle it in an effort to get his hands around the throat of Thomas Jones, who for some even stranger reason, he now saw as the source of all his problems. He had poured all of his very worst emotions into Thomas. He was too hot coffee and Thomas Jones was the ill-prepared plastic cup.

"I want you to listen to me, *senior* – I know that—"

"Professor," said Melvin samurai-slicing David's sentence in twain.

"Excuse me?"

"Professor…Peligro."

"Oh, but of course. Excuse me, *professor.*"

"Jes, jes, das okay"

"Yeah well—professor—my problem is that this

291

brochure has YOUR address on it, and I am really going to have to insist you let me take a look around. My wife would be devastated if I couldn't at the least come back with some information as to the whereabouts of—" David's words were again mangled, this time by Pedro who was standing on tippy-toes and looking over David's shoulder with a smile.

"Um. Is dat joo cars?" said Pedro through a growing chuckle, pointing to the Hummer.

"Yes—no—no, it's my wife's, but that's not—"

"Joo gotta cars like a girly no? Joo cars a pinky-pink!" David dug his nails into his palms and drew blood. Just before he became incapable of holding back any longer his desire to rip both men's throats from their neck with his hands, David's brain wrapped itself around a beaded metal cord and pulled. A light came on in a dim, shadowed corner.

"Think this is funny? Do you? So tell me this you pricks. What would happen if I dialed the number on the back of the brochure?" David's eyes were wide open and did not miss the looks of subtle surprise on the faces of Melvin and Pedro, both of whom were no longer smiling, "That's what I thought." David feverishly uncrumpled the brochure and began punching numbers into his cell-phone while panting in anticipation. Finally, when he had finished the number he raised it to his ear and looked at both men with the eyes of a lunatic and waited.

"*We're sorry, but the number you've dialed is not in service. Please check the number and try again. We're sorry, but the number you've dialed is—*"

David shut the phone with two hands and squeezed it as hard as he could.

"I HAVE HAD ENOUGH!"

"Me too," said Melvin over David's protestations and Pedro's whooping, thigh-slapping laughter before slamming the double doors shut in Drahtman's face with surprising force for his diminutive frame.

"GODDAMNIT!" screamed David pulling on his hair with two hands before pounding on the doors, "THIS ISNT OVER! DO YOU FUCKING HEAR ME, ASSSHOLE?! I KNOW THIS IS THE PLACE! I KNOW YOU'RE HERE, THOMAS JONES!! I'M GONNA FUCKING FIND YOU, AND IM GONNA FUCKING CUT OUT YOUR FUCKING—"

"WHOA! DAVEY! FUCKIN' CHILL!"

"—EYES YOU SON OF A BITCH. I'LL FUCKING RAPE YOUR—"

"DAVE! RELAX THE FUCK OUT!"

"—MOTHER AND SISTER AND DAUGHTER AND DOG AND—"

"DAVID!"

David Drahtman could not think of any other living things which might be dear to Thomas Jones that he would be able to have forcible intercourse with. His face flushed with blood, eyes red, sweat falling in sheets from his face—David fell to the ground and exhaled deeply.

"Davey-boy! You gotta fucking relaaax, pal. I mean,

c'mon, who the fuck cares. You hated that dog since your wife brought the little shit home"

"It's—not—about—the—dog."

"Then what is it, Dave, 'cuz you have got to get some pills or something, you got a real anger problem, man."

Before Drahtman could respond to Collins's entirely well-intended suggestion of therapy and psychiatric medicine, David's brain found a second light-switch on the wall of his skull and flipped it. Lying on his back in the gravel, he was looking at the six cars along the wall.

"Wait a second, Collins. Did you see inside that place? How many people were in there ...sewing or whatever?"

"I dunno—like thirty, forty?"

"And how do you suppose forty people got here in six cars?"

"Well, maybe there's another entrance"

"No way—there's nothing but trees for miles behind this block, I saw it on the GPS." David got up and ran to the fence along the side of the building. He jumped to get a look behind it. He did this a few times at different locations along the fence.

"Nope, no cars. I'm telling you, Collins, something is UP. I can FUCKING SMELL IT."

"Davey—I'm gonna have to suggest we just forget about this for a while."

"Collins—shut—your—mouth. Something seriously fucked up is going on here. Write down all these license plates. I want you to call your friend at the state police and have him find out who these cars belong to. I wanna know who the fuck is here and how all those other people got here. I wanna know everything about the Thistlestick River Technical College and I want to know it YESTERDAY!"

"Okay Dave, okay." Collins was genuinely afraid of David now.

As Collins scribbled the license plate number off of the back of a white Ford Tempo, David's cell phone rang, despite being nearly crushed to dust in his hands moments earlier. When David looked at the phone's face he found the words "Mr. Prewitt Cell" blinking on the screen.

"Yeah?" said David, finding it difficult to commence ass-kissing his superior in a moment like this.

"Mr. Drahtman?"

"Yes. Where are you Mr. Prewitt? Shouldn't you be resting?"

"Where are you, Mr. Drahtman?"

"I'm out of town."

"Get back to town immediately and meet me at the office."

"You're at the office?"

"Yes."

"You just had a stroke, yesterday."

"I am aware. Unfortunately present circumstances necessitate my coming to the office, regardless of my condition."

"Circumstances?"

"Alastor Shank was murdered last night."

<u>24</u>

It took the three hung-over, un-showered, nauseated men two hours to get the truck off the lawn and to the police station where they were to pick up Reginald Jefferson Davis IV. Rather than even attempt to park the thing in the police department lot, they pulled over a few blocks away and walked up a short hill to the trooper barracks. About fifty feet before the main door, Mike spoke.

"Anybody got gum?" he said pecking and pinching at his vest. Mike slapped his palms on different points on his chest like he was giving a base-runner the sign to steal second. He stopped suddenly when he came across a large lump near his midsection; padded and prodded the bulge a few times and stopped walking. Mike unzipped the pocket, looked into it and cursed, "Shit! Shit!"

"¿qué? lo que está mal?", said the aggravated and headachy Pablo, descending into complete Spanish.

"I've still got the pot on me. Can't go in a police station with a bag of weed. Although…" he went on still moving his fingers around in the square of black canvas, "There really isn't all that much left. How much did we smoke?"

"Fumabamos todo!" yelled Pablo.

"Yeah well, whatever—I'm going back to the truck, you guys pick him up and meet me back there, I gotta call Carter anyway 'cuz we've got his pot and he's not going to be happy about it."

Reg was still none too pleased with the New Jersey State Troopers. The acting chief made it a point to mention that the truck driver had refused food, water, and a change of clothes (which still stunk of urine). He was sitting in the corner of a holding cell by himself, while the other six or seven inmates were all sitting in the opposite corner, piled on top of one another to avoid the stench.

"Ahhhh-HA! Tole you boys dey was onna way. Ha-lay-LOO-ya. Let ole Reg' out damnit. Let 'im go!" he had begun shouting at the sight of Thomas and Pablo.
On the way out he made a concerted effort to insult every single man and woman in the barracks. A slight, bushy-haired female officer at the front desk responded by pinching her nose.

"Oh, now you can stuff it, kitty-kat, yer panties smella catfish—could smell em from ma cell, ya guldarned hussy!"

Despite the stale pissy odor that surrounded him and his tales of the justice system, they were all glad to see him back. The rig, which had been a jumbling, jangling, spine-shortening effort in perseverance for the rest of them, flew under the deft hands of Reginald. She purred and hummed warmly at his touch and roared into the open road. Before long Reg had parallel-parked on a busy city street like he was sliding a tricycle into a dog-house.

"Now git goin'. I gotta be in Richmond by sundown." He gave them five seconds to get out the passenger door and on the ground. "Well…Go! Git goin, I tole ya! I ain't got aw day ter set 'n' chitty-chat in this guldarned city."

Before they could muster good-byes the truck was weaving in and out of traffic in the lower east side of Manhattan.

When he turned around, Thomas Jones looked up at a shabby brick building stuck between two larger ones. It looked as if it had once been used as residential space but had long since had that use neglected. Several windows were boarded up, though still others were wide open. Above a green wooden door was a small crucifix.

"This is God's Demand, one of the many businesses that Jameson owns. You a religious guy, Thomas?"

"Er…no, no I wouldn't say I'm especially…no."

"Good," said Mike, without offering a further explanation. Pablo had already opened the door and was making his way inside, rubbing his temples and muttering under his breath in Spanish.

The front hall opened on the right to what was likely once a living room but now looked like a modified kitchen. There were four stove-tops plugged into an oversized power strip and corrugated steel gas lines that ran into holes carved into the plaster. A man or woman stood in front of each stove, working several pans of something that smoked and smelled like frying bread.

In the room's center was a long dining room table with six individuals, mostly young white people, not unlike the shit-shovelers, minus the stains, who were bent over plates in front of them, aiming small gas torches onto some sort of edible concoction. At the end of the table a short, dark-skinned young girl was wrapping each of the finished products in plastic wrap.

"Hey everybody," said Mike to those assembled. Several people looked up from their work or over their shoulders and hollered salutations to Mike. Pablo entered from an opening in the living room wall, which by the contrast of carpet to linoleum looked like the original kitchen. He was nibbling at something that appeared identical to what the cooks and torch-bearers were attended to.

"Grilled cheese," said Mike to Thomas, who took a few moments to make out what Mike was talking about.

"Oh—you mean…Oh? Wait, you make grilled cheese sandwiches?"

"Not just any grilled cheese sandwiches!" said Mike, picking up one from the pile and unwrapping it. "See anything unusual about this grilled cheese?" he asked, holding up the sandwich in front of Thomas's face. It certainly looked delicious, but by no means unlike any other grilled cheese he had ever seen or eaten in his life, "Look closer," Mike encouraged him.

And then Thomas saw it. It was the face of Jesus Christ staring back at him from the crusty, caramelized white bread.

"Wait a minute. How the hell did you…" started Thomas

before noticing the torches again. "You guys are burning the image of Jesus into grilled cheese?"

"Not just Jesus! The Virgin Mary…Moses…" Mike leaned over the shoulder of a younger guy with long, messy brown hair. "And Bradley here is working on a brilliant Vishnu." He paused to appreciate Bradley's handiwork, "You see, Thomas, Vishnu is especially difficult, what with the extra arms and all—great work Brad!"

"Thanks Mike," said the one named Brad.

"Sure thing. The ones with torches are art students. Pretty gifted bunch."

"Who is buying grilled cheese pictures of Jesus Christ?" Thomas asked, mystified.

"Lots of people. We put them on eBay. We had one go for $28K."

"What?"

"Yeah, the only one that we can't seem to sell is the Mohammeds, we think on account of the fact that the image of the prophet is considered blasphemous, most especially when rendered on cheese sandwiches." A few cooks at their pans laughed.

"Wow—I mean, this is just crazy—grilled cheese—"

"And it's not just grilled cheese. Toast, cakes, pies, cookies…you name it and we put the image of Jesus on it."

"Wow."

"Oh it's nothing—follow me."

They passed through the kitchen and back into what

might have been a dining room in another life. Large windows at the back let good light in the space; the sun's thumbs lit up the figures within like they were on fire. There were three young women, sitting around another, rounder table doing what looked like needlework until Thomas got closer. They were making jewelry.

"Glow-in-the-dark rosary beads," said Mike, as he kept walking through the room. They passed five or six crates full of the beads, some of which near the bottom were glowing green. "The kids love 'em."

Mike and Thomas climbed a set of stairs at the back of the jewelry room and came to a landing. A hallway darkened by three or four shuttered doors was lit at its end by a lone open one from which sunlight reached the guts of the building's upper floors. Thomas thought he heard someone crying—sobbing even—far away. Perhaps on the floors above.

They seemed to be walking towards the light but stopped at the second door on the left. Mike knocked twice and opened the door.

"This is real special…still working on it."

Behind this door were two older men in white coats, both of whom were fiddling with a large white statue of the Virgin Mary. There was a third man on his back on a rolling dolly, head and shoulders slid under the skirt of the Blessed Mother like he was changing the oil on an Oldsmobile.

"Uh…what are they up to?"

"They're perfecting a prototype of a new idea our

manager Eli came up with. Any guess what it is?" Thomas had none, but then the question was answered for him. The man performing cunnilingus on the Mother of God started cursing, muffled by her alabaster hemline.

"Shit. Fuck! Get away!" And no sooner had the other doctors huddled behind a chair than the statue starting shooting what looked like tomato juice from its eyes with the force of a garden hose. Mike snapped the door closed through the cursing. They could hear the pulpy juice spattering the door as it shut.

"We're trying to perfect a Virgin Mary statue that cries tears of blood. Clearly we're still not quite there."

"Clearly!"

They made their way back down the hall to the door at the back, and Thomas could still not make out whether the muted, groaning voices were crying—or laughing? Was the building haunted? Or what? He decided to ignore it and talk about something else. "Did you ever speak to Carter?"

"No, actually, he didn't pick—" and Mike was cut off by a short bespectacled young man with a black Mohawk and a steel-barbell punched through his nostrils. Thomas winced at the sight of him. The man was eating a bowl of what looked like Fruit Loops and nearly sloshed milk all over Thomas as he walked into him.

"Whoa. Hey, Eli. Thomas, this is Elijah Willets."

"Hello, Elijah." The man named Eli balanced his breakfast in his left and shook with his right. His earlobes, punctured by what looked like black plastic half-dollars, wiggled with the effort.

"Nice to meet you Thomas. Call me Eli."

"Sure thing," Thomas said shortly, taking note of curling spirals of red and black ink inching from Eli's collar, ringing his neckline.

"Eli is the brilliant young mind that came up with the idea for God's Demand a few years back."

"Yeah man, I met Jameson at a bar and told him about my idea and he had me my own building in a week," said Eli, through a mouth full of milk and cereal.

"Really? That's great—um...so what can we—or I—help you with?"

"Oh, there's tons to do. You good with a computer?"

"Well—um, not really *good*—"

"Oh, don't be silly, all you gotta do is answer e-mails. C'mon, I'll show you," assured Eli, guiding Thomas with his free right hand into the back room. The small office space was three walls of desks and computers and a smushed brown couch with pillow and blanket in one corner. Two chairs on wheels sat in the middle of the room. On the wall was a large, framed photograph of a man strung from a parachute. By the inch-thick steel bar punched through the nostril, Thomas recognized the individual in the picture as his new co-worker.

"Skydiving huh?" said Thomas, trying to make friends.

"Oh yeah. Outside of this business there is nothing I love more. It's freedom man...*freedom*."

"Yeah, I can't imagine ever doing that."

"Fuck that dude, that—" he said pointing to the picture—"is EASY. What I really love is base-jumping. Jumping out of crazy shit, like planes and off buildings. That's where the real fun is."

Thomas's penis shot back into his abdomen at the thought of leaping off of a building for amusement.

"Enough with your hobbies, Eli, tell him what we do here," interjected Mike, his words stopping a flood of foam forming in the corners of Eli's mouth at the very mention of hurling himself from elevated structures. In his dreams, Eli was Clark Kent with a tongue ring.

"Yeah—yeah ... he's right…basically, what God's Demand does is target a very specific niche market."

"Niche market?" Thomas couldn't spell "niche," much less define it.

"Exactly," started Eli. "There is no bigger demographic that better combines the principles of massive wealth and intellectual vapidity like the Evangelical Right. So /many of them have more money than they can shake a crucifix at, and fortunately for us they are some of the dumbest sons of bitches you'll ever meet." He paused to spoon some Fruit Loops before swallowing. Cleaning his teeth with whatever power tools were in there, he watched Thomas's face with one eyebrow in the air. "You a religious guy, Thomas?"

"No—no, I wouldn't say so."

"Well that's a good thing…"

He took another bite and grimaced before putting the

bowl and spoon down on a desk with two computer monitors on it. "Fuckin' mushy…anyway it's not that you gotta be an atheist or anything, it's just we wouldn't want you to be offended by some of what you'll see here. Were basically in a situation where there's all these kids who still believe in Santa, and rather than tell them otherwise, were just gonna turn a profit of all the presents under the tree. It's certainly a better place for their money than having them hand it some monster playing pin the tail on the altar boy."

"And we make a pretty penny doing it." added Mike after a laugh, "The grilled cheese and rosary beads are only part of the operation. Up here is where the magic happens…Tell him, Eli."

"It sure does," said Eli falling backwards into a rolling chair, sliding up to one of many keyboards and opening a web browser. The home page was a white screen with a cross at the center, a halo slung over its shoulder. It was perched on a yellow triangle, beneath which read, in neat, conservative letters: *The Ministry of the Prophet Elijah and the Golden Mountain.*

"Oh Lord—" said Thomas, not wanting to even surmise what in the name of the heavenly father was going on here.

Eli clicked a menu item that said *About Elijah and the Golden Mountain* and said "Here…read!" Thomas leaned over Eli's shoulder and began to read:

<u>About Elijah and the Golden Mountain</u>

It was Christmas Eve in the year of our Lord, 2000, that

something strange happened to me. At the time I was living under a different name and working as a successful attorney who had everything a man could want: money, cars, a beautiful home and a beautiful wife and family. For some reason, however, I was not happy.

It was on that Christmas Eve, while trying to fall asleep that something strange happened. I had gone to the bathroom late in the night and while sitting on the toilet, flipping through a *People* magazine, it happened: in between a picture of Britney Spears and Justin Timberlake and an article about the immortal Backstreet Boys there was a light. A bright, fierce light pouring from the seam of the magazine. In fear, I dropped it on the floor of the bathroom and backed away. Unbelievably, the light spread—filling the room until it overwhelmed me. I couldn't see a thing and I fell. But rather than fall through to the hard floor of my bathroom, I kept falling. And falling.

Finally I awoke, but still I could not see. I could, however, hear. And what I heard changed my life forever. It was my own voice, but it was not my words. The Heavenly Father spoke through my very lips and told me that I was to become his tongue and teeth. That I would be his voice on the earth. The Lord said that I had been chosen in these perilous times to act as a go-between for the maker and mankind. He gave me two tasks and titles:

The Answerer and the Builder of the Golden Mountain.

The Lord asked me to build Him a Golden Mountain with the help of his people. For each one of his children who would contribute a stone to his mountain, the Lord has directed me to answer one question.

I cannot explain how it is possible, only that it is, and his influence in my life has been dramatic. Through this website which he has provided me through his divine providence, you may contribute to the mountain. I do not know what the Lord requires this mountain for; suffice it to say that he has a plan which he has not yet made me aware of. For the golden sum of $77.77 the Lord will allow me to answer one question of yours by which I will be able to direct the Holy Spirit to give you the response you most need in your life. Each contributor will also have their name inscribed on this mountain which the faithful may observe at this link.

May the Good Lord bless and keep each of you always. In these dark and dangerous times, the Heavenly Father has asked me to send you his Eternal Love and know that your salvation is dependent on the peace and devotion you give your fellow man, and to your Divine Father. In Christ's Name.

Amen,

Elijah

"Wow." finished Thomas, "Can I see the—um—mountain?"

"Sure," said Eli, clicking the link. The page that opened was a list of names which was long enough to shrivel the scroll cursor to the size of a chink of orzo. At the top of list was a running ticker totaling the amount of the "mountain." The number was eight figures long.

"Oh my…oh my God! Who is—how do you—" Both Mike and Eli were already laughing. Eli put his hand on Mike's arm, shook his head and began to explain.

"Firstly—you shouldn't use the Lord's name in vain." Mike howled at this sentence. "Just kidding—just kidding…Anyway, yes, it is a lot of money, but it's also a complete fabrication. We've made up half of those names. The larger the community the person thinks they are joining the more likely they are to join. At this point we've got about six million from 'donors' in a secure back account. We use the grilled cheese, rosary beads, and a few other enterprises to pay the bills and we just let this mountain grow. Whenever the day comes when it's needed, it's there. In the meantime, Jameson takes care of all of us."

"So you answer people's questions? Like what kind of questions?"

"Oh, all sorts of shit. Have a seat and we'll get you started. I need all the help I can get."

Thomas pulled up the second rolling chair and sat next to Eli. Mike put his hand on Thomas's shoulder from behind.

"Listen guys, I'm gonna go grab something to eat. You okay, Thomas?"

"Sure thing, man."

Between the two of them, Eli and Thomas answered hundreds of emails and processed the payments of $77.77 for each. There were some individuals, Thomas noticed, who asked many questions, paying over and over again to speak to what they believed was the creator of the universe. Some wanted to know when they would find true love. Others wanted to know how old they would be when they would die (Eli said these were his favorite). Still others were interested in the inner workings of the universe; the meaning of it all. On a dry-erase board behind the monitors, Eli had a list of easy answers to certain questions which were repeated frequently.

Q: WHAT IS THE MEANING OF LIFE?

A: To fulfill thine potential and use thine gifts to make the world a better place than when thou found it.

Q: WILL I GO TO HEAVEN?

A: If you follow the four demandments: Train Hard, Eat Your Vitamins, Say Your Prayers, and Believe In Yourself

Q: WHY DID YOU HAVE TO CAUSE THAT EARTHQUAKE/TORNADO/ FLASH

FLOOD/OUTBREAK OF VENEREAL DISEASE?

A: Because thy Lord works in mysterious ways. And because thy sexual practices art too much prolific. If the Holy Father did not prune the bush, the bush wouldst die. If thou wouldst not maketh so many children, the Lord would not have to do so much damned pruning. Doth thou thinkst the Heavenly Father enjoyest spending his afternoons gardening? I am the way, the truth, and the life. Not the landscaper.

Thomas very quickly got the hang of playing God. It was no more than a matter of being relatively honest with his best advice and sprinkling in a generous dash of "thous" and "thines." As an added bonus, a healthy dose of underhanded humor seemed to be expected. Thomas doubted seriously that the average retired super-Christian was going to get the Star Wars references he was sneaking into every other answer.

"Yeah, I don't know if the divine creator would sign his emails 'May The Force Be With You'" said Mike, who had been standing behind Thomas for a few minutes, drinking a glass of orange juice.

"Oh, I'm sorry – I just—"

"Relax pal, it's cool—Jameson once told a guy his goldfish was the reincarnation of Saint Francis. It's all in good fun. These people take themselves way too serious to think they're being had."

Eli laughed knowingly, like he had been sitting next to Jameson that day.

"Hey, I was just wondering Mike, you know—I left my car in Thistlestick River, and I don't know how I am getting home tonight," said Thomas, catching sight of the dusty sun slowly pouring off between skyscrapers beyond the window's glass.

"Yeah, I figured that would come up. Usually every Saturday night we all have dinner together at the home of a few old friends of Jameson's. It's close by and since we normally end up playing Monopoly till the sun comes up, I just crash more often than not. You'll be more than welcome to tag along."

"Oh. Yeah? You sure?" Thomas was excited, but didn't know if it was medically advisable to drink alcohol two days in a row.

"Absolutely man, you're gonna love the food too—these ladies can COOK!"

"Yeah dude. It's serious." said Eli over the sound of his clicking keyboard keys. He stopped at the sound of more sobbing from above, and Thomas was glad that he wasn't the only one who had heard it. Eli sighed dramatically. "Goddammit!" he blasted, grabbing a baseball bat which was leaned up against the corner desk and stabbed at the ceiling a few times with it. Thomas didn't understand the sudden, violent batting practice and gave Eli a moment to breathe and sit back down.

"I had been meaning to ask that, what exactly—" began Thomas cautiously, but he stopped cold at the sound of a door just outside theirs opening and closing. The individual who had come from that door pushed theirs open. Cleo was standing in the frame.

"Well, well. If it isn't Mr. Jones!" she said, though it looked like her pillowy lips hadn't moved. In contrast to the last time he had seen her she was wearing a gray tank top and sweatpants. Her hair was up and the faintest sheen of sweat painted her collarbones and brow the color of glass. "Providing salvation to the many, I see?"

It took Thomas a few moments to close his jaw, blink, and comprehend what she had said. He answered like a six-year-old who had been asked if he had eaten all his peas.

"Yup!"

"Gooood," she said without the slightest hint that she had noticed that Thomas had regressed thirty years at the sight of her, "I'm glad to hear you're getting on well." She turned to Eli, "And for you my be-dazzled friend, I wonder if you would at all mind not interrupting us. We've got quite a lot going on right now and we have to stop every time you smash your little stick into my floors." Eli still hadn't turned around to acknowledge her and was clacking away absently. He let her stew for a moment before answering.

"Yeah."

"Wooonderful. Just wonderful... Michael." She nodded to Mike. "Mr. Jones..." she looked at Thomas, smiled and closed the door with nary a whisper of wood shuffling wood.

"Hmmmm. Trying to get on that eh?" said Mike looking at Thomas, whose eyes were still fixed on the closed door.

"Oh, of course not. She does, work—here—then?"

"This week she does," offered Eli.

"Her actual position is in the main office, but Jameson has

had some issues with the operations upstairs, and she has been asked to oversee it until he returns from his trip."

"And what goes on up there—I had been meaning to—"

"I'll tell you now man, stay away from that bitch. She's trouble. Fucking…" Eli was spitting and clacking at the keyboard with such ferocity that Thomas was surprised Eli hadn't put a finger through the thing. He looked at Mike for an explanation. The ponytailed one simply shook his head and mouthed the words *DON'T ASK*.

"So what *does* go on upstairs?" Thomas asked, changing the subject.

"Porn" both men said together.

"Huh? She a—a—porn star?!"

Mike and Eli answered that question very differently. Mike said "God no!" and Eli said "probably." Mike shook his head again.

"No, she is not a porn star. The porn industry was one of Jameson's first business ventures. Porn makes more money every year than all four major American sports combined, so it is definitely a lucrative business, it's just a very small part of what Jameson does now. I think he keeps the operation for old time's sake. He started his porn company in high school."

"Jesus!"

"Yeah, I know. I suppose he was popular with the ladies. Anyway apparently the um—actresses—have been getting a little out of control, and Cleo is here to get them under control."

"She's the right choice to teach a bunch of whores."

313

"Oh Eli, cut the shit," said Mike quickly.

"Whatever, man."

When the sun was just nuzzling its blazing head down for the night and a phantom moon was materializing from the dusk and musk of mid-evening, Thomas, Mike, and Eli left God's Demand together in a cab.

"Who else is coming to dinner?" asked the new guy.

"Everyone I suppose. Pablo and Paco are in the city. I suppose Pedro and Melvin will be staying in Jersey case that Drahtman guy shows up. Us three. Cleo most likely. The lady whose house we are going to's daughter works at God's Demand. She was working one of the frying pans, I suppose she'll be there."

"And where does this lady live?"

"Close, and it's actually two ladies. Sisters."

"Oh that's nice."

"Yeah, you've also met their mother: Beulah."

"Oh really?" Beulah had scared the scrotum off of Thomas so he was hoping Beulah's daughters would be a bit less imposing.

"Yeah, Jameson has known the family for many years. I think he's known Beulah since he was a kid."

"Do these sisters work for Keepwater?"

"I don't very well know. I don't pretend to know everything that guy does. What I do know—is that Miss Marie and Miss Susan make a mean gumbo."

"What's gumbo?

<u>25</u>

David Drahtman and Bobby Collins would have torn
through traffic in the pink Hummer, running over man, woman,
and child to get the details on what in the world had happened to
Alastor Shank. They would have turned the Jersey Turnpike into
a Monster Truck Rally, would have literally driven over a road
made of newborn babies and kittens to get there faster. However,
there was one thing the two men could do nothing about: traffic.

It took hours to reach, and then cross, the bridge. It was
uncharacteristic for a Saturday, but apparently there was a jumper
on the George Washington and he was being difficult in making a
decision. If he were close enough, David would have pushed him
off and honked twice for good luck.

Sitting in traffic, the two men considered what possibly
could have happened. They knew well that Shank had a slew of
mistresses and girlfriends…perhaps it was his wife in a jealous
rage. Shank was certainly not going to win a popularity contest in
the business world; maybe his vicious handling of business, and
ruthless attitude towards his competition had earned him a
bloody end. Even still, what if one of the many little people

Shank had smashed under his toe in his many years at Ohmco had finally snapped under the weight of undeserved impoverishment and shot him dead on his way to lunch one day. Prewitt wouldn't say much, only that Shank was dead and it was by no means natural.

One thing that they were sure of was that Shank would have a will written out and that someone had just become very, very, very, very, very, very, very rich.

When they had finally managed to maneuver themselves into their building, crawl through an elevator shaft and finally tear through the office door of their direct superior, they found Prewitt behind his desk, being fed pudding by a nurse whom David was familiar with only by breasts the size of ottomans. Prewitt was in a wheelchair, still wearing a hospital gown, and looking no better than he had a day earlier. Remarkably, he looked a good sight better than David and Bobby, both of whom had gone without food, soap, or a decent night's sleep. Their hair was crusty and pointing in every nautical direction and their clothes stunk of rat-sex. Still Prewitt looked better than both of them, as well as—no doubt—Alastor Shank.

"Mr. Prewitt!" they exclaimed in tandem after bursting, knockless, through the door, much to their employer's surprise. He spat rice pudding across his desk like a hail-storm of snot-rockets.

"Gentlemen! I should at least expect the courtesy of a knock!" spat Prewitt with drippy lips. The nurse was so shocked that her cinder-block boobies were still trembling at the sight of them.

"Uh—"

"Sir, we apologize, but—forgive us for being so shocked—but…what in the world happened?"

"The details—Mr. Drahtman—are a matter for the police. Needless to say, the founder and chairman of this company was found dead in his home yesterday morning, brutally murdered."

"He was murdered?! You're sure?"

"Unless you think Alastor Shank was capable of grossly mutilating his own body—yes, I am quite sure."

"Mutilating?"

"Again…these are details for law enforcement to consider. We—as in the three of us—have more pressing issues to attend to." He finished by turning a porridge-puddled face up at the barrel-chested nurse. She took the meaning of this correctly and tottered from the office.

"Mr. Shank was found yesterday morning. His funeral will be tomorrow, and following that event will be the reading of his will. As you are all well aware, Mr. Shank was childless." Both men nodded.

"Hence, his will shall be quite the matter of contention. The man was a multi-billionaire. His wife, whom he certainly wasn't a great fan of, will no doubt be given consideration regardless. However, I would be remiss if I thought the two of you were of the belief that she would be receiving the gross total of his sums." David and Collins were still nodding like bobblehead day at Yankee Stadium.

"I think it is safe to say that that the weasel Battlefax will stand to gain from this as well."

"So it's true they are related?" asked David.

"It is. Somers's parents were killed in a fire when he was a child and Shank's wife Marjorie—at the time his only known relative—took the boy in. Shank, to my understanding, was not at all pleased with the arrangement. You see, Marjorie Watershed-Shank is a powerful, domineering woman and was wont to have her way. I wouldn't be surprised to learn she forced the boy on Shank for his employment."

"Fucking little bastard," remarked Collins like a professor of comparative literature.

"Indeed, Mr. Collins, indeed. The problem for us is two-fold. Firstly, young Mr. Battlefax was no doubt aware of the arrangement for the three of us to handle the situation with Mr. Melendez. If that rodent of a man does take over the operation of the business than I would be shocked if his first actions weren't to investigate our progress in the matter. I know for a fact that the young man strongly dislikes me personally, and as for you two—I think it's safe to say he's no great fan of either of yours."

"Huh? Why—what's he got against me?" stammered Collins, clearly insulted.

"Oh I am sure it is nothing personal, but you are both high-ranking employees and clearly better qualified to run this enterprise than he is. He will see you as threats."

"Prick."

"Indeed…indeed. So I need you both to focus your efforts on that restaurant. You mustn't fail to pry the goods from Mr. Melendez. If you fail, we are all doomed."

"And what's the second problem?"

"The second…problem…is not so much a problem as it is a fall-back plan. In the event that things do not go as planned and we are, for whatever reason, without financial security—I have recently come upon some news which may provide us an opportunity to remain comfortable from a fiscal sense." At this his pale, sickly pupils darted around in eyeballs the color of putty, as if checking his surrounding for spies and terrorists. He leaned over the desk and said, a bit softer, "Wetra International is going public…"

"Huh?" said Collins. David looked at him like he was a donkey with a suit on.

"Where did you hear this?"

"I have my sources, Mr. Drahtman. Suffice it to say the initial offers are going to be absolutely tremendous. Fortunately for us, not many know about this at the moment. What I am suggesting, gentlemen, is that three of us combine our efforts and make an enormous offer for the business. Something in the arena of a half of a billion dollars. We would be grabbing a stranglehold of control on their business and ensuring our security in the event that something goes wrong with Melendez *or* the reading of the will."

"That's a lot of fucking money," offered Collins.

"It's money that you have, and trust me I've checked. The three of us have the money; there is no safer place for our funds than in an immensely sound holding company like Wetra."

"What does Wetra even control?"

"Well, no one knows the exact figures because they've been private for so long—" began David, drool pooling in the pits of lips at the very topic of being a controlling partner in Wetra.

"The Chairman and Founder, a man by the name of O'Brien, can quite easily move funds and money around at will, but the general consensus among industry insiders are natural gas, securities and interests in agriculture, mining, and capital finance. The company is perfect, gentlemen, and I suggest we move quickly to pool these funds."

"I agree." said David instantly.

"But we're not buying the whole business?" stuttered a still undecided Bobby Collins. Both of the other two men in the room laughed, David a bit louder than Alexander.

"No—asshole," spat David with indignation, "they're not got sell the whole thing, obviously. Something like forty-nine percent, so they still have control and central powers. Besides, the company should be worth hundreds of billions of dollars, the three of us can't afford it. "

"But a half billion is—"

"Great because it's gonna be more than almost any one group will be able to grab. We'll have a vote on everything that a stockholder can exert control over. It's a brilliant plan Collins...I encourage you to get on board." David sold Collins—a lady in a pair of white, silk gloves—a turd Popsicle.

"Oh I dunno guys, that's a LOT of fucking money. That's everything for me."

"Same here," snapped David quickly.

"Fine."

"Let's do it," said David putting his right hand, palm turned down out between the two of them. Collin's cold, clammy palm cupped David's, which was topped by the trembly, liver-spotted chicken's foot of Alexander Prewitt.

Prewitt, Drahtman & Collins was born

<u>26</u>

"WHO YOU!?" bellowed the channeled spirit of Thor and Jupiter in the form of the frail, rickety hobble horse that was Beulah. Ancient in every regard, she batted eyelashes like long white whiskers—awaiting a response from Thomas, who was standing before Mike with an open mouth that spoke no words.

"Uhhhhhhhmmmm…"

"Beulah, this is Thomas Jones—you met him earli—"

"OH FOW DA DAWGS?! YES! YES!" she turned, apparently satisfied by the results of her investigation, directly in the arms of the biggest, blackest woman Thomas had ever seen. She straightened out her mother and arranged her in a dining room table's head and ran up to the two men with a big, face-swallowing grin.

"Come in dearies, come in!" she said, swiping at a small yellow-haired cat with her foot and a mutter, "I heard we had a new boy, huh?" she said to Mike while planting a big purple kiss on his cheek before pulling Thomas into her arms. "My name is

Miss Marie…Welcome! Welcome! Come in—come in…" She kissed him and then led him into the living room of a decent-sized apartment in Brooklyn.

The living room smelled of sweet old ladies and hot food. Miss Marie was wearing a purple blouse and skirt and big purple slippers with dachshunds for heads. From a kitchen the men could hear the sounds of a running faucet, and clinking of glasses. A larger replica of the dachshunds on the end of Miss Marie's feet came scampering into the room and immediately began hopping up on Thomas's leg. He smiled politely.

"Get off him Fritzy, get off him! Shoo! Shoo, silly dog." The dog gave a half-hearted whimper and then sat at attention besides his owner's thick ankles, tongue out, tail wagging.

She invited Mike, Thomas and Eli to sit on a big, squashy, flower-print sofa. She waddled off for a moment after holding up a finger (to let them know she was leaving) and returned with three glasses of pink lemonade on a tray.

"Hot! Yeah?"

All three men gave her various responses that all meant they agreed that the city was stifling in this time of year. No sooner had she parallel parked her caboose in a small, matching loveseat than the doorbell rang. Just as Miss Marie left towards the door (offering them a finger once again), her sister burst through a cloud of steam at the kitchen's opening. She was wearing a large red apron with a picture of a tabby cat on it and two oven-mitts which she was using to move steam away from her face. When the clouds cleared Thomas saw a quizzical look on her big brown face as she looked straight at him.

"Who's he?" she asked Mike

"Oh this is Thomas, the new guy…Thomas, this is Miss Susan." Thomas stood as if to go shake her hand.

"Stay set mister, I ain't got time for huggin' and kissin', there's cooking to be done now." She turned and shuffled her way back into the steamy kitchen, yelling into it, "Etta, get your behind down here and help with the bird dammit!"

"Etta's Susan's eldest daughter," Eli whispered to Thomas.

Thomas felt someone sit on the armrest besides him. When he turned Cleo was sitting beside him looking down with eyes the color of the earth. She had one hand on his shoulder and he immediately put a throw pillow over his erect member. She was still wearing the same get-up she had been earlier and her right nipple was eye-level to Thomas. She smiled to greet him without words before calling to Miss Susan and asking if she needed help. She did. When Cleo passed him there were two figures behind her, Pablo and Paco, who smiled and waved at Thomas. Pablo clearly felt better than he did earlier.

Thomas quickly found out what gumbo was. If you counted Marie's cat Fritzgerald and Susan's cat Hamhock there were thirteen of them scrunched up and squashed together around the dining table. Both pets sat at the feet of their owner awaiting the obligatory table scrap

In clockwise order Beulah at one head of the table, Pablo, Paco, Thomas, Mike, Eli, Marie (at the foot), Susan, Etta, Freddy

(Etta's son and grandson of Susan) and Cleo sat and broke bread. As Thomas would later know to be the norm, Beulah led a raucous prayer that those non-believers in the room kindly abstained from.

Gumbo, a traditional dish in the Southeastern United States, most notably and famously in Louisiana, is a thick stew composed often of poultry, sausage and local seafood, accompanied by the traditional *mirepoix* of bell pepper, onion, and celery, thickened in a variety of ways—but most popularly, as it was this evening, by that gelatinous cucumber—okra. It is typically served on white rice which was the only thing that looked familiar in his bowl to Thomas. Where Miss Marie and Miss Susan come from the dish is also made hot enough to "sear the seat off a sasquatch," Mike whispered in his left ear. He also said Marie had confided in him that she was convinced that her mother made her gumbo hotter and hotter as she moved into her eighties and nineties—when her tongue was about as useful for tasting food as a computer keyboard.

"AHHHH," Beulah sighed heavily after a first messy spoonful, like John Bunyan sitting down to supper after a long day riding his forty-ton blue ox. Her whole body was jittering with the effort and Thomas thought the weight of each spoonful might dislocate her shoulders.

Thomas—who was probably the only one who hadn't eaten at all that day—set himself to digging into his first gumbo. Thomas's Irish and English background did not give him the mouth for this cuisine, and he was none accustomed to the not-so-subtle use of the chiles and what tasted like straight-up supermarket hot sauce. Eating baked beans for breakfast and pickled eggs for lunch does this to a gene pool.

His face turned the color of a cherry snow-cone and he started sweating like one that had been left out on a sidewalk in New Delhi. Cleo, sitting diagonally across from Thomas, laughed with a mouthful of andouille and crayfish. He thought he heard Eli sigh, but then convinced himself it was just the sound of Marie blowing on her forkful at the head of the table. While everyone seemed to be enjoying it, no one did more than Pablo and Paco—whose own genetic taste evolution had provided them with tongues of stainless steel. They washed down the soup with cold beer from clear bottles and smiled widely between bites. Beulah was egging them on.

"YEAH! S'GOOD! YESSIR!" she pounded the table in approval of their gusto.

They exchanged stories, one of which included Mike showing everyone the picture of Thomas being sexually molested in a photo booth by a tractor-trailer dressed up as a young female. Everyone thought this was hilarious, and since Thomas's face wasn't getting redder unless he found a Cherokee uncle on his family tree thanks to Beulah's hot sauce, he didn't even blush. It could be said he laughed a bit inside, despite being on the whole mortified by the experience.

Susan's eldest daughter, a beautiful late twenty-something, with skin the color and smell of coconut bark, fidgeted with her own child. About seven years old, Freddy was a mover and a shaker. Even more so than his great-grandmother, who kept taking swings at him with a second spoon she was holding for some reason in her right hand. He didn't want to sit at the table and kept insisting he desperately needed to attend to pressing issues related to national seven-year-old security on his Xbox. Neither she, nor any of the strong females that surrounded him, were having any of it, however—and kept putting food on his plate and insisting he hadn't taken a bite.

Despite Eli's anti-Christ superstar personality, he was getting along quite well with the Southern Baptist to his right, Miss Susan. The two were discussing cornbread recipes while taking turns giving greasy pieces of fish to her greedy little feline, Hamhock. The cat was pretty enormous, much like her owner.

At one point Thomas almost choked to death when he thought he felt a foot brush the inside of his leg. Cleo wasn't paying any attention to him as she was in an animate discussion with Beulah about her incredible eyewear ("DON' NEEDEM! EYES FINE!"). But since the only other people that could've done it without a go-go gadget leg were Etta (and her seven-year old son), Thomas ignored it and shoveled a mighty forkful of rice, sausage, and brown broth. He got used to the heat after a while and really began to take to it. Thomas was deeply impressed with himself.

Eventually, after a long meal, quite a number of frosty bottles of Mexican beer (Marie kept it here for the seven sons of Consuela Peligro) and a bottle and a half of red-wine—properly iced—for Thomas and Cleo, Eli stood and excused himself to the bathroom rubbing his hand over his distended stomach and belching. While Beulah and her daughters certainly harbored no ill will towards Elijah, they were certainly more suspect of him than any of the others on account of his be-pierced and oft-tattooed exterior. Beulah hardly waited for him to turn the corner.

"BOY SMASH 'IS HEAD INNA TOO'SHED?" she always acted like it was the first time she had seen the man.

"Mama!"

"GOTS EARS LIKEA HOUND!" she shook her head disapprovingly.

"Shhh, woman, he's a sweet boy, he'll grow out of it," Marie whispered heavily. Beulah looked down at her great-grandson and shook her second spoon in his face, splashing gravy on his face and then waved it towards the bathroom.

"NONE O' THAT? Y'HEAR? NU-UH!"

"Yes gray-gamma." the boy was absolutely mystified by Beulah. Like she was a creature from outer-space. He stared at her momentarily and her eyes, blinder than Braille's—met his.

He woke not long after from this trance and, noticing his mother was now leaned over in conversation with Mike about Freddy's schooling, leapt from his seat, and bolted away under the table, right through Thomas and Michael's chair.

After Freddy was in bed (or at the very under least his covers and playing with his PSP) and the table cleared, the adults sat about for a while chatting aimlessly over coffee. Eli, Cleo, Mike, and Thomas played Monopoly. Thomas was running away with the game and had just purchased his fourth railroad when the phone rang and Miss Marie announced from the receiver's caller ID that it was Jameson. She sounded pleased to hear from him.

The conversation seemed unimportant as Marie's end of it sounded like little more than a string of "Yes dear"s and "of course, Love."s

While they spoke Eli rolled an eight, landed on North Carolina Avenue and had to stay at Cleo's hotel, a steep $1275 a night. This cleaned him out entirely and he took his beer and left the table.

Both Cleo and Thomas made quick work of Mike until he was left with Baltic Avenue and Water Works. By one in the morning, when no one was left in the room but those who were playing the game and Mike who was watching it, re-filling a shot glass with Jagermeister continuously, Cleo had bought and sold Thomas on a stupid trade which cost him control of the pivotal orange-red corner of death. Mike's protestations had to be shushed by Cleo who thumbed over her shoulder to two sleeping Mexicans sharing a sofa-bed while re-filling Thomas and her glass. She even went and got the ice once.

Eventually Mike fell asleep in his seat and Thomas gave up at two-thirty.
Thomas took his place on a blanket on the floor and politely offered the small loveseat to Cleo. He was on the floor, just getting comfortable when Cleo rolled on top of him and put her tongue in his mouth.

Our hero was no Casanova, we are sure, so after first fighting back the sounds of exploding neurons in his brain, he composed himself and got his hands around Cleo's smooth, braless spine. They rolled around, madly swishing tongues darkened by red wine in each other's cheeks. It was no small miracle that Thomas did not ejaculate the very instant she wrapped her long fingers around his member.

What followed was the sort of awkward, messy, drunken herky-jerky hand-job that always seems far sexier when you've drunk a box-full of crappy wine. She wiped her hands on his chest and fell asleep in his neck; her thick, un-coiled hair draped across his face. It smelled like everything he had ever wanted anything to smell like.

She was so unconscious that she wasn't awakened when Thomas sprouted a second, immediate erection twenty seconds after his first ejaculation. It kinda nudged her in the stomach for a minute or two suggestively, but alas—to no avail—and then gave up.

Sometime around sunrise, as the first chirping birds were yawning and stretching their beaks wide in the dewy morning air, Thomas had to use the bathroom. He grudgingly eased Cleo to the pillow beside him and got off the floor.

The bathroom was fluffy and primpy and embroidered with clashing kitty-kats and canines. The toilet-seat cover had a great black cat on it as Thomas lifted it, considering what sort of argument ensued over that prime real estate between the two sisters. The shower-curtains as least were a gaggle of dancing dachshunds.

In the few other times in his life when he had pulled something so miraculous as his tryst with Cleo, Thomas always had a strange practice of congratulating his penis. A sort of hunched over pep-talk when Thomas gave his penis head his highest praise and when his penis head agreed Thomas would nod his head for him. "Did you know how sexy you are?!" he would say…and then in response his penis would nod vigorously. Thomas continued this tradition before pointing him downwards to take care of business.

When Thomas looked up at the wall behind the toilet, he saw the strangest thing he had ever seen in his life: a small brass frame held within it the portrait of a ruddy, chubby white man with a great walrus-like moustache who was holding a polished red apple in his left hand. He looked pretty damned familiar.

Thomas Jones had found a painting of his great-great-great grandfather in the home of two black grandmothers from Brooklyn.

27

David awoke early on Sunday morning to prepare for the
wake and subsequent reading of the will at the offices of Ohmco.
His wife had been wearing black since she had found out about
the dog and this did not exclude her pajamas. She looked like a
sleeping ninja when David left her in bed.

Drahtman would also be wearing black that day, for
entirely different reasons. The wake service was at St. Patrick's
Cathedral: an absolutely royal locale for the reposition of a
corpse, befitting the defenestrated remains of Charles V. Strange
it was for this reason that a man without a monarchy would
receive this treatment. Especially a notoriously vicious and
loveless human being like Alastor Shank.

Under the impression that he would be able to escape his
house and family by leaving so early—and also stand to plant his
flag in a better spot on line to drool over his mutilated husk at the
church, David crept downstairs in all black. He had his shoes in
each hand so as to be more silent going down the stairs on sock-

foot.

He was quickly disappointed that he would not be leaving
unnoticed. Halfway down the first landing he could hear the
snapping and popping of paint-bull guns. His sons were outside
with them already…at five in the morning.

Of all his family, David despised his sons least. They
never seemed to ask anything of him, and only were a problem
when they were trying to burn down the house, frame their sister
for capital crimes, or otherwise destroy his property. This
morning they had cornered a small bird and shot it to death with
neon-green paintballs. They ran up to their father with it and
showed him proudly. Rubbing each of them on the head, David
passed them and made his way to the Hummer.

In the strictest sense, this "wake" was really more like a
lying-in-state. Whereas most baptized Catholics are viewed in the
humble setting of one's local funeral home, Alastor Shank's deep
involvement with the Roman Catholic Church had earned him a
place of great honor. The church itself was shut down (on a
Sunday) for visitors to come and view the remains. David
thought this was odd when he heard, since from how Prewitt
described it, Shank had been torn apart; "brutally mutilated" was
the way his boss (and new partner) had described it. Seemed a bit
graphic to have an open-casket for a man who had been cut to
pieces.

St. Patrick's was carved out of the clay of the earth by the
finger-nail of the creator. Its inside's intensely detailed surfaces,
etched and lined and scoured with the work of the making of the

universe, looks like an enormous lung. Its exterior is a many spired, neo-gothic monstrosity—a jagged, dramatic, wizard's castle sharing the street with Radio City Music Hall. At its center façade is a colossal, circular rose-window that looked like ten thousand pagan symbols from antiquity. That place pulsed and breathed with magic, mystery, and the breath of God, and was no different that morning than it still is today.

That building, however, had no hold on David Drahtman, who walked directly through its doors—ignoring holy water and leaving genuflection for the pussies.

He had stopped for breakfast on the way to the church, not having eaten for forty-eight terrible hours before. Due to this delay there were already a few people here before him…but not many. He belched up greased, porky air as he made his way to the far right corner of the structure, ignoring the history of the galaxy which was inscribed on the walls and floors around him. There he found Bobby Collins, looking much better than the day before, sitting at the end of a pew.

"Sup Bobby…" he said as he squeezed in beside Collins.

"Oh hey Davey…not too much," Drahtman had never heard Collins so soft-spoken. He very much approved of church-Collins. He considered the odds of him making it through the afternoon without swearing at an inopportune moment: "I'm so very sorry for your fucking loss Mrs. Shank." When Collins went to shake his hand, David held out his fist for a "pound" like they were the starting point guard and power forward in the NBA Finals.

As David sat, Bobby talked, and David ignored—gazing around the room interestedly. The coffin, a sleek black number than looked more like a nuclear submarine than a body-box, stood on the altar, its bisected lid open. David could not see in it for the angle, and the procession to view the body had not begun. Beside the coffin was a great oil painting of Shank, looking very severe in a high-backed, black leather chair, scowling like an angry rhinoceros. He was frightful, even in death. A priest, in deep violet vestments, milled around behind the altar making whatever preparations were necessary.

David could see, sprinkled throughout the front row, other people he knew well. Marjorie Watershed-Shank was plopped into the first pew in all-black, her wiggly little legs hanging off the seat like a ten-year-old girl with the body of Humpty Dumpty. Behind a black veil inlaid with lace baby's breath, her lips moved quickly. She was speaking with someone beside her whom David could not see. Behind Mrs. Shank was her husband's be-siliconed secretary, Marigold Humphries, who looked like she was going to be working on location today shooting a film called *Four Gang Bangs and a Funeral*. She was wrapped tightly from nipple to asshole in a cocoon of what looked like nothing more than tinted Saran-wrap. Several rows behind her he saw Somersworth Battlefax, also in all-black, with big, eye-of-a-dragonfly, black sunglasses. He was flanked by several large men with earpieces who looked like the Secret Service, but were more likely some form of corporate security guards. At the rear of the building David saw something he had

335

definitely expected: cops. Lots of cops. There were uniformed officers and scrappy looking detectives, all no doubt keeping eyes peeled like potatoes for suspicious activity.

While his head was still turned he saw the rotund figures of the company's secretaries, Miss Marie and Miss Susan, making their way through the door. Susan was speaking to Marie with her normal tone of irritability, but Marie was shushing her with a finger, and pulling her along by her arm.

"Surprised they're not wearing stupid fucking cats on their funeral clothes," said David to Collins, cutting him off in the middle of an explanation about the mystery of his wife and the Econo Lodge. Ignoring David's remark, he continued.

"Sooo…I need help moving some shit, you know—to the new house. I gotta be out by Tues—"

"Move what shit? To what house?"

As Collins went to re-explain, Alexander Prewitt rolled up to them on a motorized scooter, coming to a jerking stop and propelling his upper body forward and nearly out of the chair but for a seatbelt his nurse had installed for just this reason. Both men yelped in shock at the sight of a man rolling up like a mechanized jack-in-the-box from the industrial age. People around them turned and cast looks of great offense at the sound to the grown men.

"Mr. Drahtman…Mr. Collins," said Prewitt like there wasn't anything strange about progressing more and more into a robot as the hours progressed. They heard clopping and panting behind them and Mr. Prewitt's garden shed-breasted nurse came galumphing towards them, sweating a storm of salt-water from her portly, dappled brow.

"Wow! Mr. Prewitt, that chair is fucking *awesome*!" hollered Collins. The entire room turned to look at Collins who was still gaping, unaware, at Prewitt like had just seen gravity discovered.

"Indeed Mr. Collins…however…" he turned to his nurse, who was still trying desperately to catch her breath, and hung an eyebrow on his head before stating the obvious, "Virginia, will you please give us a moment?"

"Of course, Mr. Prewitt," she said like she was quite tired of being told to leave the room every five minutes like her parents were discussing S-E-X.

"Virginia?"

"Her name, Mr. Drahtman. Do you expect me to call her by something else?"

"Does it go in reverse?" went Collins.

"It does…Mr. Drahtman, I wonder…" he continued once the nurse Virginia was off admiring a stained-glass window, "if you noticed our young friend Master Battlefax?"

"Yeah, with the bodyguards or whatever."

"Precisely. He seems to believe he may have reason to be worried for his safety at his uncle's funeral services."

"I don't get it though—"

"Nor I, Mr. Drahtman…but it is certainly most interesting…"

After an hour or so of the room filling, slowly, with people who were under the impression they either might meet

337

useful contacts in coming to the wake, or were hoping for a piece of the great golden pizza pie that was to be served at the conclusion of this service, a priest stood.

For less than ten minutes the priest described the wonderful majesty of the afterlife and gave accurate directions to find the road which would lead the seeker there. He also said some apparently sincere words of condolences to a woman who seemed, by her million dollar smile, not to need them, before asking the congregated executives to form a line and pay their last respects to the man named Shank.

Virginia refused to let Prewitt walk up the altar steps without her help so she walked alongside the scooter while he, Collins, and Prewitt waited to reach the coffin. Once Prewitt had reached the steps, his nurse lifted him out of the chair with hands under armpits. He was shook and weak, but he could stand if he had to. Collins, who stood behind Prewitt, took this occasion to get on the scooter and move it out of the way of the rest of the line. With a smile wrapped three times around his head he scooted the machine five yards and got off, looking back at it longingly over his shoulder as he walked back to his place on line.

When Prewitt was placed on his knees in front of the coffin, Drahtman could finally get a decent look at Shank. Besides the pale, pasted-on look of the skin, and the shadowy hollows that were growing ever larger round his eyes and beneath his emerging cheekbones, Alastor Shank looked relatively intact. There certainly was no obvious sign of "brutal mutilation" on his face.

When Prewitt was lifted from the floor, Virginia crossed herself momentarily and guided the wobbly old man back towards his vehicle. Collins followed, openly weeping and sobbing over the body despite, to Drahtman's knowledge, never having so much as been in the same room as Shank before now.

"OHHHH FUCKING HELL BOSS! POOR FUCKING BASTARD! OHHHHH HO HO HO OHHHHHHHHHH." David rubbed his temples as Virginia had run back up the steps and was now dragging Collins from the coffin, prising his fingers from the lip of the coffin, not unlike the way she just transported the stroke-addled body of Alexander Prewitt.

Drahtman fell to his knees. It made him feel vulnerable and uncomfortable and most of all…weak. The stench of embalming fluid and a slowly drying piece of person filled his mouth and throat. David put his right hand over his mouth and tried to avoid retching. Breathing from a small pocket of air in his cupped hand, David tried to look sincere. Perhaps not so sincere as Collins did—but…still sincere.

Looking still for any sign of what might have happened to Shank, David took notice of his hands. They too were in perfect condition for a pair of hands that belonged to a dead human being. The nails were long and gray and he wore no rings. Surely Marjorie didn't want to bury anything good with the old dog. After another few seconds, David could no longer handle the stink and got up, crossed himself backwards and walked off the altar.

As he tried his best to not look like he knew who the

openly weeping man was next to him, David watched the procession at the altar and tried to listen to the conversation burbling all around him, while blocking out the honking spit and slobber of Bobby Collins blowing his leaking nose into a Kleenex the nurse Virginia had pulled from her purse.

He noticed the two security guards who had come with Battlefax standing around, perfectly erect, before the coffin. He took this to mean that Somers himself was at the front of the line. This held up the line significantly, and David noticed the whispers of growing impatience spreading in the crowd. Finally, the two large men in dark suits walked off the altar. In a creepy and altogether unsettling way, they walked in a fashion that occluded Somers. Like he wasn't even there, invisible behind a wall of black-suited muscle. David only got a look at the side of his pale, tightly-drawn head and white-blonde hair again when he was in a pew, parallel to him. His eyes were shut, but not with the calm of prayer. His eyelids were folded and tense, scrunched and squeezed. His lips were thin and colorless and the veins in his snow-white hands were like iron cords keeping the whole thing together. Tight, straight, and stiff as bone.

David watched the rest of the room make their way to Shank's body. Miss Marie and Miss Susan knelt for a minute beside one another. Marigold Humphries took her time and seemed truly shaken by the affair, as did the four or five local cops who were next in line, enjoying the show as she leaned over the coffin and kissed Shank's mottled brow. Her entire vagina hung like a half-pound of roast beef from between her thin thighs and plastic dress. The holy water in its tin basins boiled at the smell of pussy in the house of God.

It was still another pair of long, Christian hours before the church-face had emptied itself of all the poison she had held that morning. Prewitt, Drahtman, and Collins took the same town car (Prewitt's rental with a lift for his scooter) back to the offices of Ohmco. The reading of the will was to take place in Shank's office as the sun began to slowly set itself at odds with mid-afternoon.

Not unlike his waking, Shank's second service of the day was a collection of high-browed hopefuls standing in line for a handful of Shank's horded gold. Rather than routed rows of ancient wood, the cavernous, glass-capped expanse was spaced and columned by tin-metal folding chairs, each holding a dream of unwelcomed inheritance. Each, the locus of a dream deferred—or even still—one many times realized. One fulfilled on the strength of worthiness divine.

The room, which David had only this week occupied for the purpose of impressing himself upon the late chairman, was transformed for the occasion. The mini-golf course and the hot dog carts were gone, replaced by a cordoned wrestler's ring of black velvet—strung betwixt stainless steel poles—which, when reflecting the dressing of those in attendance—were blacker than the velvet—the night—and the very center of the heart of Alastor Shank. The room was composed of shadow.

Alexander Prewitt was certainly no spring chicken. In fact, he was no chicken at all; he was a very, very old monkey.

And in his many, many monkey years he had seen altogether too many of these "readings." While Collins mingled and mourned his way through the room, Prewitt gave Drahtman the details on what to expect from the execution of one's will.

According to his superior, David learned that what would follow was that a lawyer, most likely a counselor whom Shank was familiar with in his lifetime, would take center stage behind Shank's twenty-ton slab of marble desktop. The man (or woman for that matter) would unseal what would no doubt be a very large envelope—and read its entire contents. Prewitt told David that you could get a feel for a man's promises to the afterlife by the thickness of his last testament on this earth. Something more like a phonebook would no doubt mean the departed had a distinct opinion on the final resting place of each one of his possessions. The thicker the man's package, the more precise his ideas were in regards to the rightful home for each element of his life's work.

It was therefore most unsettling for all in attendance when Shank's lifetime attorney, a wide-bodied man with a hair-piece so ridiculous that it could have lived undetected as a squirrel if it was so inclined—pulled the hinged lid on a safe-deposit box and removed nothing more than a single letter-sized envelope. David's eyes widened, his pupils gorged on the fat of excess photons…saw *through* the envelope. It was, at best, a single sheet of paper.

David, ever the detective, scanned the room for a response. The first thing he noticed was that his was not the only head pivoting on its neck at potentially dangerous speed. In the room's rear row were the only two police officers who had managed to get passed security and into the reading of the will. One was wearing a tweed jacket and a hairline that seemed to be running in fear from some follicle-eating monster of the underworld. The other was bronzer than a medal, and had a long black pony-tail slicker and sleeker than spun sunshine dipped in crude oil. It glowed and consumed light in the same breath. Both men were scribbling notes on small, coil-wired pads and whispering to one another cautiously.

Suddenly, both men's eyes became fixed on the same spot, and both of their jaws slackened and loosed. David followed the invisible laser-line to the top of Marjorie Watershed-Shank's brillo-pad head, which just now had peaked over the rows behind her. She was standing—her over-filled water balloon was quite unsettled by something and leaking on the floors and windows. Drahtman heard a chuckle of utter nonchalance, and then her grayed, tightly-woven head disappeared amongst those behind her.

David thought he saw the side of Battlefax's face, chewing at his cheek-flesh like bubble-gum made of blood… but it instantly vanished behind an immense black shoulder; strung with transparent telephone wire traversing a woolen trunk to an ear-bud in off-white.

"Okay, ladies and gents, for those of you who don't know me, my name is Charlie Castleford and I was fortunate enough to know Alastor for much of my adult life. I also was blessed to have served as his attorney for the better part of the last four decades and so the task of the reading of the will has fallen to me. Before I read from what is a truly brief document I would like to give me condolences to Marjorie, who has—"

"GET ON WITH IT, CHARLES." The words burst in a ball of fire from behind the veil. Her face was shaking to force her lips into a curl. One could almost hear teeth sink through her tongue.

Flustered, but not surprised, Charlie went on. "Uh—yes—yes ma'am…" The attorney held the thin envelope in one hand and with the other used a brass blade to cleave glue from paper. The room was silent like a time before time. The shifting sift of paper on paper. The crispy de-creasing sheathed the air with its dry mouths and bright white light. Castleford adjusted a pair of spectacles over his pale hazel eyes, cleared his throat in his hand and spoke slowly.

It was fortunate that he spoke so carefully and slowly, for the document was lines long:

"I, Alastor Alabaster Shank, do hereby bequeath my estate as follows:
To my wife, Marjorie Watershed-Shank" at this his wife held back her veil so that the whole of the room could see her piggy features sweat out the wait of a sentence, "I leave my boat, the *S.S Empyrean*, so that she may sail out to sea at her earliest convenience. The remainder of my worldly assets, interests, and possessions are hereby bequeathed to my nephew, Somersworth Omicron Battlefax. May he ever look after the things I have made

344

in my life and may long his own life last into the many, many futures…." he paused and his eyes flicked to something on the bottom of the page that David could see was written by hand in three lines. It looked, bestill his black heart; like a poem. Marjorie was standing, mouth open, piggish fists clenched and trembling at her side, "And here at the bottom—I haven't the foggiest what this means but I assume he wanted this read, It says:

Summer comes much veiled
Relish anew, infinite as madness
Youth bore under raking feasts
As others hunger
We've reaped.

"I am certainly not one for poetry – but that certainly was an interesting little ditty if you ask me! Anyway—that's all so if you—"

In one flurry of motion, Battlefax stood and instantaneously vanished amidst his guard while Mrs. Shank threw a white corsage and her veiled, black hat to the floor and began cursing her husband's name and jumping up and down, stamping the floor to death with tiny black spikes. The phalanx of black guards swept from the room, presumably containing the new Chairman of Ohmco, and Mrs. Shank fell to her hammy knees and screamed his name in rage.

David Drahtman and Bobby Collins walked while Alexander Prewitt rolled from the room and into an elevator where, due to the space Prewitt took up in his chair, they were left on their own.

"Well, that was fucking insane," started Bobby.

"Indeed it was Mr. Collins, and I believe that things are due to change in due course. Mr. Drahtman, if I am not mistaken the Melendez family will be returning in two days' time. This means that tomorrow—"

"I'm gonna call the inspector back and follow the plan."

"Precisely. If we lose the restaurant, I can assure you we will each be exterminated from this company by nightfall. It is safe to assume that Chairman Battlefax will be keeping an eye on the situation and waiting for the slightest hiccup in our plans."

"What a fucking asshole that little prick is"

"Yeah, but it's cool—we've still got Wetra in our back pocket if something goes wrong."

"Mr. Drahtman! Do not assume that we can simply afford to play games with the Melendez situation. We stand to benefit wildly from Wetra, but it is nothing more than a back-up plan. Our jobs and our futures depend on Ohmco, not Wetra!"

"Okay! Relax, Mr. Prewitt or you'll have a fifth stroke."

"A fifth?" spluttered Bobby.

"I am QUITE relaxed Mr. Drahtman! Just do your job and all will be well."

"Yeah, all right. Just calm down."

They exited the elevator, two walking—one puttering—and returned to their respective offices. Bobby Collins called a moving service. Alexander Prewitt called his nurse. David

Drahtman called Safety Inspector Shudenbacker of the New York State Department of Health.

28

Hours before, Thomas was wakened by the bathwater-speckled, towel-shackled body of Cleo standing over him, looking down with smiling eyes, a steady bead of water raining on his face from her long, wet, locks. He was clutching the framed portrait of his ancestor although Cleo didn't seem to notice as she kicked him in his side with one bare foot and made her way to the kitchen.

When Miss Marie and Miss Susan had entered the living room early the morning after Thomas had his crank yanked by the most beautiful woman he had ever seen—they were both wearing all black and looked like they were going to a funeral (which, incidentally, they were). Marie turned off into the hall closet and Susan came hurtling up to Thomas.

"Say—boy! You seen the picture from over the toilet?" said Susan, clearly perturbed that some form of gnome that feeds on picture frames had stole off into the night with her priceless possessions (which she kept above an appliance which housed the collective poop of the family). Thomas was watching Cleo's toweled behind wiggle as she rummaged through the refrigerator and so was ill-prepared to hide the frame which was sitting on his lap. Susan saw it, waddled to him and snatched it from his crotch. "Hey! What do you think you're doing boy! New guy thinks he's gonna take my things and not tell me first? No sir!" she then caught sight of the half-dressed Cleo in her refrigerator, "AND YOU! PUT SOME CLOTHES ON DAMNIT!"

"Oh—I'm sorry Miss Susan—but it's so strange. You see, that man in the portrait—do you know him?"

"That *man?* That man is a saint. And his name is Frederick Terwilliger Jones. And *why* his portrait is over my toilet is none of your business."

"Yes—see that's what I mean. That man is my great-great-great grandfather, and I just don't get how you came to have a copy of that portrait. The same one hung in my house as a child—"

"WHAT?" Susan bellowed. Marie came running—as fast as her wide-bodied frame could take her—into the room with three coats on each arm, clearly alarmed.

"Whatever is the matter Susan—hollering at this hour?" it took Miss Susan a full minute to close her mouth and then re-open it with the intention of forming a sentence.
"He," she started, pointing at Thomas, who was standing now in his stained boxers and covering a thunderous morning erection with a throw-pillow that had a kitten with a pink bow in its hair on it, "He—is a Jones."

"'Course he is, Miss Susan, now that's a name that plenty people got, not just you and I."

"Your name is Jones, too?" asked Thomas, completely bewildered by the entire situation.

"No—Marie…he is *the* Jones. Frederick's great-great-great grandson."

Marie dropped six coats to the floor and her jaw nearly beat them there.

Dr. Clarke Carter woke early on the morning of August 5 in the Wildwood home of Thomas Jones. Today was the day.

He hadn't slept well at all. In fact, he hadn't slept well since Mike left with all his weed. Carter had taken it on himself to try and find some more, but eighty-year-olds don't necessarily find locating illegal narcotics to be an easy task. The average teenagers assumed he was a cop and told him to suck their dicks. It was getting desperate for Dr. Carter, but thankfully— there was one thing which calmed all else: today was the day.

Carter put Jones's mother's immense red plastic frames on and walked barefoot to the kitchen where he poured himself a glass of orange juice. He had taken to wearing Thomas's pajamas, which were too short for him and looked like Capri pants on the elderly, white-haired doctor. He was quite a sight that morning. But after nearly fifty years, his waiting was nearly over. In a few hours the machine would shut itself off and there would be nearly a trillion dollars in diamonds under the lid.

Not wanting to take any chances, the doctor spent the remainder of the morning sitting by the machine in a lawn chair, reading the paper, drinking orange juice—which made him think of vodka. Which made his mouth water extensively. He was, however, able to calm himself with reminders that there were more important and pressing issues on this most glorious of days.

He checked his watch far too frequently. He finished the crossword on a nine-letter word for a spineless aquatic animal (jellyfish) and finished Thomas's orange juice before having to walk to the corner convenience store for antacid to ease the searing pain in his esophagus which had been gouged by the river of acid that is a half-gallon of orange juice. At the very least he was getting his vitamin C intake for the week before noon.

Jameson Moxy said goodbye to a small group of people, closed the door to his helicopter and instructed the pilot to take-off. It was a short trip from Queens to Thistlestick River, where he was going to check in on the "Technical College." It had been a long, long day for Moxy, who had been in the chopper since before the sun had risen that morning.

The trip from Mexico was long and painful. His ass-cheeks felt like they would be sore for a month and a half after the abuse of a six-hour helicopter flight. He also couldn't hear very well at all due to the punchy, rattling sound of the propellers.

It was, however, a necessary trip—both financially and morally. There was simply no way to do what they had needed to do in the States.

Beside him, Jonathan stared out the window and down below to the disappearing park where they had landed the chopper to drop off their partners, a family of three. They were both in desperate need of hot food and a cold shower, but that would have to wait. Today…after all, was the day.

Before the sun set today, Jameson Moxy would be a trillionaire, and everyone who worked for him would be immensely wealthy as well. Jonathan had asked Jameson not to give him any of it. He had enough money and Jameson had always been generous to him, he felt, to a fault. But Jameson knew well that his ginger-haired friend was being modest. That, and he knew well what Jonathan wanted more than anything else in the world. And he intended to get it for him. Since Jameson had known him (high school) Jonathan had wanted a limousine. In those early days, they planned to use it as a portable hang-out—where they could keep stocks of booze on hand at all time. It was no doubt a strange request, but one Jonathan, ever the modest man in his adult life—would not fulfill for himself for fear of being seen as self-indulgent.

What Jameson wanted, was a bit more extravagant. And as the coast of Long Island disappeared beneath them, he was reminded of that wish.

Jameson wanted an island. He wanted a piece of land out in the middle of the ocean somewhere, and he wanted to build

homes and factories and roads and create his own city. He
wanted to build the perfect little nirvana somewhere out in the
great blue beyond. And he wanted Jonathan to be the chief of
police, fireman, and admiral of the navy.

Before long, they had safely landed on the helipad and
disembarked the chopper. Pedro and Melvin (Pedro did most of
the talking) brought him up to date on the incident of the day
prior with Drahtman, and Jameson congratulated them all on a
job well done.

"You've handled it perfectly, but I am willing to bet that this was
not the last we hear from David Drahtman. Constant vigilance,
boys! We're keeping the sign up until I tell you otherwise. No
dogs. No dogs for the foreseeable future." Pedro looked a touch
disappointed but nodded still.

As the four men walked through the back property they
heard the plaintive mooing of wild forest cows and Jameson
smiled.

"Yes Mr. Shudenbacker, my name is Reynaldo Melendez
and I am the owner of Cocina Criolla. When I returned home
this morning I found your card on the door and I hurried to the
phone to call you. Whatever seems to be the problem, sir?"
David feigned the most grave concern he could, stewed it with
the salt of a Spaniard slow to sentence the Anglo-Saxon to

speech. The inspector, a man with a squeaky, crackling voice chirped back with the scantest touch of suspicion in his bird-like voice.

"You are Mr. Melendez, you say?"

"Yes sir, Reynaldo Melendez, son of Hernando" quoted David directly from the blue folder Shank had handed him earlier in the week.

"I was under the impression that your restaurant would not be re-opening until Monday morning..."

"Well, we cut our trip short some. Couldn't stand to be away from the kitchen. You know?"

"I'm sure...And where did you and your family go?" This flustered the unflappable David; even he hadn't expected such pleasantries from a man whose job it was to be as stiff and severe as possible. David, uncommonly muddled by this question, blurted the first thing that came to mind.

"Uhhh—Canada, actually."

"You are, I take it, of Hispanic descent?"

"Sí."

"And you were in Canada? For the weekend?"

"Um—yeah, we got some fam—" he was halfway through the word when he realized what he was saying, "—mmmmily."

"I wasn't aware there was a large Latino population in Canada."

"Oh sure...in Toronto...tons of us....And I'm only half Puerto Rican...my mother is Canadian."

'I see…" David hadn't performed this poorly at work in ages, "Well, Mr. Melendez, the reason for the visit was that I received some very serious complaints about your establishment and I will need to conduct a search of the premises…first thing tomorrow morning. Say nine a.m."

"Oh sure thing, I'd be happy to let you look around. We got nothing' to hide sir!"

"Very well. We shall see in the morning then."

"Sí! Sí, senior!"

It was in the mid-nineteenth century that Marie Elizabeth Jones and Susan Roberta Jones's great grandmother left from North Carolina on a horse-drawn wagon for the north, manned at its front by Frederick Jones, patriarch of the Jones clan. He had given them his name and Marie and Susan's ancestors lived and worked in his home for near fifty years.

When they finally had saved enough money, they bought land and raised their children in the bright light of overwhelming providence. Frederick Jones had given them many gifts, none the least of which was their freedom.

It happened, as it often did, that the black and white Joneses drifted apart through time. One thing, however, was not lost to time, and that was the tradition that every member of the black Jones family would continue to their deaths: the remembrance of Frederick Jones on his birthday with the dressing of his grave with white flowers.

When Marie and Susan had unclenched their fat arms from around his neck and ceased painting his face with purple lipstick, they forced him to sit on the couch. Thomas, still holding the pillow over his softening erection, did so obediently—astonished by these revelations.

Both women hustled—raced, even—to their kitchen and nearly tossed Cleo through a wall. They returned with a pitcher of lemonade and a glass of ice for Thomas and sat again on either side of him, one stroking his head, the other his back.

After Cleo was dressed and recovered from her tussle with the sisters, she shortly pulled Thomas by his hand and out of the living room—towards the bedroom where she locked him in and told him to dress. The sisters hailed accusations of nefarious activities at her and warned her to unhand their new favorite human.

As the pair left for work, Thomas could hear them hollering after him.

"If you ever need ANYTHING boy you come to Miss Marie and Miss Susan and we'll make it okay. You can count on us, little Thomas. Count on your aunties!"

Thomas left with his left hand in Cleo's but he was now less concerned with the beautiful woman who was dragging him down a stairwell with the same hand she had used to jimmy-rig his driveshaft only hours before. His mind was elsewhere: with his two new relatives. His twin African-American aunts from

Brooklyn. Thomas racked his mind for any rap lyrics he could recall from managing teenagers all his life. He quickly found this to be an undeniably racist train of thought, and resumed imagining sticking his penis in all sorts of other crevices which were hidden throughout Cleo Daniel's lithe, steaming body.

High-noon in Wildwood, and Dr. Clarke Carter was chewing a handful of mixed berry-flavored antacids in a green lawn chair, reading the sports section.

Carter had no idea who Shakweel O'Neal was (as Carter pronounced it out loud) but he'd be damned if he'd ever seen a larger man in his life. His hands were the size of trash can lids. As he considered the feet of the giant, the doctor heard the sound he had been waiting for all his life. The soft whirring of the diamond machined stopped with a click, and a gentle tone pulsed three times.

He dropped the paper, spit pink bits of antacid in the high grass and walked to the machine's front, where a small footstool had stood since they had arrived. Re-positioning the discarded reading glasses of a wildly insane woman who wanted to give her own son a blowjob, Carter gingerly toed the steps of the stool and raised his head over the beveled ledge of his precious, precious creation.

Each of his hands unlatched thick metal clasps with the

balls of his thumbs. Pneumatic lifts slowly raised the ledge and let the sun's tongue lap full and fat along the mouth of the machine. When she had extended to her fullest, the lid—bent on its nine-inch hinges—cast a slivery half-moon shadow over its contents.

A breeze, altogether innocent on any other day or in any other locale, found its way underneath the half-hinged lid. It fell within the machine's aperture and lifted a shovel-full of fine, brilliant white dust into the air and blew it into Carter's face and hair and mouth. His tongue turned to sandpaper, crusted and corroded by a hard sugar made of diamond. It cut his gums and collected underneath his lips. Carter shook his head and a few thousand dollars in diamond took flight around him, lighter than air—a nebulous fog of unimaginable wealth.

Straightening himself and spitting blood in the grass, Carter lifted his upper body over the lip of the machine and got a better look: to the hilt, it seemed, she was brimming with diamond sand. Eyes tearing and hands shaking, the doctor pushed his hand in the beach of white light and to his surprise, found solid ground an inch or so below the surface of that richest silt.

Like he was erasing a message etched in the beach, Clarke Carter swept his cupped left hand through the glassy slag and drew a gutter in its center. Through the midpoint of this avenue of diamond dregs and flecks of blood Carter saw his own face. Glass. As firm and flat as an ocean frozen over.

Feverishly, he dove atop the machine; knees dug into the silt and swept away the remainder of the dust. The lawn looked like winter. His hands like the son of God. He stood atop it.

A circular, mirrored surface, fifteen feet in diameter, stood below him. The machine had not created trillions of diamonds. It had created one massive diamond, worth trillions. The good doctor wept, and fell back to his knees, leaning on the lid.

Given its conical, top-heavy design, the shock of the tall, elderly man against the lid of the machine gave it a slight rock. When it compensated by tilting back in the other direction it caught the stool which bent and crumpled beneath the machine's massive inertia. It rolled off its end and to the right, away from the dismantled, green-metal foot-stool. Carter was flung from its top and the whole of the machine came to the ground and rolled in a tight circle 180 degrees in the glassy lawn.

As Carter squealed and screeched in horror at the sight of fifty years of research lying belly-up in a backyard, his trepidation was overrun by a horrifying sound.

A crunching, crackling, sound, like ten thousand ice cubes being unclenched from their trays at once, filled and pounded out drumrolls in his skull. He thought for a moment this was the machine itself combusting from within—but he was wrong.

In one brief moment, the block of diamond in the machine cut loose from its womb, and slid smooth and perfect to the grass like a glass elephant calf from the mechanized vagina of a stainless-steel pachyderm.

What was lying on the lawn of Thomas Jones' house now was something that you only see in video-games and comic-books. In action-adventure films and wildly fantastic novels. It was the perfect diamond, a snow-cone of glass ten feet high and thirteen across. It looked like what would happen if you multiplied the following about a hundred thousand times:

Jameson Moxy hung up the portable phone in Thistlestick River. He had been waiting to hear this story retold to him by the sisters Jones'.

"'Sup?" asked Melvin, with one thick white eyebrow cocked over his left eye. It was a sign of their friendship that Melvin offered even this much outward concern for Jameson.

"The Jones sisters have discovered their connection to our little project."

"Yup," offered Melvin before returning to his work of moving a pallet of black canvases to a back-room of the facility.

Jameson sat in a small chair behind a leather-working station which was un-occupied and stared at the phone. Reveling in the mystery of the universe, he dialed a number to distract himself. Checking on Carter was always a good idea. He was fragile, even with all the weed he had sent him down there with. As the phone rang, he wondered if it truly was wise to trust a recovering alcoholic and former traitor to the government with such an absolutely earth-shatteringly important project. As it continued to ring, he imagined the doctor running off to Cuba with his white over-coat pockets filled with Jameson's diamonds. As it rang still more, Jameson realized that it was, indeed, still ringing. Dr. Clarke Carter hadn't picked up the phone. And this was most unusual.

29

  While David Drahtman had certainly not *ignored* the fact the he looked absolutely nothing like a Puerto Rican, he had done little to solve the problem. He had, fortunately, made one serendipitous mistake in his otherwise disastrous conversation with Inspector Shudenbacker the day prior. By attempting to explain his inexplicably retarded decision to say his deeply Hispanic family had been visiting family in *TORONTO*, he had at least given cause to explain his decided lack of melanin. No matter then that Latinos make up less than two-and-a-half percent of the racial demographic in that city. Clearly, they were a vocal minority, those Drahtmendezers.

  Still, David did not look remotely near half Puerto Rican. He was a German Caucasian by descent and his skin was whiter than Hitler's undershorts. Drahtman found inspiration in his daughter's bathroom. He had only been using this bathroom because his wife was vomiting ceaselessly in their own toilet out of grief. That, and his daughter had not come home the night before. As he squelched whitening tooth-paste on his brush, he noticed a small can of spray-on tanner.

It took him about a minute to decide this was his only hope, strip to his birthday suit, and dispense the entirety of the canister on his Snow White body. He now looked like a last-place finisher in a body-building contest from the year 1977. He was golden. The color of a new penny.

On his way through his daughter's bedroom back out to the hallway he grabbed a thin red handkerchief he was sure his daughter used as a winter jacket and tied it around his head like Rambo. Like Rambo about to mow the lawn.

Settling on the fact that there was no other solution to the problem, he dressed again, smearing bronzer on his sleeves, socks, and collars and sped from the house lest his vomit-stained and tear-smeared wife see him and take him for her masseuse.

But he didn't make it out.

"HONNNEEEEEYYYY!"

David was not above running for his life, but he was trying desperately not to sweat off his tan.

"Staci—I'm very late—I need to get going." he couldn't see her, but she was nearby, around a hallway somewhere in the guts of the home.

"Where ARE YOU?! You didn't get dressed up here!" She was getting closer, as her voice and the intermittent *arf* of her remaining dog would attest

"I know Staci, I used Sophie's room."

"Oh that's right, she's away."

"Away?" He didn't care where she went or why and was

frankly surprised this even came out of his mouth.

"I don't know, for the week —with friends"

"Lovely—well, I'll be going—have a nice—"

"David! What are you WEARING?"

He heard her voice shriek on high and then be snuffed into sweet silence by the fitting of door in frame. He scampered like a frightened bunny into his wife's truck and sped away.

The tanning spray was not comfortable. It felt as though he had been buttered like an ear of corn and the heat of the first week of August did little to ease his suffering. David sweated ferociously and creeks of grease and liquid sunshine formed on his brow. *Now* he looked like a Hispanic-Canadian. One battling to the death with his internal race-conflicts.

David parked behind the restaurant less than twenty minutes before the inspector was scheduled to arrive. His tanning session has cost him more time than he had thought. Further, knowing full well that the inspector had seen his wife's truck and would not soon forget the look of such a contraption, he had to park well out of sight and hoof it to the restaurant.

The back-door was still cinched shut by the laundry hamper and David quickly shoved it out of the way. The door eased open without its handled lock and David prepared himself by covering his mouth and nose and shutting his eyes for the assured horror within before pushing forward. He wished Collins could have been here for this and David could have made him go first.

Strange…but there wasn't a rat to be found. This was all

at once distressing and a relief. On one hand, his investment had seemed to vanish into this air. On the other, he wasn't losing toe and shoe in the maw of a million rodents. All around him a hundred images of the Virgin Mary winked at him.

Drahtman remembered the plan and relaxed: of course they weren't just sitting about the kitchen where he left them; they were of course spread throughout the basement and pantries and fridges ingesting the restaurant's food source like a frenzied flock of locusts.

David pushed through the heavy, swinging steel kitchen doors and entered into the dining room. Again, not a rodent to be found. He unlocked the front door, sat at a table and waited..

He thought he heard the scurried patter-step of four black feet behind him. When he swung his head promptly, smattering a painting of the Blessed Mother with a splash of bronze dots from the tips of his black spitting cobra locks, he found nothing.

He had nearly nodded off into his shirt when the sound of a car door slamming nearby startled him back on to his feet. He walked quickly back and forth in each direction, trying the come up with an idea of what he should be doing. David had never worked in a restaurant and so did the only thing he knew how to do in one: he picked up a menu and read it casually while tapping his right foot and whistling.

The inspector knocked on the door and David came all too lately on the fact that the Inspector wasn't going to kick in the door like the A.T.F at a cult compound. His last name was

Drahtman, not Koresh. Strangely, as he opened the door at that moment, his name also wasn't Drahtman. It was *Melendez*.

"Oh hello, Inspector Shudenbacker, how are you on this fine morning?," David sprawled in the daylight as he swung the door open and held open two arms in a display of fundamental welcoming. The inspector took a solid thirty seconds to get over the look of him, decide that he was just going to ignore it with a momentary, three-centimeter flick of his chin, and crossed the threshold

"Mr. Melendez?" said the thin, stringy man. He was freckled in blotchy spots of tan and tope and was balder than David's two sons. His suit was straight out of 1955 and his spectacles looked like they belonged to Harry Potter's paternal grandfather. He was an odd, smug creature that looked like and acted like a weed in a three piece suit. Shudenbacker said David's fake name like he was talking to a homosexual, Islamic, left-wing child molester. Amazingly, Drahtman was none of these. Or at least not just yet.

"The one and only!" replied David, far too excitedly, again swinging his arms wide as if he was expecting a big hug from the man (when in actuality he was compensating for the sub-conscious desire to have the inspector look at the entire restaurant and leave no stone unturned in his effort to find the swarming nest of rat children which David knew was living like a brain tumor in a fifty-pound bag of onions somewhere in the goddamned restaurant).

"Very well then, Mr. Melendez," he began through beaky

lips, chirping each word in a small, cockling way as he drew a clipboard from behind his checkered, woolen blazer. Not surprisingly, his jacket was in black-and-white. "I will be inspecting each portion of the restaurant in succession. You will follow with."

"Of course!" exploded David joyfully.

"Yes, well then, we may as well begin in the dining room."

"Oh, but of course…"

The inspector could have inspected the room by turning his head to the left and right once or twice; it was that small. Ever the mean little hummingbird, Randall Shudenbacker was sure to put his head underneath every table and chair. It looked as though Shudenbacker would have given him a ticket for religious impunity on behalf of the décor, but not for a rodent. At least not in this room.

The inspection went on, with David opening every door with brimming enthusiasm, but was each time disappointed by an inexplicably spotless restaurant. Even the cabinets and refrigerators which David thought would be stocked to the ceiling with bed-bunks full of Muppet-sized rodents singing show-tunes in every nook and cranny—were empty. Shudenbacker even employed a thin, polished metal flashlight. Still, every corner was clean. Clean, and empty. He was beginning to worry so much his tan was melting off face in a wash of sweat and bronze goop.

Finally, the inspection having gone smoothly as can be

and with nary a checkmark from the ostrich-man, David got the chance he had been waiting for: the basement.

They must have immediately cut and run for the cavernous recesses of the ancient building where no doubt a century of scraps and specks of food caked the floor. Where, surely, there would be bags of salt and sugar, honey and syrup. Food stores the rats would have consumed furiously; humping like manic black rabbits in the late April.

David skipped and trolloped down the steep, paper-thin wooden stairs into the burgeoning darkness, ears peaked for the din of a saucy, sodium- and saccharine-fueled orgy.

It was, then, so unfortunate for David when his feet found the concrete bottom of the building and he did not step on pile of pulsing rat-flesh. Nervously and with his breath markedly shortened, David swung his arm blindly in the air in search of the thin, beaded metal cord which likely hung from somewhere above his sweaty, golden head.

The sound of a million, inch-wide church-bells ringing jangled about him just before that of a cinching *click*.

In the center of the room where the lone, dim, blue-white light bulb was a halo of light. It fell like spotlight on a rat with a belly the size of a grapefruit touching on the floor over his feet. He was the size of a small dog and despite a lack of sweat-glands his black fur seemed greasy and slick. Strangest off all, the obese rat was alive, staring up into David's face. His little rodent-hands and arms were held out in front of him, up at David with palms turned up in a sort of look that said *"Whadya want from me?"*

The rat looked up, exhausted, like he was nailed to the spot by the weight of his immense frame. David thought he saw him blink twice, before he closed his eyes for the last time and fell backwards, dead in the center of the spot's light.

His brain swallowing what he had just seen, David hardly noticed when a thin column of light flickered and waved wildly, cutting through the darkness and painting the black with the color of white walls, steel shelving, and non-perishables. When Shudenbacker reached Drahtman's shoulder, his pencil of light met the inverted tee-pee of the bulb. Shudenbacker clucked his tongue on the roof of his beak and scolded David like he had stolen another kid's lunch money.

"Now, now Mr. Melendez…" he said over the chicken-scratch scribble of pen on pad. "A rodent in a restaurant can carry all forms of viscous diseases, all manner of sickness." He finished as he leaned over and stared into the face of the fat, black rat. "And most especially when dealing with an animal of this size, we are taking a great risk."

David Melendez had been so dumb-founded by the sight of the lone rodent that he had not even responded to the clucking chicken at his shoulder, pecking at him with a ball-point beak. He had spent the intervening moments staring at the spot of light where the rat lay, mouth cracked. David had yet to even consider the true significance and consequence of this event; he was still attempting to explain to himself the results. He would have had an easier go of explaining the creation of the universe to his wife than to make sense of the situation in the basement of

Cocina Criolla.

Despite the discovery of this one, fat, rat Inspector Shudenbacker seemed generally unoffended. He tore a pink piece of paper from his clip-board and handed it to David, who simply held it—not breaking his view of the rat. He seemed to be waiting for its soul to rise from the rat's mouth with wings and a halo defining the afterlife.

Shudenbacker took a few more cursory swings of his flashlight into the blackness, seemingly satisfied by the discovery of the lone offender. He told David, who wasn't listening, that he had thirty days to remit payment of the fine or he would face further penalties.

Shudenbacker was gone for hours before David looked at the sheet. It was for one hundred dollars. David sat, beside the rat and lay on his back. Both heads turned back and to the left, the pair rested. David napping, the rat rotting.

Perhaps it was the smell that eventually roused David from his bedtime with the parasite. There were a handful of black ants, the first to the party, trying to squeeze their beady little heads between the rodent's eyelids to feed on the yolky soup of his decomposing eyeballs. Then again, perhaps it was his phone. Drahtman opened it without checking who the caller was and grunted into the receiver.

"Davey BOY!" Collins was certainly feeling better than he had in a few days. David grunted back into the phone a monosyllabic expression of greeting, "You sound like a fucking MESS pal! Where the fuck are you?! How did it go with the spicks uptown? You take care of the filthy fucks?"

"I don't know what happened, Collins. I need to call you back. The situation has changed."

"Oh shut the fuck up, everything will be all right. I've got some good *fucking* news for you Davey!" Hoping the good news would be that Collins had invented a time-machine on his lunch break, David croaked an expression of unimpressed inquiry.

"I spoke to my boy down at the state police." David's ears peaked like a prairie dog on the lookout for predators. His filthy bronze eyebrows arched ever-so-gently. Collins had paused. He was clearly awaiting David's interest to spike. He bit.

"And what did you find out?"

"'Member the white car?" said Collins so quickly on the heels of David's question that the sentences could have been mating.

"Yes, I remember the car Collins…now just tell me what you called to tell me goddammit."

"Registered to a Jane Jones, 47 Beach Boulevard, Wildwood New Jersey…Gotta be the wife, right?"

On Bobby's end there was a long pause. On David's end, however, the situation was quite eventful. Drahtman's mind exploded with color, the stuffy air of the basement cooled and a breeze swept through its subterranean walls and found him. A lipless grin spread across his face, baring his many gummy teeth and bleeding tongue—David held the phone out in front of him and squeezed it. His eyes began to fill with sympathetic water. His face trembled with the force of how it felt to be him.

You see, for David Drahtman, everything that had ever gone wrong in his life was someone else's fault. For him, this week would forever be the worst of his life. So bad that he on at least four occasions this week wished desperately that it was his last. And yet, now, there was peace within his black-raisin heart. Nothing cooled and calmed David like vengeance, and for David everything about this week could be traced back to Thomas Jones. By extension, all his life's sadness and pain were a gift from Thomas, and David now had tracked the evil to its lair. Had found a way to make good on all the bad.

"Stay—where—you—are," he said into the phone, slowly and evenly.

"Yeah man. 'Course. You all right?" said a concerned Bobby Collins. David hung up on him.

The phone call had come from Ohmco. David was going to work to collect his help, and then they were going to destroy a man completely. His heart, wrinkly and crumpled, sung a song and skipped a beat with unbridled and overwhelming joy. Like black canaries were pumping from his ears in song.

<u>30</u>

Thomas Jones was telling a fifty-three year old dentist that her feelings for one of her patients was entirely normal and not immoral, but that she may want to consider halting the practice of unzipping his trousers while he was under anesthesia when the phone rang. Eli answered.

The conversation lasted less than thirty seconds and Eli didn't say more than a sentence.

"We need to go uptown," he said, still in the process of re-holstering the phone. "In a little bit. Jameson's moved the meeting up to today."

"Oh yeah? What do you think it's about?"

"I have no idea," Eli muttered as his fingers clacked away furiously like a pair of dancing albino tarantulas on the keyboard.

Thomas clicked "send" and processed the dentist's credit card before opening another email.

Dr. God,

Why did Daddy have to go away?
Samantha, Age 9

His emotional matrix, fizzling and shooting sparks, ignored the fact that this nine-year-old apparently had stolen her mother's credit card to ask God in heaven why her father was no longer among the living. He checked the card and indeed, it belonged to an individual whose name was not "Samantha."

Dear Samantha, began Thomas. In comparison to Eli's flash-dancing arachnids, Thomas's hands were like a duo of jerking, trembling house spiders than had just been stepped on.

Dear Samantha,
Your Daddy is here with me in Heaven, at peace. And one day when you grow up, you'll get to see him again. But for now, know that I love you, your Daddy loves you, and your Mommy loves you too.
Love and Kisses,
God.

Now, to be fair, Thomas Jones had had a long day. He had hardly slept and had spent the last six hours solving the great questions of existence for several hundred desperate believers. This letter was certainly not his best, but it sure seemed to be the right answer. What do you say to a child whose father is dead? Thomas didn't right well know and just as he had opened the letter again to consider some editing, Eli had shut down his computer and demanded they get going. He was getting less and less tolerable by the moment, that one.

Thomas just closed his eyes and clicked "send" before following Eli from the room.

"Should we grab Cleo?" said Thomas—pointing a thumb at the thumping, creaking ceiling above them.

"She's got her own car."

For whatever reason, Thomas assumed that the office they were heading to was going to be the same one he had interviewed in nearly a week before. He was both right and wrong.

The men pulled Eli's car in front of the same building, across the street from the same Hispanic men pulling longingly from brown-bagged bottles of beer on their front stoop. It seemed like a decade ago, but only six days before, Thomas Jones had been mugged by some of those people's children. He stroked at his rib gingerly and swallowed three Vicodin without water, their waxy casing painting a dry path across his tongue. He wiped his shirtsleeve at his tongue to lift the bitter cast from his mouth.

When Eli entered the building with the small paper sign the room was just as Thomas had last seen it: generally empty. The afternoon sun, settling low in the sky cast a dull gray light on the bare floors of the lobby. Not waiting, Eli opened the room to where Jameson's desk was. Thomas assumed they were the first people here because the office too was completely empty. It did not appear to faze Eli, who opened the door at the rear of Jameson's metal desk; the one Thomas suspected was a bathroom.

There was no toilet in this room, however. It looked oddly like an elevator, a terribly old thing which shook and wobbled badly when Eli got in the thing. He stared at Thomas, not speaking. He got the clue.

Not having a front door that wasn't attached to the floor below them, Thomas watched in horror as the cement walls, laced with metal piping and thick black wire rushed passed their faces as the car rose ever upward. Eli was unshaken by this and bit his nails distractedly as the elevator shook and bobbed, scraping along the walls and squealing like a subway car in a sewer drain. As sudden and violently as the trip began, it ended—coming to a stop who knew how many floors above.

When it stopped swinging about wildly in its shaft the car was behind a great black door —sheathed in what Thomas did not identify as carbon-graphite. It looked like bullet-proof superhero armor. The knob was a ball of black stone with a great "D" carved in its face. Thomas was impressed, most of all by the doorknob. For Eli, this was a touch less mind-blowing. He twisted the knob hard and pushed, shoulder-first, through the door.

The main room looked like the inside of a night-club. There was an immense island bar at the center of the room, populated by remarkably beautiful men and women sharing laughter and cocktails. The lighting was low and the music, high. As they approached the island bar, Thomas's head turned rapidly on a swivel, taking in the sight of the place. By a door to the extreme right, a figure in a black suit and tie yelled towards Eli, waving a hand.

Eli waved back, and then turned to Thomas.

"C'mon."

Thomas followed.

The man was talking to another person wearing the exact same get-up; both had dark sunglasses on and smelled like lilies. The door behind them had a glass pane in it, with the word *GRIMSURANCE* painted across the wired glass.

"Name's Joe Spinelli," said the man named Joe Spinelli, as he held out a hand to Thomas, who took it and shook feebly. Joseph's black hair was shaved to the skull and Thomas was unnerved by not being able to see his eyes. He spoke low and slowly and had the air of a man who preferred the company of werewolves to human beings. As dark and unsettling as a thunderstorm in the French Quarter, Joe Spinelli nodded to the man he was speaking to. He didn't speak in response, but patted Joe on the shoulder, waved to both Thomas and Eli and made his way back to the elevator door with a folder under his arm.

"Big day," Joseph said to Eli, "Elaine Bodicemeyer went last night."

"Really?" said Eli, interested. "Wow, you guys are getting good!"

"Seems so," said Joe, scratching at an itch behind his ear. "Two months after signing is below average."

"Not bad? What was the policy?"

"Two million. Jeff is on his way to the family's house now with the bill."

"Oh, I doubt they'll miss it much."

"You wouldn't think so."

Thomas had absolutely no idea what was going on. Eli didn't seem ready to offer an explanation, but when Joe saw Thomas's look of mystification, he grinned slightly and offered to clear the thing up for him.

"Of course. I'm sorry, Thomas. I run Grimsurance for Jameson—it's basically a life insurance business."

"Uh—okay— so what's so crazy about that?" said Thomas, doubting roundly the idea that a life insurance business owned by Jameson Moxy was going to resemble anything remotely close to what one might find at Prudential.

"Nothing. Rather than crazy…I would call this life-insurance venture—unusual."

"How so?" Thomas offered, filling the void in the air left by Joe's suggestive and carefully worded remark.

"Firstly, we don't offer life insurance. We purchase it for people and pay the bills for them. It is free to people who want it. They sign a contract saying that a portion of the payout will go back to us at the termination of the policy."

"The termination of the—"

"When they die."

"Oh—then—but—but how do you —"

"We bill the estate, which is where our friend was going."

"Why did a rich old lady want more life insurance?"

"Because she loved her family, and it was a bargain. We don't charge them a penny, we pay their life insurance bills and when they die, their families get what is essentially 'free money'."

"Is this legal?"

"Yes, but it wouldn't be if too many people knew what we are doing."

"So you look for the people who are closest to death and offer them free policies?"

"Exactly," said Joe from behind his glasses. "A fast learner, no?" he said to Eli, who nodded marginally. "That's precisely how it works. We go to hospitals dressed as professionally as possible." He said gesturing with one hand to his clothes, "and find the deadest and most often poorest people in the building and offer them and their families our services."

"That's friggin' brilliant."

"Well I sure wouldn't call it stupid." Joe smirked.

As Thomas laughed at this comment, the men turned their heads to the sound of a door slamming from directly across the room. A man in a long plush purple robe had entered the room holding a bottle of something in each hand. His black hair was slicked back and stubbly bracken broke evenly across his face. He had a fat, black cigar in his teeth. The man removed the cigar with a pinky and took a swig from each bottle before proclaiming loudly to anyone who would listen, "IT'S ME, BITCHES!"

Many people at the bar cheered this announcement like first-graders heralding the arrival of Santa Claus, but Thomas could hear Joe audibly sigh.

"I have to get back to work gentlemen. Thomas, it was a

pleasure meeting you." Joe shook his hand limply before retreating back to the office of Grimsurance.

When Thomas looked back, the man had his arm around four women and was demanding a round of shots for everyone in the room. He caught Eli and Thomas in his line of sight.

"YO! GET OVER HERE, MARILYN MANSON!!" he was talking to Eli. Eli smiled unconvincingly and beckoned Thomas to follow. He spoke under his breath as they made their way across the room.

"Trick Jackson. He's the manager—"

"His name is Trick?" Thomas was again seriously considering legal name change.

"Lord no, it's prolly something like Rupert, and he changed it to look cool. The man is a menace, but he makes a lot of money for everyone."

"I see." When they got close enough, Thomas noticed a familiar face next to Trick—Crank, the blonde coke addict who had driven him to the hospital. Crank was laughing as hard as a human possibly could at something Trick had said. When he got closer he noticed that Crank had two enormous bottles of beer duct-taped to each hand. He took swigs from each and laughed again. This time, apparently at nothing.

"Trick, how are you?" said Eli, offering a hand. Trick punched his hand with his fist.

"What the fuck is going on, you little freak?! You look good; did your mommy take away your staple-gun?" Crank howled and slammed the bottom of a forty on the bar repeatedly.

"Pretty much!" Eli seemed to be able to laugh of Trick's barbs relatively easily. "Listen Trick, this is Thomas"

"What's cracking, Tommy?"

"Well – actually—" started Thomas before he caught the stare of Crank, who had noticed him.

"OHHHH SHIT!! WHAT THE FUCK IS UUUUPPPP MANG!" screamed Crank, rushing over to Thomas and jumping on him in embrace, sloshing cool beer in his hair. Crank was on so much coke that talking to him made Thomas's teeth numb. A large group of people laughed at this encounter and swilled their own drinks.

As Thomas was drying his head with his shirt-sleeves he felt a finger run along his spine from top to bottom. He turned, yelping in fear, and found Cleo Daniels's eyes within his own.

"Hello, Thomas."

"Oh… Hey! Hey, Cleo. How are you?"

"Fine, Thomas. Couldn't wait for me? You in a rush tonight?"

"What? Oh! Oh—well—" and now he dropped to a whisper, "I wanted to wait but Eli said we had to go."

"You shouldn't listen to Eli, he tends to get himself into trouble with his mouth," Cleo said without the pretense of a whisper. Eli easily could have heard her, and this made Thomas's stomach do somersaults.

"So what's the deal with this Trick guy?"

"As yes…Mr. Jackson…" she sighed. "Mr. Jackson deals

with all the operations which involve our pretty substantial stable of young ladies. That is, the women who don't work for me on the fourth floor downtown."

"So…the, um, non-porn stars."

"Don't give his girls too much credit, they're not all that more scrupulous than mine. I still do work for him occasionally, but less and less since I kicked him in the balls for touching me once on the job."

"Oh my good—"

"Most of the girls are more than happy to sleep with him, but I find him repellant. There's something to be said for humility," she finished staring right into the back of Thomas's eyeballs with a twinkle and a wink. Thomas sat on a barstool to cover his erection.

"So—um—what's this meeting about then?"

"Well, I'm not really sure, but I assume it's about what we were supposed to meet about tomorrow. For whatever reason, Jameson moved it up to tonight. It makes sense since I know Trick has got a lot on his plate tonight and so do most of the people you see at the bar. Even Grimsurance will be busy tonight. More people die on Mondays than any other day of the week."

"Really? I didn't know that."

"It's true," she said, smiling, "I'm gonna go say hello to a friend." She pointed to another door in the far corner with a similar glass pane. Thomas couldn't read the writing from this far away. Once Cleo had kissed him softly on his cheek and sauntered off, he squinted hard. Before he could focus on it, Eli bumped his arm with a shot glass full of amber fluid and nodded to him.

While Thomas was as experienced with Vicodin as one can be, he was not one (in the past) to have to worry about mixing alcohol with pain-killers. He had drunk more in the last six days than he had in his entire life. But on the other hand he had also had more non-self-initiated sexual activity this week than ever before, so he had to weigh his priorities. Needless to say, the night—still early—was getting off on a precarious foot. After about an hour of drinking and conversation (or at least for Thomas—watching conversations), two double black doors opened at the rear wall and Jameson walked out. His appearance silenced the room—even Trick and Crank, who shushed some of the drunker young ladies on their laps. He was wearing a white suit and looked like he was going to his First Communion. Beside him was Jonathan. Jameson lifted a megaphone to his mouth and spoke.

"My friends! The meeting will begin in my office in five minutes. Managers only, please. The rest of you just sit back and enjoy yourselves. Be careful though, ladies, we have a long night ahead of ourselves and we all need to stay alert!" He handed the megaphone to Jonathan and retreated back into the office. Jonathan followed, leaving the doors open.

Thomas made his way towards the doors when he saw Cleo doing so, coming from the door at the corner. He took the opportunity to get away from the insults and degradation of Trick

Jackson, who was holding court at the office bar with a female's ass in each of his hands. Crank, finished with his two forties, was now trying desperately to get the things off him. It was hard work, what with no hands. Thomas had never seen Crank so unhappy. Trick, on the other hand, looked delighted.

"FUCKING ASS!! HAAAAHAHAHA!!"

Everyone laughed and pointed at Crank like he had came to school with no clothes on. Thomas seized his chance and walked briskly to cut off Cleo, who was among several people milling about the entrance to the office. Thomas couldn't shake a feeling of acute dizziness. His legs felt like they were sinking into the floor, and Cleo—no doubt the most religiously beautiful woman he had ever laid his hands on—looked, if possible, even more stunning. Thomas held his glass in front of his crotch and spoke to Cleo who had watched him walk up.

She took his glass from him, tilted back her head and drained it. When she handed him back his glass she ran her pink tongue over her throw-pillow lips. She wiped her mouth with the back of her hand and Thomas had a small-scale orgasm.

When they entered the room, Thomas Jones thought he had entered a cathedral. The ceiling, somehow, was twenty feet higher in this room than in the main barroom and the back wall was composed of tremendous windows that stretched to the ceiling in curved points. To the left and right of each were great, dark-red suede curtains which were pulled open to let the slowly dying day lay about the room.

The non-windowed walls were dressed in infinite

bookcases. A ladder on wheels stood up against one of them. In the center of the room was a black desk in the shape of a half moon. Behind it, in a high-back black leather chair, sat Jameson. Jonathan stood behind him, looking as serious as ever. Before the desk was an arrangement of squashy couches and plush sofas which filled slowly as Jameson watched. There was room for about twenty.

Jameson was smoking; blue whirls of smoke played with Thomas's vision. When he had sat beside Cleo, he took stock of the others in attendance. Everyone was here. Melvin and Pedro sat beside each other, and behind them were what Thomas took to be the remaining six sons of Consuela Peligro, though Thomas only knew three of them personally. Eli sat in a corner with Joe Spinelli and another man Thomas didn't know. Mike was standing at the rear of the room by himself, sipping from a green bottle, looking around the room carelessly. He caught Thomas's eye and smiled over a mouthful of beer and waved his bottle at him casually. Trick Jackson and Crank made their way in last, Crank's hands still taped to two bottles of shitty beer. The only person who was missing was Clarke Carter, whom Thomas assumed was still sitting in his house, waiting for the diamond machine to burst open.

When Jameson was satisfied with the attendance, he nodded to Mike, who put his bottle on the ground and closed the doors, stifling the sound of horns and snare drums coming from the bar.

Jameson put out a cigarette and sighed longly with his

eyes closed. Then he stood.

"Friends…I have asked you here this evening for many reasons. But before I begin let me tell you that I have never been prouder of anything in my life than I am of what we, as a family, have created. I love each of you more than you all may ever understand. You have been, to me, proof of the goodness of people—evidence that in a world as sundered and cynical as ours—one so compromised and contemptible—that there still remain some who will do what it takes to set some things—even the smallest of things—right again in their time on this planet."

"HELL YEAH, SHUN!" screamed Jackson, and there was a murmur of agreement from the rest of the crowd. Some hooted and all applauded, others clapped. Crank clanked his bottle hands together in approval.

"I thank you. I thank you all. Each of you has been so committed to our collective vision that it is astonishing to me we ever had to consider this day a possibility. The heartless wealthy of this country have been bled and siphoned by our actions. That upper crust is weak and undernourished. It is dying. The time when the poor could do nothing but be bought and sold by soulless, greedy, monsters is drawing to a close. And we have you to thank for this progress. This week we shall wage the final blow and sever the head of many of our greatest enemies, and in doing so protect ourselves from a society which was built to destroy our work and support the weight of those demons that would see harm come to us. We have done great good in the world. And I wish it could go on forever."

Many seemed to be confused by his words.

"Tonight however, will be a night of change." The room's celebratory nature softened, "Tonight and tomorrow, and the rest of this week will be a time of great transition for our company.

"Two things have changed in the last week, friends. Firstly, I have reason to believe that our safety and security has been compromised in a number of ways. Information from individuals both new and old to this company has proven what I always feared: that we are on the cusp of being discovered. Each of our businesses is at risk of exposure and destruction.

"Long ago, when this business began, I put in place a protection which I hoped to never need. It appears now that the enemy is at our gates, and the time is right to enact this guard. Later this week, we will all become very rich—but we will also become unemployed. As confusing as I know that sounds, I promise it will all be clear soon enough. I can promise each of the people in this room total protection financially and personally. I only ask that you each continue to use your prodigious skill-sets to continue work as normal until the moment arrives. Tonight, specifically, I hope that we will all put our hearts and souls into the work at hand, so that we can get as much good done before the end arrives.

"Please trust, that I have your best interests at heart and that not one of you will be forgotten—and each shall get what they deserve." His brilliant brown eyes swept the room. Jameson grinned as he did so, meeting each pair of eyes in turn. When he found Thomas, he smiled even wider, bared some teeth and nodded so imperceptibly that might may have missed it if he blinked.

31

David honked. He laid both elbows on the horn and stabbed at its internal mechanisms. He wanted the thing to sing like a symphony. As if by manipulating different pressure points on the snow-tire sized steering wheel he might find the spot that sprung to life an orchestra. Like a thousand trombones being blown through by hurricanes. The cars before him and beside him were driving far too slow to be entirely coincidental. They all knew him—they all knew where he was going and wanted to stop him. He checked his rearview so frequently it looked like he agreed vigorously with something someone kept saying.

Over and over and over and over again.

Oh, how David Drahtman honked that horn. The sun was the shape and shade of afterbirth. A low, fat patty of red, flat on the back of the horizon. Bloody shoulder-pads on the mountain monster. In this fading, internal light one car stood out among all the rest. It was pink. It was large. And it was on a mission.

If the Loch Ness Monster had fallen from the sky and landed in the middle of the freeway that night, David would have punched the truck through its ribcage and come out the other side with his wipers on. He had to get to Manhattan, and then to Jersey. In another time David might have not even made the effort to pick up Collins. Nowadays, for some reason, he felt he needed him.

The events at the restaurant were beginning to vine and coil around his brain. The soft whir of spun rubber to road had lulled his mind even though his heel still fed the floor. How in heaven and hell did over a thousand rats disappear, leaving nothing but their fat uncle behind? How did a stench so thick and overpowering that it was still sewn into the fiber of his wife's upholstery manage to dissolve into that of honeysuckle and rose-water in the course of four days? He knew one man who could explain it, and it took all the strength in his bloodless, black-souled body to keep himself from exiting at the Cross Island Parkway to visit the residence of Stanley Crabbitch.

David pushed on.

When he had parked—sprawled across three spaces like a ten-ton man getting a suntan—David walked briskly and angrily towards the elevator. He threw the keys to the attendant. He didn't toss them. It was more like a split-finger fastball with a high leg-kick.

David's face forked and folded with each passing moment. The stress on his skin was profound; a vicious scowl was being tattooed in shadows on his brow. He looked, at this moment, like something that lived under a child's bed.

In the lobby, light was being chased from the room in

horizontal tracks of black and white. It was mostly empty, which David expected for suppertime. Strangest of all was that both of the lobby secretaries were still there. Miss Marie and Miss Susan didn't stay later than necessary, as they typically watched their grandson on schoolnights. The young Freddy Jones, however, wasn't with them.

David did not have time to hear how the computers were down, or the voicemail was backed up, or be troubled with some other inane detail in the life of a receptionist. He strode briskly past them, cutting molecules in twain with quick slices of his arms. As he passed them, David offered a nod and perhaps an ever-so-slightly cocked corner of his mouth. A third of a smile.

For some strange reason, they didn't respond with hugs, kisses, or chocolate chip cookies. Both women stood straighter than David had ever seen them—so much so that the effect was to make them appear much taller, like cobras unwinding, and stared through him with flame in the air. It was a look of unabashed revulsion. Like David's middle name was Osama.

Was he supposed to get them new staplers? Did they want a raise? Were both of them still actually menstruating? Did he even give a shit in the absolute slightest?

No. Yes. No. No.

David punched the up elevator button directly in the nose. He waited five seconds before he started tapping his foot and sighing heavily. He checked his watch nine times to find out that it was 7:30. He checked it again ten seconds later and it was 7:31. When it opened he walked, alone, into the elevator and punched another button in the shnoz. This one said 87 on it.

But the elevator didn't stop on 87. It stopped on the second floor. And then the third floor. And the fourth. The elevator was stopping at every single floor, opening for about ten seconds to wait for no one, since the building was nearly empty, and then closing. By the time the elevator had done it five times, David took to repeatedly jabbing the door close button. His finger blistered and lip bloody from being bitten, it took Drahtman twenty minutes to make his way to his floor.

Sucking on his finger and whimpering for a mother whose ashes he had lost sometime in the last twenty years, David's hand fell from his mouth when he reached the 87th floor. The scene inside was enough to give even the healthiest horse a massive pulmonary embolism.

Directly before him was his employer, Alexander Prewitt, staring up with big water-balloon eyeballs from his scooter at an encroaching mass before him. At his handle-bars was Virginia, the nurse, breasts like bulwarks at the beach, looking vicious with her eyes squinty and tense.

What they were looking up and into was hard to see, because the object of their sight was occluded from view by nearly a dozen broad-bodied men in black suits—ears stuffed to the lobes with white ear-pieces—transparent phone cords vanishing within folds of muscle and fabric.

To the right of this scene was Bobby Collins, staring with

389

a look of shock and disbelief. His mouth was open like he was waiting for his mommy to feed him mashed bananas. A pile of paper pooled at his feet, clearly dropped outright from two upturned hands. He looked not unlike the rat whose last vision in life was the face of David Drahtman. Just like him—except sweatier—and wearing a suit.

Collins cricked his neck and saw David watching with a pair of question marks whirling in his urinal trough eyeballs, but did not respond otherwise—he simply revolved his neck back to where it had stood—and stared on still at the scene which David was just now beginning to be able to hear clearly.

"Did you think I wouldn't find out, old man? That I didn't know what was before you?" said a voice that growled like coals in the bottom of a bonfire. It was white, orange and black all at once and smoke embraced every syllable. This was not the Somers that David had known. Not a sniveling parasite; feeding on bones at the heel of his master. This was a base monster, feasting — nay, gorging himself, on the humidity of fear in the air. Flashes of white hair and skin the color of ash popped and sparked between chubby arms and rolls of black neck fat. Battlefax was trembling—quaking. He was sweating, and a long, white finger was pointing from the center of his heart, on a downward angle at the face of Prewitt. Despite his own shaky and tearful demeanor, Alexander's chin and nose were in the air. He was not going down like an animal.

David didn't know what the fuck to do. He tip-toed behind the mass of blackness and literally dragged Collins from his spot in the office and pulled him towards David's door. He swiped his card key and they slipped within, avoiding the attention of the gathering and quietly slid the door's lock shut with a soft *click*.

"Whatthe*fuck*isgoingonoutthere?" rapped David, neck jutting out and head leaned up into Collins's face. He pointed aimlessly behind him with a shivering fingertip. It took his colleague some time to respond.

"He knows something's up, Davey. That little bastard—"

"Knows what Bobby?"

"He knows that whatever happened today at the restaurant happened. There's no sense hiding in here. He knows and we're all gonna be fired."

"GODDAMMIT! GODDAMMIT," David swore and pulled at his hair; he kicked his desk. And then he kicked it again. As he was winding to kick a third time when he was stopped by a half-second's sound of rushing water, and then the forceful spritz and spray of his overhead sprinkler system. Everything in the room was being pissed on by the shower-head in the center of his ceiling.

What was left of his tan was now all over the front of his shirt like a smock in a kindergarten classroom. Collins, oblivious, was sitting on the sofa in David's office, being rained on—his thinning blonde mane washed down his brow.

If Collins wanted to commence another fit of hysteria he could, but even if he was going to be fired, he wasn't going to be burned alive doing it. Given that neither of them were smoking bongs in the room—it wasn't like they were the only ones soaked to their assholes right now.

David pulled at the door-knob. It didn't budge.

"Craziest thing Davey…" started Collins, staring off through the spontaneous thunderstorm and talking to each drop as it blew passed his lips. "My daughter—you remember her?"

David wasn't listening. He was pulling and tugging and pushing and shoving at the door of his office. He swiped his keycard again and again and again. A red light blinked on the transceiver and the door remained stiff and serious in its rejection.

"My daughter…the wife told me that she thinks I'm dead. You know, not being there for so long and all. She said that God told her I was in heaven. Crazy, huh?"

"I think that's a great idea, Bobby, let's talk about it tomorrow—but *first*, why don't you give me a hand with this door." David spat distractedly. Bobby didn't respond. David didn't need Bobby Collins. He didn't need anyone. Recalling his A-Team, GI Joe moment earlier that week, David stood back a few paces. He then ran full speed into the door and drop-kicked the knob, only to discover that office doors in billion-dollar corporations are far sturdier than in the back of 110-year-old restaurants.

As he fell cursing and clutching his ankle, David rolled on his back and cried out loud. It was a mix of sorrow and inspired fury. Putting his front teeth squarely through his bottom lip in agony, David was distracted when, over the sound of thunderous rainfall, he heard a curious—yet definite—*click*.

It wasn't as if Battlefax's guard stormed through the door. Not at all as if they rushed into the room in search of a victim. It appeared more like they were poured in the room. Like oil, tar, and smoke—they filled the space until David could not see behind them. One of the largest walked to the sprinkler and tore it from the ceiling, leaving a serrated wound in the plaster from which a steady finger of cold water pushed a puddle into the carpet. The immense man tossed the fixture and its attached wall-scrap onto the couch beside which, David was sure, sat Collins.

At their front, seemingly without warning or provocation, the guard parted like a curtain of flesh and wool. Bright white against the black fabric, Somersworth Omicron Battlefax crept from behind the clouds and stood over David.

A jet-black overcoat, far too big for his slight frame, was cloaked around him, pulled close at the neck by ten ghostly-white, near translucent fingers. His thin lips vibrated, flickered and pursed. Somers's eyes, large and black as the inside of a womb, shook and flitted on David's dripping face.

"Mr. Drahtman…" he clucked his tongue and scolded him wordlessly "…plumbing troubles?" Battlefax finished by fluttering his eyes about the office, soaked to the soul. "You really should do something about this…"

David forced a laugh as his eyes searched Somers's for a sign of his intent. A whisper of sincerity.

"It has been a very disturbing week, Mr. Drahtman…"

"Yes—yes it had Somers, I am very sorry about—"

"Sir. David, Sir. I'm sure I noticed you at the execution of the will? You are aware I am the new chairman of Ohmco?"

"Yes…sir." His insides burned at the taste of the word.

"Excellent…even more disturbing, perhaps, than the passing of my dear uncle has been the behavior of some of his most trusted associates."

"Oh?" David feigned ignorance.

"Imagine my surprise, David, when it was made apparent to me that rather than the Melendez family having sold their restaurant—or at least having it taken from them, as my dear, dear uncle requested—but instead…" he paused here to swallow, blink furiously, and shake off a tremor "…instead, David, that Reynaldo Melendez has just purchased new floors and lighting fixtures for his property—to be installed this coming weekend!"

"I—sir—I had no—"

"YOU…" Battlefax's entire head was a blur of hate and white light; his eyes were closed tight, folded within their hollow sockets. "YOU—WILL—NOT—SPEAK!" He leaned now, down into David's wet, scratched, bronzed face and spoke slow and low like cooking fire, "Unless spoken to…do you understand me?"

David couldn't muster a murmur in defiance. Apparently, control of the conversation now pumping lifelessly in his hand like a dying animal, the guard broke open behind him into a semi-circle, giving its master room.

And Somers filled it. He began to stroll, casually even, along the rim of this wreath, coat-tail whipping like a cape at his

394

heels.

"And do you know, Mr. Drahtman…how I knew this?"

"No, I—"

"OF COURSE NOT! You know very little, of course…but allow me to inform you, Drrrrahtman. I know this, because they PURCHASED THE MATERIALS FROM US!" Battlefax paused in his prancing and stared directly into David's eyes. He walked purposefully across the semi-circle, back in to David's face, "You just couldn't believe my confusion…how could a family on the very cusp of impoverishment, shadowed by the impending death of a child, burdened by the ever-approaching cost of coffins and tombstones—find time to shop for floor-boards and fluorescent wall sconces? I'll tell you how Mr. Drahtman—because you and your colleagues failed my uncle. And you failed me. I do not know how it happened, or what has become of the boy. But I will find out David, I promise you that. For now, however, we must consider the state of the company."

Battlefax drew back from David, stretched to his full height and back-peddled four steps before turning and continuing his circular pace.

"You see, David, we cannot have individuals in our inner circle who will repeatedly fail in achieving the vision of this corporation. Your services will no longer be needed, Mr. Drahtman. Your pension and other benefits are hereby revoked and I will expect your personal effects gone by sunrise."

"Somers…please," David pleaded before he saw twin flames erupt in the black pits of his employer's eyes.

"David…you will cease using my first name. I am now Chairman Battlefax. It is with great pity I even allow you the use of the word 'sir'."

David gave no response. He was defeated. Demolished. Unrecognizable.

"Sunrise, Drahtman." He turned his back to David and the phalanx collapsed around him and poured towards the door. From within he heard a last, parting shot, "Take this trash with you."

He was referring to Collins, still staring at nothing, hair wet and thin around his eyes, lips parted slightly.

Through the still-open office door, David watched the black cloud thunderclap its way past the still sitting Prewitt and Virginia, who had been watching from behind David's door. Prewitt had a box of his personal possessions on his lap and stared with enmity at the passing storm. It swept into an elevator and disappeared.

Drahtman's soggy steps met the stiff, dry shag of the main office. Apparently, only his office was troubled by the spontaneous sprinkle. Silent, and broken, David led the addled Bobby Collins towards Prewitt. They did not converse. The four of them, Virginia included made their way to the elevators and entered.

This time, the elevator seemed to be moving without a hitch. It did, however, stop once on its way to the lobby. The 70th floor, the women's gym and lockers. Someone apparently was waiting for an elevator there.

When the doors opened there was a small figure, whose face was hidden behind several cardboard boxes, leaned against her chest. At the top of them was a green gym bag, which teetered right above her head. When she had pushed into the car, fingered a button and the doors had closed, she lowered the boxes and bags and stood. Dana Jenkins had been cleaning out her locker.

Due to the crowded conditions of the car, Dana was pressed tight up against the man who had entered the elevator last: David. Her breasts were pushed into his sternum, and they looked at each other wish surprise and speechlessness. The car moved ever-downward and David prayed over and over again that this ride would end sooner rather than—"

With a jarring lurch, the car stopped dead between floors thirty and thirty-one. The lights within went black and the elevator moved no more. And this time, it seemed, it would move no more.

Each of the occupants had a reaction to this event, most of them were swear-words and sighs. The only person, surprisingly, who didn't spout obscenities was Collins, who gave a curious "Hmmmm" when the car made it clear that it had no intention of resuming activity.

David frantically snatched his phone from his pocket and opened it. No service. This wasn't unexpected; they were in a five by five steel rectangle within a ninety-story-high, enclosed shaft of cement. He used the light of the phone's display to find the emergency intercom, where he should be able to contact someone who could help.

Try as he did, there was no answer. Miss Marie and Miss Susan must have finally left for the night. It seemed that for the time being, the five of them were going to be stuck—together.

32

As the room began to disperse following Jameson's puzzling speech, Thomas caught sight of his boss waving at him, beckoning that he come over for a chat. Much of the crowd was gone and Jameson was now waving towards several other people, until the only ones that remained were Mike, Cleo, Eli, Melvin, Jonathan, and—of course—Thomas Jones.

"Friends, I wish to be a bit clearer with you few who have been so faithful and instrumental to our work."

Thomas was genuinely touched that he had been invited to this latter meeting, though he couldn't for the life of him discern why he had been asked in the first place. No one spoke a word of thanks at this, but rather waited for him to continue, which he did.

"The situation is thus: I have reason to believe that our little secret in Wildwood is in danger. Firstly, earlier today it was made plain to me that someone had requested a license plate check on a Ford Tempo registered to our newest addition,"

Thomas gasped like a schoolgirl as Jameson swung an open palm beside him, displaying our hero like an item for auction. He seemed to catch Thomas's expression of horror, and quickly reassured him.

"As Thomas will tell you, that vehicle is registered to his sister, Jane, who lives not far away in the same town." He paused and looked thoughtfully at Thomas, who now feared for his sister's life.

"As it happens, Thomas, you're sister has unwittingly provided herself with her own protection, which I will explain later. She will not be in any danger for the time being, even if Drahtman can find the home."

"I don't understand. How will she—what—"

"Please trust me Thomas. All is fine for now. As for *why* this all has happened, much of it was my fault entirely. I knew that Mr. Drahtman was going to investigate following the demise of his pet and neglected to account for his level of contact, cunning, and coercion. It appears Mr. Drahtman has some level of internal knowledge within the New Jersey state police."

Still no one spoke.

"The larger issue at play is that I have recently become aware of a reason to suspect that David's former employer was aware of Dr. Carter's little toy. Whether or not that information had been passed along to our friend David is another thing entirely. We know that his motive for seeking out Thomas is independent of the machine, but we cannot be sure he does not have an ulterior reason for heading south."

In the intervening pause someone spoke. It was Mike.

"Wait, Jameson—why are we working then? Let's get in the chopper and go there now. I'm sure Carter won't be able to do much about this guy if he gets there."

"An excellent point, Mike. Even more problematic is the fact that Dr. Carter has not answered the phone at the house since yesterday morning. I am concerned for him, though I cannot fathom what possibly could have gone wrong. Fortunately we have been able to immobilize the threat of Mr. Drahtman for the time being. He will be no trouble to us until morning. This is why I am quite confident that the very important work of this evening can be executed safely."

"Wait…Carter is missing? What about the machine?"

"This is an issue, certainly, but I am sure all will be revealed when Thomas and I arrive tomorrow morning."

Thomas choked on his tongue.

"You and I?!"

"Yes, Thomas, you and I. We will travel early tomorrow via helicopter and uncover the situation at your mother's home. If needed, we will also deal with Drahtman."

"Deal with him? How?"

"Oh I have plenty of ideas. But that is not for tonight! Tonight we all have great work to do …" A strange voice did a strange thing. Very rarely, in fact never before, had Thomas heard someone cut Jameson off mid-sentence. It was Melvin.

"Jameson…how did they know? It seems rather unlikely that this information is so easily acquired. What I mean to say is—doesn't it appear that someone with pretty comprehensive knowledge of the business must have assisted them?" The only person in the room who wasn't shocked by not only Melvin's words, but the fact that he had just spoken so many of them was Jameson, who nodded agreeably at Melvin.

"It does appear, old friend, that there is a leak in our circle of trust. Someone had been aiding the enemy. And that person, whoever it is, shall pay the king's ransom for his transgression. For now, though, I do insist we keep to the present. We have work to do tonight and all of us are behind schedule as it is. To the cars."

Without an argument, all of them turned and made their way out of the office. The island bar and its clubbish atmosphere was still and empty. The music had gone and the dimly lit room, only minutes before bisected by laser-lights, was loud with white overhead lamps. Like closing time. Its many beautiful occupants had abandoned their stools, and only the bartender remained to clean up after them.

While he certainly trusted Jameson, Thomas couldn't imagine what kind of protection his sister had in place. Was his housekeeper sister going to chase him down with a dust-buster? Assault him with a feather duster? Poison him with Windex and impale him on a mop-handle? Thomas didn't have time to further mull the possibilities, as the crowd exited the building they were surrounded by long black limousines.

Thomas Jones had never been in a limo. He had never gone to a prom and never married. So it was with childlike awe and wonder that he crawled within the cavernous, leathered tube that is an authentic stretch. A fleet of them clogged the small street that wrapped the front of Keepwater's building, and the Hispanic men who sat across the dusty little side road were pointing and yelling and drinking with vigor at the sight of them. They seemed to expect celebrities to exit the lengthy vehicles. Like the Academy Awards were being held on a tight, one-lane strip of city street on the lower east side of Manhattan.

Thomas had no idea where they were going; he was far too overcome by his surroundings. Chrome track-lighting lined the roof and a stocked bar was imbedded in one wall. There were no fewer than five television screens and the music was louder than necessary. The windows—to Thomas's unbridled delight—were tinted, and besides Cleo and Mike, he knew no one else in the vehicle. Nine of them were stunning, long-legged stripper types. For the first time in his life, Thomas considered the feelings of another woman with reason. He wondered if Cleo thought he was meant to stare only at her long legs. She gave him no guidance, so Thomas glanced swiftly at an unnamed canyon of cleavage and turned away. He liked Cleo. More than that, he hoped she liked him.

When they reached their destination, the laughing harem of half-dressed women hurdled from the limousine and wobbled up the door, passing a long line of club-goers waiting to enter. The sign overhead was made of thin blue neon piping and said "EXPOSITION."

All of the women, Cleo, and—remarkably—Thomas,

were waved within by a man the size and shape of an African-American Jabba the Hut. Thomas had never met him, but he assumed Cleo's arm around his sufficed as identification. Thomas heard those at the front of the line groan as he passed, and he felt a fleeting sense of privilege. His lips dripped with saltwater and his hips opened so that it could even be said that Thomas Jones was *strutting*.

If there was one thing Thomas Jones would never, ever be able to do well, it was dancing. Surely there were many thing he wasn't exactly adept at—among them athletic competition, interior decorating, and public speaking. There was, perhaps, nothing at all that Thomas was less able to do competently than dance. Curiously, Thomas nearly always recognized his deficiencies and avoided them accordingly. Dancing, however, was something Thomas seemed to feel he was relatively gifted at.

It was for this reason that not moments after having purchased a pair of drinks (for a near-offensive thirty dollars) for himself and the woman who had lassoed his penis a night earlier, he pulled her by her hand to the center of the dance floor.

The club was a sort of super-trendy, post-modern mish-mosh of lasers, squashy velvet sofas and mirrored floors. The music was unrecognizable to Thomas. It was written, composed, and recorded on a computer and the only actual musical instrument that was involved in its construction was the voice of a human. And even that was debatable.

Thomas, however, could not care less. The DJ could have been spinning *Sounds of Nature* and he still would have been performing the same, strange, dance. Thomas gyrated, twisted, and pumped his limbs forcefully. Vodka swished and splashed from his first martini as his body contorted and coiled, bended and bounced. Lubricated by liquor and pain medication, his rib felt like warm putty. He moved freely, madly and passionately. His eyes squinted and his tongue wagged. He tried to moonwalk and it looked like a video of the hundred-meter dash at the Special Olympics played in reverse.

When he paused in his tribal undulations to sip from his glass, he caught sight of Cleo, who seemed to be laughing without opening her mouth. She smiled broadly and swayed to the music like a person who actually had rhythm and a sense of musical timing. Thomas wanted to shove his face into hers the way one dries his face in a towel after a shower. He resisted, and resumed his standing grand-mal seizure.

When both glasses were drained, Thomas grabbed hers by the stem in a manner that was just nearly smooth. He sauntered away from her as suggestively as possible and made his way to the bar, leaving Cleo in a wake of unintentionally intentional sexiness.

Clubs in Manhattan, or in any major city for that matter, are notorious for the virtual impossibility of obtaining drinks. You could stare at walls full of booze for an hour and watch iced glasses swirl past you and never get your hand on a beverage. For the price they were asking, you might think they would be more concerned with service. Alas, for Thomas, it was easier to find a drink in a camel's footprint than at a place like this. Being in front of the crowd meant nothing for an under-dressed middle-aged man. Martinis made their way to breast-possessing teenagers a mile away, to the bartender's spiky haired coke dealer, or—as was fortunate for Thomas at the present—to Trick Jackson.

As Thomas stood an inch behind Trick, trying to get the bartender's attention, he was run into by a pair of men who couldn't have come across as more homosexual if they were wearing assless leather chaps and dragging each other across the room by one another's penises. They laughed, apologized absently over their shoulder as Thomas lost his balance and fell face-first into Trick Jackson's back.

Trick wheeled around with one fist cocked two feet over his head and an eye squinted like he was shooting skeet. When he saw Thomas, Trick held back, but still squinted—now with two eyes. As if Thomas were a mile away, rather than bumping nuts with the guy in a club, albeit blamelessly.

"What the fuck are you doing, new guy?" Trick wasn't as welcoming and genial as his co-workers. As salty as he could possibly have been, Thomas was still not quite up to the task of physical combat with a lunatic like this man.

"Oh—I am so sorry—these two guys ran into me—I kinda tripped…"

"Yeah, well—don't trip. It makes me look bad."

"Oh, of course, sure thing. I'll do my best."

Trick turned back around without a word and hollered down the bar to the tender. After nodding to an unseen figure hidden behind a mass of body-glitter, short-skirts, and highlights he paused and turned back to Thomas.

"Listen, shun. I'm sorry—it's just not a good night. Let me get you something." He yelled again over the music and babble of a gaggle of the ladies beside him. As they waited, Thomas tried to offer his help as kindly and carefully as possible.

"Well...maybe I can help? What exactly is the problem?" Trick found this suggestion humorous, as his laugh attested. He took a drag from his black cigar (which Thomas was sure was prohibited in a club) before speaking.

"Nah my dude, I don't think you've got the body for this kind of work—" another pull, "—and it's not that big a deal. The new girl never showed—and I don't like the way that reflects on my staff."

"Well, have you called her? I could—" but Trick turned away from Thomas as his voice trailed off into the humming thump of music and foot on floor. Trick pulled two small rocks glasses with ice and brown booze over a few blonde heads and handed one to Thomas.

"Yeah, so this bitch never showed, and we're one short. I don't like to be short girls...and what fucking pisses me off most is that we've got a perfect replacement right here in the building—but she won't work."

"Oh yeah? Who?"

"That fucking cunt Daniels."

"Don't ever talk about her like that again."

Thomas had said those words with an unintended and unexpected tone of warning and anger. It came out so quickly he hadn't realized he had said it. Like he had been possessed by the spirit of a professional wrestler. A pirate. A five-star general with balls made of cast iron. Trick raised both of his black brows and Thomas couldn't tell if it was surprise or the onset of an ass-kicking that would make his mugging earlier in the week look like a game of patty cake by comparison.

Already past the point of no return as far as he could tell, Thomas took the brown drink he hadn't ordered and put it down on the bar, leaning over Trick, who was still wearing his eyebrows like a headband. He gave the man the most threatening look he could and turned his back on him.

His face turned directly into that of Cleo, whose mouth was not a fingernail from his own. He tried to apologize but couldn't move away since he was being buffeted on all sides by a migrating herd of homosexual men. He stammered, trying to think of something to say. She, who had plenty of room behind her to move away—did not. She smiled, stared through him and pecked him quickly on the mouth. Thomas's kneecaps turned to pudding snacks. He thought he heard someone cursing behind him at this display.

"Where's my drink, Romeo?"

"Oh—well, I got into a bit of a thing with—um—"

"Ahhh…Mr. Jackson is giving you trouble." As she said his name she gave a nasty sneer over Thomas's shoulder to what he assume was the observant Trick. When her eyes re-discovered his they were smiling. She peeled him off of a mass of dancing men and dragged him to a squashy red velvet love-seat—sat him

down and told him to stay. Like a golden lab at the whim of
Pablo Peligro, he did as the boss said.

She returned in under two minutes with a bottle of red wine in a
bucket of ice with two glasses. If he only knew what it meant.

They drank.

"So what the hell does that guy do?"

"Who—Jackson? He's an asshole—that's what he does."
They both laughed and clinked glasses.

"No, really."

"You wanna guess?"

"Well, yeah. I mean, I kinda have an idea."

"Oh, this I wanna hear," Cleo remarked, pulling her glass
up to her mouth.

"Okay, well—all these girls he's got working for him—I
dunno, I just thought maybe it was some sort of prostitution
ring."

She stifled a laugh and caught a mouthful of red wine
against her lips with three fingers, crowned with black polish.
Cleo composed herself.

"So you're saying I look like at one time in my life I was a
prostitute?"
Whoops. Thomas hadn't even thought it through well enough to
notice why that last sentence might be offensive.

"Oh, my God—no, no not at all. I forgot you had said
you worked for—"

"You wanna know a secret?" She cut him off, leaning into
his ear and touching her elbows beneath her bust to thrust her

breasts up. He could smell them.

"Yes." He said this probably too eagerly, but truth be told Thomas would have preferred this secret to knowing what happened after death.

"I was."

"You was what?"

"That's terrible English, Mr. Jones. I was a prostitute, when I was very young—at home."

"Home? Where's home?" he seemed to have missed the fact that she admitted that she had taken money for the right to shove a dick in her mouth.

"South Africa. Though I moved around a good deal. Military family. Parents passed when I was fairly young, and after the inheritance was gone I used the money to support my little sisters. When we had enough we came to the States and while I still used my body to make money, I stopped *using* my body. If you get my meaning."

"Um. Wow."

"Does that offend you?" she said with a look that gave Thomas the impression she didn't expect this knowledge was turning him off. She was right. The thought of her straddling some strange man in a car made his balls tingle. It was hot. Hot in an honorable…family sort of way. He told her so, and she squirmed her way under his arm and buried her head in his shoulder.

They drank.

"What is Eli doing?" slurred Thomas, noticing Eli sitting

with a gorgeous Spanish woman yammering in his ear. He looked unimpressed by her and was tapping away at a cell phone. The girl's lips spun blindly—face in his ear to be heard over the music. She was waving her hands and flipping her hair with every one of her many, many sentences.

"Being grumpy as always." She laughed and took a long draw from the bottle which they were now just passing back and forth. She swallowed and wiped her big lips on the back of her arm and continued, "He's got a fucking attitude problem, that little prick."

Thomas had been connecting the proverbial dots on the relationship between Eli and Cleo for some time. He had pretty much assumed that she and he had been involved, that Cleo had ended it—and Eli had ever since given her a problem over the split. He had meant to mention it but hadn't on account of basic fear. *In vino veritas* being what it is, Thomas's hesitation abated.

"So you and him used to...you know?" Cleo sat upright and stared at Thomas with her mouth open. Her teeth and gums were purple from the wine. She was not only drunk. She was drunk and insulted.

"Thomas, Eli is a little boy. I don't fuck little boys...What did he tell you?"

"Nothing, he just seems to have an attitude towards you."

"Whatever feelings Eli had for me are his own problem. The reason he doesn't like me is because I don't share his feelings about the business."

Thomas, rather than ask the obvious, simply let her fill the void.

"Eli is always suspicious that someone is out to screw

him over. He's always worried about the stupid Golden Mountain and how Jameson is gonna fuck him one day. He's an idiot. A stupid little boy." She finished and her eyes drifted over his shoulder. She waved the empty bottle over her head and gave a kind of *what are you waiting for* look to a cocktail waitress wearing an outfit that looked entirely composed of scotch tape.

"And another thing…"she began, belching in a pause before continuing, "if Jameson hadn't kept Eli back today I would've gone right up to him and told him that Eli has got to be the mole."

"You don't think?" said Thomas who had just a minute earlier become convinced a thousand times over that Eli *was* the source of the sprung leak.

"First of all, Eli does more complaining to Jameson than anybody, so he's aware that Eli thinks what he thinks. And secondly, there's no way he would've kept Eli behind if he thought it was possible he was the one. He's not stupid."

"Then who—"

"If you ask me – it's probably that asshole" she pointed the empty bottle towards Crank, who was telling an animated story to a table full of girls. Waving his hands wildly. He had bandages wrapped around them both.

"What about Trick?"

"Not possible."

"Because?"

"Because he and Jameson are cousins. And without Jameson Trick wouldn't be who he is. Financially I mean. Trick is

411

a scumbag. But he's a loyal scumbag. I could tell you stories…"

"I don't get it—you still haven't explained what this guy does?"

"Ah yes…" she said. Before Thomas noticed she was talking to the waitress appearing behind him. When she placed an identical bottle on the side table in front of their sofa, Cleo got a nasty look in her eyes and stood, if a bit wobbly.

"Excuse me….but where the *fuck* is my ICE?"

"Oh sweetie, don't worry about—"

"No! No!" she spoke to him before looking back up at the waitress. Her hair was in her face and her left breast looked ready to pop from its nest. "You see that we prefer our red wine iced. Do you?" She was truly frightening when she wanted to be. Thomas's heart skipped a beat.

"Oh, of course. I'm sorry."

"You better be, missy!"

The waitress scurried off on plastic platforms as Cleo shrugged and sat down again beside Thomas.

"Where were we darling? Uh-huh…Mr. Jackson. What this scumbag does is really pretty smart stuff. But don't give him any credit, 'cuz it's Jameson's idea."

"Okay."

"See all the girls?" She waved indistinctly around her head.

"All of them?"

"No, silly, but all the ones we came with. The ones at the bar in Jameson's office."

412

"Okay, yeah."

"Well, they are decoys. Plants. Spies."

"Huh?"

"This room is filled with cameras. Every one of our girls has one in her cleavage."

"Do you—um—have a—"

"No…I'm not working. But you can see why that would be the ideal place for it?" she said to his eyes which were turned from her, and down swimming in the pools of pink flesh and shadows that filled her top. "The women are here to test the fidelity of many of the corporate dickheads who populate places like these, trolling for ass. They tell their wives that they're at a meeting and come and try to score with a girl forty years younger than themselves."

"Uh huh…" said Thomas, looking around and noticing an odd proportion of old men in suits to gorgeous twenty-something's.

"If they decide to cheat on their poor wives and lie about it, then we blackmail the shit out of them. Pretty simple."

"Oh, wow."

"Yeah, it's big time money. You've seen the girls—they're pretty hot. But that's not all. You remember—"

"The guy in the restaurant!"

"Exactly! Very good Thomas. Though that was a special case. I had never met that man. But his wife, whom he has cheated on and abused verbally and emotionally for twenty years, is the one who approached us. The man would go on month-long trips, never calling their children. Awful. She wanted out, but needed to make sure she would get a piece of the pie. The pre-nup would only allow her anything if she could prove infidelity. So we go in, and give her witnesses."

"Because how would you know his name..."

"You are one smart cookie, Thomas Jones!" she snatched a bucket of ice from the waitress and shooed her away. She refilled their glasses with ice and red wine and tipped back half her glass in one slug. Cleo slammed the glass down and put her hands on his thighs, crawled up him like a mountain and pushed her lips over his. The breath from her nose cooled his flushed cheeks. When she pulled off of him she sucked in her bottom lip.

They drank.

Again Thomas caught sight of Eli staring blankly into his cell phone. He was wearing a black t-shirt with a large white upside down cross. Beside him the young lady had run out of gas. She was no longer talking, but sitting there staring at her toenails.

"That's some shirt he's wearing." Thomas pointed towards the prophet with his glass.

"Yeah, Eli is such an outspoken little atheist isn't he?"

"Um—well I kinda thought everyone at Keepwater was a—"

"Not at all. The Peligros obviously, and many more are firm believers. Not everyone, of course—but don't you feel Eli is a bit fucking obsessed?" His ladyfriend had the mouth of a sailor with Tourette's when she drank this much. Her head was in his lap now, her feet in the air over her. Thomas had to use every

muscle in his body to avoid doinking Cleo in the back of the head
with his hammer.

"I suppose. He certainly—"

"Oh, I shouldn't even tell you this, but I fucking hate him
so much."

"Tell me what?"

"Eli used to be an altar boy."

"And?"

"And..."

"And what? He used to—OH! Ohhhhh. You don't
mean?" Thomas caught on and Cleo's smiled widely and nodded
at him upside down from his lap, where her head was.

"Yup. It's sad, but he's not the only one who had a
fucked-up sexual past. That's why he's such a little Nazi about it.
I mean, millions of people come to the conclusion that organized
religion is a bunch of hysterical, sappy bullshit—but we don't all
harp on it for the rest of our lives. It is what it is."

"Yeah, I guess so."

"I think that's why Jameson trusts him with it. Because he
knows how angry he is about it."

"Did he ever—um, sue or whatever? Like the church that
it happened at?"

"Well, we're making a whole lot more money doing what
he's doing now then he would in a lawsuit. And I think Eli is
more concerned with finding the actual guy who did it to him."

"He's alive?"

"Sure is."

"Oh, my."

"Ok well I shouldn't say that…I don't know for sure, but I know the priest was young when it happened and Eli's turned legal like two years ago."

"Wow. I don't know what I'd do."

"Oh shush Thomas. You make it sound like he's the only one. Tens of thousands of children had the same experience and they all didn't become wanna-be antichrists. Yes, the priests should be strung up and disemboweled, but there's a bigger issue—and that's what Eli always misses. It's all revenge, and no rectification."

"Huh? You're saying the priests did this because—"

"They did it because they are sick, evil, disturbed individuals—but the bigger idea is that religion itself allows this to happen. September 11, the Holocaust, the Crusades—all of it is rooted in the fact that there is some mad, essential truth in the universe which is incontrovertible and any divergence from that line of thinking is worth killing for."

"And there isn't?"

"There may very well be, baby, but it sure isn't one that says a man has to deny himself inborn urges to be holy. It sure isn't one that says that the death of innocent strangers is the deepest desire of the creator. When we begin to sacrifice the truths that are self-evident—those that are plainly obvious by the slimmest internal investigation, because a fairy-tale said so—we're treading on dangerous ground, no?"

How this woman—this miraculous, marvelous,

magnificent woman—was able to extricate herself from the depths of a bottle of chilly red wine to spout such dialogue—such seamless, perfect speech—was tantamount to Thomas's brewing affection for her. Cleo Daniels was the saltiest person he had ever met and…most likely—the smartest as well.

Then, in brilliant contrast, she swung back her head—chin to the clouds and long strawberry chocolate locks pooling in the small of her back.

"The lights look like nipples!"

And so they did. Halogen eruptions from within flat disks of incandescence—each recessed ceiling fixture looked like a nuclear pacifier—like Homer Simpson's donut pulled from the reactor's swimmy, neon waters.

They drank.

"Don't you two look *adorable*," a voice rained down upon them from above. Their bodies—pretzeled—twisted and entwined, leg upon leg and arm in arm. When they cast four eyes up at Jameson they were one animal with two backs and a single, steady heartbeat.

They laughed at his comment in a chorused unison.

"Well…I shall leave you to one another. But before I leave…Thomas, I should warn you we shall be leaving very early tomorrow. Am I to assume you will be staying with Cleo?"

"YES," Cleo yelled over Thomas's stammering wonder.

"Very nice. I shall see you before the sun rises, my friends."

Jameson turned, and within the spread of his shadow,

two individuals more loving than ever loved pressed into one another. The music, light, and smoke around them became theirs. One that had waited long enough on the smell of backseat blowjobs and the insults of underage employees. One that had been prepared by the burn of words like like "slut," "old fuck," "whore" and "loser."

The very definition of the word.

The truest display of its merit and measure.

The essence of what it means to be a living thing.

Thomas Jones was in love.

EAT THE RICH - DILLON

EAT THE RICH - DILLON

33

David Drahtman would have rather spent his evening with his face in a deep-fat fryer filled with thumbtacks than what truly had transpired the night previously. While David had done everything in his estimable power to avoid Dana, she had no such desire. Dana—in fact—had been waiting for an opportunity to get her hands on Drahtman for nearly a week. And this was not for any of the reasons that she may have had cause to feel this way in the past.

She was actually quite disappointed she had only had time in the evening to make it back to Ohmco to fetch her things. She had been so caught up with training for her new job—and shopping for the clothing required of the position—that she hadn't been able to do what she wished: confront Drahtman in front of his co-workers and verbally debase him. To loose him of the task of manhood. Now she was going to be late for her first night in the field.

She had prayed that her parting note would do the trick, but it would never satisfy her the way it would have to say those same things to his wife. To his children. She wanted badly to destroy him completely. The evil lived within her, too. In her dizziest daydream—she would compel David to jump off of a rooftop.

And maybe that's why she took the job she did.

Regardless, Dana Jenkins did not care who the fuck was in the elevator. Her god-daughter—a nine-year-old—could have been in the car and she still would have chosen the term "small-dicked sycophant" to describe her former superior.

For David, the conversation could have been worse. First, Bobby Collins was in a catatonic, psychological coma and had nary an idea what was going on around him. Furthermore, Alexander Prewitt couldn't right well laugh at David for his penile-paralysis when he couldn't so much as consume oatmeal without giving himself a black eye. And lastly, Virginia Rowling was just too damn nice of a person to laugh at another's misfortune.

If there is a heaven—this would make her the only one in the car with a golden ticket to pass on. Before the end, she may have been able to save but one soul in that elevator—but certainly, not them all.

"You know what's the funniest part, you fucking prick? Do you? No? Goooood, I'll tell you. Your brain is even smaller than you're strange little dick...you're a fucking MORON. You always will be. Your children must be a bunch of fucking little retards....They are aren't they? You've got a bunch of stupid little retards for babies! You smug little fuck—you've ruined more than your own life. You're so fucking poisoned and stupid and small-minded that the depth of your mindlessness was too much for one generation!"

"D-d-d-Dana…"

"Can they read, David?"

"Dana…"

"Oh, that's right you wouldn't know 'cuz you can't read a fucking street sign without asking for fucking DIRECTIONS…"

David growled.

"Oh fuck you David—you're a joke—"

"YOU WILL—*NEVER*—*EVER*—matter, Dana. You will die alone and childless—and the only ones who will have known you existed at all will be the poor sons of bitches that bury you."

Typically, this sort of insult had broken Dana in the past. But it seemed—now—she was less concerned with what he thought of her. As before, her response was silence. On this occasion, however, she did respond.

From the blackness of that itty-bitty box, a curling knuckleball of spit materialized and pasted itself across David's eyes and nose.

They couldn't see each other, but in another universe Dana would have recognized him by twin flames alight in his eyes.

In that same universe, one that stunk of comic books and cartoons—the one which rolled tight in his mind—David saw himself squeezing the oxygen from her neck—saw himself watching her eyeballs fill with blood before popping. Her saw her skin go blue and mouth…finally…shut. It was beautiful music to spare him from the scratchy violins in the belly of Dana Jenkins.

After Dana had exhausted her little body, the rest of the cart heard her slump down against the doors. David hoped silently that she had dropped dead.

Within the elevator, no one had a clue as to the time or state of night. It was only when the doors opened that they came upon the fact that they had been there through the evening. The elevator had begun moving, downward. It stopped and the doors broke open.

The light, like an ocean of photons, crashed and burned against the backs of their eyes. All were blinded instantly. When David could finally blink his way back to sight, he saw two short, thick figures occluding the whitest of lights.

"OH MY! Whatever do we have here Miss Marie?!"

"Dear me! It seems these poor souls have spent their evenings in the elevator shaft, Miss Susan."

"Well I never—you poor dearies. Come out here this instant and let Miss Susan have a look at you darlins!"

David exited, followed by the blinking, flustered crowd behind him. Dana, late for work as a sex-object, took a few steps and turned before slapping David across the face with all her might. By her bitten lower lip and satisfactory grunt, one might assume that she had truly enjoyed it. She had, after all, waited quite some time to be able to unleash herself upon him. Dana would have taken a swing in the past few hours, but she was afraid she would have missed him in the dark.

While he wanted—soooo very badly—to rip her throat out with his hooves, he did not. There was someone else on this earth who, if possible, more thoroughly deserved his risking a murder conviction.

As David had slumped against elevator walls through the night—trying desperately to telekinetically remove his ex-secretary's heart from her chest, Thomas Jones was having an altogether different experience.

One of the many limousines which had deposited their party at Club Exposition had been commandeered for the task of transporting a far smaller party back to their appointed domicile. Alone within the padded, black-leather tube, Thomas and Cleo's bodies tied knots with flesh.

Thomas did not see that they had stopped, nor did he see where they had stopped. He was pushed, shoulder-blades first backwards from one of the doors before the chauffeur had made his way to the handle. Cleo directed him with her mouth, back-peddling up a small clutch of stairs, through a door which she unlocked with one hand around his back, and then up another flight of stairs.

For his blood-alcohol level, Thomas was quite remarkable as he quickly skipped in reverse up two flights of stairs with his eyes closed.

Finally, abusing his face with hers all the way, Cleo shoved him through the door to her apartment with an anger that said *How dare you not already have your penis inside me?*

The door slammed with thunder and Cleo's clothes dissolved in a cyclone of movement. So eager to pull at clothing—and finding nothing left on her own body—her hands made quick work of Thomas. She pulled his socks from his feet with her teeth and threw him on the floor. Thomas Jones did not give a *fuck*.

Through the haze and fog of four bottles Thomas got a look at Cleo as she walked over him. Her body, long and golden, was carved. Her breasts, like the tear-drops of Shiva, rose to blood-red, raspberry tips. Clusters of sex upon spoonfuls of caramel. Her long hair was pulled over one shoulder and she tied it off like she was getting ready to do some welding.

His eyes followed a never-ending mile from her belly-button southward to the center of the woman. A tight, pink "W" that Thomas could swore was actually purring drew ever nearer. His penis, in all its majesty, convulsed at the sight of her—bluer than Sub-Zero's jock-strap.

While we can all pray and wish on high that what transpired that night was the definition of "love-making"— it was not. They were far too drunk for this sentimentality, and what followed should instead have been classified as "fucking."

They pulled at one another's hair, screamed, grunted, and swallowed one another's sweat. Thomas had his penis in more holes than he thought she could have possibly had. Before they were spent, Cleo had done a handstand and a crabwalk and Thomas had her entire left foot in his mouth. She used his body like a plunger, a pogo-stick, and a piece of kielbasa. In return, he did things to her he had only ever done to a purple unicorn filled with cotton.

After five hours, they collapsed—buckled—and fell into each other with a sticky *smack*. Their bodies slid from one another and fell into a panting, smiling, cigarette-smoking pile in the middle of Cleo's living room floor. Thomas took stock of the room he had missed for the sake of swallowing her body whole with his eyes. Her ceiling was covered in stick-on, glow-in-the-dark stars.

"Pretty," he said between deep, long breaths.

Cleo laughed and rolled her head onto his chest as the sun crept in through a tapestry-draped window and laid upon them. They wore August like a bed-sheet and fell off into dreams.

David watched Dana as she strutted through the revolving doors at the office's center. Its spinning brass blurred her body until it disappeared into the earliest morning of midtown Manhattan. The air smelled like fried eggs, hot tar, and black coffee as it was whipped in a whirlwind back through the lobby's spun doorway.

As the invisible blips and bleeps of satellite signals finally found their way to David's cell phone, it began to hum and fizzle.

A night's worth of e-mails, text messages and voicemails began to fill his various inboxes like broken levees reacquainting rivers with long-forgotten canyons' beds. He was able to cycle quickly through the slough and disentangle the pointless from the important. There were missed calls aplenty from his wife, e-mails from assorted clients whom he had ignored for the entire week, and several texts. David little used his phone's texting feature and was surprised to find four of them awaiting his perusal.

There were three were from his daughter:

11:55pm—Call mom. She wnt stp bothering me abt where u r

1:15am—WTF?! U no im on vaca! Im ignorin mom from now on.

2:45am—ASSHOLE! CAAL MOM! FAACKK!!

In the midst of his daughter's increasingly incoherent messages, was one from an unknown number.

12:30am—123 Christmas Ct.

David had nary a clue as to what this meant. The number was unrecognizable, as was what appeared to be a street address and an instruction which may or may not have related to anal sodomy. David dismissed it as a wrong number and shoved his phone back in his pocket. Withdrawing his hand, Drahtman's palm came across a folded piece of glossy paper.

David clenched the brochure—squeezing it till it bled. He inhaled through his nose and got a full sense of the stink of wet laundry that surrounded both him and Collins. As his eyes canvassed the yawning foyer, he found his receptionists behind their massive, semi-circular desk. When they caught his eye they smiled. He was too far away to hear but those were more than smiles. It was laughter that trickled between their happy lips.

He hoped they both choked.

"Let's go."

"Go?"

"Yes, Bobby. We're going."

"That sounds like fun."

"C'mon." David led his co-worker, brain addled and cooked by the wood-smoke of his own, disturbed existence—through a side exit which descended to the parking garage.

Normally, the Hummer stood out quite well on its own. Its fluorescent roof stood out over the tops of the other cars like a slipped nipple at a pool party.

Strangely, its pink skull did not peek above the average vehicles which surrounded it. He knew he had parked rather poorly upon arriving, and so it should have been even plainer to the eyes.

The reason the truck did not stand head and shoulders above the others cars was because it had shrunk by about a foot since he had last seen it. All four of her massive chocolate-donut-of-the-Gods tires has been sliced open and emptied of air. The white and red heart-patterned rims were crunched up on the gravel—crackling under the weight of the Hummer. Before them were two parking attendants feverishly working at a tire jack. Behind one of the young men were four oversized black wheels. The chubby, wheezy one named Billy spluttered apologies and fell towards David. The man with the outhouse eyeballs was unable to focus on his asthmatic employee as he had just noticed another strange addition to the Hummer. Across the windshield, in what looked like purple lipstick was scrawled the words:

FOR MR. FREDERICK!!

"Who's Frederick?" asked Collins, curious and inquisitively.

"I—have—no—idea."

"Well, he sure has some fans!" Bobby exclaimed. David looked at Collins for a moment, sighed and turned towards the portly attendant.

"Billy. Fix this."

"We tryin', sir. Trying hard." He panted and clutched at his knees, "Got the tires, see? Got them now just gotta change 'em."

"Do it then, faster…and you," he said again towards Collins, "Give me your keys."

Collins handed over a jangling gaggle of keys, the center of which was notable for a neon-green bunny's foot. Soaked to the bone, it now smelled like a rabbit that had been drowned and scraped from a riverbed. It was squishy and the knuckles felt loose and broken, its tendons eroded.

Collins drove a seven-series BMW—which was nice if you were an average shmuck who just got a raise. David dreaded how insignificant it would feel to be caught in the tan-leather bucket-seats. At least the Hummer added an imaginary inch or so to your dick on the base of its sheer size. Nonetheless, David stormed off towards Bobby's spot.

"Where you going Davey?"

"What? To—the—car, Bobby."

"My car ain't here pal. Wife's got it. I've been taking trains."

David threw the keys at Collin's face, dragged him to the ground and made him assist in the removal of another broken, withered tire while the parking lot workers twisted furiously at their own.

Twenty minutes later the Hummer was re-tooled and David had cleaned the windshield with Billy's red valet jacket. As quick as possible given the circumstances, they were off. The engine turned like ten thousand chainsaws and the men pulled off into the morning astride the great pink beast—riding into battle.

"Rise and shine!" Jameson screamed down at his two butt-naked co-workers through cupped hands. It was loud, like it had been fed through a conch. The two lovers sprang up with a start. Jameson's tie, pink as pussy-lips on a prom queen, dangled and wobbled over their heads. A silken mobile for two adults who were underdressed for infants.

Cleo seemed to be unfazed by being caught in the utter buff by her employer. Thomas spat a spewing string of cusses and pulled the nearest object he could find—a two-foot high steel candleholder straight out of a game of Clue—over his exposed member.

Cleo stood quickly, perfect boobs aquiver, and rubbed her head with her palms.

"What the fuck, man? It's six in the morning."

"And Thomas and I are already behind schedule."

Thomas noticed with wonder that Jameson was engaging in a conversation with this woman—entirely flawless by the description of any man with a beating heart—without even once stealing a glance at her bare, seamless body, reflected in the morning's slanted light as it wrapped around her more tasty bits like a bikini made of sunbeams.

"Still…it's early. You don't have to yell," she mumbled, rubbing hard circles into her temples with tired hands. Her nipples swirled in the air.

"As I said my dear – we – are – *late*. You might remember I asked you if you were going to be staying at home last night?"

"Oh. Shit…I forgot…I'm sorry Jameson…"

"Hush. It's all right—just understand this is why we," he turned to Thomas, still naked on the floor, "Thomas—clothes—hurry," he turned back to Cleo as Thomas stood and scrambled across the apartment (which apparently did not belong to Cleo), collecting his scattered clothing, "why we—are so behind schedule. I actually had to do a bit of locksmithing to discover that you weren't there."

"God…It's just this was closer and I guess I forgot we had told you…" She had her sentence hacked apart by his gentle hands raised, palms toward her.

"Cleo, my love…please. It has been no great trouble. At least we have found each other—even if it is a little late."

Thomas's shirt was inside out and he was missing a sock but he still reported for duty. Jameson looked him up and down—and approved.

"Spectacular! Come Thomas…today will be an important day."

Looking over his shoulder at the woman he loved—standing naked in someone else's apartment—Thomas followed cluelessly in the wake of his employer.

When they reached the stairwell, Thomas made to go down them, and his boss the opposite. Spinning on one foot while tying his other shoe, Thomas made up the lost time and caught Jameson's tail as he reached the uppermost floor. And a ladder. He had forgotten that they would be flying today.

It might be surprising to note that, for all his many idiosyncrasies and varied phobias, Thomas had little trouble with flying. He had certainly never seen the inside of a helicopter, but if any fear were to burble and froth within him this morning at the sight of that bird of steel, it had been quickly stamped out by the taste of toe on his tongue. Thomas Jones no longer knew fear.

Except his mother. His mother still scared the shit out of him.

They were met at the chopper door by the pilot, whose face was primarily occluded by his helmet and its tinted shade. He was missing a few teeth but this didn't seem to discourage a great smile of welcome. The pilot held open the door and when Thomas peered inside he saw an unexpected person sitting within.

Eli Willets was sitting in the corner with earplugs in and a backpack. He smiled broadly when Thomas climbed aboard.

While Thomas certainly had nothing against the prophet, he would have had to admit that he was a bit disappointed that Jameson had felt it necessary to invite someone else along. His image of the day was of himself and his boss waging war on enemies unknown. Thomas calmed down and assured himself that he was certainly no Navy Seal and could use all the help he could get.

They exchanged pleasantries. Jameson followed them into the cabin.

"I hope you don't mind Thomas, but I promised Eli a long time ago I'd let him do some base jumping from the new chopper."

Eli nodded greedily over a smile.

"It's really not smart, but I don't think one little unregistered jump will do much harm."

"Oh wow. Cool. Where are you gonna jump?"

"I'm gonna try and land on Ellis Island. It'll be hard, but I can swim if I miss."
They all laughed.

When they were settled and wrapped in gun-metal headphones, the throttling punch of propeller blades dissecting the atmosphere overtook the air around them. They took off from the rooftop and, while his stomach gave a fleeting roll, it was stopped dead in its spin by a wall of salt that broke its fall.

They weren't in the air for ten minutes when Jameson and Eli exchanged facial expressions and nods. They were coming up on the Statue of Liberty, not a hundred yards from

Ellis Island.

"Now remember, just as soon as we get over her head you need to jump, that'll give you plenty of time to pull and point yourself towards the grassy parts of the island."

"Got it!"

"All right, here we go!" Jameson pulled open the chopper's door. Wind roared into the chopper's guts and cut into Thomas's face.

"ONE…TWO…" counted Jameson.

"THREE!" they said together, and Eli fell from the copter's ledge like a dead man.

Thomas tried to get a view of the prophet as he fell, tried desperately to see the chute explode into the morning air. For whatever reason: the angle, the shoddy windows in the back of the helicopter, or the hazy mist over the East River—he couldn't, and didn't—see Eli's graceful flight.

"Well…that's that," said Jameson, slamming shut the door and sitting down beside Thomas. He patted him on his thigh and smiled.

Collins slept the majority of the way down the turnpike. Neither he nor David had slept at all in the elevator, and the two of them combined had slept like less than a meth-addict in Montana for the better part of the week. Drahtman was operating on fumes, while Collins, devoid of fumes, fluid, or a frame of reference to the world around him—slept soundly.

As he pushed on, dragging the elephant ever southward, David began to consider his next move. What—on earth—did David actually plan to do when he arrived on the doorstep of Thomas Jones?

The plan, as he had imagined it, was plain: physical retribution. He had yet to decide if he actually intended to murder the man, but he was quite sure that anything short of actually cutting his heart out was going to be on the menu. Every time his mind moved to lessen the punishment—he recalled the chuckle. That simpering, snickering, sniveling giggle. He had—laughed—in—his—face. Thomas Jones deserved to die. Somewhere along the way David realized he didn't have a weapon. For a second, this was disheartening. But that sentiment quickly transfigured into glee. He was going to beat and bludgeon the man with something in his own home. If Jones was an athlete, he would rape him with a baseball bat. If he was a musician he would strangle him with his guitar strings. And if he—as David assumed—had not a single redeeming quality, he would just cut him to pieces with his own cutlery.

David Drahtman had leapt from the precipice. He was lost within the foam of his fury—the roar of a rage that cried for blood. No one fucked with David Drahtman. He had to teach him a lesson.

No matter what the cost.

It was just shy of ten o'clock in the morning when David

exited the parkway and began to meander his way forcefully through the city of Wildwood.

David hated every single stitch of it. The colors of the hotels—pastels and pale pinks and greens—looked like the Easter Bunny had been drawn and quartered before being dragged through town tied to a hundred black horses.

The smell, though David wouldn't admit it, reminded him of home. Beaches, salt-water, and suntan lotion. And that—perhaps—is why he hated it so deeply. It smelled like home.

When the corner of Beach Blvd. came into view, David spun the wheel like he was flipping pizza dough and turned the Hummer on its two right wheels. Bobby's head smacked the glass and he gave an audible yet still sleepy expression of pain.

He tore down the block watching house numbers roll by until he came to it. David stopped the car sharply before house, sending Collins's head off the sun visor and into the dashboard. This woke him up. Spittle on his chin, eyes half-open Bobby swung his head back and forth as if looking to see who had kicked him in the face. He cursed.

"Shhhh! Shut up. We're here," David whispered angrily.

The home was a simple-looking colonial with dark green siding. Interestingly, three black balloons wobbled from the mailbox in the early morning's sandy wind. Draped vertically over the side of the mailbox was a shiny silver banner bloated with the breeze at its middle. It said *"PARTY OVA HERE!"*

David wished strongly that today was Thomas Jones's

son's or daughter's birthday, though the black balloons seemed a bit morbid. He had the wildly satisfying vision of himself pissing on a first-grader's birthday cake when he heard voices from behind the home's screened front door.

"Duck!" David spat, pulling Bobby down by his tie into a slouch so that only their eyes peered over the Hummer's window pane; like crocodiles in a river of pink lemonade. They could barely make out the sounds within. What first had sounded like fighting and cursing now sounded like crying or sobbing. Something very strange was going on.

"Davey, what the fuck?! It sounds like—"

Before Collins could finish they heard three loud THWACKS followed by more moaning and cursing. If they didn't know any better, they would say Thomas Jones was beating his wife.

"The fucking guy is a wife beater!" David exclaimed gladly, "We've got him Bobby, let's burst in and give him a taste of his own medicine.

Reluctantly, Bobby Collins followed David out of the car and towards the door, crouched low and moving quickly. David was rolling up his sleeves when he heard more voices. It sounded like there were at least five or six people behind the door, all of them making strange noises and beating the shit out of one another.

The front door behind the screen was ajar and David could just make out strange shadows within. Drahtman took a moment to compose himself before hurdling up the three wooden steps and bursting through the dusty screen, blasting it from its hinges.

"AHHH—HA!!" David proclaimed, pointing to the center of the living room, before he quickly lost his sense of achievement.

What was no doubt intended by the home's designers to be a sitting room was empty of furniture. The carpet was covered from wall to wall with a plastic tarp and on top of this were at least a dozen people in various states of undressed sexual congress staring up at him. Most wore some form of black leather, some full masks with zippers for mouths. Others held whips, chains, leashes and at least one of them was holding a burning candle over the exposed breasts of a young woman wearing a tiara.

"OW! Ronny! Watch it," the woman exclaimed as the man's attention had been drawn from the steady flow of wax piling on her left tit to David's blustered expression. Collins's head was just inside the doorframe and his mouth was very open.

The awkward silence was broken when from a back room a woman appeared angrily before them all.

She was a mousy, tow-haired woman in her early thirties, small breasts packaged well in a black leather corset. High red boots met her kneecaps and she wore nothing at all to cover her bushy crotch. She had her hands on her hips and from between her legs jiggled the opposing end of a blue double-sided dildo, still glistening from wherever it had last been.

"Now what the fuck did I tell you guys? It's early now so we gotta keep it down…Ronny easy with…" Jane Jones's eyes found David's.

"Who the fuck are you?"

"I—err—well. I'm looking for Thomas Jones." It sounded more like a question than an answer. Jane sauntered up to him, big blue dick slapping against her inner thighs all the way.

"What did you say? Thomas? Thomas doesn't live here. Did he put you up to this? Come to spy on me, did you?"

"Oh no! No ma'am," David stammered as several of the entangled and black-leathered party guests began to rise to their feet.

"My brother needs to keep his nose out of my private business!" she screamed into David's face. More of the large, mask-wearing attendees began milling behind her., several tapping bullwhips and chains of stinky anal beads in their palms. One man was carrying an enormous, cherry-red paddle over his arm. David looked back over his shoulder for assistance but found that Collins was already long gone.

"No, you don't understand ma'am. I'm trying to find Thomas…"
"Well you FOUND trouble, scumbag!" Jane said, inches from David's mouth. In one swift motion she reached between her legs and slurped the business end of the two-headed blue dildo from within her. She swung it over head shook it menacingly, spraying David's face with Jane juice. Just as she launched back to crack him across the face with the dragon dong, David ducked, turned

and bolted out of the door screaming for dear life. Jane Jones and her entourage came pounding after him. Drahtman scrambled up to the driver's side door which Bobby was holding open from the passenger seat and peeled away just as a dozen half-dressed sado-masochists were pelting the side of the vehicle with all manner of sex toys. A great black condom large enough for David's twin boys to wear as long johns stuck to the side view mirror and squelched its creamy cargo all down the pink paint. They heard the crash of glass and cursed as a large brown ass paddle that looked like a fly swatter for pterodactyls tore through the rear window and landed in the backseat.

They did not speak for a long time. Collins stared straight ahead, stopping only to blink. It was a testament to their relationship that Bobby did not attempt to open his mouth. He knew better, and on the whole preferred to not be thrown from the vehicle by a sociopathic David Drahtman.

David pointed the truck aimlessly through the sandy streets of Wildwood for nearly an hour. The only sound that could be heard was the morning breeze squeezing through a glassy wound the size and shape of an oversized spatula built for spanking the asses of adult humans0.

They had been down this same block a half dozen times. David had no idea what he was doing. Out of the corner of his eyes he saw a squirrel fidgeting on the curb, looking both ways as if to test whether or not he could cross. Drahtman slowed in an attempt to lull the rodent into a sense of security before throttling the poor beast. As he waited for the animal to make up its mind,

David noticed something familiar directly behind the squirrel. It was a street sign. It read CHRISTMAS COURT.

Christmas Court was quiet…clearly too early for the pointlessly elderly residents of this shit-shack town to be up and about. They were watching church on TV—he was sure of it.

The house that matched the address on David's phone sat in the forefront of the cul-de-sac. It was dull, eggshell white and looked like it was dying. The fence to the right of the home was in tatters—a pile of plywood stacked upon itself to form a shoddy excuse for a fence. Like there was something to hide—in back.

"There she is!" exclaimed Thomas, pointing from the small side windows down on to a small assembly of art-deco style motels and beach-goers in next-to-nothing. Wildwood, from the air, was a diamond in the rough.

Where the rest of Jersey was a geographical fart on the map, Wildwood was, if not a bit cheap-looking, a sort of beautiful in comparison to the dull, drab landscape that surrounded it. In a world the color of a neglected litter-box, the bright lights of Wildwood shone madly that morning. A gemstone set into the sandy skirt of the continent. An overzealous belt-buckle set above the tattered, acid-washed denim of yesteryear.

Strangely, he seemed to see his hometown anew—as if he

truly missed the comforts of its decorative peculiarities, curiously fair-weathered inhabitants and the gentle lull of her beachheads being beaten back by the tide. Thomas looked with loving eyes on his hometown as it rushed underneath the chopper's sheet-metal underbelly. Behind him, he heard the scratchy flick of an aluminum thumbwheel on its flint. Jameson pulled his lighter, still afire, from the hot-headed end of his cigarette. Smiling, he rolled the tube in his teeth, caught it in the gap and pulled longingly. When he opened his eyes—he meant business.

"My house—it's coming up…We should pass right over it."

"Good. Keep your eyes peeled for it and tell me what you see. Look for anything unusual…notably a car that you do not recognize."

"The pink Hummer." Thomas thought he was being brilliant.

"No he won't be in the Hummer."

"How do you—"

"He won't."

It was a minute, maybe two, before Thomas could see the roof of his mother's home come into view. He eyes focused, and he found strange, strange going-ons in his yard.

David got out of the car and stood before the home.

Realizing Collins was still in the car, evidently lulled sleep by repeated trips around the block like a newborn baby girl, he walked to the open window and mashed his hand into his friend's drooly, snoring face.

When the two of them were standing side-by-side at its front, David began to speak to himself.

"Well I don't see the Ford," David said plainly.

"That fence is interesting."

"If this is his house, he must be out, probably at work somewhere robbing decent people who actually work for a living."

"It's hot today," Collins said as he began unbuttoning his shirt.

David still had no idea why he had been sent to this place, nor who had given him the information. Despite this, the coincidence of the address in his phone being in the same town Thomas Jones hailed from was too much to ignore. He had tried calling the number twice. The first time it was a song he did not recognize as the voicemail recording. The second time, the number was completely disconnected.

Perhaps more importantly, David just didn't have any better ideas.

Then he got one.

David walked to the mailbox and relieved it of its contents. An electricity bill gave him all the information he needed.

"Okay. Here's the plan: we break in and wait for him. And when he gets back we give him what he deserves."

Bobby didn't respond. Instead he began removing his shoes and socks. David ignored him. He replayed the text message in his mind before speaking.

"Well, like you said, Bobby. The fence *is* interesting. Let's go around. See what's in back."

Bobby was mopping sweat from his hairy chest with his shirt, sighing. David walked away and towards the splintered tinder that was once called a fence.

As the yard unfolded around the house's corner, it appeared entirely normal, if not a bit overgrown. Just as they made to turn the edge of the home, Collins swore.

"Fuck!" screamed Bobby, hopping on one foot. The sole of his bare left foot was gouged with many small cuts. He brushed at the wounds and a fine glass dust blew up into the air.

"What the—" David's eyes turned slowly from Collins foot to the grass where the glass had landed. As his chin revolved, he saw the entire lawn was dusted with the strange glassy slag. His eyes consumed this sight, bewildered, before it found the apparent source.

On its side in the middle of the lawn was a great steel machine, conical in shape and open at its top, the beach breeze blowing in and out of its insides, picking up more and more of the unknown substance and whipping it across the yard. Beside the structure was a similar sized mass, draped over with a large green tarp. At its corners the tarp was nailed to the ground with thick stakes.

Collins sat in the grass and tended his wounds. David walked towards the machine. Shielding his eyes to avoid the sweeping sheets of glass, he got a brief glance inside the cone and saw nothing but blackness. A cave of cut crystal and shadows. Turning his attention to the tarp, David crept—side-stepped—to a corner opposite the machine so he could avoid the sharp breeze. He tugged a corner stake and lifted the green plastic.

Just then, the sound of a helicopter flying dangerously low filled the air. David dropped the tarp and covered his face as the whole lawn's clutch of razor dust lifted in the air—a cyclone of knives. The chopper blew over the house and did not stop. When it had passed, David put his head under the tarp.

In a frenzy, eyes banging about in their sockets, sweat pumping from his pores, David shuffled up the steps of the home's back porch and attempted to kick through his third door of the week. For the second time, he was successful.

If the thing under that tarp was what he thought it was, he hadn't to ever care again what anyone thought of him. He would never need work again for anyone. He could, if he wished, pack his things and move to an island all his own.

The back door opened to a kitchen is disrepair. The cabinets and drawers had all been turned out; the fridge door was open and was beginning to stink of cheeses and meats no longer under the protection of cooled air. It looked like the home had been burglarized.

Not even recognizing the situation as one which required sympathy, David sighed. Here he was, in the home of Thomas Jones. And the—thing—in the back was his. Perhaps the people who had torn the house to pieces were looking for a diamond. They had simply underestimated its size.

The front door was unlocked and the couches were covered with bed sheets and pillows. It looked like a world-class slumber party had taken place. Like the criminals had decided to spend the night.

David, now ravenously attempting to protect the stone in the yard—which he now fully considered his—canvassed the home for any sign of life. Did he, after all, have a wife? A child? An elderly parent? He brought duct tape and a kitchen knife up the stairs.

Collins followed him—hopping and swearing—with a wooden spoon and a garbage bag.

At the landing, they could hear a strange sound coming from one of the rooms. Salivating, David pointed at the door and told Collins to open it.

It sounded like some kind of animal. A dog. Drahtman crossed his fingers and said a prayer as he watched Collins turn the knob and burst through the bedroom door.

When the door swung in—what sounded like the entire resident population of the Bronx Zoo erupted from the room and poured into their eardrums. Collins screamed and ran for his life, knocking David over on his way down the stairs before sliding a third of the way down on his ass.

Swearing, David walked in and stabbed the alarm clock with the knife. The bedroom was slept in, but clean. The curtains were drawn and strangely, David couldn't find a light switch. He pulled open some drawers and found nothing of importance. An old newspaper sat on the windowsill.

He turned the entire upper floor on its head in search of a hostage. Alas, no one was home. David had suspected that the small-minded Jones would be single and childless, and so was only marginally disappointed when he found no one to hold against their will.

David Drahtman now took possession of the home on Christmas Court and all of its property. However he had gotten it, and wherever it had materialized from—that stone made Thomas a powerful man. All the more reason to destroy him. Stealing such a thing would not be easy, as even his wife's Hummer would be of little use with such a monstrosity. He needed time. And as the hours crept on, he was losing it.

There would be no choice, David had to remove Thomas Jones and get the diamond back to Long Island. So he could think. They would wait, and when Thomas got home that evening, David would put his knife through Thomas's heart: vanquishing his enemy—and taking possession of immense, all-encompassing wealth.

And so…they waited.

When the clock neared five, David prepared himself. Not knowing when Thomas would normally arrive home, he waited—crouched—beside the front door. Collins was upstairs—sleeping. He knew the aloof Bobby would have moral issues with the act David had planned, and although his friend had been seemingly driven to madness over the course of the week—he couldn't risk Bobby's involvement in the murder of Thomas Jones.

The hour hand on the clock dragged slowly across the face of its center. The sun set. No Thomas Jones. Not yet.

David Drahtman grew impatient. He peeked and poked his restroom eyes through the living room blinds every few minutes. Still no sign of the Ford. He took a break and looked through the house for a drink. Some booze—a beer—anything. It seemed, unfortunately, that the house was free of liquor—and this made him hate Thomas even more.

The sun having long since retired over the ocean's head, there were no lights on in the house. David could not find a light switch for the life of him, and after scouring the walls by the light of his cell-phone, David threw a lamp against the wall. At the smashing, clapping sound of glass blasted on plaster, every light in the house came on, blinding him.

As his eyes re-focused, David's ears picked up a strange sound. It sounded like screaming. Cheering. It sounded like thunder underground. He knelt and touched the floor. Ever so slightly, the earth beneath him was quaking. Shouting, chanting sounds were getting closer. The world beyond the walls of the Christmas house sounded like joyous warfare.

His sight regained, David scrambled to the great bay window at the home's front and slashed across the blinds with his knife, cutting a vision of what lay beyond from the blue fabric window treatments.

Barreling—storming down the street towards the home was a mob. A screaming, raving pack of people. Where torches would have been there were lit cigarettes, where clubs and weapons should have been, there were bottles of booze. And where there should have been clothing—there wasn't very much. Nearly a thousand drunken, oversexed high school seniors were running flat out towards the house. Several pairs of shirtless boys shared the load of kegs, three others shouldered an immense bong the color of his wife's car. At least a dozen of the females had not elected to wear tops that evening. The boardwalk of Wildwood had emptied upon him and a throng of maddened, frantic young people broke upon the home. Clearly, someone had told them there was a party. And with that, the Battle of Wildwood had begun.

They hit the house like a hurricane—flooding it fully and shaking its walls to the foundation. The entire house pumped and pulsed. When the door was breached, David was overrun. The first hammered few immediately tore to the stereo and forced the volume knob to the breaking point. The sound of Fifty Cent destroyed the silence with the brain-thumping heart-beat of mindless self-indulgence. Surrounded and packed in on all sides by half-dressed, wildly inebriated teenagers, David pushed and shoved. He had no idea what was going on—but he didn't like it. He punched a sixteen-year-old boy in the face. Broke a bong taller than him in half and stumbled through the crowd. If he wasn't already awake, Drahtman needed to find Collins and get him out of there now. He needed to protect the diamond and survive the night somehow—and he wouldn't be doing it alone.

David crawled and squirmed through the fleshy gauntlet of sweaty teenaged bodies and found that the door to the bedroom was open. Collins might already be lost. As he forced his way into the room David saw Collins standing on the bed with a digital camera. He was taking a picture of four young girls whose backs were to David, all of them flashing their breasts at the camera.

"Oh for the love of God! Collins, get the fuck over here—we've got to get out back now!"

"Daddy?" one of the four over-exposed young ladies said, as she turned around, quickly re-positioning her bikini top.

And oh how right she was. The man standing before her holding a kitchen knife was—indeed—her Daddy. Sophia had, like so many of her peers, taken summer vacation in Wildwood. This is where she had gone with her friends for the week. Her eyes were bloodshot and her breath smelled like fruit-infused rum. She was profoundly shit-faced. So much so that it was a minor miracle she recognized her own father.

David's head shook. Suppressing the overwhelming urge to strangle his only daughter—he was distracted by a sound that just cut through the pounding bass of the music below them. It sounded like a helicopter. A helicopter—landing.

"STAY!" he screamed at her, before turning and sprinting from the room—threatening prom dates with his knife to clear the path to the stairs. Pushing, shoving, and blaring obscenities, he made his way to the kitchen, threw someone through the kitchen table and kicked through the half-attached back door.

He was just in time to see the helicopter take off again—a diamond the size of a mobile home hung from chains under her belly. It swept, laboring under the strain, away from the house. A tiny, pin-sized orange light appeared in the sky and fell to the earth. The cigarette butt lay, smoldering, where the diamond had been. The teenagers applauded and cheered the display.

David Drahtman fell to his knees. Defeated.

<u>34</u>

"I can't believe that worked!" said Thomas, laughing and watching his home dissolve into midnight behind them.

"The power of youth, Thomas!"

"The power of a party is more like it…that was amazing." Thomas's joy abated momentarily as he felt a jab of regret at not spending his formative years over-running houses and having sex on sidewalks.

"Whatever the reason, we are almost out of the woods. In the morning, we will have one last task to accomplish. But before we can rest for the evening we need to do something about him." Jameson pointed to the sleeping Dr. Clarke Carter who was in an alcoholic coma, dressed in nothing but his underwear and Thomas's mother's glasses. He was sucking his thumb.

They had not been on the boardwalk an hour before they

had discovered the doctor buying a tray of margaritas for seven underage girls at a bar. Having no weed left for him by the departing fellowship of Thomas, Mike and Pablo, Carter had struggled to stay balanced. He had done well until the diamond was born.

The overwhelming, mind-raking success of his life's work was simply too much for the doctor to not respond to. If anything in life called for a celebration—a trillion-dollar diamond was one of them. Dr. Carter stripped the house to the pipes in search of alcohol, but found none. Frustrated, but well aware of the availability of booze elsewhere in this town, he had left the house after tarping the stone—and had been drinking constantly since.

By the time they had extricated him from the bar—much to the displeasure of his seven girlfriends within—the night was long. Thomas wrangled him on the beach while Jameson stood atop the chopper and announced an open invitation to a party he was throwing.

"And what are we doing with him?"

"Oh, I think detox is in order."

"Oh," Thomas said uncomfortably.

"Yeah, we can only supplement his situation with weed for so long. I knew for a while that if he ever had a severe relapse we would need to intervene medically. There is a place not far from Thistlestick River where we can deposit him for a few weeks to clean up. Then we will stop at the factory to take care of some things and prepare for a meeting in the morning."

"And the diamond?"

"I have a perfect place for it. Down south. I have already arranged for Reginald to meet us in Thistlestick—where he will transport the stone to the safe location. The sons of Senora Peligro will assist."

The flight to Thistlestick took longer than it would have without the massive rock dragging beneath them.

"It would have made sense to move the diamond via helicopter in the first place, but unfortunately we did not have time to wait until nightfall—as David Drahtman could have very well been on his way at the moment. And I'm sure you can understand how this scene would look in broad daylight."

"Yeah, I was just gonna say that."

They were silent for a moment, watching the seventy-year-old doctor snore and suck at his fingers.

"Oh—I nearly forgot," Jameson began as he pulled a white envelope from within his jacket and handed it to Thomas.

"What's this?"

"It's payday, my friend. I hope you don't mind, as I have included a small bonus for the rather unexpected nature of your initial week with us."

Thomas counted out two thousand dollars in hundred-dollar bills.

"Wow. Thanks, Jameson. Thank you so much."

"You are so very welcome, Thomas Jones. I knew when we met that you would prove to be a great and significant partner in this business. And as the business itself comes to a point of transition—I want you to know that I intend to keep you on with my rather smaller plans for the future. That is, if you are so inclined?"

"Jameson, I will follow you wherever you need me to go."

"I am glad to—" Thomas cut Jameson off.

"What about Cleo?"

Jameson smiled.

"There are few people on earth who mean so much to me as does Cleo Daniels. I assure you that your dear Cleo will be with us as well."

"Good. But I don't understand. What's going to happen to the business? To Keepwater. What are we going—" Jameson returned the favor.

"All in time, Thomas. All in time…For now, we have to deal with the doctor. We should be nearing the clinic shortly."

It was not fifteen minutes before the helicopter landed in the middle of an empty parking lot. Several medical professionals looked aghast from the front doors as the monster beneath it touched gently to the ground. The pilot effortlessly pushed the chopper forward to that it landed without smashing into the package. The propeller died and Jameson and Thomas carried the sleeping doctor to the doors and laid him gingerly into a bench outside the clinic.

The doctors—a man and a woman, with mouths hanging open like cartoon characters—watched as Jameson pulled another, far-larger envelope from his pocket. He unfolded it several times and removed what had to be hundreds of thousands in cash. He gave an undetermined amount of money to one of the doctors and handed Carter's wallet to them.

"This man is a dear friend of mine and I would like him to be given the best of care. Sadly, he has once again fallen off the proverbial wagon. I have no doubt that he has the temperament and fortitude to resume a sober way of life, and ask only that you give him the chance. I believe the cash there should cover his costs."

The doctors, still showing Jameson their tongues, looked blinkingly at the money and nodded wordlessly.

"When he awakes tell him that Jameson loves him and wants him to be healthy, and that when he is ready he will be welcomed home with open arms. You will find my contact information in the wallet."

It was near two a.m. when the men reached Thistlestick River. The helicopter pilot once again deftly landed both diamond and chopper on the helipad before killing the engine.

When they were inside, the men made directly for the back wall. They walked along the doors until they reached the black one. The knobless door.

"Thomas. I am going to rouse the troops on the second floor. I want you to go in that room and empty it. I will meet you back here with the entirety of our staff."

"But how? Ya know… no knob…"

"And for a good reason, Thomas. Because this door was meant to be opened only once. Break it down," he finished, before walking off towards the stairs.

Break it down? Thomas, having dispensed with a sense of hesitancy a day ago—did what he had all his life done best—follow directions. He took a few steps backwards and brought his foot down at the hinge in a furious kick. He had never in his life felt more like a man.

There was no light within the room. Further, it was hardly a room—it was more a closet. By the light of the main room he could see a diminutive, unfinished oak table set at the center of the room. On it was a small cardboard box. Thomas picked it up. Curiosity being what it is, he also opened it. By the low light, he saw what looked like a stack of ancient papers—small leathery books with yellow pages. He couldn't read them in that light. Thomas closed the box and walked back to the great room.

Jameson's employees, the many hundreds of them, were stumbling into the room in their pajamas, rubbing their eyes. The only ones who weren't half-asleep were the ten or fifteen men exiting the White Room, who looked like they were just getting warmed up for a long day of work.

When they were assembled, Jameson—now carrying a megaphone—skipped to the top of one of the sewing counters and raised the megaphone to his lips. Behind him, Melvin stood quietly. He was dressed to the nines. He clearly was not surprised by this sudden meeting.

"Friends! I am sorry to wake you all at this hour but I felt it was necessary to give fair warning."

Mention of a "warning" seemed to have piqued the

crowd's interest.

"It is with great regret that I must inform you all…" he paused—either for dramatic effect or out of genuine sadness—before finishing, "that you are all fired." The room gasped collectively.

"I promise you all that this is for your protection. Soon this place will not be one in which you will find safe haven. All of you must be out by tomorrow afternoon. I have a fleet of busses arriving at sunset tomorrow to transport you all wherever you need to go. In addition," he said, pulling out the large, folded envelope, "I have here a parting gift for each of you. I know it is not much, but in this envelope is ten thousand dollars in cash for every one of you. I hope these funds will see you to a new job without having to suffer to greatly from your rather abrupt exit from this one."

The crowd stared, rather plainly.

"I want you to know that it has been my honor working for each of you and that you will always hold a special place in my heart. Trust—*please* trust—that this has been done in your best interest."

When the audience had filed past him, each taking one hundred one hundred dollar bills from Jameson with the assistance of Melvin and Thomas, the room fell quiet.

The three men looked at one another. Jameson sighed.

"Sleep, friends. Tomorrow is the day and we shall need our energy."

And so they did. The three men unrolled sleeping bags on

the northwest tower and slept beside one another under the stars like Boy Scouts.

It wasn't much of a sleep. Thomas was awakened from dreams of Cleo by a slap across the face from Melvin. He laughed. The man was apparently punishing himself for his dissertation two nights before by no longer using words at all – opting, instead, for applied violence and snickering.

As Thomas peered over the edge of the tower into the front yard, he saw Reginald Jefferson Davis the Fourth screaming at a group of seven Mexican brothers who were rolling a tremendous white diamond up an iron ramp and on to the bed of the truck.

"No time to waste gentlemen, we must depart shortly. The Peligros and Mr. Davis will be able to handle the job at hand," said Jameson behind Thomas and Melvin.
Back in the air, the three men sat silently as the Jersey shore skirted past them on their left. Thomas didn't know what this meeting was about, but whatever it was, he was glad to arriving at the side of Jameson Moxy.

Re-tracing steps that Jameson and he had taken only yesterday, the Statue of Liberty came into view before them. The mid-August morning was clearer than the prior day, and the aquamarine woman of the East River stood unmistakable in the sunlight.
It wasn't, after all, only the sunlight that lit her blue-green body. At her heels, another type of light swirled across the hem of her dress. Red, white, and blue; a vast horde of law enforcement

vehicles gathered at her toes, sirens no doubt blaring and lights alight.

Curling above her eternally extended right hand was a police helicopter. Jameson's pilot cut westerly to avoid getting near its official counterpart. Through his window Thomas could see quite plainly that an officer in black gear and helmet hung just above her torch, suspended by cable. He was trying to reach the faux iron flames—frozen in their one, singular flicker.

This, however, was no tourist stop. The officer was trying to clean up quite a scene on her flame. Run through by the tippiest tip of the topmost blue-gold flame was the body of Elijah Willets. The stiff iron fire cut through his spine and tore a hole in his trunk; a blue tooth stained red erupted from his broken and mangled chest. His face was blank and his eyes open. The prophet had been pierced for the final time.

A strong southern wind blasted into the parachute still strung to his shoulders, filling it like a sail. From his vantage point, Thomas could see the problem. Carved into the fabric was an enormous capital letter "D".

Thomas turned, jaw unhinged like a viper sitting to supper and stared at Jameson and Melvin—both of whom were smiling. Jameson inhaled deeply and began to speak.

"It seems Elijah had been sharing some very sensitive information with rather unsavory characters. As you may or may not be aware, Eli was not only in my employ. I had him take a position with an immensely powerful corporation under the guise of a computer intern. It seemed wise at first; not only an

459

opportunity to gain insight into the goings on at this company, but also to offer him time away from our business. I had become concerned that his intensity and conviction which he applied to God's Demand were becoming a burden. Unfortunately, I had placed him in the employ of someone who would only further fuel his anti-religious sentiments."

"Is this—like the same as—Drahtman's—"

"Please allow me to finish, Thomas. Eli's enmity toward the Catholic Church runs deep. In his effort to do further harm to those who had harmed him, Eli sacrificed too much. He had taken up with a man with great ties to the church...One whom, Eli believed, could help him find the location of a certain priest who had been removed from his clerical duties after being accused of terrible things by some of Eli's classmates. In this desperate attempt to curry favor with this man, he shared vital information about Keepwater. Eli was unaware that this man was already a target of ours. My cousin, whom I believe you've met?"

"Oh, Trick?"

"His first name is Cornelius. But let's keep that between us." Jameson smiled. So did Thomas. "My cousin had been courting him for possible exploitation by one of his ladies. Given the vast wealth Mr. Shank represented, Trick was giving him special, personal attention. Thinking his new friend trustworthy, Mr. Shank let slip that a new employee of his had discovered a plot by a group of people to build a machine."

"The diamonds."

"Indeed. That man, unfortunately, was murdered last

week. You remember my mention of it at the offices two nights ago? I asked Eli to stay so that I could gauge his reaction to the news of his death. It was, needless to say, plain that Eli knew the man well and was the only one capable of betraying our trust. Hence the situation atop Lady Liberty's lighter."

"But…you really had to kill him?" asked Thomas incredulously.

"Unfortunately, yes. Eli broke the rules, Thomas—and invalidated himself. He was a poison. A misguided young man who could not see the bigger picture. Who could not grasp the *big ideas*."

"But—what about his family?"

"His family has six million reasons to feel financially secure in his Golden Mountain. Further, they have no reason to mourn his murder, since to them—he wasn't murdered at all. Rather, young Eli died in a tragic skydiving accident. And one we regret. However, there can be no mistake—what we do is important, and to risk all this in vengeance will not be acceptable. As is always in life, much seeming wrong will accompany the right, and I hope you can do your best to understand that."

"Couldn't you have just fired him?"

"No, Thomas, Eli knew far too much."

"But the priest?! This guy deserved whatever Eli wanted to do to him. Didn't he?!"

"Yes. And when I find him he will suffer a far worse fate than what befell Elijah."

"I just don't understand—what could be so—" Jameson cut

through his words expertly and spoke severely.

"Mr. Jones. This country is in peril. 100% of it. We have allowed a trivial and silly bauble—money—to control our every action. A nexus point has been reached—one in which a wound has been cut between the rich and the poor. One in which we judge our fellow man based on his possessions. One in which lives are destroyed and families torn apart based on bank statements. There is one way to fix it Thomas, and we at Keepwater are doing everything in our power to right the wrongs. To create a society in which people do not need to die because they can't afford medicine. Where people do not need to beg. Where no one will ignore the reality of the universe and the implications of their actions because it's a good business decision."

"And how on earth are we going to do that?"

"We eat the rich alive. We eat the rich alive, Thomas. Feed on their flaws. Tear them apart using their vanity, carelessness, and brutality. Everything Keepwater has done has been to build a massive wealth which will override our enemies. Once we have become more powerful than they are we can show them the error of their ways. Show them how much suffering their fellow man has endured at their command."

"I just—"

"Thomas…listen: This is not the great quest. This is not the meaning of the universe. This is just a balancing act. We are trying to save as many families as possible from suffering because they can't afford the same things the wealthy can. We are eating the rich alive to feed the poor."

"I see."

"I knew you would, Thomas. And one day you will come to realize how much you have done to leave the world better than you found it. There is so much I have yet to explain to you. So much you don't know about why you are so special to me. The big ideas are beyond mere money. Beyond wealth and destitution. There is so much going on, so much pumping in your blood that you cannot fathom what the future will bring. There was never a classified ad taken out in Wildwood. We photoshopped your paper specifically. You were the only one I wanted. And while that may not make sense now, and you may regret my deception, I ask you to trust me. Things are going to get very strange. Stand by me Thomas Jones. There is much work to do."

"What the-"

"Not today Thomas. Soon. But not today"

The rest of the trip was quiet. Thomas hardly noticed when they had arrived atop an enormous building's helipad, high above the Manhattan skyline. He followed Melvin and Jameson down into the building, through a hallway on one of the uppermost floors. Thomas stared at his feet as he walked, still wrapping his brain around what Jameson had said. When he felt the trip stall, he looked up and found himself looking through a doorframe into a yawning conference space. Within noticed two men who looked familiar. One he had seen in a restaurant, the other just the night before—in his backyard. They were flanking an older man in a motorized wheelchair.

"Thomas, if you don't mind, please have a seat out here. I'd prefer not unsettle those within with a new face. They can be quite testy, that sort."

"Ofcourse."

"You do not mind?"

"No – not at all Jameson!"

Thomas sat in a fat brown sofa, alone in a waiting area. He thought of things to text Cleo. Everything that came to mind seemed creepy. When he finaly had sent something he thought wouldn't scare her off, he heard some noise from within the room. It fell silent again. Thomas waited.

An hour later, Jameson Moxy burst through the doors, turned and shut both large mahogany doors behind him. Pivoting he pointed Thomas back down the hallway they came from. He was smiling?

"What the fuck just happened?"

"We just sold Keepwater, lock, stock and barrel."

"What?"

"The men in that room—and let's move a bit quicker if you don't mind, Thomas—just purchased one-hundred percent of a business they assumed they had only purchased a small portion of. They are now the proud owners of a company that, unless they elect to go into the pornography, grilled cheese, life-insurance speculation, religious evangelism, dog-shit shoveling business—will be worth nothing."

"Huh?"

"Hurry, Thomas, up the ladder. You see Thomas, the

men in that room had seen a document which listed our assets as businesses, but not one of them knew exactly what they were buying. Their zeal to purchase our business was based on the fact that they knew how much money I had. They could surely turn the profit I did if they were so inclined—but as they will soon discover, they will be engaging in some nearly illegal, highly offensive, and morally reprehensible work. They will also have to find employees to do the work of handbag making, canine care, and sandwich manipulation, since we just fired the only people who knew of the business and how to do it. I should think they will be quite surprised when they inspect the premises of our factories. Don't you?"

"Well yeah…but you sold everything?!"

"Nearly. As I mentioned, the Golden Mountain has been moved into a private bank account for the Willets, and my office downtown is a private piece of real estate so I've kept that, under different names of course, although the corporations within it—Grimsurance and Cheating Hearts—were sold. Thistlestick River, God's Demand, and a slew of other businesses which are worth nothing without some serious lifestyle changes are now the property of those stuffy sons of bitches we have just left. Those men will no doubt find shit-shoveling beneath them. And so, they will find themselves with considerably thinner bankrolls."

"And what did you just make?"

"We, Thomas, just made about fifty billion dollars."

Thomas swallowed the figure and digested. Then he spoke.

"Call me Tom."

The three men skipped back into their helicopter and took off into the morning. Unemployed and dog-tired—yet—also—insanely and profoundly wealthy they flew. Thomas Jones felt remarkable.

Epilogue:

The Many, Many Futures

While many of the businessmen in that room were taken badly, none were so severely divested as Prewitt, Collins & Drahtman. In their effort to gain control of a business they could do nothing with—they had spent everything they had on Wetra. The new executive board of Wetra tried desperately to keep the business afloat but found it difficult to convince anyone to do the work required. Bobby Collins was the last employee of Wetra, and he spent the next decade caring for a small pack of dogs on his own, shoveling shit into his latter days.

Alexander Prewitt was financially defenestrated and spent his remaining years living off a nurse's income with his wife, Virginia. He never truly recovered from his last stroke and died an older, happier man. He and his wife shared a one-room apartment and, despite his past transgressions, Prewitt came to call it home until the day he passed—smiling, in a sofa, watching Judge Judy, and eating pudding through a straw.

David Drahtman was equally cleaned of his wealth, but he was saved from a life of poverty by his wife's father, an affluent diplomat who helped them get back on their feet, although they did need to sell their home and David's cars. Today David works for far less money in a small investment firm in the Bronx. He rides to work every day in a Honda and works with minorities. This makes him want to die.

His daughter still has no license, and his wife and he are beginning to age due to a lack of cash for plastic surgery. They look their age, and hate every moment of it.

Dolce tried to rape a large cat and had his throat scratched out. Staci purchased a replacement pair of pooches and named them Minolo and Blanick.

The diamond was removed and stored safely in a location deep in the heart of Texas for the day when it was needed. Los hermanos Peligro completed the task with Reginald Jefferson Davis IV, and six of them returned to New York to rejoin Jameson. Pepe, the lone standout, stayed behind to pursue a degree in massage therapy at Texas A&M, where he fell madly in love with every woman he met.

The Melendez family's restaurant was sold back to them prior to the sale of Wetra for the sum of $1. Their youngest son is recovering from his transplant surgery and their new floors look beautiful. The City Of New York found a way to begin construction of the Second Avenue Subway Line without the building, thanks to someone, somehow, buying the three buildings adjacent to the restaurant, and sealing off the basement.

The Jones sisters now call their new nephew every day, and he spends Christmas with them and his extended African family each year.

Thomas Jones and Cleo Daniels moved in with one another shortly after the events of this story and have earth-shattering sex every morning and night. Thomas has developed a foot fetish and continually tries to install Clappers in their apartment. Cleo finds them and throws them out.

The house on Christmas Court was condemned by the state and demolished following the party that ended all parties. Thomas sold it to the state and bought himself a new car.

One of the few major players in corporate American to escape the downfall of Keepwater was Somersworth Omicron Battlefax, who still runs Ohmco—the last bastion of depthless greed in the corporate landscape. Unfortunately for Somers, this makes him public enemy number one for a man named Jameson.

In the future, and there will be many, Jameson Moxy will go on with his most trusted associates in the newest and most dangerous work that is to be done. For while they had defeated some of their strictest and most deadly foes, a greater evil remains hidden in a cloak of flesh and black fabric. The many, many revelations of Jameson Moxy will unfold as they should. And most of these aforementioned souls will not live to see it's final form.

Acknowledgements

I am deeply and eternally indebted to the following individuals: The Intangible Collective, my dear friends and family who have made any and all work I have done as an artist possible. Ben, Brian, Carmen, Caroline, Dia, Eden, Edy, Izzy, Looch, Joseph, Kerri, Toma, Matty, Miles, Chevy, Peace, Gallagher, Shara, TJ, Zev, to Daniel, to Sierra, to my brother Bamboo.

To my students past and present for whom this work was worth doing. To New York University, SUNY New Paltz, and any institution crazy enough to allow me the opportunity to learn from their young minds as often as they would ever learn from me.

To my father, mother, sister, cousins, aunts, uncles.

Loved ones living and passed. To Joe, Mike, Sean, Dan, Anthony Jonathan, Danielle, Jenna, Jill, Jessica. To Felicia. To the names I've forgotten.

To those who have stuck by me when it was most difficult: Mahogany, Jive, Cristin, Shappy. You have each in your own way been an example for me as to how to live better as a man and a writer. I won't soon be able to repay all I owe you.

And lastly, to Eliza, who allowed this book to be written by keeping the lights on.

A Note About The Author

Brian Dillon is a performance poet, author, educator, and organizer from New York City. Currently a professor of performance poetry at NYU's Gallatin School, he is also the 4th ranked slam poet in the world and a writer-in-residence at the Nuyorican Poet's Cafe. In 2011 Brian finished in second place alongside his Nuyorican teammates at the National Poetry Slam. He has served as a guest host and featured poet on the world renowned Indiefeed performance poetry podcast numerous times. In his free-time, Brian is an aficionado of youth ice hockey, designer lighting, and bad music.

www.ingramcontent.com/pod-product-compliance
Lightning Source LLC
Chambersburg PA
CBHW061039030726
47504CB00002B/440